A DEADLY DECEPTION

Also by J.P. Bowie

A Portrait of Phillip

A Portrait of Emily

A Portrait of Andrew

A Self-Portrait

The Journeyer

A Portrait of Olivia

A Deadly Game

Long Ago and Far Away

My Vampire and I

Kyla's Journey

Slaves to Love

For Phil … always.

A DEADLY DECEPTION

A Nick Fallon Investigation

A Novel

J.P. Bowie

iUniverse, Inc.
New York Lincoln Shanghai

A DEADLY DECEPTION
A Nick Fallon Investigation

iUniverse books may be ordered through booksellers or by contacting:

iUniverse
2021 Pine Lake Road, Suite 100
Lincoln, NE 68512
www.iuniverse.com
1-800-Authors (1-800-288-4677)

Because of the dynamic nature of the Internet, any Web addresses or links contained in this book may have changed since publication and may no longer be valid.

This is a work of fiction. All of the characters, names, incidents, organizations, and dialogue in this novel are either the products of the author's imagination or are used fictitiously.

ISBN: 978-0-595-47768-5

Printed in the United States of America

PROLOGUE

The two young men in the black Pontiac pulled up outside the large, imposing home in the Hollywood Hills area of Los Angeles. "You sure this is it?" The speaker, tall and slim, with dirty-blond hair, his tight musculature defined under the white tee he was wearing, frowned as he stared at the darkened building. "Don't look like anyone's at home."

The other, short, stocky with wide shoulders, and a shock of dark curly hair picked up the piece of paper he'd written the address on earlier. "Yeah ..." His Texan drawl deepened as he too gazed out his car window, his brown eyes fixed on the wood-carved front door. "Accordin' to what Mike gave me, anyways. There's other cars here ... must be the place. Look ..." He grabbed his friend's arm. "The door's openin'. Let's go ..."

They climbed out of the car and walked toward where a man stood holding the door open. The man, young, blond and well dressed, with an easy friendly smile asked, "Zack and T.J.?"

"That's us ..."

The man's eyes swept over the pair appraisingly, and obviously liking what he saw, ushered them indoors. "The party's at the end of the hall," he said, closing the door. "You'll find plenty to eat and drink ... Uh, which one of you is Zack?"

The taller of the two gave him a lazy smile. "That's me."

"Good." He said his name quickly, and Zack didn't quite catch it. Not that he was interested in names ... "You'll stay with me while we auction T.J. first."

"Sounds cool …" They followed the man down the long hallway, listening to the sounds of music and voices emanating from behind a closed door at the far end. "Sounds like a great party," Zack said, feeling the need to fill the silence between the three of them. Situations like this always made him a little nervous. Once they were among the people and he had a couple of drinks under his belt, he knew he'd be able to relax. It was just the first few moments of not knowing quite what to expect. Mike, their agent, had said it was an auction party—they'd be expected to strip and pose while they were bid on. The highest bidder would own them for two hours, then they'd be paid and cut loose … no big deal. From the looks of this place, these people were loaded. T.J. and him might just make quite a bit more than Mike had told them. Zack smiled at the thought … no need to tell Mike about it.

"Here we are," the man said, swinging the door open. Every head in the room turned, and all eyes in the room surveyed Zack and T.J. as they entered. "Everyone, this is Zack and T.J., tonight's honorees. Get ready to loosen your wallets—and remember, it's all for a good cause." The large group of well-dressed men smiled in Zack's direction, then resumed their conversations.

"Over here." the man beckoned them to where a bar had been set up. "What'll it be?"

"I'll take a beer," Zack said.

"Me too," T.J. mumbled, looking around the room.

The beer was cold and smooth. The man smiled at the bartender as the two hustlers chugged their beer. "Pour them another two, Jake," he said. "Looks like they're thirsty boys. Oh, and I'll have a Manhattan."

Two more bottles were handed over, and were as quickly emptied. "Okay," Zack said, wiping his mouth with the back of his hand. "When do we start?"

"T.J., why don't you go get ready over there by that dais?" Their host pointed to a small stage in the corner of the room. "You brought your music?"

"Yeah …" T.J. handed him a tape. "It's cued in."

Zack, left alone at the bar, turned to face the stage as a blare of music filled the room, and he leaned against the bar to watch T.J. begin his slow, sensual dance. T.J. was good, Zack thought. Good on stage, but even better in private—he could attest to that. He watched as the man who had brought them in climbed onto the stage alongside T.J.

"What am I bid, folks?" he yelled into his microphone. "Come on, let's start this at one hundred dollars ... do I hear one hundred?"

Zack snorted. A lousy hundred ... Hell, he'd pay T.J. that much ...

"I hear one hundred ... two ... three ... that's it, come along gentlemen ... five, I hear five!"

The bidding finally topped fifteen hundred, and a beaming T.J. was led off the stage to meet his 'buyer'. Now it was Zack's turn. He'd worn his skimpiest bikini under his tight pale blue jeans—the one that hugged and displayed his butt to glorious effect. As the music pulsed and vibrated through the room, Zack looked out at his audience and smiled, ripping his shirt free, exposing his slim hard torso, letting his hips sway and undulate to the rhythm.

"Five hundred," someone yelled.

Yes, Zack thought, studying the bidder through half closed eyes. Tall, silver haired ... Mmm ... I want you to have me, Daddy—you're hot.

"Six ... seven ... one thousand ... do I hear fifteen?"

"Fifteen hundred!"

"Sold! Come on down and collect your prize."

Zack stood waiting, his slim tanned physique coated with a fine sheen of perspiration. Yes, it was him, he thought. The one who'd started the bidding. Nice ... obviously loaded too. This could really be my lucky night. Smiling, he jumped down from the stage, into the man's arms.

"You're beautiful," he breathed in Zack's ear. "Let's not waste any time." Zack let himself be led into an adjoining dimly lit room. He pressed himself close to the tall man's side, shivering as searching fingers caressed his bare skin. He wondered where T.J. was.

"What do you like to do?" he whispered.

"Something a little edgy—are you up for it?"

"Sure," Zack said, pulling down the man's zipper. "Anything you want ..."

"That's my boy." He took Zack's hand. "It's all waiting behind this door."

The door that swung shut behind them was thick and heavy—and the walls were insulated enough to be sound proof, so that no one in the rest of the house could hear, or would know what was happening in the adjoining room. This was a secret that the men gathered in the room maintained among themselves, admitting new members only after careful scrutiny.

T.J. beckoned Zack over. "They want us to do it together while they watch."

"Okay," Zack said. "I'm up for that." He looked at the tall man by his side. "We'll need more money, though."

"No problem, Zack." The man smiled at him. "Don't worry about a thing—I'll see that you're very well taken care of." His smile as he watched the two young men embrace, turned cold and vicious. *That's right, Zack,* he thought, *you're going to be very well taken care of, indeed.*

CHAPTER 1

Nick Fallon looked up from the paperwork he was working on as his partner Jeff Stevens strode into the office they shared. He grinned as Jeff flung himself into his chair, glaring moodily across the office at him, his handsome face unusually glum.

"Bad start to the day?" Nick asked.

"You could say that. Don't ever live with an artist!"

"Oh, oh." Nick leaned his long frame back in his chair, and waited.

"Now he wants to open a gallery in San Diego," Jeff growled. "Like the one here in town isn't enough to keep him busy, night and day."

"San Diego—that's not so far."

"Nick, Peter and I hardly see each other anymore as it is." Jeff gave his chestnut brown hair an impatient swipe. "What with his schedule and mine, it seems like every hour of every day is filled with stuff that keeps us away from each other. You have it easy. Eric has regular hours at the gallery. He's at home every night when you get there—candles lit, cocktails poured, dinner in the oven—don't deny it."

"I'm not denying ..."

"But me," Jeff continued to rant, "I get home to a dark and empty house and maybe, just maybe, there's a note saying something to the effect that he's in conference or got a sitting, or ..."

"Well, he's a successful ..."

"Or, he's having dinner with some high-powered business people that want him to design a mural for their fucking office."

"You should be proud of ..."

"And that's not all. The other night ... get this, he told me he might go to Europe for three months!"

"What for?"

"Some school in Paris wants him to coach their more gifted students."

"But surely that's quite an honor, Jeff. You should be proud of him, buddy."

"I am proud of him!" Jeff slumped back in his chair with a heavy sigh. "I'm behaving badly, aren't I?"

Nick nodded. "Yeah, something like that."

"Well, don't be so quick to agree, partner mine. You won't like it when he asks Eric to manage the gallery in San Diego."

"He's going to do that?"

"Of course he is. You know he thinks the world of Eric's management skills—never stops telling me what a great choice he made in hiring your sweetie."

"Well, San Diego's hardly at the ends of the earth."

"Yeah, but he's going to be driving back and forth till they get it up and running," Jeff told him. "And then," he added with a degree of triumph, "He won't be at home ready with your pipe and slippers!"

"I don't smoke a pipe."

"That's beside the point. You know what I mean. You and I are going to be on our own ... alone ... outcasts!"

Nick threw his head back and roared with laughter. "Oh my God! You are becoming the biggest drama queen of all time. What happened to the stable, levelheaded guy I teamed up with two years ago? If you'd behaved like this then I'd have told you to take a hike—no way would I have been your partner. What are we talking about here? You not getting enough nookie?"

"Excuse me?" Jeff assumed an affronted expression. "That's rather personal isn't it?"

"But I bet I'm right—right? Go on ..." Nick chuckled. "You can tell me. Don't be shy."

Jeff groaned. "Oh, for Pete's sake. Well, as a matter of fact ..."

"I knew it!" Nick crowed.

"No you don't. I was going to say that, as a matter of fact, Peter goes out of his way to ensure that I ... that we ... well, you know ..."

"Get some ... So what's the beef?"

"Nick, there is more to a relationship than just sex, you know."

"There is?"

"Cut it out." Jeff looked at his partner's grinning face. "What I mean is ..." The phone ringing in the outer office cut him short.

"I'll get it," Nick said. "Monica took an early lunch." He picked up the phone. "Stevens and Fallon Investigations ... this is Nick Fallon."

"Oh hi, Mr. Fallon ... uh ... my name's John Hammond."

"How can I help you, Mr. Hammond?"

"Well, I'm not sure, but I think a friend of mine was murdered."

"Have you contacted the police?"

"Uh ... no. I mean, I'm not sure if I should."

"Well, the police always welcome any information from any source when they're investigating a murder," Nick said patiently. "Quite often, that's how they manage to solve a crime."

"But I don't really know very much—that's why I'm calling you. I wondered if you would take the case. I can pay ... can I come see you to talk about this?"

"Sure. What about this afternoon, say around two?"

"That'd be great. I'll see you then."

Nick put the phone down and looked at Jeff. "Here's a guy who thinks his friend was murdered, but he doesn't seem to know how or when."

"Sounds like a challenge."

"Yeah. So, okay, Mr. Overreacting, if it's not the lack of sex, what is it you're really bitching about?"

"Quality time, Nick, quality time. We used to have loads of it."

"That's because Peter had loads of time on his hands," Nick interrupted. "You used to tell me he'd get pissed because of the time you spent working. Now, what with people lining up to commission him, the gallery and his private classes for young artists, he's a busy guy—even with Eric to help him. What you need to do, instead of getting all irritable about it is to sit him down, and tell him your tale of woe." He opened his arms expansively. "Tell him you're lost and unhappy."

"You're making me sound like a weenie."

"You're making yourself sound like a weenie," Nick said, chuckling. "Come on Jeff, you're a big, tough guy, and from what I've seen, Peter is putty in your hands most of the time."

"Oh, yeah?" Jeff laughed wryly. "That's what you think. Peter comes across so sweet and noble …"

"You're saying he's not sweet and noble?"

"Well, yeah, he is most of the time. But when he gets a bee in his bonnet about something he wants to do, watch out …" He glared across at Nick. "What are you laughing at?"

"I was just picturing Peter with a bee in his bonnet," Nick chortled.

"Yeah, well … there's nothing I, nor anyone else can say or do that will change his mind—and he's driving me crazy!"

"Jeez, here we go again with the drama," Nick sighed. "Look, call him up right now; tell him you're taking him to lunch, and that you need to talk. And don't take no for an answer."

"Is this is how you deal with Eric? You overpower the poor guy with your macho maleness?"

Nick smiled. "Yeah, that's right. You gotta show 'em who's the boss!"

"Hmm … remind me to ask Eric about that some time."

"Uh … well … of course, he'll deny it."

"That's what I thought."

John Hammond pushed his way through the glass doors that led into the reception area of Nick's office. He returned the pretty Asian girl's smile as he approached her desk.

"Can I help you sir?" Monica asked him.

"I have a two o'clock appointment with Mr. Fallon."

"Oh yes, Mr. Hammond." She put a finger on the intercom button. "Nick? Mr. Hammond is here."

"I'll be right there, Monica."

"Would you care for some coffee, soda, or water?" Monica asked.

Hammond shook his head. "No thanks. I'm good."

A second later, Nick opened the door to his office and gestured for the other man to enter. They shook hands briefly then Nick indicated Hammond should sit at his desk. Nick sat opposite him and looked at him appraisingly for a moment. He judged him to be around thirty, about five-ten and in good shape, physically. Thick, blondish hair, cut well, expensive navy blue blazer, good sense of style—obviously not short of money.

"So, Mr. Hammond ..." Nick opened a file and inserted a cover sheet. On it, he wrote 'John Hammond.' "You live in Laguna?"

"Yes. I moved here about a month ago—from LA."

"Like it?"

"Very much."

"Can I have your address and phone number?" Nick wrote down the information as Hammond recited it to him. "So, how can I help you?"

"Well, I brought this with me." He handed Nick a page from a newspaper. "I still get the LA Times to keep in touch with what's going on, and I came across this report which kind of startled me."

Nick looked at the grainy photograph of a pleasant looking young man under which the name, Robert Landon, was printed. "This is your friend?" he asked.

Hammond nodded.

The header read; 'Body of Man Found in Laurel Canyon Identified'. Nick scanned the report that stated police had released the name of a man found by some children playing in the woods in Laurel Canyon. He had been dead for approximately three months. Police were checking missing person files. Foul play was suspected. At present, there were no suspects.

"Mind if I make a copy of this?"

"No, go right ahead." Hammond looked relieved. "You'll take the case then?"

"Just a sec ..." Nick got up and took the page to Monica for her to make a copy. He sat down at his desk, and studied Hammond for a moment. "What is it exactly you want me to do? The cops already have the case."

"I just want to know how this happened to him."

"Call LAPD."

"I did already, right after I talked to you. They wouldn't give me any information. They asked me a bunch of questions, and when I couldn't answer any of them, they wouldn't give me the time of day."

"Just how well did you know this Landon guy?"

"Not well, really." Hammond looked embarrassed. "We ... uh ... we met in a bar in West Hollywood. He seemed really nice; we talked up a storm and then ... well, I'm not into casual sex, so I asked him if he'd like to have dinner at my place. He said yes, so we fixed up a date for about three days later. He seemed pleased about it. I fully expected him to show up."

"But he didn't ..."

"Right. I was kind of surprised. I mean, not that I'm any kind of a catch, but we just seemed to get along, you know."

"Did you call him?"

"Yes. I left a message on his cell that night—then I tried again the following day. He didn't return my calls, so I just presumed he'd lost interest and I kinda just shrugged it off." He paused for a moment, looking away. "I did go back to the bar where we met, thinking maybe he'd be there and I could call him a jerk ... or just maybe he had a good excuse ... been taken ill or something. But he wasn't there on the two occasions I went back, so I gave up."

"Which bar is this?"

"Uh, The Racket on Sunset. Anyway, my transfer to Laguna was in the works at the time, so when it came through, I guess I forgot all about Robert, until I saw that report in the paper. It struck me as shocking, that he might have been on his way over to my place when he disappeared."

"Did you tell the cops that?"

"Uh … no. I'm a little wary of letting the police know of my sexual orientation."

"But you don't mind telling me?"

"Well …" Hammond seemed embarrassed. "I figured from your ad in the local paper here that you and your partner are both gay … so I felt I could trust you, if you know what I mean."

"You're half right. My partner, Jeff Stevens, is gay—but I'm not."

"Oh …"

Nick chuckled. "Sorry, my sense of humor."

"Oh, okay."

"You're not out?" Nick asked.

"Not totally; not at work, anyway. And the cops—they don't ever hold anything back. They're just liable to come barging into my office, and start asking all kinds of questions."

Nick shot his prospective client a knowing look. "You sound like you've had some experience of this."

Hammond nodded. "I got arrested in Griffith Park a year ago. It was humiliating. They made me feel like I was the lowest thing on earth."

"Yeah." Nick grimaced. "They have a way with them, sometimes."

"Will you take this on then?" Hammond looked anxious.

"Why do you care about this guy, Mr. Hammond?" Nick asked. "Why are you so keen to find out what happened to someone you barely knew?"

"I guess it's the not knowing what happened to him that night. This is going to sound juvenile I know, but I really liked Robert. You know when you feel that first spark, and you just can't wait to see him again? That's how I felt about Robert. Can you understand that?"

Nick was quiet for a moment or two, reading the seeming intensity in Hammond's eyes. Then he nodded. "Yeah, I can understand that. I've been there. Fortunately for me, it worked out and we're still together."

"That's great …"

"Yes, it is." Nick stood and walked to the window, looking out for a moment. "Okay, I'll do some snooping around, talk to my contact at the LAPD, find out what's going on, if anything. If it looks doable, I'll go ahead. You should know our terms …"

"That's OK, whatever it costs."

"Nevertheless, take a look." Nick pushed a sheet of paper toward Hammond. "We like our clients to know upfront what it'll cost them. Traveling expenses are extra, just so you know, but I'll check in with you about that."

"That's fine …" Hammond gave the paper a cursory glance. "Seems reasonable enough."

"Good. Okay, Mr. Hammond …"

"Please call me John."

"Fine, John. But I'm still Mr. Fallon."

"Oh …"

"Just kidding, John … again." Nick held out his hand. "Jeff, my partner, tells me I have the worst sense of humor of anyone he's ever met. See …?" he added as Hammond shook his hand. "Didn't even make you crack a smile."

Hammond chuckled. "I think the term for you is 'dry'—as far as the sense of humor goes, that is."

Nick grinned as he showed Hammond to the door. "I'll be in touch, soon as I have something"

"Thanks, Nick." He smiled at Monica, who gave him a little wave along with a sweet smile.

"Is he gay?" Monica asked after Hammond had closed the door behind him.

"Yep …"

"Wouldn't you know it?" Monica complained. "Why is it that all the good looking guys turn out to be gay?"

"Hey, your guy Reg, is good lookin'" Nick teased her. "Are you telling me something here?"

Monica laughed. "No. I guess there are some who are spared for us poor women."

Nick picked up the copy of the report John Hammond had brought. "Thanks for doing this," he said. "Did you read it?"

"Yes. Sounds like a really sad story, for sure."

"Right—and just how sad, I hope to find out."

Driving his Lexus into his garage, the silver-haired man sighed with exasperation as his cell phone jangled on the seat beside him. Glancing at the name of the caller on the ID screen, he barked, "What is it?"

"Did you see the paper this morning?"

"Didn't have time …"

"They dug up Robert Landon's grave."

"Oh, yes? Now what?"

"I don't know. They ID'd him from his driver's license …"

"Yeah … body must've been in pretty bad shape by now."

"So, what d'you think?"

"Leave it alone. There's really nothing to connect him to me. Did you cover your ass?"

"I talked to the other guys. They said they were OK with the story if the cops question anybody."

"Good. Okay, keep me informed—and keep your mouth shut."

"That's not what you used to say."

"I'm saying it now." He snapped his cell phone shut, and climbed out of his car, slamming the door behind him.

Jeff stepped into the darkened hall of the house he shared with his lover, Peter Brandon. With a heavy sigh, he flicked on the lights that bathed the living room in a mellow glow. Trudging through the room, he entered the kitchen, tossing the mail he had collected on his way in onto the counter. He opened the refrigerator door, pulled out a can of beer, perched himself on a barstool, and looked around, a gloomy expression darkening his handsome features.

Another night on his own stretched before him, and he felt the first prickle of irritation at the thought of it. Okay, he could have gone to a movie, he could have called a friend and gone out for a drink—he could have done several different things, just as he used to do back when he was single. But dammit, he thought, I'm not single—haven't been for years! Yet now, he might as well be just that again.

He hadn't told Nick the real problem earlier; the fact that he felt Peter and he were drifting apart. He hadn't wanted to admit that to Nick or anyone, and least of all himself. But that sad thought remained uppermost in his mind, no matter how many different ways he tried to analyze it. For weeks now, he and Peter had been at odds, and for the first time since they had been together, they had actually gone for several days without talking to one another—something that, at one time, Jeff would never have believed possible.

And it wasn't just the lack of intimacy that Nick had joked about, yet he had lied to Nick, not wanting to appear a total loser. That male, macho pride had kicked in, refusing to allow him to acknowledge that it had been some time since he and Peter had last made love.

How had all this happened? For the umpteenth time, he let himself wonder just what had been the catalyst that had thrown them both into this unbearable situation. Not so much a single event though, rather a slow process of going their separate ways due to conflicting schedules and work-loads. It was ironic that what Peter had complained about early in their relationship, had of late, somehow reversed itself. Now, Peter was the one whose time and interests were spent elsewhere, and when Jeff allowed himself a petty moment, he would argue that he had always made time for the two of them to be together alone. Now, he groused to himself, it seemed that the only time they spent together was in the company of high-falutin', la-di-dah, mega-powered art dealers, who fawned over Peter with sickening sycophancy.

Jeff had admitted to himself that he was jealous—not of Peter's success. He deserved every part of that. The guy was talented ... more than that, gifted really. No, he could never be jealous of the renown Peter had garnered for himself. But he sure as hell could be jealous of the amount of time Peter felt he had to give those gushing flatterers—people he would have laughed at, once upon a time. Jeff threw back the last of his beer and stood up. Suddenly, he didn't want to be in the house alone, watching TV or reading a book. Picking up his car keys, he strode from the kitchen into the garage. He'd go for a ride, stop at a restaurant, gaze at the moon over the ocean … something, anything to try to stop these insidious thoughts of failure that pervaded his mind. Because that's what it is, he mused bitterly; yet another failure to hold a relationship together. Until Peter, he reckoned his track record had been lousy. In the years Peter and he had been together, he thought he'd finally struck gold. It had all seemed to good to be true—and now, it sure looked like it was.

He cruised along Coast Highway, the top down on his Porsche convertible. It was a beautiful evening, a sultry breeze coming in from the ocean, lending an almost tropical scent to the air. He parked near the beach, then strolled toward a bar and restaurant he and Peter had said they must try sometime. That was when Peter had time to spend alone with him of course, he thought, kicking a pebble out of his way. Well, guess what? He'd try the darned place all by himself.

Soft music and subdued lighting greeted him as he pushed open the door to the restaurant. It was obviously a quiet night. Only a scattering of tables was occupied, and the bar was empty, save for one man sitting at the far end. Jeff nodded at the bartender, ordered a beer, then sat on the edge of the barstool. He felt suddenly uncomfortable. What the heck was he doing here? Why hadn't he just called Peter to find out what time he'd be home? They could have talked like Nick had suggested. But Jeff's invitation to Peter to join him for lunch had gone down like a lead balloon. No, he was just too busy to stop for lunch—another time, perhaps. Jeff had slammed the phone down and stomped around the empty office, fuming none too quietly.

"How's it going?" The voice from the far end of the bar, jerked him from his mental tirade.

"Oh, just fine," he replied.

"You look kinda mad."

"Sorry, I was just thinking about something."

The man slid off from his barstool and approached Jeff, a sympathetic smile lifting the corners of his mouth. A nice mouth, Jeff thought, returning his smile.

"John," the man said, holding out his hand.

"Jeff …" He took the other man's hand, pleased by the warm and firm grip. "Buy you a drink?"

John sat on the barstool next to Jeff. "Sure … a beer, thanks." He gave Jeff a keen look. "You look familiar. Have we met before?"

"Don't think so. You live in town?"

"I moved here just recently."

"Like it?"

"Very much. Big change from LA."

"That's for sure. I lived there for a time …"

The bartender delivered their beers, then went back to wiping glasses at the far end of the bar.

"Cheers …" John said, holding up his glass.

"Cheers …" They clinked glasses and smiled at one another.

"I'm going to have a bite to eat later. Care to join me?"

Jeff looked around him uneasily. "I should get home …" He threw back his beer, immediately feeling the buzz. He stood, looking at John as if seeing him for the first time. "You live near here?"

"Yes …" John pulled a twenty from his wallet and left it on the bar. "Let's go."

They walked outside to where their cars were parked. "I'll follow you," Jeff said.

"Right … just don't get cold feet half way there."

"I won't." Jeff climbed into his car, waiting for the other man to pull away from the curb. In the short space of time that it took them to reach the gate-guarded complex where John lived, Jeff must have told himself a hundred times to turn around and go home. In the six years he and Peter had been together, what he was about to do had never even crossed his mind. Why now, just because things weren't going so well? Did he have to prove something to himself—maybe that he was still desirable or something? This is nuts, he thought. Go home!

Instead, he followed the car through the gates that swung open upon their arrival, and parked in a guest spot John gestured to. He walked slowly over to where John stood waiting, and gave him an apologetic look.

"I'm sorry," he said. "I'm afraid I can't do this."

John's puppy-dog smile faded, his face etched with disappointment. Jeff felt like the biggest heel in the world.

"Sorry," he said again.

"Just come in for a drink ... if only for a few minutes. I'd really like the company. God, does that sound like I'm way too needy?"

Jeff found himself relenting under the guy's sad smile. "Okay, just one drink, then I really should go." He followed him along the path that led to his front door. Once inside, John raced to the kitchen and produced two beers.

"This OK?" he asked.

Jeff nodded and took the proffered bottle. "Nice place," he said, looking around.

"My company's paying for it till I buy something."

"Well ..." Jeff lifted his bottle in salute. "Here's mud in your eye."

"You are very good looking," John said, stepping closer. "Do you find me attractive?"

"Uh ... yeah, sure." Jeff started to step back but found he was backed up against the kitchen counter. "I really should go ..."

John took another step toward him and kissed him hard on the lips. "Please don't go," he whispered. "Let me make love to you, Jeff."

Despite himself, Jeff felt a sudden jolt of lust sweep through his body. He put his beer down on the counter and pulled John into his arms, crushing the other man's lips with his own. He could feel John's arousal press against his thigh, and fingers fumbling with his belt buckle. He looked down as John knelt before him and, with an almost quiet reverence, released Jeff's erection. Oh, this could be so easy, Jeff thought, carnally. We could do it right here—and who would know?

You would know—that's who!

Jeff gasped as those words resounded in his brain. "Jesus ..." He pulled John to his feet, more roughly than he intended. "I'm sorry, John," he said, seeing the man's startled expression. "I just can't do this. I have a lover ... this would be wrong of me."

Anger flickered through the other man's eyes. "Then don't tell him."

"I can't do that. I don't want to cheat."

"Jeez!" John turned away with a bitter laugh. "The guy's not only gorgeous, he's honest too. Just my luck to pick up someone with ethics."

"Sorry." Jeff pulled his zipper up, and fastened his belt.

"Don't be, I understand. Too bad there aren't more like you around." John's smile was tight. "Well, if you ever change your mind ..."

"Thanks. I'd better go."

John walked him to the door. "Your boyfriend is one lucky so and so," he said, opening the door. "Tell him that from me."

"Uh ... in what context exactly?"

"Right ... maybe not a good idea. Well, you know where I live, if you ever change your mind."

The traffic on Coast Highway was light as Jeff sped north toward home. *What the hell was I thinking,* he berated himself, slowing at a stoplight. *Have I gone completely crazy? Going to some strange guy's house with a fucked-up notion of having some kind of a quickie—Jesus, I must be out of my mind. Thank God, John hadn't been some kind of a jerk who'd have made a big scene about being let down like that. He had every right to get upset, you leading him on like that and then—'Oh I'm sorry, so sorry, I just can't cheat'! What a weenie you're becoming ... a total dweeb! At thirty-five years old, you should be showing a little more maturity, for Chrissakes.*

The light changed, and he accelerated forward. The dashboard clock read nine-thirty. Maybe Peter would be home by now, and they could have that talk. He pushed a little harder on the gas, and then cursed as he saw the flashing lights in his rear view mirror.

"Oh, for fuck's sake," he groaned, pulling over to the side. He reached for his registration from the glove compartment. "Good evening, officer," he said, handing over his license and registration.

"Good evening, sir." The cop gave him a searching look. "Know what the speed limit is on this stretch?"

"Uh … yeah … forty-five, isn't it?"

"It's *thirty*-five, and I clocked you at sixty. Step out of the car sir, please." He put his head close to Jeff's and sniffed. "Been drinking have we?"

"Just a couple of beers."

"One moment, please sir." He walked back to his car, presumably to check Jeff's license and registration, then Jeff's heart sank as he saw another patrol car pull in behind the first one.

"Oh shit," he muttered. "I'm in a world of trouble now."

CHAPTER 2

Nick looked across the living room to where Eric was rearranging a collage of small prints he'd recently picked up at a street fair. Eric was wearing only a pair of shorts, and for a moment, Nick let himself enjoy the view. The sight of Eric's sleek muscularity never failed to fill him with admiration—and lust. He noticed, with a deal of satisfaction, that the puckered scar on Eric's back was fading from its former livid color to a less startling pink against the light tan of his skin. Remembering, he fingered the scar on his shoulder, the result of what had happened that day.

Six months before, a crazed drug dealer, bent on avenging the death of his youngest son, had shot both Nick and Eric. For a time it had been touch and go as Eric's life had hung in the balance, but by some miracle, he had survived, and was now completely recovered. Nevertheless, the scar was a constant reminder to Nick of the near-death experiences they had both encountered that day. A day when he had thought Eric was lost to him forever. Even now, he shuddered at the memory.

"How many more times are you going to play with that?" He stood up and stretched, trying to shake himself free of those haunting memories. "It looked great the first time you put 'em up on the wall." Ever since they had moved into their new home, Eric had been finding ways to 'enhance the ambiance' as he put it.

"No, it's not quite right ..." Eric stepped back and surveyed his handiwork. "See, that one on the right is off balance. Aagh!" He'd been so intent on his project he hadn't heard Nick sneaking up on him from behind, until strong arms lifted him and swung him off his feet. He shivered with delight as he felt Nick's warm lips press against his neck. "Sorry, was I ignoring you?"

"Yes," Nick growled, turning him around in his arms. "Jeff warned me about this only today."

"About what?"

"About you, and Peter, giving us the cold shoulder."

"What on earth are you talking about?"

"Jeff ..." Nick tickled Eric's ear with his tongue. "He's all shook up about the way Peter's got no time for him anymore."

"That's crazy ... was he serious?"

"I think so. He said that Peter's opening a new gallery, and going off to Europe and they have no 'quality time' these days."

Eric, trapped in Nick's arms, squirmed to free himself. "Nick, this isn't like Jeff." He stepped back from his lover's embrace. "He's usually always so supportive of Peter's projects."

"Yeah, well this time he feels left out. I told him he was being a drama queen. So, is he?"

"Well, Peter does have an awful lot on his plate."

"So, you're goin' to San Diego?"

"Maybe ..."

"When were you going to tell me about this?"

"There's nothing definite yet."

"But you haven't even mentioned one word of it." Nick stared hard at Eric. "I know San Diego's only an hour or so away, but according to Jeff, you're going to be running both places at once. Isn't this something we should talk about?"

"Of course it is." Eric put his arms around Nick's neck and held him close. "You know I wouldn't do anything without talking it over with you first. It's just in the initial stages—nothing is certain yet."

Nick grunted, pulling Eric even closer. "I think you should talk to Peter, and have him say something to Jeff before things get out of hand. Damn …" His cell phone ringing made him release Eric, and hurry into the bedroom where he'd left it earlier. "Nick Fallon …"

"Nick, it's Jeff. Did I catch you at a bad time?"

"No, no … what's up?"

"Nick, I'm in jail, down in Niguel."

"What? What did you do?"

"Speeding … and I'd had a few beers."

"Oh, man …"

"They'll let me pay bail and leave, if I can get a ride."

"I'll be right there."

"Nick, don't tell Peter."

"Jeff, you need to straighten things out with him."

"I know … just let me do it my way. Okay?"

"Right. What about your car?"

"They've impounded it. Is Eric there? Maybe he can come with you, and drive it back."

"We're on our way."

Nick was decidedly grim as he and Eric drove south on Coast Highway toward the Laguna Niguel police station. "I don't like this, Eric," he said, his jaw clenched in a tight line. "This isn't like Jeff at all. He must be really upset to get himself in trouble like this."

Eric nodded, adjusting the gray sweatshirt he had hastily pulled on. "I don't get it. What did he say exactly—about him and Peter?"

"He said Peter's so busy these days they hardly see one another."

"Yeah, Now when I think of it, Peter talked about it the other day," Eric remarked. "He was upset at having to cancel something they had planned weeks ago. He said he knew Jeff would be pissed, because he'd already made some comments about Peter being too busy these days." He looked at Nick as he continued. "I know Peter's really caught up in what he's doing. Maybe he thought Jeff would understand like he usually does."

"Well, Jeff getting himself thrown in the slammer is a sure sign that all is not well. I just hope they don't go after his business license."

"Jeez, they wouldn't, would they?"

"It's a possibility—maybe he can talk to his buddy McKenna." They fell silent as Nick pulled into the parking lot outside the police station. They both blew a sigh of relief when they saw Jeff standing outside, talking to a tall African-American man. "That's a good sign," Nick muttered, as he pulled up alongside the two men.

"Nick, Eric …" McKenna gave them a solemn-faced greeting.

"Thanks for coming to get me, guys." Jeff looked tired and morose. "Sorry for this …"

"It's no problem, Jeff," Eric said. "We're just glad you're all right."

"So, what's the scoop?" Nick asked, getting straight to the point as usual.

"Louis arranged my release," Jeff told them with grateful look at McKenna. "Lucky for me, he happened by the station on his way home, saw me being processed, and used his powers of persuasion to get me off the hook, for tonight."

"On condition that you don't try anything this stupid again," McKenna said, without smiling. "Now, let your friends take you home and, whatever's buggin' you, put it to rest."

Jeff nodded. "Thanks again, Louis." They shook hands, and the detective held out Jeff's key

"Which one of you is driving Jeff's car?"

"I am," Eric said, accepting the keys.

"Okay, take is easy." McKenna turned to go. "Talk to you later, Jeff."

The three friends stood for moment silently watching as the detective made his way back into the station."

"How are you?" Nick asked.

Jeff dug his hands into his pants' pockets and hunched his shoulders before replying. "I feel like a total jerk, if you must know. A stupid-ass jerk." He looked at his friends miserably. "I can't believe I let this happen."

"It's not the end of the world, buddy," Nick said.

"Oh, what … I'm being a drama queen again?"

"Something like that. Get in the car."

"Nick, be nice," Eric protested. "Jeff doesn't need to feel any worse than he already does. Maybe I should drive him home."

"I'll be nice," Nick said, rolling his eyes. "Jeff, *please* get in the car."

"That's better," Eric chuckled. "Okay, I'll see you guys in a few."

"Uh, Eric …" Jeff looked a little shamefaced. "Do me a favor. Let me drive when we get near the house, would you?"

Eric paused for a second to look at Nick, who nodded. "Sure," he said. "Have Nick pull over round the corner from your house, and I'll stop behind you."

With a muttered thanks, Jeff slumped into the front seat of Nick's car and gazed vacantly out the window.

"Jeff," Nick said, as he pulled out of the parking lot. "I know I said I'd be nice, but you really have to pull yourself together. Peter's going to know somethin's up if he sees you like this."

"I know, I know. I just feel like such a fool."

They drove in silence for a while, Jeff lost in thoughts of how he was going to explain all this to Peter, when his court date came in the mail. Involuntarily, he groaned out loud.

"Jeff," Nick glanced at him and drummed his fingers impatiently on his steering wheel as he spoke. "Is there more to this than you've told us?"

"What d'you mean?"

"Just what I said … is there something you haven't mentioned?"

"No … no, of course not." Jeff shifted uncomfortably in his seat. "I … I was just thinking of how to tell Peter what happened. That's all …"

"He'll understand," Nick said. "Everybody slips once in a while. We've all done dumb things in our lives. I know you consider yourself a paragon of virtue, Mr. True Blue and all that jazz, but you are still human … I think."

"I'm trying hard to see the humor in what you just said," Jeff muttered.

"What I'm trying to make you see, is that going out and having a few beers because you were feeling neglected, does not make you a loser. Okay, so getting stopped by the cops maybe wasn't too smart …"

Jeff managed a laugh. "This is supposed to make me feel better? Don't ever try your hand at counseling."

Nick chuckled. "You know, Jeff; when we first met you kinda had me fooled too … like I believed the sun shone out of your ass. Mr. Squeaky Clean. It's quite invigorating to find you can fuck up like the rest of us."

"Okay," Jeff growled. "Enough with the jesting at my expense. I know you're never going to let me forget this. Just let me explain it to Peter first, before you make it the topic of the day every time we're all together."

"As if I would," Nick protested, laughing.

"Yeah, as if you would. Okay, this'll do. Stop at the corner there."

Nick pulled over and waited for Eric to climb the hill from Coast Highway and park behind them.

"There he is," Jeff muttered, with some relief as headlights lit up the interior of Nick's car. "Thanks again, Nick. I'll see you tomorrow." He was just about to walk to his car, when a vehicle he instantly recognized, rounded the corner. "Oh *crap*," he muttered.

Peter tooted his horn and came to a stop alongside them. "What're you guys doing lurking in the dark?" he asked, chuckling. "Why is Eric driving your car, Jeff?"

"They needed to talk," Eric said quickly, getting out of Jeff's car. "Some investigative stuff, you know. We're just on our way home."

"Oh, okay." Peter looked puzzled. "Why don't you come up to the house?"

"Uh … we've really got to get home."

"Right," Nick said. "Let's go, Eric. See you, Peter."

"Okay, goodnight." Peter waved, and sped off up the hill.

Jeff, watching him go, shook his head. "There he goes, like a bat out of hell—and he never gets a ticket!"

John Hammond turned out the lights in his living room, and padded barefoot through to his bedroom. He was still irritated by the fact that he hadn't been able to persuade Jeff to stay. The memory of the encounter they'd shared was still fresh in his mind.

What a hunk, he mused, throwing his clothes onto a nearby chair. Those intense gray eyes ... and why did he look so familiar? He was almost certain he'd seen him before somewhere, although he was sure they had not actually physically met. That was going to bug him till he remembered.

Climbing into bed, he lay looking up at the ceiling, his mind churning with the possibilities the night might have held, had Jeff not left in such a hurry. He's everything I like in a man, he thought—built, beautiful sexy smile, and not a cheater. Too bad about the last part, he reflected, with a rueful grimace. He knew he wasn't going to get any sleep until he remembered where he'd seen Jeff before. A sudden thought occurred to him.

He reached for the Laguna Beach magazine he'd left on his nightstand earlier, and flicked through the pages till he found the advertisement for Stevens & Fallon Investigations. He'd chosen them for the job of finding out what happened to Robert, because he'd seen the rainbow motif that ran across the bottom of the ad. He'd felt he could be comfortable dealing with a gay investigator, rather than someone who would take his money, then sneer at him behind his back

The photograph of the two men was quite small, and Nick, the one he'd met earlier in the day, was in the foreground. He was hot ... not classically handsome like Jeff ... a bit more rugged. Now, his eyes widened as he peered at the other man in the photo. He was right, it was Jeff—the man he'd held in his arms just a matter of hours ago was Jeff Stevens, Nick's partner.

"Oh my God," he said aloud. Not a very good likeness, he thought as he peered at Jeff's picture. He's much better looking in real life. So, *that's* why he looked so familiar. "Oh, Mr. Stevens," he said with a chuckle as he fell back on his pillow. "It looks like we *will* be seeing each other again!"

Jeff stripped off his shirt and pants, threw them into the laundry basket, and stood, for a moment, looking at himself in the bathroom mirror. "You look like hell, chum," he muttered, before turning on the hot water in the shower.

"Are you all right, Jeff?"

He frowned as he heard Peter's voice from the bedroom. "Yeah, I'm fine," he replied. "I'll be out in a minute—just taking a quick shower." He stepped under the hot spray, letting the water beat down on him, while he tried to make sense of the nightmare this evening had become for him.

"If I could turn back time," he whispered with a rueful grimace. He soaped himself vigorously, in the hope of eradicating the feelings of guilt that lingered on in his mind, like so many wicked whispers.

When he went back into the bedroom, a towel wrapped around his hips, Peter was sitting on the bed looking at him expectantly. For a moment, the two men gazed at one another in silence. Jeff began to feel a steady pulse throb in his right temple.

"So, what were you guys up to earlier?" Peter asked, breaking the silence.

Jeff sat beside him. "We need to talk."

"Okay. This sounds serious."

"It is ... and I want you to hear it from me, first." He cleared his throat and looked away from Peter's steady, blue-eyed gaze. "I got into a little trouble tonight ..."

"What kind of trouble?"

"Well, I'd had a few beers, and I got stopped for speeding on Coast Highway."

"Oh, no." Peter put his hand on Jeff's arm. "Did they breathalyze you?"

"Yeah, and it came up a little over. The cop was a real dick, and hauled me down to Niguel to book me. It could have been worse, but Louis McKenna was there ... he got them to release me. I called Nick, and he and Eric came to get me. I was embarrassed as hell, and I asked them to drop me off round the corner, so I could drive up to the house in case you were home. That's what we were doing when you came by."

"I see ..."

"The thing is, they wouldn't drop the charge, so I'm going to have to go to court, pay a fine, maybe have my license suspended—all because I was an ass, and didn't come straight home after I had that couple of drinks."

"But why were you out drinking alone, Jeff? You don't ever do that."

"That's a long story …"

"I want to hear it." Peter moved closer. "I've never seen you like this. Tell me what's troubling you, please."

Jeff looked into Peter's eyes, trying to discern whether the concern he saw there was for him, or for something Peter feared he would be unable to control. Finally, he said, "Do you know how long it is since we last made love?"

"Not that long, surely."

"Long enough, if you can't remember. I remember. It was the last time we were out together, for dinner and a movie. We saw 'Capote'."

Peter nodded, remembering.

"Then we came home," Jeff continued. "And you started nuzzling me, like you do—or used to. I remember it like it was five minutes ago, although it's been over a month."

"No, it can't be that long ago!"

"Yes, it can—and it has been. And Peter, tonight was just one more example of how much I hate what our lives have become."

Peter gasped with dismay. "How much you *hate* our lives?"

"What our lives have *become*, Peter. Look, no one is prouder of your success than I am—I was impressed by your talent the first day we met. When I saw that seascape over the fireplace, I was in awe of you, and what you could do. I still am, but for some time now we've been drifting apart, and you're so damned busy you haven't even noticed it. We've gone for days without any conversation because you're either not here, or you're too tired when you do get home. Today, when I called to ask if you'd have lunch with me, Eric answered, and you didn't even bother to take my call—just told him to tell me you were too busy. You used to bitch at me about how much time I spent at work, but I can say this with complete honesty—I always found time for you, and never refused to take a call from you."

Peter stared silently at Jeff for a long moment, then his eyes slid away, and for a time it seemed as though he was studying, in great detail, the pattern on the bedside rug. When he lifted his eyes to Jeff's again, they were filled with tears.

"I had no idea you felt this way," he whispered.

"I know you didn't. That's why I wanted to take you to lunch today, so we could talk about it. Instead, I go get drunk, end up in the slammer, and have to call Nick to come get me."

"Why didn't you call *me*, Jeff?"

"Because I figured you'd be in some high-powered business discussion, and the last thing you'd need to hear was that your loser boyfriend needed bailing out of the pokey!"

"You're not a loser, Jeff." Peter leaned over and kissed him gently on the lips. "That word could never be used to describe you."

Jeff pulled him into his arms. "Stop being so nice to me. Let me indulge myself in my self-pity a tad longer." They fell back on the bed, in each other's arms, and Jeff kissed the tears from Peter's eyes. "I'm sorry ..."

"No, *I'm* sorry," Peter interrupted. "Sorry I hurt you, and even more sorry I was too blind to see that you were worried about what was happening to us. I feel like a creep."

Jeff silenced him with a long, hard kiss. "You're back," he said, his voice husky with emotion. "Back where you belong—in my arms."

"Mmm." Peter snuggled closer. "Now, let me make up for all those times I should've been paying much more attention to you."

"That might take all night."

"You have somewhere to go?"

CHAPTER 3

Monica buzzed through on Nick's intercom. "Nick, Joe French on line one, returning your call."

"Thanks, Monica." He picked up. "Hi Joe, how's it going up there in Lalaland?"

"As crazy as ever. What can I do for you?"

"That guy they found in Laurel Canyon recently." Nick looked at the newspaper report in front of him. "Robert Landon ... d'you know the one I mean? Are you handling the case?"

"No, lemme find it ... hang on a sec." Nick could hear the sound of keys being painstakingly tapped. "Yeah, here he is ... case is being handled by Detective Morales. You know the deceased?"

"No, but I have a client who says he does."

"Oh yeah? Tell him to give us a call."

"He says he did that already, and got blown off. Whoever he talked to wouldn't give him any information about how or when Landon bought it."

"Well, we're in the business of taking information, not giving it out to people over the phone—especially since we haven't been able to contact his family yet. Who is this guy?"

"His name's John Hammond."

"D'you think he might know Landon's family?"

"Doubt it ... they only met once, in a bar. I don't think they'd have been into swapping family stories at that point."

"Gotcha. So what's his interest?"

"Well, apparently they had arranged a date, dinner and whatever, at Hammond's apartment, but Landon never showed up. My guy tried contacting him a couple of times after that, but no luck. Then three months later, he sees Landon's picture in the paper, along with the report of his body being found. He's curious, I guess, about what might have happened."

"He died, is what happened," Joe said, curtly. "So, your client wouldn't have any useful information."

"No more than you can get in a couple of hours conversation in a bar. Hammond says he's not into casual sex, so nothing passed between them, so to speak, on that first occasion, other than talking."

"Right ... doesn't sound like he'd give us anything we don't have already."

"So how was he identified?"

"His driver's license was found in his wallet ... no credit cards, no money ..."

"Cause of death?" Nick asked.

"Blow to the back of the head, the report says ... base of the skull was crushed."

"Murder, then."

"Looks that way, but no sign of a weapon. He had to have driven, or been driven up there ... been tailed or met someone there. Robbery could've been a motive. The body's not telling us much. It was in a bad state of decomposition."

"But if he was on his way to John Hammond's apartment in Westwood," Nick mused, "Laurel Canyon was really out of his way."

"*If* he was on his way there. We don't know he disappeared that particular night."

"What about where he lived, or worked?"

"Bob's been checkin' that out ..."

"This Bob Morales; d'you think he'd mind me checking out the scene?"

"Probably, but I'll have a word with him. Just make sure you go through me before you go up there. Bob's an okay guy, but a little prickly at times."

"Thanks for the advice. I'd appreciate your help there. Okay, good talking to you, and thanks for the info."

"Likewise ... tell Jeff I said hello."

Nick put the phone down and looked across at Jeff's empty desk. Hmm, just where *is* my errant partner, he wondered. Hope he hasn't gone off on another bender ... and why do I still have that sneaky feeling he didn't come totally clean last night? Just as he was about to call Jeff's cell phone, he heard him talking to Monica in the reception area. Well, he sounds a deal more chipper today, Nick thought, getting up from his desk. Maybe he got a little, last night.

"'Mornin', Jeff," he sang out from the doorway.

"Hey, Nick." Jeff steered him back into the office, and closed the door behind them. "Thanks again for what you and Eric did for me last night."

"Everything OK?" Nick asked him.

"Yeah. I told Peter what happened. He was kinda surprised ..."

"Of course he was," Nick interrupted. "He had you up on that pedestal."

Jeff scowled. "Don't start that again, please. Anyway, we talked things through and we're good. I'm going down to San Diego with him this morning. He has a business lunch down there and wants me to go with him. Hope you don't mind looking after things here ... we should be back around five or so."

"No problem. So, the San Diego project is a go?"

"He still has some things to straighten out ... lease terms for the gallery ... that kind of thing. I think Peter's a bit nervous about some of the details."

"So he wants you to sit in and listen?"

"Something like that."

"Feels good to be needed again, eh?"

Jeff sighed. "Is it that obvious?"

"Hey, whatever floats your boat. I'm just glad you guys have talked finally." He punched Jeff lightly on the arm. "Have fun in San Diego. Oh, I almost forgot. Joe French said to say hello."

"He called?"

"No. I called him regarding this new client I have ..." Nick filled him in on the details and showed him the copy of the newspaper report. "I think I need to go up and view the scene where the body was found ... hunt around a bit. Joe said he'd clear it with the investigating officer."

"Don't you think forensics would have swept the area clean by now?"

"Most likely. Still, I'd kinda like to take a look-see. Sometimes they overlook something."

"Well, good luck with that." Jeff turned to go. "I'll see you later ... and Nick ..."

"I know." His partner grinned at him. "I'm the greatest."

"Uh ... yeah. In your dreams." They laughed together. "But seriously," Jeff added, sincerely. "You are a great friend."

"No more than you've been to me, buddy," Nick said. "Now go, before we get maudlin and start cryin' in our beer. See you later."

After Jeff left, Nick called Joe French again, asking him to get an okay for him from Morales. "Tell him to call me on my cell, Joe. I'm going to get an early start and head up there now."

"Will do, Nick. Just go easy with Bob Morales—he's the sensitive type."

"I'll be the soul of tact," Nick chuckled.

On his way to LA, he called Eric at the gallery to let him know where he was headed. "Did you see Peter this morning?" he asked, after he'd filled Eric in on his itinerary for the day.

"Yes, he seemed to be in good spirits," Eric told him. "But then, Peter's generally pretty cool. Even when he's pissed off, he can act calm—most of the time anyway. He did say Jeff was going to San Diego with him today."

"Right. So it looks like they straightened things out between them."

"Yeah ... you know, I'm still kind of surprised at Jeff going off the rails like that last night. It seems so out of character for him, don't you think?"

Nick chuckled softly. "Yeah, it's hard for us to think of Jeff as being anything but Mr. Steady. Don't think I haven't pulled his leg about all this ..."

"Oh, I bet you have. Don't rub it in too hard, Nick. He's got to be cringing inside every time he thinks about it."

"I hope that's all he's cringing about," Nick said.

"What d'you mean? Oh darn," Eric lowered his voice to a whisper. "I have to go. There's a customer waving at me."

"Well, wave back."

"Can't ... gotta go ... Bye!"

The traffic was flowing at an easy pace on the Interstate 405 as Nick headed north toward Santa Monica Boulevard. His cell phone rang just as he was making the turn onto Laurel Canyon Road.

"Nick Fallon?" The voice was rough and terse.

"That's me," Nick replied, guessing it was Morales with the unfriendly attitude.

"Joe French says you wanna snoop around my investigation."

"If it's OK with you, of course," Nick said carefully. "I promise I won't get in the way of your forensics team. I used to be a cop ..."

"Yeah, Joe told me," Morales interrupted. "Well, lucky for me, they're done here, so there's nothing for you to contaminate. But there's nothing to see, neither, so you're wasting your time."

"Well, I'm almost there, so if it's all right with you, I'd still like to view the scene."

"Suit yourself." He gave Nick the directions. "I'm getting ready to leave, so unless you're here real soon ..."

"Actually, I can see you up ahead. That's me in the blue BMW." Nick pulled over to let the forensics truck pass, then he swung his car round to where Morales was standing. The detective looked nothing like his voice had suggested. From the roughness of his tone, Nick had expected some down-at-the-heel flatfoot out of love with his work, but Morales was young, tall, slim, well dressed in a dark blue suit, pale blue shirt, open at the neck. His thick, black hair was neatly cut. He was wearing sunglasses, which he did not remove as he held out his hand.

"Bob Morales," he said, his attitude more than slightly challenging.

"Nick Fallon." Nick took the detective's slightly damp hand in a firm grip. "Thanks for letting me come up here."

"So, you used to be a real cop."

"Instead of a make believe one?" Nick asked, chuckling.

"Instead of a *private investigator*," Morales replied. "I don't like you guys getting under my feet."

Nick sighed. "You know, when I was *real* cop, I found PI's to be very useful sometimes. Maybe you should broaden your horizons a little."

"Yeah ... well ... like I said, you won't find anything here to help you. We've already been through this area with a fine tooth comb."

Nick looked down the narrow path that led to the crime scene. "Joe said the dead guy's wallet had been emptied. You think it was a robbery turned violent?"

"Seems to be, but it's early days yet."

"So, you're open to some different scenarios."

"Of course. The guy could've been killed somewhere else and dumped here."

"What about his car?" Nick asked.

"We haven't been able to trace that yet."

"My client told me it was black Corvette convertible."

Morales looked surprised behind his sunglasses, which he now pushed back on his forehead, and gave Nick a long, hard stare from dark brown eyes. "This guy, your client, what else does he know?"

"Not enough apparently. When he tried talking to one of your guys, he was given the old heave-ho."

Morales ignored the dig. "So what else has he told you?"

"Just that they met at a bar and arranged to have dinner two or three nights later. Landon was a no-show, so my client is assuming he disappeared on his way over to his place."

"These guys gay?" Morales asked, pulling his sunglasses down to cover his eyes again.

"Uh huh …" Nick stared through the black lenses as though trying to read the expression in Morales's eyes. "Does that mean you won't be in such a hurry to catch the killer?"

"I treat all my cases the same, Fallon. What they do in their spare time isn't my concern."

Nick grimaced. "On the contrary, I would have thought what murdered people do in their spare time is very much your concern."

"You know what I mean. Sure, the emphasis on the case will shift because of Landon's proclivities, but I'll check on all the information I get from the coroner—just like I always do." He turned to go, then pulled a card from his top pocket. "Have your client call me," he said, handing over his card. "Maybe he knows something he hasn't thought of yet."

"His name's John Hammond," Nick told him, glancing at the card. "I'll have him call you tomorrow."

"Right. And Fallon—you come up with anything, let me know right away."

Nick watched Morales leave with some relief. It suited him just fine that the detective didn't want to stick around. He really hadn't wanted some young, overbearing cop, huffing and puffing, and breathing down his neck every step he took.

He walked down the narrow footpath that led to a densely wooded and secluded ridge. Signs of recent digging showed him where the body had been found. According to the report, Landon had lain in a shallow grave, until some kids, playing Pirates of the Caribbean, and looking for buried treasure, had unearthed something that had sent them screaming back up to the road, and all the way home.

Nick walked slowly around the perimeter of the area, deep in thought. Three months ago, Robert Landon had come here and perhaps stood on this very spot. Had he come to meet someone, or had he been taken here against his will? Was he already dead when he arrived here? If he was on his way to meet with John Hammond, why come up here? Had he received a call that had persuaded him to postpone his dinner with Hammond? But then, if that were the case, why not call and say that he had to take a rain check?

The police seemed to think that robbery was the motive. Could have been—his wallet had been emptied, but that could be a cover for the greater crime of murder. Nick hunkered down by the shallow impression in the earth that had held Robert Landon a secret for almost three months. He gazed up into the branches of the trees that stood, like silent sentinels, guarding that very secret. What had they seen and heard that night? An argument, a covert meeting, sex maybe? Nick took out his camera and snapped some shots of the scene. He would run these off on his computer later and keep them in the file he'd started. He stepped back to get a better shot of the grave, and stumbled backwards over a small rock imbedded in the ground.

"Shit," he exclaimed, as he landed heavily on his butt. He glared at the rock belligerently, and kicked at it with his heel. The rock rolled away, revealing something that looked like a silver case lying partially covered in dirt. Nick peered at it … a cell phone. How in hell had forensics missed this? he wondered with amazement. That fine-tooth comb Morales had bragged about was obviously missing some teeth! He lifted the phone from the dirt, using only his thumb and forefinger on the top and bottom edges—there just might be some usable prints left even after all this time. Carefully, he pressed the talk button with his car key and listened with some satisfaction to the dial tone. Amazingly, after three months, the battery was still charged. If this was Robert Landon's phone, it might still contain the last few numbers he had called on the night he was killed.

Quickly, he pulled his own cell phone from his jacket pocket, punching in the number on the card Morales had left him. "Hey Detective," he said when Morales answered. "I found something up here … a cell phone. It might've belonged to Landon."

There was total silence on the other end for what seemed like an eternity. Nick had a satisfying vision of Morales silently mouthing curses, within the confines of his car.

"You there?" Nick asked, holding back his laughter.

"Yes," Morales growled. "Stay where you are. I'll be right there—and don't touch it!"

Nick chuckled as he put his phone away. Oh boy, he thought, heads will roll for this one. At the same time, he knew his discovery gave him an edge in this investigation. Morales owed him one, and Nick was determined to collect.

CHAPTER 4

Hammond had said he'd met Landon in a bar on Sunset—The Racket. Nick was unfamiliar with the area, not ever having lived in Los Angeles. He'd visited West Hollywood exactly twice before. Once when Jeff and Peter took him and Eric for a night out on the town, and once when their close friends, Andrew and David, planned a celebration to mark their tenth anniversary together. Still, he found Sunset easily enough, and Morales had told him which block he'd find The Racket on.

He grinned as he remembered the frustration on the detective's face when he'd returned to pick up the cell phone Nick had uncovered at the crime scene. Nick, looking as sympathetic as his self-satisfaction would allow, had listened while Morales had ranted about inefficiency, lack of expertise, and any other deficiency he could think of.

"Well hey," Nick had said, trying not to look smug, "I just got lucky, tripping over that rock, I guess. Otherwise I wouldn't have spotted it either."

Morales mumbled something that sound almost like 'Thanks', but Nick couldn't be sure.

"Maybe if there's something of interest on there," Nick said, watching Morales slip the phone into a plastic baggie. "You could let me know?"

Again, Morales mumbled something. Was it 'Sure'?

Nick pulled into the parking lot behind The Racket and climbed out of his car. Glancing at his watch, he noted it was just three o'clock. Too early for the place to be jumping, but the bartender who served Hammond and Landon that night might just be there. He pushed his way through the door and stood for a moment, getting his eyes adjusted to the gloom inside.

A voice came to him through the darkness. "Hi there, what'll ya have?"

Nick found his way to the bar. "Just a coke, thanks."

The bartender, an older man with gray hair in a brush cut, gave him the once over, obviously liking what he saw. "New here, eh?"

"Just passing through … I live in Laguna Beach."

"Nice." The bartender held out his hand. "Bernie … Bernie Kaminsky."

"Nick Fallon. You're from New York?"

"How d'ya know?"

Nick grinned. "It wasn't hard. I lived there for a time."

"Yeah? I pegged you for a Pittsburgh native."

"Very good. That's where I'm from, originally."

Bernie nodded, filling a glass with ice and coke. "That accent's hard to lose, all right."

Nick looked around the dimly lit bar. Like he'd suspected, the place was empty but for two guys sitting at the far end of the bar, deep in conversation. He pushed the photograph of Robert Landon toward the bartender as he put Nick's coke in front of him.

"You recognize this guy, Robert Landon?"

Bernie picked up the photo and gave it a long hard stare. He looked back up at Nick, with a sad expression. "Sure do. Robert's the guy found up in Laurel Canyon. Read about it in the paper."

"He might have been in here a few nights before he was murdered. D'you happen to recall seeing him?"

"Oh yeah, he was a regular here … must've been coming in here for a couple of years or so. Nice guy." He gave Nick a wary look. "You a cop?"

"Private investigator. My client says he met Landon here and they made a date for a few nights later …"

"Oh yeah? Who would that be?"

"Name's John Hammond, fair hair, sharp dresser …"

"John Hammond?" For just a moment, something akin to dislike flickered in Bernie's eyes. "What else did he say?"

"Just that Robert Landon didn't show up for their date."

"Well, I don't really remember him from the night he said he met Robert here," Bernie said slowly. "But one night he came in, madder than hell, asking me if I'd seen Robert. I said he hadn't been in, and he went storming out of here like a witch on a broomstick. Jeez … I'm just glad he didn't make a habit of coming back."

"So you never saw him again?"

"No, thank fuck. I see so much crap in here at times, it's hard to keep track of all the drama."

"Anybody else who might know Landon come here?"

"One or two. Frank, can't miss him—a redhead. They worked together, I think. Yeah, that's right, and the other guy too. They were always talkin' about stocks and such."

"Did they say what office they worked out of?" Nick asked with interest.

"Not that I recall—but then, I find that stuff a drag. Believe me, there're a lot livelier conversations going on here at times."

Nick chuckled. "I bet. So, do these guys still come here?"

"Frank, the redhead … he comes in one in a while by himself. Kinda shy … doesn't say much after hello—at least not to me."

"And if you can't talk to a bartender …"

"Right, us and hairdressers—we get all the scoop!" Bernie looked at Nick with sharp eyes. "So, this client of yours, is he a suspect?"

"Not that I know of. He came to me wanting to know what could have happened to Landon."

"Well, if it's the guy I'm thinking of, he was truly pissed off at Robert. Somethin' about being stood up, and all the trouble he went too, and blah, blah, blah. What an ass. I wouldn't have thought for a minute, he was Robert's type."

"Yeah, I got the impression he wasn't too happy ..."

"An asshole," Bernie muttered, looking over Nick's shoulder at a new customer. "What it'll be?" he yelled.

"Thanks Bernie," Nick said, leaving a twenty on the bar and turning to go.

"Yeah, any time. Don't be a stranger ..."

Nick walked outside into the glaring sunshine and quickly rammed on his sunglasses. Well, well, he thought. That was interesting. I think young Mr. Hammond has some 'splainin' to do when I talk to him next time.

Peter looked across the table at Jeff and smiled happily. "Thanks for coming with me today, Jeff. You were a big help."

"I didn't do much," Jeff protested.

"Yes, you did. You sat there looking like my stalwart bodyguard, and *nobody* was going to argue with my concerns about all the loopholes in the lease!"

They were sitting in Mo's, a famous bar and restaurant in Hillcrest, San Diego's 'boy's town'. Sitting amid a crowd of lively and good looking men, and chilling out with a cold beer and a hamburger, was the ideal antidote to a boring morning spent with business executives trying to convince Peter that the only place for his gallery to find any prestige at all, was in their 'fabulous' new building. Peter had not been that impressed with the building's cold exterior, but had liked the location at an intersection on bustling University Avenue, Hillcrest's main street.

"You think you got it all hashed out then?" Jeff asked.

"For the main part, yes. I'm going to have Johnny check out all the fine print when we get back." Peter leaned forward in his seat and took Jeff's hand in his. "I've been giving a lot of thought to what you said last night, and I want you to know that from now on, you will be my top priority in life …"

"Peter, I'm sorry I laid all that on you."

"Don't be—especially the laying part. Ouch, I didn't mean this to be humorous, but you know what I mean."

Jeff chuckled and squeezed his hand. "I like you humorous."

"Anyway, I realized something after you had gone to sleep." He paused for a moment as if collecting his thoughts. "I realized that all the time you were unhappy with our relationship, I didn't have a clue. I think I said last night that I had no idea you felt this way, and I didn't Jeff—and that's what makes it so bad. There I was, running around, totally absorbed in what I do—totally *self*-absorbed really, and never giving a thought as to how this was affecting you. While you were in the shower this morning, I spoke to Mom, and as always, she asked how you were, and I told her what you had said."

"Oh great!" Jeff groaned. "You told Eve I was whining? Thanks, Peter."

"You know what she said?"

"Tell him to take a hike?"

"No!" Peter laughed. "She said, 'Never, I repeat, never take your relationship with Jeff for granted.' I said I didn't, and she said, 'Well, why does he feel this way?' Like it's all my fault—which of course it mainly is."

"No, Peter …"

"Let me finish. She then went on to haul me over the coals, saying that she knew, only too well, what you had to put up with. The way I could be withdrawn and uncommunicative when I was working on some project or other. Apparently, even Andrew has bitched about this to her on occasion. Added to that, I am stubborn, opinionated, and far too mouthy. If I didn't know that my mother actually loved me, I would have been rather put out by all this crucifying.

"Then she said something that almost made me cry. She said, 'Do you know that when Phillip died and you were in a coma for three years, I wondered if I'd ever have you back again. When I did get you back, and saw you so lost and alone, I prayed that you would meet another who could love you as much as Phillip did—and Jeff is the answer to my prayers. So, my boy—don't mess this up!'

"When I put the phone down and thought about what she had said, I was devastated. For the first time, since I fell in love with you, I was faced with the possibility of losing you, Jeff—all through my own carelessness."

"Is that why you were so quiet on the way down here?"

"Yes. Did you think I was being my usual uncommunicative self?"

"No, I just thought you were tired, after last night."

They laughed together. "You know ..." Peter ran his fingers across the back of Jeff's hand. "Too bad we're meeting friends for dinner tonight, or I'd suggest we stay in San Diego."

"I would love that," Jeff said. "But let's save it for another time." He signaled the waiter for the bill. "We'd better hit the road. You know what the traffic can be like, this time of day."

As they left the noise and gaiety of the restaurant behind them, Jeff's mind was filled with everything Peter had said—especially what Eve, his mother, had told him. Jeff knew that Eve loved him, regarded him almost as another son, and he loved her for that in return. But as they drove toward the freeway that would take them home to Laguna, he could not help but think that, should she ever know about his actions of the previous night, it very possibly would destroy her respect for him—and for that reason he knew he could never trust anyone with that knowledge. He would have to live with that secret for the rest of his life, and pray that no one ever found out.

Despite heavy traffic on the southbound freeway, Nick arrived back in Laguna around six o'clock. He stopped by Peter's gallery knowing that Eric would be just about closing up shop. He tooted his horn as he pulled up outside, and waited until Eric appeared in the doorway.

"Hey, you with the cute buns," he yelled. "Wanna go for a ride?"

"My car's out back," Eric told him.

"We'll pick it up later. Come on, let's go!"

"Okay, give me a minute to lock up."

Nick turned up his radio while he waited, and whistled a slightly off-key accompaniment to Michael Buble's rendition of 'Come Fly With Me'.

"Come fly with me, baby," he sang as Eric jumped into the car.

"You're in a good mood," Eric remarked, kissing him on the cheek.

"Aren't I always?"

"No."

"True," Nick said with a rueful laugh. "And after driving from LA I shouldn't be, but seeing you standing there looking good enough to eat, gave me something to look forward to."

"You say the sweetest things. So, I guess the 'ride' is straight home?"

"Well, I thought I'd take you to dinner first, but if there's something else on your mind ..."

"*You're* always on my mind," Eric said, rubbing Nick's thigh. "Sometimes, I just can't wait for the day to end, just so I can be home with you. Is that what they call being co-dependent?"

"Who gives a shit what *they* call it?" Nick chuckled. "As long as you're co-dependent on me—that's just dandy." He covered Eric's hand with his own. "We haven't been out on the town for some time, so how about a romantic dinner down by the ocean? We can watch the sunset, and then I'll take you home, and you can be co-dependent all over me."

Eric laughed aloud. "You *do* say the sweetest things—a tad off-the-wall, but sweet."

They drove down the coast to a restaurant Jeff and Peter had introduced them to, and which had fast become a favorite of theirs. It was a slow night, so they had no problem securing a table by the window where they could look out over the ocean, and enjoy each other's company. The wine and their meals were, as usual, as impressive as the view, but after they had settled the bill, and sat lingering over coffee, inevitably, the conversation got around to Jeff and Peter.

"What were you saying earlier today about Jeff," Eric asked "You know, when I had to run and attend to a customer?"

Nick was quiet for a moment or two, as if wondering whether his suspicions were justified or not. "I think Jeff was holding back on a part of what happened the other night," he said finally. "I have a feeling there's more to it than he told us."

"Meaning?"

"Meaning, I think there was someone else in the picture."

Eric's eyes widened. "Surely not. Jeff's not the type."

"I wouldn't have thought so either, but I also wouldn't have thought him the type to go out drinking on his own, and get stopped for speeding. He was depressed about his relationship with Peter, and even though I tried to make light of it, and kid him a bit about being a drama queen, I could tell he was really upset."

"Well, they seemed okay today. Spending the day in San Diego, just the two of them, might just be what they needed. Some time to talk, and work things out."

"Yeah, you could be right," Nick said, slowly. "I hope I'm wrong about what I was thinking—and you know why? Because Jeff is the kind of guy, that if he screwed around—even just once out of some kind of desperation—he would punish himself for the rest of his life."

Eric nodded his agreement. "I know what you mean. He could never just shove it to the back of his mind, pretending it never happened. God, I hope you're wrong about this, Nick."

"So do I, babe." His eyes searched Eric's sad expression for a moment, then he said, "But you know what? I couldn't live with that either."

Eric smiled at him, touching his hand gently. "That I believe." He looked at his watch, then at Nick with mischievous eyes. "You know there's almost a half hour before the sun sets. We get a terrific view of it from our bedroom window."

Nick grinned. "Even lying on the bed …"

Eric got to his feet. "Let's go," he whispered. "I have a sudden urge to become very co-dependent!"

CHAPTER 5

Nick's routine early morning run was important to him. He felt it set him up for the day, and he hated it when unexpected things got in the way. That's why he was up and out the door most mornings before six, running along the beach, burning up the sand with his long, loping stride. Added to that, he enjoyed the solitude of his run. Early on in their relationship, he had mentioned this to Eric—and he, sensible soul that he was, had not ventured to impinge on Nick's private time. So it was decidedly irritating for Nick to find that, this morning, he was not alone as he pounded along the shoreline at his usual sharp clip.

"Hi!"

The voice was vaguely familiar, but Nick, with his usual habit of ignoring that which he found annoying, did not respond.

"Nick, hi!"

Oh, for Pete's sake, he groaned mentally, glancing to his right. John Hammond. He slowed down to a walking pace, managing a quasi-friendly smile.

"Good morning, John. I didn't know you were a runner."

"Hope I'm not disturbing you," John said, puffing mightily, obviously glad that Nick had slowed the pace.

"No, that's fine," Nick lied, stripping off his tank top and using it to wipe his face and chest. "Actually, I'm glad you're here ... saves me a phone call."

"Oh yes?" John tore his gaze from Nick's perspiring chest and looked up, his baby blue eyes filled with questions.

"Yeah, I went to the bar where you said you met Robert Landon."

"You did?"

"Uh huh. I talked with the bartender, Bernie ... remember him?'

"Can't say I do, but then I was only there a couple of times."

"Well, he remembers you very well, John. He said you were in there, red-faced mad, yelling about how Robert had stood you up. Now, if I recall rightly, that's not how you explained it to me."

"Well, I was upset."

"Uh huh … but I think you said you went there just to ask him why he didn't show—not to cause a ruckus."

"I … I think the bartender was exaggerating."

"Well, not that I'm an expert, but it's been my experience that bartenders see so much that not a lot of it bothers them after a while. For Bernie to actually recall you being there, makes me tend to believe you were pretty obnoxious."

"Obnoxious?" Hammond stepped back as if offended. "I really resent that, Nick."

"Okay …" Nick closed the space between them, towering over Hammond in a way he knew would intimidate the other man. "Just so you know, one of the criteria I insist on from my clients, is that they are always honest with me—and John, that means no bullshit! If you are not completely on the level, you'd better find someone else to handle this investigation."

Hammond' eyes seemed to do a three hundred and sixty degree swivel as he tried to look everywhere but into Nick's intense stare. Then he did something that Nick found completely amazing. He leaned forward, and put his forehead against Nick's chest.

"I'm so sorry," he said, his voice barely a whisper.

For a moment, Nick stood transfixed, taken aback by this strange and intimate gesture. A second later he jumped as he felt something warm and moist swirl around his right nipple. Hammond was licking him!

"Whoa!" he yelled. "What the hell was that, John? What are you doing?"

Hammond looked up at him with a slow smile. "I just couldn't resist," he said after a moment. "You have to know how attractive you are."

"So you go around licking the nipples of every guy you find attractive?"

"Hardly …"

"Right, hardly. Okay John, that's it. Go find yourself another private investigator to annoy." Nick turned on his heel and strode off. "I'm done here."

"Wait!" Hammond ran after him. "You can't do this!" His voice took on a hysterical edge. "You can't just drop the case, you bastard!"

"Get lost!" Nick shouted over his shoulder, before breaking into a fast jog along the beach.

Eric was preparing breakfast when Nick got home. He heard the door slam, and then something that sounded like, "Stupid s.o.b ... what an ass!"

"Who's an ass?" Eric asked, as Nick stormed into the kitchen.

"That new client of mine ... John Hammond. I just ran into him on the beach—only now, I think he was stalking me."

"What?"

"Yeah. Get this, out of nowhere he comes on to me, starts sucking on my nipple."

"*What?*" Eric gaped at him, then he chuckled. "Jeez Nick, can't I let you out of my sight for an hour, without some guy molesting you."

"It's not funny. The guy's a total jerk—and he hasn't been straight with me either."

"Definitely not straight with you," Eric said, grinning.

"All right, smartie pants, enough of that." Nick flopped down on one of the kitchen chairs. "I just couldn't believe it."

"Well, it's not the end of the world, Nick. I mean, he just made a pass at you. It was probably innocent enough." He paused, then asked, "You didn't hit him, did you?"

"No, I just told him to take a hike." Nick glared up at him. "How come you're not mad with this guy? If you came home, and told me some guy was out on the beach trying to put the make on you, I'd be out there look-ing to pop him one."

"That's why I don't tell you when guys try to put the make on me," Eric said, trying not to laugh. "There would be bodies lying all over the place."

Nick chuckled, relaxing a little. "How many do you figure?"

"Oh, hundreds ... on a daily basis." They laughed together, and Eric came and sat on Nick's lap. "Which nipple did he lick?"

"The right one ..."

Eric leaned over and fastened his lips on Nick's left nipple, flicking at it with the tip of his tongue and bringing it to attention. He smiled into Nick's eyes. "Can't let that one feel neglected, now can we?"

"Difference is," Nick said, his voice soft and husky, "when you do it, I *like* it."

Eric shifted on Nick's lap. "I can feel you liking it." His lips met Nick's in a kiss that was tender at first, but was soon fired by lust and desire. "Shall I put breakfast on hold?" he asked in a whisper against Nick's mouth.

Nick nipped gently at Eric's lower lip. "That might just be the best idea you'll have all day."

"Good morning, guys!" Monica looked up with a smile as Nick and Eric entered the office. "Eric, you not working today?"

"Yeah, I'm on my way." He stepped round Monica's desk to give her a hug. "How's Reg?"

"He's good."

"He's gay," Nick said, straight-faced.

"What?" Eric looked at Monica, who shrugged and shook her head.

"Monica says that all good lookin' guys are gay—ergo, Reg is gay." Nick picked up his mail, then sauntered into his office while Eric and Monica rolled their eyes at each other.

"Will you please do something about his sense of humor?" Monica said. "The jokes are getting lamer with every passing day."

Eric grinned at her. "Oh, he manages to make me laugh sometimes."

"Yeah, but I'll bet that's more of a hands-on job, isn't it?" Monica giggled.

"Hey you two out there, cut it out!" Nick yelled. "Have *some* respect for the boss, for Pete's sake!"

"I better get going," Eric said. He peeked into Nick's office. "Bye, *boss*."

"C'mere you," Nick growled, getting up from his desk. Eric ran into his arms, and held him tight.

"Thanks for giving me such a great start to my day," he whispered. "I love you."

"Love you too." Nick held him close, nuzzling his neck, inhaling the clean scent of his after-shave. "Call me later."

"I will. Bye."

Monica buzzed through at that moment. "Nick, there's a Detective Morales on line one, for you."

"Thanks, Monica." Morales ... that's a surprise, he thought, picking up the phone. "Hey, Detective, how's it goin'?"

"Good, Fallon. Listen ..." Morales spoke as if he was in a hurry. "I said I'd give you any info we got from the cell phone you found, so here it is. There were several messages in the phone's memory, mostly from a guy named John. Is that your client?"

"Yeah ... or rather, he was my client."

Morales seemed not to hear what Nick had just said. "Anyway," he continued, "some of these messages are like off the wall, y'know? He starts off on the first couple of messages being real nice and concerned, but the ones that he'd obviously made the following day were like ... Jeez, kinda crazy."

"In what way?"

"Well, like screaming at the top of his lungs, calling Landon a son-of-a-bitch for not showing up, that kind of stuff ... stuff like, 'Just wait till I see your sorry face in that bar again'. And oh yeah, get this, 'You won't look so cute without your teeth'."

"Jeez, what a vicious queen," Nick muttered.

"Tell me."

"Any messages from anyone else?"

"Yeah, Landon's mother. She didn't sound too friendly either, but in a different way. She was pissed he hadn't called in a while. She even left her number—'In case you've forgotten it', so that was a break for us."

"You've informed her?'

"Yeah. She took it real hard. I asked her if he'd ever mentioned a John, but she said her son never spoke of his friends in Los Angeles."

"Where does she live?"

"Houston, Texas. She lived in New Orleans for years, but she got evacuated after Katrina."

"So that's where Landon is from. New Orleans."

"Right."

"So, what do you think?" Nick asked.

"I think we need to talk to this client of yours."

"John Hammond, that's his name. Here's his phone number." Nick waited while Morales wrote it down. "He's a bit of a screwball, I think."

"A screwball capable of murdering someone?"

"I don't know. He's obviously got a short fuse." Nick told Morales what Bernie the bartender at The Racket had said. "He called him an asshole, for the way he'd been in there screaming at the top of his voice."

"Hmm. Seems Hammond starts screaming when he doesn't get what he wants."

"Yeah, he's a bit of a hysterical queen. Listen Morales, I had words with John Hammond earlier this morning, and I quit the case—told him to find someone else."

"Why'd you do that?"

"Personal reasons. He's just too weird, frankly."

"You think he could have done it?"

"Because he was mad Landon didn't show for dinner?"

"People have been killed for a lot less."

"True, and obviously Hammond has a temper. But then, why would he come to me asking if I'd take the case, if he'd done it?"

"Yeah, he'd have to be really crazy to do that."

Nick hesitated for a moment then said, "I could call him and say I'd reconsidered. He might just want me back." He looked up as he heard voices in the outer office. One of them sounded like Hammond. "Oh, for ..." he muttered under his breath. "Hey, can I call you back? Somethin' here I need to take care of."

"Sure. Let me know what you decide."

Monica buzzed as he hung up. "Nick, Mr. Hammond is here."

"Send him in, Monica. Thanks."

Nick leaned back in his chair as Hammond appeared in the doorway. He stood awkwardly for a moment, his eyes everywhere but on Nick.

"Take a seat, John," Nick said, not getting up. "What can I do for you?"

Hammond sat opposite Nick, fidgeting for a moment or two before he said, "I came to apologize." He finally met Nick's unwavering gaze. "I behaved badly this morning. I don't know what got into me, Nick. It was really stupid of me to think you wouldn't mind if I … uh, got close to you in that way. You see, I'm kinda lonely here. I don't know anyone in Laguna, apart from you and the people I work with—and they're a bunch of deadbeats. There was a guy I hooked up with the other night, but he flaked out on me at the last minute. So, I know it was a dumb move, but it was not meant to upset you, believe me. I overstepped the mark, and I am truly sorry." He sat very still after he had finished talking, looking at Nick with an abject apologetic expression on his face.

Nick cleared his throat. "Well, John," he said, quite enjoying the moment. "You certainly are a man of many surprises. But first, your apology is accepted."

"Oh, thank goodness," he gasped, reaching for Nick's hand to shake. "And you'll still work on Robert's case?"

"Yeah." Nick pried his fingers loose. "But I have some questions for you, John. You have a few minutes?"

"Sure." Hammond looked at him expectantly.

"Robert Landon's cell phone was found at the crime scene, and the battery had just enough juice left in it to hold some messages in its memory card."

"Really? His cell phone …"

"Right, and John there are several messages from you on there."

"Oh, God." Hammond buried his face in his hands. "Oh, God," he repeated.

"Yeah, I'm afraid some of those messages are a bit incriminating. A lot of screaming, use of obscenities, threats etc."

"I was angry, Nick. I didn't mean any of it."

"Like when you were in the bar?"

Hammond hung his head. "Yes, like then too." He looked up at Nick through tear-filled eyes. "I really, really didn't mean any of that, Nick. Please believe me. Surely, you don't think that I could have killed Robert, do you? I could never kill anyone!"

"Okay, John, calm down. Take it easy … just relax." Nick leaned forward in his chair, and lowered his voice as he spoke. "The LAPD have listened to those calls, and they want to talk to you."

Hammond half rose from his seat in alarm. "They think I did it because of those messages I left when I was mad. Oh Nick, what am I going to do?"

"Stay calm, is what you're going to do," Nick told him. "You tell them what you told me—that you were upset because Robert didn't show."

"Oh God, they're going to look at me, and sneer at the homo. Shit, I hate this!" His eyes filled with tears again, and Nick began to feel genuinely sorry for him. The guy was a weirdo, no doubt about it, but he was a scared weirdo, and now he was looking to Nick for help.

"I'll go with you when they question you, John," he said, quietly.

"Will I need an attorney?"

"Not right away … only if they charge you. If that happens, I know a guy who can represent you. Johnny Pedersen—he's really good."

"Oh Jesus, how did this happen? How could they have …" Hammond broke off and buried his face in his hands again.

"Take it easy, John." He got up, walked into the reception area, and asked Monica if she would bring Hammond a cup of coffee. He paused as he saw Hammond sitting slumped in his chair. Putting his hands on Hammond's shoulders, he squeezed gently and said, "Look, why don't I call Detective Morales? He's the one in charge of the case. I'll tell him you're available anytime to talk to him. That way, he's half way to believing you have nothing to hide."

Hammond nodded. "If you think that's best … and if you'll be there."

Morales listened to Nick as he told him that John Hammond was in his office, willing to talk to the police about the messages he'd left on Landon's cell phone.

"Okay, Fallon. Tell him to report to the Santa Ana police precinct on Harbor at three this afternoon. I'll meet him there and take his statement."

"Mind if I come along?" Nick asked.

"I guess that's OK. Just make sure he shows—otherwise I'll have a warrant made out for his arrest."

"Don't worry, he'll be there." Nick put the phone down. "Okay, we're meeting him in Santa Ana at three this afternoon. Hope you don't have any other plans."

Jeff, feeling decidedly grumpy after a long disposition session at the County court house, parked his car in the tiny lot at the back of Peter's gallery in downtown Laguna. He sat for a while, going over again in his mind what he was going to say. He had decided that, regardless of the consequences, he was going to tell Peter what had really happened the night he got the speeding ticket.

He had tried putting it to the back of his mind, telling himself that what is unknown cannot hurt, but that reasoning just wouldn't let him rest. It didn't sit well with his conscience, and he knew that his guilt might eventually drive a wedge between him and Peter. He knew, only too well, from his line of business, that the truth had a nasty habit of biting you in the ass when you least it expect it to.

With a heavy sigh, and a feeling of trepidation, he got out of his car and headed for the gallery's back door. As he approached the door, it swung open and Eric appeared carrying a large box filled with garbage.

"Hey, Jeff." He threw the box into the dumpster by the door. "You just missed Peter."

"His car's here," Jeff said lamely, looking at his partner's vehicle with an accusatory glare.

"Yeah, his client's driving him over to her house. She'll drop him back here when they're done."

"Will he be long?"

Eric gave him a look of concern. "Rough day, Jeff?"

Jeff's shoulders slumped a little as he answered. "You could say that. I've got a lot on my mind."

"About the DUI? I thought Johnny could take care of that for you."

"That, and something I ..." He broke off, looking away from Eric's worried expression.

"Jeff, what is it? You want to come in and talk for a while. Get it off your chest?"

"I can't, Eric. You're Peter's friend, and ..."

"I'm your friend too, Jeff." Eric gripped his arm. "You look like you need to talk. Whatever you tell me will go no further, I promise."

"Not even Nick?"

"It you don't want me to." He frowned. "Is it really that bad?"

"It could be." Jeff hesitated, wondering if he should really do this. Eric was their friend, yes—but he was also Peter's right hand man at the gallery. Peter trusted Eric implicitly—he had said so several times. Would Eric feel that Peter's trust in him was compromised if Jeff made him a part of this situation? He stared into Eric's light blue eyes, at his open and expressive face. How would he take this, he wondered.

"Jeff ..." Eric stepped forward, putting his arms around Jeff. "I've never seen you so upset. If I can help in any way ..."

Jeff laid his forehead on Eric's shoulder, and gave in to the comfort his friend was giving. "Oh Eric," he sighed, "I have truly fucked things up."

"What do you mean?"

Jeff stepped back, out of Eric's embrace. "I can't make you a part of this," he muttered.

"If it'll make you feel better, then you can," Eric said quietly. "Come on inside. I've closed the gallery already. Everyone's gone."

Jeff nodded, and followed Eric inside. He slumped down on one of the chairs in the back studio gazing about him as if he were seeing the place for the first time.

Eric sat next to him. "You've been seeing someone else ... is that it?"

Jeff flinched involuntarily, shaking his head. "God, no ..."

Eric breathed a sigh of relief, thinking Nick had it wrong. "That's all right then," he said. "I had to go to the worst thing I could imagine, other than you robbing a bank or something." He patted Jeff's arm. "So what is it?"

"Well, I haven't been seeing anyone else, but ... something did happen the other night." He paused for a moment then, taking a deep breath, he continued. "I met this guy in a bar, the night I got the speeding ticket. I went back to his place. I knew I shouldn't but I was kinda buzzed, and I was mad at Peter, and shit, that's just a bunch of excuses, I know ... but the guy was nice and he kissed me. He wanted to give me a blowjob, and Jesus, Eric—I was ready to give in to the whole thing, when I suddenly couldn't, you know? I kept thinking of Peter … how this was some kind of betrayal. Anyway, I told the guy I had to leave. I felt like such a loser, Eric." He covered his face with his hands, and let out a long sigh of despair.

"Ever since then," he continued, looking up at Eric. "I've been racked with guilt. Peter's been so sweet since that night. I told him about how I felt as if our relationship was no longer important to him, and how at odds I was about it all—and ever since then he's just been incredible … and Eric, I feel like a giant, fucking *rat!*"

Eric smiled sadly. "You're being way too hard on yourself, Jeff," he said.

"Am I? What I did was …"

"Human," Eric interrupted. "What you did was to act on an impulse. You were feeling down, and right or wrong, you were mad at Peter for making you feel this way. You were tempted to do something to hurt him."

"But he's the last person I want to hurt!"

"I know, Jeff." He looked at his friend for a long moment before he said; "So, you're going to tell him?"

"You think I shouldn't?"

"To be honest, I don't know." Eric walked over to the small fridge in the corner. "Like a beer?"

"Yeah, please."

He popped the tops off two bottles, handing one over. "I'm never sure what's best in these circumstances. Honesty is great—and I know you're an honest guy, Jeff. It's probably killing you right now, having to keep this inside you."

"You could say that," Jeff said, after gulping his beer. "This is something I never thought I was capable of. Not that I'm patting myself on the back or anything, but I've never cheated before. Even when Joey, my ex, was screwing around all over the place, I never cheated on him."

"You haven't *cheated* on Peter … not really. You didn't go through with it."

"But the intention was there, Eric."

"Right, but you realized in time that it wasn't what you wanted to do. You didn't really cheat. Cheating, in my book, is when you deliberately go out looking to get laid—and do the deed. You didn't do that. Like I said, you were acting on impulse." Eric sat beside him again and squeezed his arm. "Don't torture yourself with this, Jeff. Look on it as a moment of madness, and put it aside."

Jeff stared at him for a moment or two. "Let me ask you this. If Nick did what I did, and you found out later—how would you feel?"

"I'd be pissed, of course. But how would I find out?"

"Someone could tell you."

"But no one's going to tell Peter," Eric said with a shake of his head. "No one. I promise you. Only you and I know about it, and it stays right here in this studio."

Jeff let out a long sigh. "Thanks, Eric. Maybe you're right. Why give Peter any more than he's got on his plate already? All I'd be doing is trying to make myself feel better, I guess. Maybe it's best that I just try to live with it."

"Don't try to live with it, Jeff—try to forget it ever happened. And what did happen really?" Eric shrugged his shoulders expressively. "So, you kissed a guy ... he tried to give you head, but you stopped him. End of story." He looked at Jeff mischievously. "I feel sorry for the other guy, if you must know. I bet he was not a happy camper, being cut off in mid-stroke as it were!"

Jeff managed a chuckle. "You have a way with words, young Eric."

"Nick would agree with you on that. Speaking of whom ..." He rose and threw back the last of his beer. "I'd better get home and start dinner, before he gets there, ravenous and rapine."

Now, Jeff laughed out loud. "Boy, that conjures up a pretty picture, I must say. Where is he anyway?"

"He had to go to Santa Ana with some client. The cops wanted to talk to him about a murder in LA."

"Oh, right." Jeff threw his empty bottle into the wastebasket. He put his arms around Eric and hugged him close. "Thank you for being in my corner. I truly appreciate how you've tried to make me feel better."

"I hope I succeeded," Eric said, kissing Jeff's cheek. "You and Peter are both great guys, and I would hate like hell to see anything come between you. So, do me a favor and hang in there."

As they released each other from their hug, they heard the gallery front door open and Peter call out; "Eric? You still here?"

"Sure am," Eric yelled, winking at Jeff. "And I've got your better half here with me."

"Oh good," Peter said, walking into the studio.

Jeff stood staring at him, taking in his blond handsomeness, the startling cobalt blue eyes that sparkled when he smiled, as he now did—and he thought; *What would I do, if I lost him?* He felt a shudder course through his body, and his mouth become dry with a sudden fear that enveloped him.

"Jeff, what's wrong?" Peter asked, his smile fading.

"Nothing, nothing … just a shitty day at the County court house."

"Well, I'm outta here," Eric said quickly, grabbing his keys. "See you tomorrow, guys."

They waited until Eric had closed the door behind him, then Jeff took Peter in his arms. "I love you," he whispered. "I love you."

Peter kissed his lips tenderly. "Are you still upset about the other night?" He nibbled on Jeff's earlobe. "You're only human you know," he chuckled. "You're allowed to make mistakes like anyone else."

"That's what Eric said."

"Oh yeah? Is that what you were talking about?"

"Uh huh. He said I was being too hard on myself, but …"

"And so you are." Peter patted Jeff's butt. "Come on, let's go for a drink at The Cedars. Andrew and David said they'd meet us there if we were in the neighborhood—and as we are …"

"Okay." Jeff let himself be shepherded out the back door. This was probably a good idea. Let's get back into our old routine, he thought. Perhaps, surrounded by good friends and buoyant conversation, he would eventually forget that he had come so close to messing up his life. Maybe Eric was right. There was no good reason for Peter to know what had happened—nothing *had* happened. He'd walked away from it, and like Eric had said earlier, "End of story".

CHAPTER 6

"So what happens now?" John Hammond gave Nick a searching look, as they pulled up alongside his car outside Nick's office.

"Well, I think Morales has let you off the hook," Nick said.

"That *fuck*," Hammond snarled. "Did you see the look on his face when he realized I was the one he arrested in Griffith Park a year ago?"

Nick grimaced. "Yeah, we could have done without that ..."

"He's a moron," Hammond interrupted. "A typical, ignorant, bigoted ass-hole, who shouldn't be in law enforcement. I couldn't believe it when he threw my arrest in Griffith Park in my face, in front of you. Did you see that gloating look on him? God, I wanted to punch that smirk right off his stupid face."

"Take it easy, John ..."

"He went out of his way to humiliate me," Hammond seethed. "One day, he might regret that."

"You need to forget about it," Nick said. "He might be a jerk, but he's just doin' his job. It was those messages that got him interested."

"Oh God, I can't believe I said all that crap," Hammond moaned. "When he played those back to me, I could have just died!"

"Yeah ... well, better keep a leash on that temper of yours, John. Don't go railing at people you hardly know."

"Thanks for the advice," Hammond said, his jaw tight. "So, is this at a dead end?"

"It needn't be," Nick said slowly. "If you want me to keep going, I thought I'd go back up to that bar, and talk with Bernie again. I have a hunch that Landon met with someone there, apart from you. Did he leave at the same time you did?"

"Uh … no … I don't think so." He paused, as if trying to remember. "I think he said something about going to the restroom, just about when I was leaving."

"You don't think going to the restroom was just a line to get you in there with him?"

"I don't do that kind of stuff, Nick," Hammond huffed.

"No?" Nick raised an eyebrow. "You sure do *some* stuff, as I recall."

Hammond flushed with discomfort. "I apologized for that."

"So you did, but John …" Nick leaned in closer to the other man. "Please don't take me for an idiot. I know what guys do, remember? I'm one myself. You found Landon attractive. You wanted to have sex with him, right? You just wanted it to be on your turf, not in some seedy washroom where it would all be over in a few minutes. That's fine, but answer me this. If Landon had really pushed the quickie idea—would you have turned him down?"

Hammond's eyes looked down from Nick's intense stare. "Why are you asking me this? What has this to do with anything? I'm paying you to find out what happened to Robert, not to get some third degree about my sex life!"

Nick shifted away from Hammond and shrugged. "Okay, I didn't mean to get you all riled up. I was just trying to get a picture of what happened between you guys … how you both felt when you said, see you later. That kind of thing …" A sudden thought occurred to him. "If you left before him that night, how did you know what kind of car he drove?"

Hammond was quiet for a moment or two, then he sighed and said, "Okay, I guess you'd better know this. We did it in the bathroom. It wasn't very good. I wasn't very good. That's why I asked him to come over. I had this need to prove to him … something … I don't know quite what … that I could be better than that, perhaps. He seemed eager enough. Yes, he said, that would be great. We walked out together to the parking lot, and talked a while standing by his car. But now, I figure he was probably laughing up his sleeve. That's why he never showed."

"You see, John," Nick said, staring out the window. "That's the problem I have with you. You don't tell me the whole story, until I squeeze it out of you. Why?"

"Because I'm embarrassed, I suppose."

"Embarrassed about what? That you had sex with some dude you found attractive, and who wanted to do it with you? That's what makes the world go around, so they say. Were you safe, I hope?"

"It didn't get that far. Like I said, it wasn't very good."

"Are you telling me the truth this time?"

"Yes! Jeez," Hammond muttered. "How many more times do I have to humiliate myself by talking about this?"

"If you'd been upfront about it all in the first place, we wouldn't have to be going over it now."

"I told you all you needed to know!" Hammond snapped. "I certainly wasn't going to pour out my soul to some ... some ... cop *wannabe*, who thinks he knows everything about me because I happen to be gay—when all he knows is just so much *shit*!"

"You really shouldn't be that hard on yourself, John." Nick's voice was loaded with sarcasm.

"Shut up!" Hammond raised his fist, his face contorted with anger as he lunged at Nick. Nick grabbed Hammond's wrist and squeezed until the man cried out with pain. "Stop," he whimpered. "I'm sorry, I'm sorry ..."

Nick released his hold on Hammond's wrist, and stared him down. "Is this what happened the night Landon died?" he rasped, ignoring Hammond's gasp of dismay. "You caught up with him somewhere, you argued—and that temper of yours took over?"

"No, no, no!" Hammond was sobbing now. "Nick, I'm sorry I came unglued like that. I never saw Robert again after that night. I told you I could never kill him."

Nick nodded, his mouth set in a tight line of dislike. "We're done here," he said. "Go home, pick up your phone book, and find yourself another private investigator."

"No, please. I said I'm sorry."

"Sorry doesn't cut it this time." Nick got out of his car, and walked round to the passenger side. He opened the door, staring down at Hammond with dislike. "Get out, John. Go home, and don't bother to call me again." He watched as Hammond crawled out of his car, his shoulders hunched with misery.

"Nick, I'm really sorry ..."

"So am I, John. Sorry I wasted my time with someone as screwed up as you. When and if you get your story straight, go tell it to someone else. Better still, forget all about Landon's murder, and get on with your life."

Nick got back in his car, started the engine and drove away, leaving Hammond alone in the parking lot, staring after him with desperation in his eyes.

Eric, totally involved in the latest edition of Ideal Home magazine, almost jumped out of his skin, as the front door slammed with such force, the whole house shook in protest.

"Not again," he muttered, throwing the magazine down. Boy, he thought, if I ever wanted the quiet life, I chose the wrong guy to live with. He chuckled at the thought, then sat back, waiting for the explosion to come.

Nick stormed into the living room, and glared at him. "Asshole!" he yelled.

"I beg your pardon?" Eric raised an eyebrow.

"Not you."

"I should think not." Eric rose and hugged his man. "Can I fix you a drink while you tell me of this latest drama?"

"Yes—and make it a double." He kissed Eric on the nose. "Thank God I have you to come home to."

"So what's the deal?" Eric asked, pouring Nick a healthy shot of Dewars on the rocks.

"That jerk, John Hammond," Nick growled. "He is one demented soul!"

"What did he do this time—try to get in your pants?"

"The guy is nuts," Nick said, ignoring Eric's comment. "And a liar—one minute he's 'Oh, I'm not into casual sex', then he's admitting he sucked dick in a toilet. When I pointed out the holes in his story, he tried to sock me one. Jeez, but I'm glad to see the back of him."

"He does sound like he's loony toons," Eric remarked.

"I don't know what he is, to be honest," Nick confessed, throwing back his Scotch. "One minute he's got me feeling sorry for him, and for what reason, I don't know. Next minute, I want to break his stupid neck. He is so fucked up."

"Do you think he's the murderer?"

"I don't *think* he'd go that far. He's got a temper, without a doubt, but I don't think he has the nerve to match it."

"So, he fired you?"

"No, I fired *him*. But y'know something? I'll bet you anything you like, that he's either on the phone tomorrow, or banging on the door, saying 'I'm sorry, Nick. I'm so sorry'. God, if I hear that one more time."

"What'll you do if he does call you?"

"I honestly don't know, Eric. Part of me will want to tell him to go to hell, but I'm the curious type you know. I guess that's why I like this business. A part of me wants to know what happened to Landon; another part wants to know just what makes John Hammond tick. He comes across as a screwball, but there's something about him that intrigues me. The dark side of him, I guess. There's definitely something goin' on in that devious little mind of his." He paused, and grimaced. "Is it the Scotch that's making me think like this? Because I'm beginning to hope that he does call me tomorrow. How crazy is that?"

Eric grinned at him. "You are a sucker for punishment," he chuckled.

"Yeah ... by the way, did you see Jeff or Peter today?"

"Uh ... yes, as a matter of fact. Jeff came by the gallery, and Peter met him there. They were going out I think."

"Hmm. I'm getting the impression my partner is avoiding me. Monica told me he hadn't been in the office all day."

"He did say something about a deposition."

"Oh, yeah." Nick nodded, remembering. "That's right. Still, he usually checks in with me at some point in the day." He crunched on a cube of ice thoughtfully. "You wanna know what I think?

Eric had a very good idea what Nick was about to say …

"I think that I'm right about what I mentioned the other night at dinner. He was with someone the night he got that DUI."

Bingo. Eric looked at him with wide eyes. "Oh, surely not," he muttered weakly.

"I know it's hard to believe—our Jeff being unfaithful. But there was just something about the way he was acting that night … so jumpy and nervous. Not at all like his usual calm self. I tell you Eric, he was up to something." He peered at Eric. "What's wrong? You've gone kinda red in the face. Wait a minute, he said something to you, didn't he?"

"Nick … I …" Eric mumbled.

"Son-of-a-gun! He told you, didn't he?" His eyes narrowed with accusation. "And just when were you going to tell me?"

"Nick … he asked me not to say anything."

"Forget that." Nick poured himself another shot. "Come on, let's hear it."

"You're making me betray a confidence."

"I know … shoot!"

"It was nothing, really."

"It had to have been something, Eric. Come on, tell Daddy."

"Promise me first, that you will never tell Jeff you heard this from me."

"Yeah, yeah, I promise … now tell me."

"He met some guy in a bar. They went back to his place … they started to fool around, and then Jeff put a stop to it, and left. That's it."

Nick started to laugh. "*That's it?*"

"Don't joke about it, Nick. Jeff feels pretty bad."

"Of course he does. I bet he's racked with guilt."

"Right. He was going to tell Peter."

"Is he nuts?"

"Well, you know Jeff—terminally honest."

"But if that's all it was, why get Peter in an uproar over it?"

"That's kinda what I said. I just hope it was good advice."

"Of course it was, babe. I mean, it would've been different if he'd plowed the guy, sworn undying love ..."

"Nick, for Pete's sake. If Jeff tells you about this, don't make a big joke out of it, please."

"Oh, he'll tell me. After I squeeze it out of him."

"Nick, please ..."

"I won't involve you, don't worry."

"God, now I feel terrible," Eric moaned, grabbing Nick's drink, and gulping it down.

"Hey, get your own," Nick protested, chuckling. "Now don't get all worked up about this. Like you said, nothing happened—well, almost nothing ..." He started to laugh again. "And you know what, babe? You caved way too easily. You were just dying to tell me that story, now weren't you?"

"You are evil, Nick Fallon!"

Nick's laughter became fiendish. "I am, ain't I?"

Next morning, Nick called Monica and told her he was running later than he had anticipated. "And Monica, if John Hammond calls, take a message and tell him I'll get back to him soon as I can."

"Oh, he called already, Nick," Monica informed him. "Soon as I got in. He sounded really upset."

"Yeah, he's good at that. Anyone else?"

"No, that's it for now."

"Okay. If Hammond should happen to stop by, tell him to wait in my office. I should be there in about a half hour or so."

"Will do."

"Jeff there yet?"

"Yes. He and Peter are in the office."

"Jeez. What are they? Joined at the hip all of a sudden?"

"Excuse me?"

"Never mind. Just me being my nasty self as usual."

"D'you want to speak to Jeff?"

"No. Just tell him I'll be in shortly."

"Okay, Nick. See you later."

Nick put the phone down and grimaced at the thought of dealing with John Hammond again. And what was with Jeff and Peter all of a sudden? Well, maybe they were trying to make up for that spot of trouble they both figured they were having. Peter was obviously going out of his way to spend more time with Jeff—but at the office? That was a bit unusual. Maybe they were planning to take a few days away alone. A good idea, under the circumstances.

He pulled on a crisp white cotton shirt and a pair of his khaki pants, then studied himself in the mirror. He grinned to himself, remembering how, last night, he'd had to placate Eric's fears of Jeff ever finding out that he had spilled the beans. Eric was such a softie … except where it counted, he thought carnally. His wardrobe completed, he wandered into the kitchen, and poured himself a cup of coffee to go. If Hammond showed, and still wanted him to stay on the case, he would drive up to LA later and talk again to Bernie, the bartender at The Racket. Nick was pretty sure that Bernie just might have some more dish on Robert Landon.

Monica looked up from her computer as the heavy glass doors by her desk swung open, and admitted Nick's client—a very nervous looking John Hammond.

"Good morning," he said. "Monica, isn't it?"

"That's right." Monica beamed at him. "Nick said for you to wait in his office."

"He did? Oh, I didn't know he was expecting me."

"I told him you called earlier," Monica said. "Go right in. Would you like something to drink?"

"No, I'm fine, thanks." Hammond pushed open the door to Nick's office and walked in. He froze, as the two men seated at the desk opposite Nick's, looked at him. One, a good looking, fair haired man with startling blue eyes smiled pleasantly, while the other stared at him with something akin to horror.

Yes, Jeff, Hammond thought, *it's me. Surprised?*

"Hi," Jeff said, recovering quickly. "Can I help you?"

"I'm here to see Nick."

"Oh, right. He'll be here in a few minutes. Why don't you make yourself comfortable, over there." He indicated the chair by Nick's desk. "Can we get you anything to drink?"

"No thanks." Hammond's smile was cold. "So, you must be Nick's partner. Stevens, is it?"

"That's right, Jeff Stevens. This is Peter Brandon." Jeff held out his hand. "And your name is …?" Peter was in the act of rising from his seat to shake Hammond's hand, when to his amazement the man slapped Jeff's hand away.

"My name is John Hammond," he hissed through tightly clenched teeth. "Have you forgotten that already?"

Peter looked at Jeff for some kind of explanation, and was bewildered to see his lover's face grow gray with shock at Hammond's outburst.

"Jeff?" Peter rose from his seat. "What's going on?" For a moment or two, time seemed to stand still as all three men regarded each other with varying degrees of dislike and suspicion. Peter was the first to speak. "I thought you were Nick's client," he said, feeling a tension build inside his chest.

"I am." Hammond looked squarely at Peter as he replied. "But Jeff and I share a different kind of relationship."

"What?" Peter stared at Jeff, shock and dismay registered clearly on his face.

"Bullshit!" Nick, who had arrived in time to hear Hammond's words, strode into the office. "What the hell are you trying to do here, John? Didn't I tell you, last night, to find someone else to pester? Now you're in here trying to get between my partner and his boyfriend. Just what are you playing at?"

"Ask him!" Hammond yelled, pointing at Jeff. "He's the one who picked me up, and asked if he could come back to my place. I didn't force him to have sex with me!"

"We didn't have sex," Jeff said, almost in a whisper as he looked desperately at Peter. "I stopped it before it got to that …"

"Liar!" Hammond rasped. "You were all over me, kissing me, begging me to give you head. You said that he ..." He pointed at Peter. "... He wouldn't put out anymore!"

"Stop this!" Jeff looked at him aghast. "Why are saying that? You know none of it's true. I told you I couldn't go through with it—I apologized ..." He broke off as Peter turned on his heel and left the office, flinging himself through the outer doors. "Christ," Jeff muttered. "I have to go ... have to stop him." He tore after Peter, leaving Nick and Hammond glaring daggers at one another, while Monica sat at her desk, her mouth wide open.

Nick took a step toward Hammond. "I'd like to break your neck, you little freak."

Hammond glared at him with defiance. "I should have you arrested for all the threats you've made since I hired you for this job. You think you can bully me with your macho attitude? Well, you're wrong. I'll file a police complaint."

"Go right ahead," Nick said, folding his arms as he sat on the edge of his desk. "The police are going to find you very interesting, after I get done telling them all about you."

Hammond looked nervous. "What do you mean?"

"Well, for starters that you withheld evidence under questioning by Detective Morales. You told him that you and Landon only talked to each other in the bar that night, arranging to meet some days later. You didn't mention that the two of you did it in the toilet, now did you? He might see you as the kind of person who tells lies in order to mislead him in his investigation. I don't think he'd like that, do you?"

"Nick, I *hired* you, remember? You should be in my corner...."

"Only if you were still a client of mine, which you no longer are, remember?"

"Nick ..." Hammond's shoulders slumped with seeming despair. "Okay, I'm sorry."

"Jesus!" Nick growled. "Don't start that again. I've never heard anyone say, 'I'm sorry', so many freakin' times. You are one sorry individual, you know that, John?" He looked at Hammond intently. "When you met Jeff in the bar the other night, did you recognize him?"

"No. How could I?" Hammond hedged. "I'd never seen him before."

Nick sighed. "See ... there you go again, John ... lying to me. You told me on our first meeting, that you had seen our advertisement in the local gay rag. There is a photograph of the two of us, me and Jeff, right in the middle of that ad. Okay, so maybe you didn't recognize him right away— a dimly lit bar and all that. But, when you were so close to be ... uh ... *kissing* him, am I expected to believe that it didn't click inside that busy little brain of yours, as to just who this fellow was that you were rubbing up against?"

Hammond's eyes slid away from Nick's intense stare. "Okay, I thought I'd seen him before somewhere ... and after he left, I remembered the advertisement. I checked it out, and it was him."

"So, knowing that he was my partner, and that you could very well bump into him here in this office, you still came barging in without an appointment. Let me ask you this, John. Was it your hope that you might just run into the man of your dreams?"

Hammond was silent for a moment or two as though thinking out his words carefully. "Initially, I wanted to see you ... to apologize *again*, for what happened last night. Although I still think you were out of line the way you treated me."

"Get on with it," Nick growled. "Don't look for an apology from me after what you did in here today."

"That ..." Hammond shook his head. "I lost control, I guess. You're right, I did come hoping that I'd see Jeff again. I really liked him, you know."

"You liked him so much you wanted to bust up his relationship with Peter, by lying about what really happened."

"How do *you* know what really happened?"

"Because he told me all about it," Nick lied. "Except, I didn't know it was you he'd dallied with."

"So, it's his word against mine!" Hammond said, with returning defiance.

"Yeah, like there's any competition there," Nick chuckled. "True blue Jeff, Mr. Honesty himself, against John Hammond, inveterate liar."

"I wouldn't expect you to believe me," Hammond huffed.

"How the hell could you? If I was to start counting the variations of the truth you are so adept at, I'd need more than my fingers and toes to keep score."

Hammond turned away, his face burning with anger and humiliation.

"You know, of course," Nick said quietly, "that I expect you to tell Peter the truth, don't you?"

Hammond cringed. "What?"

"That's right. Once Jeff and Peter clear the air between them, as I'm sure they will, I want you to retract your story about Jeff being 'all over you' as you so nicely put it."

"Nick, believe me, it wasn't all my doing."

"I believe you, John. That I do believe. Jeff and Peter were having a little trouble. Bad communication was all it was, but my partner was feeling blue enough to go out and have few drinks—and suddenly, there you were. And to be fair, John, you're a cute looking guy, and Jeff was just about buzzed enough to make that fatal slip."

"Gee thanks," Hammond muttered. "You're great for my ego."

"Forget your ego, John, and do the right thing. Jeff and Peter have been together for several years now. They've weathered a lot of setbacks in their lives—and frankly, I do not want to see either of them unhappy. Understand me?"

"And if I won't do this?"

Nick fished a business card out of his wallet and held it up in front of Hammond's eyes. "Your friend, Detective Roberto Morales, gets to have another chat with you. Or maybe you'd like that? He *is* kinda hunky."

"Very funny, Nick."

"That's me, the Joker. Until you piss me off."

Jeff caught up with Peter in the parking lot.

"Peter, *wait*." He gripped his lover's arm. "Please, hear me out."

Peter turned and looked at him through eyes that seemed to have turned to blue ice chips. "Say what you have to, then let me go."

"Not here. Let's go somewhere we can be alone, and ..."

"No. Right here will do." Peter broke free of Jeff's grip. "Just so you know, I have no intentions of listening to some half-baked excuses about how lonely you were, and how I was not paying you enough attention—because if you dare try that tactic, I will punch your lights out!"

"I'm not going to try to excuse what I did," Jeff said quietly. "No excuse in the world would cut it, I know that. What I want you to know is that John was lying about what happened."

"You mean, you didn't pick him up the night you got the DUI?"

"No, that part is true, but ..."

"Then there's nothing more to say, is there?" Peter interrupted. "You picked him up, you went home with him—the rest I don't want to hear. So if you're done ..."

"Dammit, Peter, let me finish."

"You *are* finished, Jeff. *We* are finished." He started to move toward his car.

"No!" Jeff put a restraining hand on his arm. "You can't mean that. Not after everything we've been through together."

"Right." Peter's eyes welled with tears. "After everything we've been through together ... and here, all this time, I thought that it meant something to you."

"Of course it does, Peter." Jeff ran his hand through his hair in desperation. "Please, don't walk away without at least listening to what happened."

Peter turned away in despair. "God, don't you get it?" he cried. "I don't *want* to know what happened, Jeff! I don't want to hear about this guy tearing at your clothes, and you ... doing whatever you did. I just can't deal with that, I'm sorry."

"Peter, please believe me—*nothing* happened. All right ... he kissed me, wanted to give me head. I stopped him, told him I couldn't go through with it ... that I had a lover. He was cool about it, or so I thought at the time. I left—*and that was all.*"

They stood gazing at one another for a long moment, Jeff's glistening eyes searching for forgiveness, and for trust. Then Peter shook his head sadly.

"I just can't forget that you went back to his home, Jeff. Did it seem like a good idea at the time? I mean, just what did you think was going to happen?"

Jeff heaved a great sigh of remorse. "I told him before we ever went inside, that I had changed my mind. He looked so hurt ..."

"Oh, my God!" Peter laughed bitterly. "And good old, big-hearted Jeff Stevens just couldn't let him down, is that it? Let me tell you something, Jeff. That guy in there is a manipulating son-of-a-bitch. He wanted you ... he still wants you. I don't blame him for that; I don't blame him at all. But you ... you betrayed our trust in one another. I may have been a bit neglectful recently, and for that I am truly sorry. I thought in my naiveté, that we had gotten over that ... but let me tell you, that in the time we have spent apart, I have never, ever, considered getting close to anyone else."

"Peter ..." Jeff's eyes filled with tears. "I just don't know what to say, other than I am so, so sorry. Just please believe me when I say that I love you, and that I'll do anything to make this up to you."

Peter stepped back as Jeff reached for him. "I need time to think about all this," he said, pulling his car keys from his pocket. "And, as you know, I have a ten o'clock appointment at the gallery. I'll call you later." With that, he strode off toward his car.

Jeff watched him go with a sinking heart. He wanted to run after him and stop him, beg him not to leave it like this, but he found he could not move. It was as though he had become transfixed by the enormity of what had just passed between them. He had never felt so empty in his life. He watched as Peter drove his car out of the parking lot, without looking at him, then he turned and retraced his footsteps back to the office.

Avoiding Monica's sympathetic expression as he passed her, he walked into his office, and sat down heavily at his desk. He looked across the room to where Nick and John Hammond were standing.

"So John," he said, his voice drained of all emotion. "Are you happy about what you did today?"

"Uh, Jeff ..." Nick cleared his throat. "John has something he wants to say to you."

"Well, isn't that nice?" Jeff showed his teeth in a mirthless grimace. "Too bad that I don't give a flying fuck what he wants to say. In fact, if he doesn't get out of my sight in two seconds flat, I may just kick his sorry ass all the way to the Mexican border!"

"Wait, Jeff ... just hear him out. He wants to apologize for what he did ... and he also wants to talk to Peter and ..."

"Are you out of your mind?" Jeff yelled, jumping to his feet. "You think I'd want that freak anywhere near Peter again?"

"Hey, wait a minute," Hammond protested. "You're not exactly Mr. Innocent in all this ..."

Jeff bounded from his desk, his face dark with rage. Before Nick could intervene, he had grabbed Hammond by the lapels of his blazer, and yanked him off his feet, pulling him up so that their faces were a mere inch apart.

"Get out of my sight, you little creep," he hissed. "If you ever come any-where near me or Peter again, I will break you in two!"

"Jeff, let him go," Nick said, getting between them. Hammond stag-gered back as Jeff released him. He looked wildly around him, his face white with fear.

"You're *nuts*," he yelled, straightening his jacket. "I'm calling the cops!"

"Okay, John." Nick hustled him outside. "Time for you to go, I think."

"That guy is a *lunatic* ..." Hammond was still yelling as Nick marched him out into the parking lot.

"That guy is dying inside, because of what you did," Nick told him. "I guess having you stick around wasn't one of my better ideas. You'd better go."

"Just like that?" Hammond screeched. "I should forget that he threat-ened to *kill* me?"

"He didn't mean it," Nick said calmly. "He's probably sitting at his desk right now, filled with remorse at having treated you so badly. Anyway, you're not going back in there to find out. Go—and I'd listen to Jeff's advice if I were you. Don't try to contact him again."

"Don't worry!" Hammond sneered. "He's even *meaner* than you!"

"Boy," Nick couldn't stop the chuckle that escaped his lips. "Never did I think I'd hear anyone say *that* to me!"

"This isn't funny!" Hammond raged at him.

"You're right, John. It isn't funny at all … Okay, so what d'you want to do now?"

"What do you mean?"

"I mean, what you came here for this morning. You want me to keep going on this case or not?"

"Are you *serious*?" Hammond looked at him in amazement. "You said yesterday, you thought I did it!"

Nick sighed. "I don't think you did it, John. I think maybe the one truth you told me yesterday, was that you didn't kill Robert Landon. But you know what? I'm kinda intrigued by the case—and I have a hunch that I'll find some answers at The Racket. So, if you still want to find out what happened to Robert, I'll go there again and do some more snooping."

"Well …" Hammond hesitated. "If you'll keep that maniac away from me."

"Jeff's not a maniac. At least … not when he's in a good mood."

"There you go again, making fun of it all, Nick." Hammond glared at him. "I don't know if my nerves can stand anymore of this."

Nick shrugged. "Okay, suit yourself. Let me know if you change your mind." He turned to go.

"Wait …" Hammond seemed to struggle with himself for a moment or two. "Okay, I guess I'd still like to know what happened to Robert," he said finally.

"It might give you some kind of closure," Nick suggested.

Hammond nodded. "Okay, Nick. Let me know what you find out." He paused for a moment. "I really am very sorry for what happened in there."

"I'll be sure to tell Jeff and Peter that," Nick said, trying to keep the sarcasm out of his voice. He watched Hammond walk to his car, climb in, then with a desultory wave of his hand, he drove away.

When Nick returned to the office, Monica was standing behind Jeff massaging his shoulders. The warning look she gave Nick said, 'Go easy'.

"I guess I lost it back there," Jeff said, his voice thick with stress.

"You could say that."

"Sorry, Nick."

"Jeez, everybody's sorry." Nick threw his arms in the air. "Sorry, sorry, sorry—that's all I've been listening to for the last few days. Sorry, sorry, sorry! Christ, now you're at it."

"*Nick*." Monica muttered. "Don't ..."

Jeff took hold of her hands and smiled gratefully. "Thanks, Monica. That felt great."

Nick stared at them both, then with a heavy sigh he sat on the edge of Jeff's desk, and put a comforting hand on his shoulder. "So, what happened with you and Peter out there?" he asked, gently.

"What you'd expect, I guess." Jeff's expression was bleak. "I think I've blown it, Nick."

"Naw ..." Nick squeezed Jeff's shoulder. "He'll come around, once he's had time to think things through."

"I don't think so."

"Me and Eric'll talk to him." He looked at Monica for help. "What d'you think Monica?"

"I think you should all give Peter some space for a time," she said, sitting by Jeff. "It was all so emotionally charged in here—everybody yelling and accusing. And it all came out of the blue. I mean, it had to have been a tremendous shock for him. John Hammond just coming out with all that stuff ..."

"But it was all lies," Nick reminded her. "Well, nearly all ..."

"Just give him time to realize that," Monica persisted. "Right now he's hurt and bewildered—and probably just a little mad."

"He'll get over it," Nick muttered.

"Why should he?" Jeff pushed his chair back, and stared at his two friends, his face pinched with despair. "Why should he get over it? Why should he believe I was telling the truth? For all he knows, I could just have been trying to worm my way out of a very sticky situation."

"He knows you better than that," Nick said.

"Does he?" Jeff's lips twisted in a wry grimace. "I bet that right now, he's wondering if he knows me at all."

Eric knew as soon as Peter slammed his way into the gallery that something had gone terribly wrong—and he intuited, with a sinking feeling in the pit of his stomach, that he also knew exactly what it was. He had seen Peter angry before, but he had to admit he had never seen him so pale and shaken.

Eric took an involuntary step back as Peter stormed up to him. "Did you know about this, too?" he demanded, with a searching glare that negated any avoidance of the question.

"Know about what?"

"About Jeff screwing around with some guy!"

"He wasn't screwing around, Peter …"

"Oh!" Peter moved in for the kill. "So you *did* know about it. Everybody, but me, knows about it."

"Peter, wait a minute, before you go flying into the air about this …"

"How long have you known?'

"Only since yesterday. I …"

"I saw you yesterday. Why didn't you tell me?"

"*Tell* you?" Eric looked at him appalled. "Do you really think I would do that—after Jeff begged me to say nothing, not even to Nick? You think that I could be the one to blab what he told me in confidence?"

"You are supposed to be my friend, as well as my employee," Peter said through tight lips. "That means we owe each other a degree of trust."

"I am your friend," Eric interrupted. "And you can trust me, Peter … you know that," he added, ignoring Peter's snort of disgust. "I just didn't want this to blow out of all proportion. What Jeff told me was … well, it was more of a temptation really, rather than cheating. Nothing really happened."

"He went back with the son-of-a-bitch, Eric. He initiated the pick-up, for Christ's sake. He *wanted* to do it!"

"But he *didn't* ... that's the important part, Peter. He didn't do anything. He left, and was on his way home to you when the cop stopped him. Peter, please see it that way—don't go looking for all the ulterior motives. He was tempted, but he loves you too much to go through with it. That's what you have to remember."

Peter stood staring at Eric for a long time, his breath coming in shallow gulps as he tried to control himself. Finally, he turned away, looking out through the gallery windows to the street that was beginning to show the first signs of the busy day ahead.

"So tell me, Eric," he said, his voice sad and subdued. "If Nick had done this, how would you feel about it?"

"Jeff asked me the same thing."

"And?"

"I would be upset, of course. Angry, *hurt* ..."

"But you would forgive him?"

"Yes, I would."

Peter nodded, then walked away toward the back studio, Eric following quickly behind him.

"Are you going to call him?" he asked.

"Not just now." Peter picked up the coffee pot, and poured himself a cup. "I need time to let all this sink in."

"Peter ..." Eric put a gentle hand on his friend's arm. "When Jeff was telling me about what happened, he looked destroyed. He told me he was racked with guilt, and he said the same thing you did—the intention was there. Quite honestly Peter, I think he'll have a harder time forgiving himself, than you will have forgiving him."

Peter allowed himself a small smile. "You might just be right about that, Eric." He took a sip of his coffee. "I just can't get over the fact that earlier we were just sitting in the office talking ... about what, I can't remember, when this guy walks in, says he's client of Nick's ..."

"Wait a minute." Eric looked at him with wide eyes. "He was Nick's client? Was his name John something-or-other?

"Yes, Hammond, I think. Why?"

"That's him—John Hammond." Eric could not control the laugh that escaped his lips. "That idiot made a play for Nick on the beach the other day. He started licking Nick's chest!"

"*What?*"

"Yeah. Nick came home ranting about what a jerk he was. I thought it was funny, of course, which did not please my fella at all! And here's the thing, Peter ..." Eric paused, remembering. "Nick told me, just last night, that Hammond is a total liar."

Peter was silent for a time, seeming to digest what Eric had told him. "I have to admit," he said slowly, "Jeff's version of what happened was completely different from the other guy's. Jeff said he stopped it before anything really happened, beyond the fact they kissed. While Hammond said Jeff was all over him, begging for it ... saying I had cut him off."

"Oh, come on!" Eric snorted with derision. "Does that sound like Jeff, for heaven's sake? You surely don't believe a word of that?"

Peter shook his head. "No, I don't believe that."

Eric smiled at him. "Good. Now, when you get ..."

A tapping on the glass door at the front of the gallery distracted them both. Peter glanced at his watch.

"Ten o'clock," he said with a sigh. "I have that appointment with the LA Times reporter. Another interview where I have to look happy and smile pretty for the camera. Shit. Why today?"

Eric gave him a quick hug. "I'll go let him in." "You'll be just fine—and so will everything else."

CHAPTER 7

"Back so soon?" Bernie, The Racket's resident bartender gave Nick a grin as he walked up to the bar, feeling his way through its habitual half-light.

"Couldn't wait to talk with you some more," Nick said, putting his foot up on the bar rail. As his eyes became accustomed to the gloom, he could see the bar was much busier than the last time he was there.

"I've become very popular these last couple of days," Bernie remarked. "Coke?"

"You remember everyone's drink?"

"Just the good lookin' ones," Bernie said, with another grin. "And Nick, you definitely rate."

"Thanks." Nick accepted the Coke. "Join me?"

"I'll have a Scotch later, if that's OK."

"You bet." Nick passed him a twenty. "So, what's making you so popular?"

"Well, first you the other day, then yesterday this Detective uh ... Mor something ..."

"Morales?"

"That's him. He came in asking 'bout Robert, same as you did."

"Right. He's the one heading the investigation."

"Yeah, well it's not going to get solved with him on the case."

"What d'you mean?"

"He's too antsy to be investigating a gay guy's murder, for Pete's sake. All the time he was talking to me, he was acting like he had a giant itch up his butt. The jerk kept looking around, nervous as hell."

Nick grinned at him. "Morales is terminally straight."

Bernie grunted. "Nine times outta ten, those terminally straight dudes are closet cases. Anyway, I told him to relax. Wasn't anybody here going to put the make on a cop—unless he was in uniform!"

"Good one," Nick said, chuckling.

"Yeah, well he didn't appreciate it ... never cracked a smile. Asked me a bunch of questions about Robert, and who he talked with, etc. Kinda like you did, 'cept I didn't tell him as much as I told you."

"You didn't?"

"Nah ... none of his business."

"But if it helps him ..."

"I'm telling you, he's hopeless." Bernie leaned across the bar and lowered his voice. "I asked him if the department ever found out what happened to the two hustlers who disappeared. They were regulars here, and suddenly they were gone. 'Course the cop hadn't a clue—dumb asshole."

"They hang around with Landon?"

"Can't say they did," Bernie replied, thinking back. "No, Robert was either on his own, or with his two buddies."

"So, tell me Bernie …" Nick leaned closer to the bartender. "What d'you think happened to the two hustler guys?"

"I don't know …" He broke off as a customer entered the bar. "Hey, Frank, what'll it be?"

Nick looked at the pale, slim, young man who had appeared at his side. Red hair, Frank … could he get this lucky?

"Just a beer, Bernie." Frank gave Nick a sidelong look and smile.

"Can I buy you that?" Nick asked.

"Frank," Bernie gestured toward Nick. "This is Nick—he's a private investigator from Laguna Beach."

Nick held out his hand. "Nice to meet you."

The hand that took his was warm and soft, and felt very vulnerable, as though the minutest pressure from Nick's big hand could crush it. The eyes that met his were sad and trusting.

"Hi Nick," Frank's voice was no more than a whisper. "You a friend of Bernie's?"

"He is now," Bernie said, winking at Nick. "He's investigating Robert's murder."

"Oh." He took the beer Bernie slid toward him, and raised the glass to his lips. His eyes met Nick's over the top of the glass.

Nick smiled. "Would you mind me asking you a few questions?"

"Not at all," Frank replied. He looked at Nick's Coke. "You don't drink?"

"I think I might just have a beer …"

"Good. Let's go sit over there." Frank indicated a table in the far corner of the bar. "It's quieter over there."

Beer in hand, Nick followed Frank to the table, sitting opposite him. "So, you and Robert were close?"

"We were good friends," Frank said, a trace of bitterness in his voice. "We worked together for three years; we came here a couple of nights a week, just to unwind, you know. It can get pretty stressful dealing with some of our clients."

"I bet," Nick commiserated. "People can get real touchy where money is concerned."

"Robert used to make me and Steve laugh when he'd imitate some of the more crass examples."

"Steve?"

"Our supervisor. He's straight, but he'd come here sometimes with Robert and me …"

"Frank …" Nick stared intently into the young man's eyes. "What d'you think happened to Robert?"

"He was murdered …"

"Yes, I know that. But you knew him pretty well. Did he ever say to you he was worried about someone threatening him, at any time?"

"No." Frank shook his head. "This was a total shock to me, Nick … to all of us here, and at work. Robert was a good friend to me. Before I met him, I would never have been able to come into a bar like this. I was far too nervous; but he took me here, introduced me to Bernie and some of the regulars. This became like 'Cheers' to me. You know, like the TV show re-runs—everybody knows your name? I just can't imagine anyone wanting to hurt Robert, let alone kill him." His eyes glistened with tears as he looked at Nick. "I still can't believe it, sometimes, it just seems unreal. Sometimes I look at the door, expecting to see him come through … Jesus, I'm sorry." He reached for the napkin under his glass and wiped his eyes with it.

Nick waited for Frank to compose himself then he asked, "Did you ever see Robert with a guy by the name of John Hammond? Fair hair, 'bout five ten, sharp dresser."

Frank shook his head. "Doesn't ring a bell …"

"Bernie tells me two hustlers disappeared about the same time as Robert. D'you remember them?"

"Oh yeah, but I never talked to them." Frank averted his eyes for a moment. "Forgive me if I sound like a prude, but what they did kind of appalled me. I could never figure why two nice looking boys would do something like that."

"Takes all sorts."

"I guess. I just found it … sick."

"Anyone else Robert spent a lot of time with?" Nick asked.

Frank's mouth twisted with dislike. "There was a guy called Tom. Whenever he was around, Steve and I would find a table over here, away from the bar. We couldn't stand him—always hustling drinks from Robert … hanging on him like they were best friends."

"But Robert obviously liked him."

"Yeah, I'll never understand that."

"What did this Tom look like?"

"Tall, dark good looking I suppose, if you like rough trade."

"Could it have been a sexual thing with him and Robert?"

"Probably. Robert never talked about it. I think he was a tad ashamed of it." He paused as if he had suddenly remembered something.

"What is it?" Nick asked.

"You mentioned someone earlier—a fair-haired guy."

"Yeah, John Hammond."

"Now, when I think about it," Frank said slowly, "Robert mentioned he had a date with a guy he'd met here. They were going to have dinner. Robert seemed really jazzed about it—and he did mention the guy was blond. Nicely put together, was what Robert said."

"Sounds like my client."

"Your client?"

"Robert never showed for the date," Nick explained. "John Hammond, my client, figured he'd just been stood up, until he read the newspaper report about Robert Landon's body being found in Laurel Canyon. He asked me to find out what I could about his death."

"Well, I hope you find the son-of-a-bitch who did it." Frank threw back the last of his beer. "Can I get you one?"

"No thanks, I'm driving. Let me just ask you this, Frank. Robert told you he had a dinner date. How long after he told you that did he disappear?"

Frank bit his lip, thinking. "It can't have been more than a day or so. He didn't show for work on the Thursday. I remember it being that day because we always get a huge download on the computers on Thursdays, and I was cursing 'cause Robert wasn't there to help. Steve called him at home and left messages, then after work, I went over to his apartment to see if maybe he was ill. His car wasn't there, but I rang the bell anyway. Of course, there was no one there. I went back the next day—still no sign of him. That's when Steve filed a missing persons' report with the police."

Nick got ready to leave. "Thanks Frank," he said, taking the young man's hand in his own. "You've been a big help." Frank couldn't quite mask his disappointment that Nick wouldn't stay for another drink, but he walked over to the bar with him.

"So, two more?" Bernie asked.

Nick shook his head. "Just one for Frank. I have to get going."

"Please find Robert's murderer," Frank said, accepting the beer.

"I'll do my best, Frank. You take care." He turned to Bernie. "Thanks again for the information, Bernie."

"Yeah …" Bernie lifted his hand. "Don't be a stranger."

Nick glanced at his watch as he left The Racket. Ten to four. As he drove, he mulled over what he'd learned in the past hour. Morales had been in there talking to Bernie. So, he was also looking for a connection between Landon's disappearance and The Racket. Did he know about the two hustlers disappearing? He pulled Morales's card from his inside pocket and punched in his number.

"Hey, Morales … Nick Fallon. How's it goin'?"

"Okay," Morales did not sound happy.

"Got any more leads on the Landon case yet?"

"Nothing I'm gonna tell you about."

"Aw, Detective. I thought we had an agreement."

"What are you talking about?"

"I found the cell phone, remember?"

"And I told you what was on it, remember?" Morales sounded ready to hang up. "That's all you get."

"What about the two hustler kids that disappeared around the same time as Landon?"

"What about them?"

"Do you have any leads on them—names, addresses, next of kin ... that kind of thing? You know, the kind of stuff you get paid to do."

"Don't get smart with me, Fallon."

Nick bit back a chuckle. "So, you got nothin' on them?"

"Do you know how many hustler kids disappear every year from Los Angeles, Fallon? If we were to follow up on every single one of them, we'd have no time for anything else."

"But these two," Nick persisted. "These two, disappearing at the same time as Landon—all three of 'em patrons of the same bar. Doesn't that make you curious, or did you just put it down to coincidence?"

"Look," Morales said, his impatience evident in his tone. "The bartender at The Racket said Landon came in the bar, with more or less the same couple of friends, each time. He didn't bother with hustlers ..."

"In the bar."

"What?"

"He didn't bother with them in the bar, Morales, but what about out on the sidewalk, on the way to his car? Hustlers can be very determined guys at times—especially as the night grows late, and they haven't scored."

"You talkin' from experience, Fallon?"

"Shouldn't you have followed that stupid remark with, 'Heh, heh, heh?' You're forgetting I was a cop, Morales. Yes, I'm talking from experience!"

"Okay, so where are you going with this?"

"Two possibilities," Nick said. "One, the hustlers murdered Landon, buried his body—then took off, in his car. Two, someone else murdered all three of them, and took off in Landon's car."

Morales was quiet for a moment or two. "All right," he said finally. "I'll buy either one, but how do you prove it?"

"We have to find the hustlers—either dead or alive."

Morales groaned. "That's like finding needles in a haystack."

"Do you have anything on Landon's car—the black Corvette?"

"Not yet. We've got the license number on our stolen car list ..."

"But of course, after three months, it could be anywhere." Nick drummed his fingers on the steering wheel as he thought. "Did you talk to the guys he worked with?"

"Yeah." Nick heard the rustle of a notepad's pages being turned over. "Let's see, the two that seemed to know Robert Landon best were Steven Blackwell, his supervisor, and a co-worker, Frank Jessup."

"How did they seem to you?"

"Okay. They'd hang out with Landon at The Racket from time to time."

"Yeah, I spoke to Frank at the bar this afternoon. Did he tell you about some guy named Tom hustling drinks from Landon all the time?"

"No, he didn't," Morales said, sounding annoyed. "What else did he tell you?"

"He remembered Landon mentioning my client, and the fact he was meeting him for dinner later in the week, which makes me tend to agree with John Hammond's original thought that Landon was murdered on the night they were supposed to have dinner."

"What makes you think that?"

"Because Hammond told me they'd set up the date for Wednesday night, and Frank said Robert Landon didn't show on the Thursday. So, looks like he was murdered sometime after he left the office on the Wednesday. Now, if we could just find out where he was in those couple of hours between the time he left the office, and when he was due over at Hammond's apartment …"

"Okay, Fallon …" Nick could tell Morales was anxious to wind up their conversation. "I have to go … but, keep in touch if you find anything else new."

Nick pressed the 'end' button on his cell phone and sighed. Why was he getting the idea that he was doing all the work here? Like Bernie said, Morales was useless … didn't seem to have a clue. Why? Joe French had said Morales was an okay cop. Then, why was he showing so little interest in solving this case? Could it be pressure of some kind? Nick was sure Morales had many other cases on his desk. The LAPD was almost always stretched beyond its capabilities. Too much crime, too few police officers. Or could it be he just didn't want to spend a lot time on a case involving a murdered gay guy? Nick hoped it wasn't the latter reason, but his cynical nature reminded him that all too many times, cases like this were put on the back burner, unless there was someone, maybe like himself, asking enough questions to keep it from being forgotten.

Eric heaved a grateful sigh as he locked the door to Peter's gallery. He couldn't wait to get home. It had not been a good day. Peter's bad mood seemed to have escalated as the hours went by. Jeff had called a half dozen times and Eric, having had to field most of the calls, was emotionally exhausted. Peter had finally agreed to speak to him after Eric had practically begged him to do so, and the side of the conversation Eric could hear, had been tense and non-productive.

Behind him, he heard the jingle of Peter's car keys as he walked the length of the gallery.

"Eric?"

"Yes, Peter?"

"I'm meeting Andrew for a drink. Want to join us?"

"Uh, no thanks. I was kinda looking forward to a swim when I get home. Hope you don't mind."

"That's OK. You've probably had enough of my gloomy face for one day."

"Peter ..." Eric hesitated for a moment. "I don't want to sound like I'm trying to tell you what to do, but shouldn't you and Jeff talk about all this before it gets too difficult? The longer you avoid it ..."

"I know, I know." Peter looked at his friend through sad eyes. "I just want to make sure I am totally calm, when that moment comes. You know me; sometimes I say things in the heat of the moment that I regret later. I don't want to do that. This is far too important for me to just stand there and yell accusations. I've done that already."

"Does Andrew know?"

"Mmm ... I called him and cried on his shoulder over the phone. He thought I was joking at first."

"He's known you guys since the beginning."

"Yes." Peter leaned against the doorframe and closed his eyes. "You know, Eric ... if you, or anyone, had told me this would happen one day,

I would have never believed it. Even my so-called psychic sense never pre-pared me for this."

"But, Peter ..."

Peter stilled him with a hand on his arm. "I know, Eric ... you think I'm overreacting, and I probably am. I only wish I could convince myself of that. I wish I could say it doesn't matter, but each time I think about it, I can't get it out of my mind that Jeff was the one who wanted it to hap-pen."

"No, that's not true! I mean ..." Eric hesitated as he saw Andrew cross the street in front of the gallery. "I mean ... he wasn't thinking straight. He was upset and ..."

"It's OK, Eric," Peter said, squeezing his arm. "I know you're rooting for us—and I love you for that."

Eric opened the door to let Andrew in. Andrew, completely aware of what he had just walked into, gave Eric a quick hug, then wrapped his arms around Peter, holding him tight. Eric stood, silently watching these two best friends communicate their love for one another.

"Well," he said after a moment or two had passed. "I'll be off ..."

"Sure you don't want to join us?" Peter asked.

"No, no. You guys go and talk about everything. Nick will be home, prowling around the kitchen, looking for bones and scraps ..."

Andrew chuckled. "Does he know what you say about him when he's not around."

"Absolutely," Eric said with a grin. "He encourages this scary image of himself." He hugged Peter. "Please let tomorrow be a good news day!"

When Eric reached home, he was surprised to see Nick had not yet returned from LA. The outside lights were on, bathing the exterior in their artfully placed glow, but the inside of the house was in darkness. Eric turned on two or three lamps, then shucking off his clothes and walking outside, he dove into the pool's cool invigorating depths. He swam several lengths without pausing, then turned and floated on his back, gazing up at the darkening sky, dotted here and there with a few early stars.

He loved this house, almost as much as he loved the man with whom he shared it. When Nick had brought him here, soon after the trauma that had almost cost both of them their lives, he had fallen in love with every stone, every room, and every part of it that made it their home. The horror that had been Francisco Garcia was each day, fading from Eric's mind, just as the scars from the madman's bullet were fading from his body. Time, he thought now, could calm and heal all things. He could only hope that it would also prove true for Peter and Jeff.

He rolled onto his stomach, and swam the few strokes to the edge of the pool, where at eye level, he could see a pair of well-formed bare feet.

"Were you spying on me, sir?" He grinned up at Nick who stood, naked, at the pool edge.

"I was enjoying the view."

"So am I ..." With an impish smile, Eric reached out and grabbed Nick's ankle in an effort to pull him into the water. When all that accomplished was a low chuckle, he resorted to some underhanded tactics. Standing up in the water, he ran his hands in sensuous movements up Nick's legs until, with a satisfied curl of his lips, he saw the beginnings of an impressive erection before his eyes.

Nick knelt down, placed his hands under Eric's armpits, and hoisted him out the pool in one quick, easy motion, then enfolded him in a crushing embrace.

"Oh, dear God," Eric groaned as the heat generated between their bodies overwhelmed him with carnal desire. He yelped as he found himself falling backwards. Still locked in each other's arms, they hit the water with a tremendous splash. Eric clung to Nick as they surfaced, laughing like boys. He wound his legs around Nick's waist and smothered him with kisses. Nick held him, his hands under Eric's butt, supporting him as their bodies meshed together.

"Mmm," Eric murmured. "I like this version of water aerobics."

Nick smiled happily. "Funny how the sight and feel of you, can make even the crappiest day seem worthwhile in the end."

"That's sweet," Eric said, kissing him on the lips. "Was it a crappy day?"

"Driving to LA and back in the rush hour, ain't the greatest." He lifted Eric up onto the pool edge, then pulled himself up beside him. "How was *your* day?"

"Pretty tense. Peter hasn't talked with Jeff yet."

"Where is he?"

"Having a drink with Andrew."

"Well, that's a good thing. Andrew might just talk some sense into him."

"I don't think it's going to be that easy, to be honest. Peter seems to be hung up on the fact that Jeff admits he was the one who initiated the pickup."

"Well, somebody had to."

"*Nick* ..." Eric punched him lightly on the arm. "Don't let Peter hear you not take this seriously."

"You know, babe ... the more I think on this, the crazier it gets."

"Meaning?"

"Meaning, they're both overreacting to the situation."

"Easy for you to say. You didn't have that idiot Hammond screaming in your face about you begging for a blow job!"

Nick shook his head, remembering. "Boy, ain't that the truth."

"Well then ... *that's* what caused the problem. I can imagine how Peter felt at that moment."

"Mmm ... but none of it's true. Anyway," he said, deciding to change the subject. "I talked with a couple of guys in LA who knew Robert Landon."

"Oh yeah? You getting any closer to what happened?"

"There's a couple of things I passed by Morales, the detective handling the case—but I don't know ... he's a strange one."

"In what way?"

"Well, I try to tell myself he's probably got a bunch of other stuff to deal with, while me—I have a vested interest in solving this. But he's just way too half-hearted about it all. You know, it's like, why bother? It's just another dead fag ... no big deal."

"So, he's not going to bother his ass."

"Well, he's not going to go out of his way, by the look of things. I think I'll call Joe French in the morning ... see if I can get some info from him."

"Good idea." Eric stood up. "You hungry?"

"Whatcha got?" Nick grinned up at him.

"Lots of things—and a surprise dessert."

Nick jumped to his feet and wrapped his arms around Eric. "Can I have the dessert first?"

Nine o'clock found Peter and Andrew walking slowly from the bar they'd been sitting in for the past two hours. Andrew had listened with a great deal of sympathy, while Peter had given him his version of the events that had led him and Jeff to this situation.

"I think I've told you everything as fairly as I could," Peter said as they approached their parked cars. "I've been trying not to put my spin on it, but of course, it's hard not to get emotional. When I let myself think about the two of them ..."

"That's what you mustn't think about," Andrew interrupted. "If you dwell on that part of it, it's going to make it harder for you to forgive him, and get on with your lives. Because you are going to get over this, Peter. You and Jeff have come too far together to let something like this ruin it all. Look at it for what it is—a mistake. That's all, just a mistake. We're all allowed to make them, aren't we? Even Jeff ..."

"Even Jeff," Peter murmured. "I suppose, in a way, there's a lesson here."

"And what is it?"

"Don't expect too much from the person you love—then you won't be disappointed."

"Oh, Peter." Andrew shook his head. "That's just way too cynical. Jeff is a wonderful guy. From the first day I met him, six years ago, I knew he was the one for you. Right now, you're angry and disappointed, but let's face it—it could have been a whole lot worse."

Peter nodded. "I suppose ..."

Andrew hugged him tight. "Don't look so miserable. I was hoping our talk would help you feel better about it all."

"It'll take time, I guess," Peter said, his head on Andrew's shoulder.

"You should talk to him tonight."

"I don't know if I can. I'm afraid I'll say all the wrong things, and make it worse."

"Try, Peter."

Driving home, Peter was filled with apprehension about just how he would deal with he and Jeff being alone, finally. Sometimes it was hard to believe that any of this had really happened. In the early morning, when they had awakened, he and Jeff had made love in a sleepy, unhurried way, enjoying the warmth and comfort of each other's body, reveling in an intimacy that only total involvement can bring. He wondered how it would feel to make love to him now, knowing that John Hammond had held him his arms, had kissed his lips, had put his mouth around his ...

"Jesus." Peter wiped the tears from his eyes with the back of his hand. Stop thinking about that, he told himself. You have to get over that, or there will never be a moment when you look at him and not think, were you telling me the truth? Was what you said happened really all there was to it—or was it as Hammond described it—you all over him, tearing at his clothes, begging for a blowjob? Oh God, how had it ever come to this?

He felt a momentary relief as he pulled into the garage and Jeff's car wasn't there. Good, he thought. It'll give me time to calm down a bit ... think of how I'm going to handle this ... of what I'm going to say. He pushed his way through the garage door, and into the kitchen. The lights were on, and his eyes immediately fell on the note propped up by a coffee can. His hand trembled as he picked it up:

Dear Peter,

If anyone had ever told me I would, one day, be writing this kind of letter to you, I would have laughed in their face. I know today was a horrendous shock for you—and for that I am deeply sorry. I know that I will never forget the look of disappointment on your face, when I admitted that I had picked up John Hammond in a bar, and gone back to his place.

Why did I do it? I have asked myself that question a million times since it happened. I know you feel betrayed by me—and rightly so. You said you didn't want to hear excuses. I respect that, and will offer none, for really, now when I think of it, it would only make me sound pathetic. Pathetic— not a word I have ever felt I deserved, until now.

I think it's probably best that I get out of your hair until you have had time to think things through. I called Rob, and asked him if I could stay with him. Maggie is visiting her folks with little Robbie for a few days, so I won't be in anyone's way. I know Nick will be mad, but I didn't want to involve him and Eric in this—at least not anymore than they already are. They are our working partners as well as our friends—it just wouldn't be fair.

I feel like I have created chaos in all our lives with this stupid mistake. I hope that you can forgive me, and will allow me to be a part of your life again. Every moment away from you will seem like a lifetime—does that sound too corny? Believe me, I mean it, every word. You are the most important man in my life—you are my life, and I will always love you,

Jeff.

CHAPTER 8

Eric rolled over in bed and encountered an empty space. He opened his eyes and squinted at the radio alarm on Nick's nightstand. Six … already.

"Oh, I don't wanna get up yet," he complained to the ceiling. So don't, he told himself closing his eyes again. Nick would be out there running on the beach … probably trying to figure out his next move on the Landon mystery. He'd be home shortly, ready for breakfast. Eric groaned and sat up, rubbing his eyes. Nothing else for it … He slipped out of bed, and padded to the bathroom. He wondered how Peter and Jeff had fared last night. He was pretty sure Andrew had given Peter some sound advice. Whether he took it or not, was another thing altogether. He could be the most stubborn pain-in-the … But, try as he might, Eric could not imagine the two of them parting company—not over something like this, anyway. Yeah, Jeff had screwed up. Jeez, but he just couldn't see that somehow. Then again, nothing had really happened. It could have, but it hadn't.

"So," he said aloud to his mirrored reflection as he rinsed his hands and face, "Peter just has to get over it, that's all."

He pulled on a pair of shorts, wandered into the kitchen, and started fixing a pot of coffee. He switched the radio on to his favorite jazz station, then hearing the thump of the morning newspaper being thrown against the front door, he went to bring it in.

The phone ringing gave him a start. Who the heck, at this time of the morning? He peered at the caller ID. Peter ...

"Hi, Peter. You're up and at 'em early this morning."

"Did I wake you?"

"Uh, uh, I'm fixing coffee. You OK? Did you talk to Jeff last night?"

"No ... when I got home, he'd gone."

"Gone ... where?"

"He left me a note saying he was going to stay with his buddy, Rob."

"So, are you going to call him there?"

"I was kinda hoping he'd call me."

"Peter, don't let this go on too long. You guys have got to talk."

"I know, I know. I didn't sleep a wink last night thinking about ... about how it would be without him."

"That's not going to happen," Eric snapped. "I will personally beat the crap out of both of you, if you let this destroy your relationship. I mean it, Peter!" He was rewarded by the sound of a faint chuckle on the other end.

"Hey, what kind of a friend are you?"

"The best kind!" Eric said, laughing. "Why don't you come on over, and have breakfast with Nick and me?"

"Only if you promise not to beat the crap out of me."

"Oh, okay ... I promise."

"See you in a few, then."

Nick repeatedly pounded up and down the stone steps that led from the beach to the Coast Highway. He liked to finish off his run by forcing his heart rate to the max, and he'd found this particular exercise to be beneficial. The sweat poured from him as he forced himself into the final climb. At the top, he dropped down onto the concrete, waiting for his breathing to return to normal. He'd been thinking while he ran—thinking about all the possible scenarios that surrounded Landon's murder. Something didn't fit, and he wasn't quite sure what it was. He'd had a thought, and the more he thought of it, the better he liked it. Only problem was how to convince the person to help him out ... Peter.

When Nick had first met Peter in New York, he had been more that just a little skeptical about the psychic intuition Jeff claimed Peter had. He had, in fact, been rude about it. So, it had come as a moment of truth for Nick when Peter's psychic ability had saved him and Andrew from his ex-partner who'd held them at gunpoint in a New York hotel room—with the intention of murdering them both. Since then, he'd seen Peter in action two or three more times, again getting him, and several other people, out of tight spots. There was no doubt now in Nick's mind; Peter could perhaps prove to be very useful in a case where there were so few clues.

Nick knew, however, that when Peter had one of his psychic 'feelings' as he called them, it could leave him drained and nauseated. Jeff had told Nick he didn't want Peter involved in this kind of thing again, as the side effects worried him, and no one seemed to know what the long-term effects would be.

Well, he could only ask.

"So, did Jeff say how long he'd be staying over at Rob's?" Eric asked, handing Peter a mug of coffee.

"Thanks." Peter sipped his coffee then shook head. "He said something about getting out of my hair for a time."

"You have to call him."

"I don't know ..."

"Peter!" Eric exclaimed. "You cannot let this silence between the two of you grow and ... and *fester*. Because that's what will happen, the longer you let it go. The more you put it off, the harder it will be to pick up that phone. Please, please call him today."

Peter's lips twisted in a wry smile. "I think I may have to, just to get you off my back," he said, not without humor. Then he sighed and closed his eyes for a moment. "It's so hard, Eric. I know you said I shouldn't dwell on what he did, but rather on what he didn't do."

"He didn't do anything, really," Eric injected.

"Well, we could go round and round on that forever, I suppose. The fact is, I just can't get past the thought of him actually picking that guy up. I know it's my hang up, and I'm sorry that I can't be more open-minded about it, but …" He broke off as the front door slammed with a resounding crash.

"Hey guys, I'm home!" Nick yelled from the entryway.

"Like we wouldn't notice," Eric said, laughing.

"Does he always do that?" Peter asked.

"Not always—just when he's mad, or in a really good mood. We'll find out which it is in a second."

"I hope you guys are saying nice things about me," Nick said, walking into the kitchen. "No hugs," he added, as Peter started to get up. "I have to shower. Don't want to mess up that nice clean shirt you're wearing. Whatcha doing here this early anyway, Peter?"

"Eric invited me for breakfast. I hope you don't mind."

"Hmm." Nick raised an expressive eyebrow. "When I come back, you can give me the real reason. See ya."

Eric smiled at Nick's departing back. "He's in a good mood, I think."

"Jeff said in his note that Nick will probably be upset he went to Rob's place," Peter remarked. "He just didn't want to get you guys deeper into this mess. I, on the other hand, seem to be doing just that."

"Hey." Eric took his hand. "We're your friends. You've always been there for us, now it's our turn."

"And there always seems to some drama going on," Peter said, with a rueful expression. "I mean, we've just gotten over you nearly dying on us, and now this …" He paused, slowly shaking his head. "You know, I just heard what I said—and I can't quite believe I equated what happened to you, with what's going on between Jeff and me. God, Eric, how shallow can I become?"

"You're not being shallow, Peter—but if I may speak my mind here, I think you're being just a tad stubborn."

Peter grimaced. "One of my more endearing qualities, I know. But am I being stubborn by trying to understand why he did it? That's what I keep coming back to, Eric. Why did he feel so compelled to go back to that guy's place?"

"He'd had a few ..."

"Is that all it takes, then? To me, that just makes it worse.'

"Well, there were other factors, of course. He was pissed off."

"Yes, I know all about that," Peter interrupted. "And I'm not denying that he had reason to be. We talked about that before I found out about ... the rest of it."

"Look ..." Eric took Peter's mug to the coffee maker for a refill. "I know it sounds like I'm always defending Jeff in this, but I do understand how you feel too, Peter. No one likes to think of the person they love being with someone else." He put the mug down in front of Peter, and sat opposite him. "But, I'm going to say this, and then you can act on it anyway you want. If you can't put this behind you, you are going to lose Jeff—and that, my dear friend, would be a tragedy—for you, for him, for all of us who are your friends."

Peter sighed and covered his face with his hands. "Jesus, Eric," he whispered. "I know you're right. I know it ... and I also know I couldn't bear it."

"Then talk to him," Eric said gently. "Talk to him, without recriminations. You know Jeff has tortured himself enough. I bet he didn't sleep one wink last night."

Peter nodded. "That would make two of us."

"What's this?" Nick demanded, walking back into the kitchen, after his shower. "A wake? You both look like you're ready to start weepers anonymous."

Eric glared at him. "We were talking, Nick. Would you please be a little more sensitive right now?"

"Okay. You can both hug me now."

Peter smiled as he watched Nick and Eric embrace and kiss. "You two," he said, teasing them. "You should go to your room."

"What—and leave you out?" Nick opened his arms to him. "Come here, now I'm all clean and shiny."

Peter stepped into Nick's arms and felt the warmth and comfort expressed in that hug. "How'd it go with Jeff last night?" Nick asked gently. "Or should I not ask?"

"Not well, I'm afraid. He wasn't there when I got home. He's staying over at Rob's."

"Oh?" Nick frowned as he accepted a coffee mug from Eric.

"He felt it would be unfair to involve you guys in this any more than you already are," Peter explained.

"And of course, he's known Rob since junior high," Eric added, feeling he had to.

Nick turned his frown on Eric. "I know that," he snapped.

"Don't get mad."

"I'm not mad."

"Jeff said you would be."

"I'm not mad! Quit telling me I'm mad!"

"Okay," Eric said, laughing. "You're not mad."

"That's right." He looked at Peter. "So, what are we going to do about all this?"

"W … we?" Peter stammered. "Uh … well, I didn't know *we* were going to do anything."

"Of course we are," Nick told him. "We're all in this together. You kick Jeff out of your life, we're all screwed!"

"Nick, for Pete's sake," Eric groaned. "This isn't funny …"

"Of course it isn't funny!" Nick agreed. "But right now, you two have got yourselves all wound up into that 'oh woe is me' syndrome. That isn't going to solve anything. What you need, Peter, is something to take your mind off your troubles—and I have the perfect proposition for you."

"You do?"

"Nick," Eric protested. "What are you doing?"

"What I am doing," Nick said, his arms spread expansively, "is giving Peter a chance to put his problems aside, and take on something much more important!"

"*And what the hell might that be?*' Eric asked, sarcasm dripping from every word.

"Robert Landon's murder," Nick said, with a deal of satisfaction.

"Robert Landon?" Peter looked at him, blankly.

Nick took a step back. "If I say the name John Hammond to you, you won't hit me will you?"

"You just did," Peter said, a pained look on his face.

"Yeah, sorry ... well, see he's the guy who hired me to find out what happened to his friend Robert Landon ..." Nick filled him in on the rest of the details, along with his sorties to The Racket in LA, and his conversations with Detective Morales. "I already get the feeling that Morales is going to drop the ball on this," he added.

"Just another gay guy murdered," Peter remarked, with a deal of bitterness.

"Exactly." Nick knew Peter would relate to these circumstances, as his own lover's murder had gone unsolved by police. It wasn't until Peter hired Jeff to take on an independent investigation that the men responsible for Phillip's death were brought to justice. He felt a momentary twinge of guilt at having to remind Peter of that terrible time, but quickly brushed it aside, when he saw he had his attention.

"So how do you think I can help?' Peter asked.

"I thought, maybe you could come with me to the crime scene. See if you feel anything, get any vibes, you know ..."

"Nick, this isn't the time for that," Eric interrupted. "Peter's got enough on his plate."

Nick gave Eric the evil eye. "Can we let him make up his own mind, please? Peter, I know Jeff doesn't like you doing this stuff. He told me it can kinda drain you, and I don't want to put you through any more stress."

"Which is exactly what you are doing," Eric said, annoyed.

"It's OK, Eric." Peter smiled at his friend. "I think I can handle it. When do we leave, Nick?"

"Hell, right now, if you're up for it. I can have you back in Laguna before lunch."

"I don't believe this!" Eric yelled. "Nick, you cannot be serious. Peter, you should be trying to straighten things out with Jeff, instead of gallivanting up to LA!"

"Calm down," Nick said, rolling his eyes. "Jeez … Peter can call Jeff anytime he wants. I said we'll be back by lunchtime. What's the big deal?"

Eric looked with exasperation from one to the other. Then he threw his arms in the air. "Oh, I give up. Do what you want. You guys always do, anyway. What does it matter what I say or think?"

"It matters a lot to me," Peter said, taking Eric's arm and giving it a gentle squeeze. "Nick's right though. This will give me something else to think about. When we get back, I'll call Jeff—I promise."

Eric hugged him tight. "I just want you guys to make it right with each other."

"I know, and believe me, I want that too."

Nick shuffled his feet. "Don't I get a hug?" he whined.

"No, you don't," Eric said tartly. "I'm still mad at *you*."

"Aw, c'mon," Nick chuckled. "You know you can't stay mad at me for more than two seconds."

Eric glanced at Peter. "You know, the sad thing about what he just said is—he's right." He put his arms round Nick. "Drive carefully—and look after my friend!"

"Okay, boss." He kissed Eric's neck. "I'll drop him off at the gallery when we get back, then we can all have lunch."

Peter began to get nervous on the drive up to LA. He wasn't sure what was unnerving him the most. The experience that lay ahead, when he would try to invoke his somewhat erratic psychic ability, the inevitable confrontation with Jeff—or Nick's supersonic driving.

"How does Eric stand it?" he asked finally.

"Stand what?"

"Your damned driving is what! You're making me a nervous wreck."

Nick grinned at him. "Well, I said I'd get you there and back before lunch."

"I thought you meant by that, I'd be able to eat lunch."

"We're almost there ... next exit."

"Just be thankful for small mercies," Peter muttered.

Once off the freeway, Nick slowed to a more respectable speed, and Peter could breathe more easily. "So, tell me something about this Robert Landon," he said. "What have you been able to find out so far?"

"Well, according to everyone I've talked with, Landon appears to have been a regular guy. I think that Bernie, the bartender at The Racket, might even have been a little in love with him."

"Oh, yeah?"

"Mmm ... He told me, in his opinion, John Hammond wasn't nearly good enough for Landon. It was the way he said it, that made me wonder."

"I tend to agree with him," Peter said wryly.

"And I also think there might have been a darker side to Landon," Nick continued. "He hung out with some guy named Tom who, also according to one of Landon's buddies, was just rough trade looking for a free drink."

"Did he put out for the drinks?"

"He could have. Landon's friend, Frank, seemed to think it was sexual thing."

"So, he didn't show for his dinner date with ... you-know-who, but how do we know he intended to keep that date?'

"Only a guess on my part. He told his buddy, Frank, that he had a dinner date, kinda described John—then next day he didn't show for work. He either changed his mind, or ... and this is what I think happened, he met someone who changed his mind for him. Either by choice, or by force. What I don't get is where the body was found. He was on his way to Westwood, and Laurel Canyon is nowhere near the route he should have taken."

"Unless he was taken by force."

"Right—or had some damned good reason to change direction. The body was found in Wildacre Park, a little ways off the road. We should be there in a few minutes."

Peter felt a flutter in his stomach at those words, and at the same time, a sense of déjà vu. He'd made this trip before; almost for the same reason.

Only that time, he'd been in the car with Jeff, and they had visited the scene of Phillip's murder. He'd only known Jeff a few days, but even then, he'd begun to feel the attraction between them. An attraction that would grow and blossom into a love that brought happiness back into his life, and helped him recover from a tragedy he'd thought he would never overcome.

"There it is, up ahead," Nick said, bringing Peter back to the present. "We can park off the road, and walk down to where they found him."

Peter sat quietly while Nick parked the car. "You OK?" Nick asked him.

"I'm fine," Peter said, feeling beads of sweat gather on his forehead. "Let's do it."

They walked down the rough path to the clearing that still bore the traces of the shallow grave where Landon had been unearthed by treasure hunting children.

Nick hunkered down on his long legs, his back against a tree trunk. "Okay, I'll stay quiet, while you do your thing."

Peter smiled. "You make it sound like I can turn it on, anytime I want."

"Ssh," Nick admonished him. "Concentrate!"

Peter lifted his head, staring up into the branches of the pine and eucalyptus trees. They swayed above him in the gentle breeze that had sprung up since he and Nick had entered the clearing. Without knowing why, he stepped closer to the place where Robert Landon had been buried. He closed his eyes, and waited … and felt nothing.

"I think there have been too many people trampling around here, Nick, since the incident. I can't seem to get close to anything."

"Don't give up so easy," Nick said. "Give it a little time."

Okay, Peter told himself, concentrate … take it easy … just let it come. Nothing.

"Sorry, Nick … I'm afraid there's nothing here for me to connect with."

He shrugged with resignation, looking over to where Nick had propped himself. But the man who stood leaning against the tree was not Nick. He was tall, with dark, almost black, curly hair. He was wearing black jeans, a yellow shirt open to the waist. His smooth, muscular chest was coated with a fine sheen of perspiration. He smiled, a seductive, lascivious smile. "I knew you'd come," he said, walking with a panther-like step toward Peter. "I knew you couldn't resist."

"I … I don't know who you are," Peter stammered, stepping back, away from the man.

"I'm everything you desire, Robert. Why don't you just give in to what you crave?" He reached for Peter, grabbed his arm, pulled him in close. His mouth was on Peter's, crushing his lips, his hands tearing at Peter's clothes …

"*Nick*," Peter screamed, trying with all his might to wrestle the man away from him. "For God's sake, help me!"

Nick watched with interest, as Peter seemed to jump back from the spot where Landon had been buried. His eyes widened as Peter started what almost looked like some sort of dance, weaving back and forth, his arms and legs flailing as if at some unseen target.

"What the …" He jumped to his feet. "Hey Peter, are you all right?"

Then he heard him scream.

"Christ!" Nick leaped forward, covering the distance between himself and Peter in two or three bounds. "Peter!" He grabbed his friend by the shoulders, straining to stem the violent movements he seemed unable to control. "Peter, cut it out!" Suddenly, as if all his strength had been sucked out of him, Peter collapsed in Nick's arms.

"Peter …" Nick gasped, holding him upright. "What happened?" He gazed with apprehension at his friend's ashen complexion. "Jesus, I'm sorry …"

"No, I'll be OK in a minute or two," Peter panted. "Just let me sit down." As Nick lowered him gently to the ground and sat beside him, Peter was gripped by the sudden thought that Jeff would be furious when he found out what had happened here. "There was a man here … tall, dark brown curly hair. He called me Robert; started pawing me, slapping me around …"

"Jesus," Nick muttered.

"Nick, there's something very strange about this. I have the weirdest feeling that the man they found in that grave, was not Robert Landon."

CHAPTER 9

Nick stared at Peter, with an expression that was both confused and incredulous. "What makes you say that?"

"Just before you grabbed me," Peter explained, "I saw the look on his face change. It was as if he had been shot, struck … something that stopped him dead in his tracks."

"The coroner said Landon had died from a blow to the base of the skull," Nick said.

"Yes, that could have been it. It was like … bam … instantaneous. The look on his face was just total shock. But it wasn't Robert Landon."

"How can you know that?"

"Because, he called *me* Robert. Either Robert Landon killed him, or someone else who was also here."

"But you couldn't see anyone else?"

"No, just the dark haired guy. That was enough, believe me!"

"You're OK now?" Nick asked with concern.

"Yeah, I'm getting there. I'll be OK in a couple of minutes." He was suddenly gripped by an idea. "Hey, you carry a notepad and pen or pencil, don't you?"

"Yeah, in the car."

"I could draw this guy for you."

"*Great.*" Nick jumped to his feet. "I'll be right back."

Left alone, Peter glanced around the clearing with a feeling of unease. Something sinister remained. He felt a wave of nausea overwhelm him. He bent forward, certain he was about to throw up. He retched, feeling his gut spasm, and a cold sweat break out all over his body. Behind him, he could almost swear he heard a crunching of leaves, as though someone had walked quickly away—but when he turned his head to look, he could see no one.

"Here we go …" Nick burst into the clearing, then on seeing Peter's sickly pallor, he dropped to his knees beside him. "Did something else happen?"

Peter nodded. "There was some kind of presence, but I couldn't make it out. I could hear something, like footsteps going away from here."

"Jeez, Peter. I am sorry for putting you through this." Nick looked at his friend and felt like a heel for causing him this distress. Maybe, he should have listened to Eric.

"That's OK," Peter said, breathing a little easier. "I'll be fine. Let me have the notepad."

With consummate skill, he quickly drew a head and shoulders thumbnail sketch of the man he had seen just minutes before, then he handed Nick the notepad. Nick studied the likeness carefully, letting out a long low whistle of appreciation.

"That is incredible, Peter. Anyone who knows this guy will recognize him immediately from this." He paused. "One more favor?"

Peter smiled and looked at him expectantly. "Okay …?"

"I'd like to show this to Bernie at The Racket." He glanced at his watch. "'Cept, the bar won't be open yet. He gave me his home number," he mumbled, fishing in his jacket's inside pocket. "Here it is …" He flipped open his cell phone and punched in the number. "Bernie? Hi, Nick Fallon. Good, how are you? Listen, I need a favor. Can you meet me somewhere that's convenient for you in say, a half hour? I'm up in Laurel Canyon right now. That'd be good … see you there. Thanks." He looked at Peter. "He's going to meet us at the coffee bar next to The Racket. He's pulling an early shift there anyway. Let's go."

Together, they started back to where Nick's car was parked. "This is great, Peter," Nick said with enthusiasm. "I figured you'd come through with something—but this is incredible."

"I'm glad I could help. But Nick …" Peter gripped his arm. "Whatever happens, don't tell Jeff about this. He'll be pissed."

Nick grinned at him. "Does that mean you're gonna make up with him?"

"Yes." Peter chuckled, punching Nick lightly on the shoulder. "Even though you made that sound like we were a couple of teenagers, instead of grown men!"

"Great! Eric will be ecstatic."

"You think Jeff will be too?"

"Yeah—he'll probably crack a smile." He unlocked the car doors with his remote. "If I'm right about who this guy is that you've drawn," he said with a deal of satisfaction, "Detective Morales is gonna shit!

Bernie, a mug of coffee in front of him, was already seated at the coffee bar, when they arrived. He looked slightly disappointed when he saw Nick was not alone.

"Who's your friend?" he asked pointedly, giving Peter the once over.

"This is Peter Brandon," Nick said. "My partner's boyfriend. You want a coffee, Peter?"

"Please … just black."

"You look familiar." Bernie moved in for a closer look. "I have to start wearing my glasses all the time, looks like." He took Peter's outstretched hand. "You sure are cute. Wait, you were in People magazine, right? And that woman's show—the one that's not around no more. Olivia somethin' … Now, I remember. You're the psychic guy … the artist, right?"

"That's right," Peter said, smiling. "But, I prefer artist to psychic."

Bernie beamed at him. "Oh, but I love all that stuff."

"Well, you'll love this, Bernie." Nick put his and Peter's coffee down on the counter and produced Peter's sketch. "We were just up at the place where they found Robert's body. I asked Peter to come get a feel for the scene—he's good at that kind of thing."

"Yeah, that's what I read," Bernie exclaimed. "You helped the police a few times, right?"

"*Anyway* …" Nick pushed the notepad toward Bernie. "You know this guy?"

Bernie picked up the notepad and squinted at the sketch. "Sure I know him. That's Tom Skinner. He used to hang around Robert a lot."

"I knew it," Nick said, under his breath. "I take it he hasn't been in the bar either, since Robert disappeared."

"That's right. No big loss there though. He was a snake in the grass. Where d'you get this drawing, if you don't mind me asking?"

"Peter drew it a short time ago."

"You did? Man, that's amazing!" He stared at the sketch again. "I mean, you've got him perfect. What was he doing up there—snooping around or something?"

"He wasn't up there, Bernie," Nick said. "At least, not in the physical sense."

"You mean …" Bernie's eyes widened as he looked at Peter with admiration. "Oh wow! You mean this is a *psychic* drawing? But then, that means that Tom is dead? Holy crap … another one."

"Well, we're not sure of that yet, Bernie."

"Like I said …" Bernie shrugged his shoulders in dismissal. "No big loss!"

As he and Peter sped back down the I5, Nick called Morales.

"What now?" the detective growled after Nick identified himself.

Nick winked at Peter as he turned on the speaker on his phone. "Boy, you really need to take some self-enlightenment classes," he said, chuckling. "You talk to everybody like that?"

"Only to ex-cops who have nothing else to do but waste my time."

"Well, you may not consider this a waste of time after what I have to say, Morales."

Nick gritted his teeth as he listened to the overly emphasized sigh the other man exhaled in his ear.

"So, what've you got, Fallon?"

"You might have to help me on this one."

"I thought you said you weren't going to waste my time!"

"Just listen for a minute, OK?" Nick said. "Don't go off the deep end and hang up on me—just listen."

"Get on with it."

"Are you one hundred percent sure that the body found buried in Laurel Canyon was Robert Landon?"

"What the hell are you talkin' about? Of course it's Landon. He had photo ID on him for Chrissakes!"

Peter plucked nervously at Nick's sleeve. "I could have been wrong about this."

"Who's that with you?" Morales demanded.

"Just a friend," Nick said. "He's doing a thesis on the interaction between real detectives and make-believe ones."

"You know, Fallon, you are too smart for your own good!"

"I know. But back to the matter at hand."

"There is no matter at hand. You asked me a dumb question and I've answered it. That's it!"

"Wait … have you had positive ID on the body?"

"Do you mean, did we ask his mother to identify him? Well, here's something you should know. There wasn't enough of his face left for her to identify. So, rather than put the poor woman through any more trauma, we felt it better that we didn't force her to look at what was left of her son!"

"So, the answer is no—you don't have positive ID. What about dental records?"

"The results haven't come back yet."

"Okaaay …" Nick drew a deep breath. "Are you a betting man, Detective?"

"What?"

"Because I will bet you anything you like, that those dental records do not match Robert Landon's. When you get the results, call me … and I'll tell you who the guy is!" Before Morales could say another word, Nick hung up. He leaned back in his seat with a smug smile. "Peter, my boy," he said. "I love you!"

Peter looked at him in amazement. "But Nick, what if I'm wrong? Isn't that going to make you look … well, dare I say it … stupid?"

"It won't be the first time buddy, or the last, I'm sure." Nick grinned at him. "I mean, here I am convinced that what you saw back there is for real. That the guy you drew is the dead man. A lot of people would say I'm nuts. But they don't know you, Peter. They don't know what you can do. I do—I have seen the proof of it, and I have total faith in your ability. Okay?"

"If you say so, Nick."

"Peter, are *you* a betting man?"

"Not really ..."

"Too bad," Nick drawled. "Because I'd bet you your new gallery in San Diego that Morales is on the phone right now, hollerin' for those dental records to be on his desk immediately—if not before."

Jeff pulled up outside Peter's gallery and peered in through the glass trying to see if he could spot him inside. "He might be in the back," he muttered, climbing out of his car. He pushed a couple of quarters in the parking meter before walking up to the gallery door. He had more or less been bullied into this by his friend Rob, who had told him, in no uncertain terms, that the only way to fix this dilemma was to confront it face-to-face. He had decided not to call ahead, just in case Peter gave him a hundred and one excuses about why they should not meet. So here he was, he thought, about to beard the horse in the stall—no, that wasn't right. What was that expression? Anyway, it didn't matter, because he could see by the look on Eric's face that Peter was not in the gallery.

"Hi Eric ... he's not here?"

"Uh ... no. He went up to LA with Nick."

"Huh?" Jeff looked at Eric for more of an explanation.

"I'm not sure I should tell you this ..." Eric hedged, his cheeks beginning to glow.

"But you're going to, aren't you? Why on earth would they go up to LA together?"

"You won't get mad, will you?"

"Not at you ... presuming you are innocent in this," Jeff said, his lips twisting in a wry smile.

"I am, Jeff—totally innocent. Nick asked Peter for help in that case he's working on ... you know the one John Hammond is involved in ..."

Jeff flinched visibly at the mention of Hammond's name. "And just how does Nick think Peter can help him with that?" he asked, tersely.

"Uh … well … they were going to the crime scene, and …"

"Oh, dear God," Jeff said, almost in a whisper, clenching his fists.

Eric backed up a step. "You said you wouldn't get mad."

"I'm not mad, at *you*." He sighed and looked around the gallery as if he could find inspiration in the myriad of Peter's paintings that lined the walls. "I've asked him not to do this anymore, Eric. It takes something from him each time. The last time he looked so ill, pale, shaken. I just don't want him to go through that again."

"I know," Eric said, quietly. "I told him he shouldn't go."

"But he couldn't let Nick down, right?"

Eric nodded. "Nick said they'd be back by lunch time."

Jeff glanced at his watch. "Well, they should be here any time. Why don't I just wait for them then?"

"Oh, Jeff … please don't make a scene," Eric pleaded. "You know Nick's temper when he thinks he's right—and even when he's not. Things are bad enough right now …" He broke off as they heard voices in the back of the gallery. "Jeff, they're here."

Jeff smiled at him calmly and stood, his arms folded, waiting for Peter and Nick to enter the gallery. Eric ran to the front door and locked it, turning the sign to read; 'Out to Lunch'.

"Hey, Jeff buddy!" Nick yelled with forced gusto on seeing his partner. "How's it goin'?"

"Just fine," Jeff replied, looking past Nick, to where Peter had stopped at the reception desk. "Peter," he said, walking toward him. "I would really like to have some private time with you, so we can talk. Is that all right?"

"Yes, yes … that's fine." Peter tried to smile, but found his face muscles were strangely unresponsive, except for a nervous tic by his mouth he'd never had before.

"Okay, that's great," Nick yelled. "Hey Eric, let's get some lunch. We'll see you guys later!"

"Will you stop *shouting*," Eric hissed at him.

"What are you so uptight about?" Nick asked, as Eric grabbed his arm and hustled him out of the gallery.

Peter looked into Jeff's eyes, trying to read what hidden emotion he would have to deal with first. He wanted to throw himself into Jeff's arms and have done with all this misery. He wanted to feel Jeff's powerful body pressed against his, to feel the strength and comfort emanate from him, envelope him, as it had done every day since they had been together.

"Jeff," he said quietly. "I know you're angry ..."

"Angry doesn't even come close," Jeff interrupted.

Peter's eyes flashed. "So, now we're mad at each other. You with me, because I helped Nick out ..."

"That's not the reason, and you know it," Jeff cut in, his tone curt. "I didn't want you to use your psychic ability again because of what it does to you—because I *care* about what it does to you. Don't you get it? And Nick knew that, dammit. Believe me, he and I will have words about this later."

"There's no need for that," Peter told him. "Nick thought it would take my mind off ... off the other problem. Give me something else to think about, and in a way, he was right. I think the intensity of what happened today did make me reconsider my own petty perspectives on what is going on between you and me."

"What do you mean?"

"I mean, I think I was overreacting to our situation." He looked at Jeff for a sign of understanding, and was glad to see some of the tension go from Jeff's body. "I think I was in shock from that Hammond guy just blurting it all out in front of us both. And according to both Eric and Nick, he was lying about most of it."

"Yes, he was."

"And today, up there in Laurel Canyon ..."

"What *did* happen?"

"Let me just finish my thought first. You know better than most, what those experiences can do to me—and today, it was one of the worst."

"Aw, Peter ..." Jeff reached for him, and he let himself be drawn into Jeff's arms. "Why did you do this to yourself? I'm going to punch Nick on the nose."

"No, you're not ... because, here's the part I remember most clearly. As soon as it was over, my first thought was of you, and how mad you'd be when you found out. I'd forgotten all the stupid things I said to you yesterday. All of that seemed suddenly unimportant. What *was* important was that I was more concerned about your reactions than I was about the way I felt at that moment, bad as that was. Am I making any sense?"

"I think so." Jeff tightened his arms around him.

Peter let out a long shuddering sigh. "All I know is, I couldn't bear it, if you and I ... if we couldn't get beyond this. Nothing is more important to me than that ... than you."

Jeff's lips found Peter's, holding them prisoner in a kiss that surpassed almost every kiss they had ever shared before, and when it ended, it was only so they could catch a breath and start again. What an idiot I almost was, Peter thought, to ever think, even for one millisecond, of letting this man go. Locked in their embrace, captured by Jeff's strength, enraptured by his scent, his sheer all-consuming sensuality, Peter closed his eyes, surrendering to the joy and exhilaration that surged through his body.

Still holding him, Jeff asked; "Do we need to talk some more about what happened?"

Peter shook his head. "No, not about John Hammond."

"What about your trip with Nick?"

"Yeah, that ..." Peter frowned, remembering. "That was, in a word, scary." Together, they walked into the back studio.

"I'm still mad at Nick," Jeff said.

"Don't be. I didn't have to go. But what I saw there was pretty terrible—the end result being that Nick is convinced the body they dug up there, isn't Robert Landon at all. We met Bernie, a bartender at The Racket. He identified the sketch I drew as this guy, Tom, who used to hang around Landon a lot."

Jeff stared at him in silence for a moment or two. "You've had a busy day from the sound of it," he said, finally.

Peter nodded. "Anyway, Nick called the detective handling the case and he, of course, thought Nick was talking out of a hole in his head. He did admit, though, that they hadn't had the dental records results—so, Nick kinda gloated over that one."

"He would," Jeff remarked, wryly. "But you still haven't told me what you saw."

"When we got there," Peter said, "I didn't think I was going to be much help. Nick was sitting at the base of a tree watching me, and I think I said something to the effect that there had been too many people milling around. Then, this guy was standing where Nick should have been. He called me Robert, started mauling me … I was yelling at Nick to come help me, when the guy just stopped dead, like someone had shot him. Then, I must have blacked out 'cause then Nick was holding me, trying to calm me. I felt like all the strength had gone from me. I collapsed. I think I scared poor Nick. He went quite pale …"

"Jesus, Peter." Jeff took his hand. "Promise me … *promise* me that you will never do this again."

"I promise." He leaned into Jeff so that their foreheads touched. "I love you, you know," he whispered.

Jeff sighed, gathering him in his arms. "My worst fear in all of this was that I might never hear you say that again."

"You'll hear it, over and over," Peter said with a gentle laugh. "So many times that you'll tell me to shut up."

"Never," Jeff murmured. "Never, for as long as we live."

Eric gave Nick a stern look over the top of his burger. They had picked up lunch at the corner café, and brought it back to Nick's office.

"You're in a world of trouble with Jeff, you know," he said, pausing to wipe his mouth with his napkin. "He was madder than a hornet when he found out where you and Peter had gone."

Nick grunted. "He'll get over it. Besides, the way Peter came through today with his psycho stuff is gonna blow this case apart."

"Psychic, not psycho." Eric tapped the back of Nick's hand with his forefinger. "You know, you're becoming way too manipulative. That's not nice, especially with your friends."

Nick's eyes widened. "Me, manipulative?"

"Yes, you ... using Peter like that, telling him it would take his mind off his troubles."

"Well, it did didn't it? Man, he was amazing." Nick leaned back in his chair and propped his feet on the desk. "He could see this guy, Eric—and the guy was trying to slap him around."

"Oh my God, Nick!" Eric looked at him, appalled. "What did you do?"

"At first all I could see was Peter weaving about. I thought he was just fooling around till he yelled for help. He was actually trying to fight the guy off. I ran over there, and he just kinda collapsed in my arms ..."

"Nick ..." Eric looked troubled. "Have you ever considered what this might do to Peter? You know, what he goes through in those moments could have some damaging effects on his mind. That's why Jeff doesn't want him to do this anymore."

"Jeff has used Peter's abilities in the past," Nick said defensively.

"I know, but the last time, he said Peter looked so wiped out, it scared him."

"Well, I won't ask him again."

"I don't think you'll get the chance, quite frankly."

"Well, I know you don't approve ..." Nick demolished the last of his burger, and threw the wrapper in the trashcan. "... And I know I'm gonna get some flack from Jeff, but I tell you Eric, without Peter's help, this case could've grown cold. I'm going to give Morales till tomorrow noon, to get back to me—then I'm calling him, or Joe French."

"But if that isn't Robert Landon in the morgue," Eric asked. "Where is he?"

"A very good question, my dear Eric. Peter said that the guy in his vision called him Robert, so that places them both at the scene. But from the account Peter gave, I'd have to say there was someone else there— someone who put a stop to this Tom guy by braining him from behind.

Peter couldn't see anyone, but there had to have been a third party some-where. He thought he could hear someone else moving about."

"God, what a nightmare, Nick. I can't believe you put Peter through this."

"C'mon, Eric … cut me some slack here. Peter's a grown man … he could've said no."

Eric sighed and stood up. "Yeah, I guess you're right. Just don't forget what you owe him." He looked at his watch. "I have to get back. I'll see you later." He turned to go.

"Eric …" Nick grabbed his arm. "Don't stay mad at me. Okay, I prob-ably shouldn't have done this …" He pulled Eric into his arms. "Say you're not mad."

"You're not mad."

"Eric, *c'mon.*" Nick nuzzled his neck, then he smiled as he felt Eric's arms encircle his waist. "Forgive me?"

"Yes, I forgive you," Eric said. "I just hope Jeff will too."

When Eric returned to the gallery a few minutes later, Peter and Jeff had gone, but a note had been left on the table in the back studio.

> *Eric,*
> *I've gone for the day—hope you can cope. You have my cell number if you have any problems. Don't worry; Jeff is with me. You were right—every-thing is just fine. You're the best.*
>
> *Love, Peter.*

Eric smiled, and walked to the front of the gallery to unlock the door. Thank God, he thought, they'd both been sensible enough to put all this crap behind them, and get on with their lives.

CHAPTER 10

"Joe, do me favor, will you?"

Joe French looked up from the paperwork spread across his desk and saw Bob Morales striding toward him. He did not look happy, Joe thought.

"What's up?"

"I'm kinda pressed for time, this morning," Morales said, laying a folder on Joe's desk. "Would you mind calling your buddy in Laguna and filling him in on this report?"

Joe opened the folder. "You mean Jeff Stevens?"

"Uh, no ... the other guy."

"Nick Fallon?"

"Yeah, that's him. Have him call me on my cell when he gets a chance. He's got the number." With that, Morales turned and walked quickly away.

Joe watched him go, his lips pursed in amusement. In the time it had taken Morales to walk over here and ask him to call Nick, he could have picked up the phone and done it himself. And this business of not remembering Nick's name ... what was that about? He glanced at the report ... dental records. He scanned the report—a non-match for Robert Landon.

Huh? A non-match? Frowning, he found Nick's number and punched it in. He smiled as he listened to Monica's, as usual, sunny greeting.

"Hey, Monica. How're those guys treating you down there?"

"Oh, hi Joe ... just the usual," she said, chuckling. "You know, mayhem and disaster all over the place."

"That good eh? Is Nick there?"

"Uh huh. Hang on, I'll put you through."

"Nick Fallon."

"Nick, how's it goin?"

"Good, Joe. You lookin' for Jeff?"

"No, as a matter of fact, I'm playing messenger for Bob Morales. He asked me to call you."

"Is that a fact." Nick leaned back in his chair, and grinned. "He couldn't call me himself?"

"He said he was in a big hurry."

"I'll just bet he was. So, what's the message?"

"I have a dental report here on Robert Landon."

"Oh yeah?" Nick flipped his phone to his other hand, and leaned forward in his chair, feeling the first twinge of excitement. "And ...?"

"According to this, it's a non-match on Landon."

"Yes!" Nick yelled. "I knew it!"

"What does this mean, Nick?"

"It means that the body they found in Laurel Canyon is not Robert Landon, Joe." Nick could not contain his laughter. "Oh man, I bet Morales was sick."

"He didn't look too happy," Joe agreed. "Jeez, he's going to get some flack for this—he was the one who okayed releasing Landon's picture to the press. So, how come he's letting you know this?"

"Well, it's a bit of long story."

"I have the time."

Nick filled him in on what had happened when he took Peter to the scene of the crime. "He even managed to draw a sketch of the guy, Joe. He's amazing."

"That he is," Joe said. "We'll need that sketch, Nick."

"Right. I'll fax it to you right now—or should that be to Morales?"

"I'll see he gets it. By the way, he said for you to call him when you get the chance."

"Gee, you think he wants to thank me?"

Joe laughed. "Don't hold your breath, my boy. Hey, you have a name for this guy?"

"Tom Skinner."

"Okay. Nick, I'm gonna talk to the Super about this. Just to keep everything on the level."

"Gotcha. Talk to you later, Joe."

After he hung up, Nick took the sketch to the fax machine, and sent a copy to Joe's office. He glanced at the glass entry doors as they swung open.

"Morning, Monica," Jeff said, as he passed through the reception area, ignoring Nick completely.

"Oh, oh …" Nick sighed, waiting for the fax machine to finish its job. "Looks like I'm in the dog house, Monica."

"I think I'll take an early lunch," Monica said, reaching for her purse. "I don't think I could stand another shouting match in here."

"But what if I need you for protection?" Nick whined.

"Call Eric," she said, heading for the door. "Good luck."

"Oh well," Nick muttered, heading for the office he shared with Jeff. The two men looked at each other for a moment, then Nick fell to his knees and flung himself across Jeff's desk. "I'm sorry Jeff—totally and abjectly sorry!"

"This is not *funny*, Nick …" Jeff's expression and voice were cold. "Not at all funny."

Nick stood up then walked over to his own desk. "I know it's not funny. I was just tryin' to break through the ice a bit. You know, the stuff you're covered in right now. C'mon Jeff, I really am sorry for using Peter like that. I promise I will never ask him again."

"You better believe you won't." He fixed Nick with a hard look. "You know, you're my friend as well as my partner, Peter's friend too—so it really doesn't sit well with me that you, in your usual cavalier fashion, just ignored my concerns about him using his psychic abilities. I told you last time, the effect it had on him …"

"Jeff," Nick interrupted. "He could've said no."

"But he didn't, because he would've felt he'd let you down." Jeff stared at him, his normally warm, smoky gray eyes now turned steely. "Didn't you care about how it might effect him? He told me it was one of his worst experiences."

"Jeez …" Nick shook his head. "Is he OK now?"

"Do you really care, Nick?'

Nick bridled. "Of course I care. What kind of dumb-ass question is that?"

Jeff was silent for a beat or two, then he got up out of his chair, and walked to the front of his desk, where he stood, motionless, gazing at Nick as though gathering his thoughts. The tension between the two men was so intense, neither one heard the doors to the reception area open quietly.

"Nick," Jeff said finally. "I think it might be better if we parted company."

"*What?* What the hell are you talking about?"

"I'm talking about you and I severing our partnership."

Nick looked at him, his expression a mixture of near laughter and incredulity. "You can't be serious, Jeff. You'd give me the heave-ho over something like this?"

"Something like *this*, Nick?" Jeff glared at him. "Is that how you see it? Something trivial that you don't give a rat's ass about? We're talking about the well-being of the one person who means everything to me ..."

"Who means everything to you," Nick repeated slowly, getting to his feet. "Who means so fucking much to you that the other night you went back to some stranger's house, looking to get laid!"

"Don't even go there, Nick." Jeff clenched his fists in anger.

"Oh, I'll go there, all right," Nick said, his jaw tight with suppressed rage. "Does Peter know what you're doing now?"

"I don't need Peter to help me run my business."

"No, but you need him for just about every other fucking thing, don't you?"

"That's enough, Nick."

"Oh please," Nick sneered. "Don't stand there acting all holier-than-thou in front of me, after the scene you caused in here yesterday. You've obviously forgotten, but it was Eric and me who stood by you. Eric practically begging Peter not to throw you out—and this is the thanks we get? Well, you know what, Jeff? You can take this lousy business—and shove it up your ass!"

"So get the fuck out of here!" Jeff roared.

"*Stop this, both of you!*"

They stared, startled, at the person standing in the doorway. Monica advanced on them; her eyes glistening with unshed tears.

"What d'you think you're doing?" she demanded, wiping her eyes. "Both of you acting like two big, stupid, testosterone-driven jerks—screaming at each other like idiots!"

"M ... Monica ..." Jeff stammered.

"I thought you were taking an early lunch," Nick said lamely.

"I was, and then I got to thinking that you two would probably end up in a fight—and of course, I was right." She stood there, all five feet, two inches of her, glaring up at her bosses.

Jeff was astounded. In all the years Monica had been his secretary, not once had he ever seen her lose her temper—and certainly not with him. This was all Nick's fault, dammit!

"This is all your fault, dammit," he yelled at Nick. He backed up a step as Monica slapped him on his arm. "Ow!"

Nick looked at her, amazed. "How long had you been standing there?" he asked.

"Long enough to hear both of you say heinous things to one another—and you're supposed to be friends!"

"Well, he started it!" Nick muttered, then flinched as Monica raised her hand again, in his direction this time. She turned to Jeff and gave him a mean look.

"If Peter knew what you were trying to do, Jeff, he'd come unglued," she said, waving her finger in his face. "Had you really thought this through? Do you know the repercussions you and Nick splitting up would bring? Not just from the business angle—but all your friendships? Eric, Peter, Andrew—they'd be heartbroken ... David, not to mention Peter's mother ..."

"She's right, Jeff ..."

Nick was cut off by a glare from his partner. "You stay out of this," he growled. "You're the one who caused the problem."

"No, he's not," Monica said. "True, he showed poor judgment in asking Peter that favor, but he's right, Jeff ... Peter could've said no. He chose not to, out of friendship, and that I think is admirable. Come on, Jeff; you and Nick are friends. You get along great as partners. What on earth would be gained by dissolving your partnership?"

"She's right, Jeff," Nick said, again. "Look, I said a lot of shitty things there ..."

"Yes, you did," Monica agreed.

"*All right.*" He cleared his throat. "And for that I apologize. That was just my big mouth. You know how I can get."

Jeff nodded. "Uh huh."

"But you did kinda ask for it ..."

"Nick!" Monica did slap him this time. "This is not the way to apologize. I should bring Reg in here to referee. He'd most likely knock your heads together! Now ..." She looked from one to the other. "I want you both to kiss and make up."

"Sorry," Jeff shook his head. "No can do."

"Yes, you can do!" Monica said, placing her hands on her hips. "You'd better do—both of you—or, I quit!"

Nick shrugged. "Great ... you can come with me to my new office."

"No way. I work for both of you, *together*—or I don't work for either one of you."

"*Monica,*" Jeff groaned.

"Okay," she said. "I am going to my desk, and I will shut the door so you two can talk, and I mean *talk*—no yelling. Understand? When you are through talking, you will tell me your decision—and of course, mine rests with yours." With that, she turned and left the office, closing the door behind her.

The two men surveyed each other silently from their own ends of the office. Then Jeff walked behind his desk and sat down. Nick chose to sit on the edge of his desk, and began to hum tunelessly.

Jeff cleared his throat, fixing his eyes on a marble paperweight to his left. "Nick ... uh ... I may have been a bit hasty there ..."

"Mmhmm," Nick agreed.

"It's just that I was really concerned when I found out what you two were doing up in LA. Plus, Peter had a really bad time, last night."

"He did? What happened?"

"Nightmares—lots of them. We were up till about five, before he could finally relax."

"Oh, Jesus." Nick's shoulders sagged. "Now I feel like a total shit. I'll call him ..."

"No. He doesn't want you blaming yourself. Nick, what I said earlier ..."

"That's okay." Nick pushed himself off his desk, and walked across to where Jeff sat. He held out his hand. "I said some pretty nasty things that, of course I didn't mean. You know that, don't you?"

Jeff took his hand and stood up. "Monica's right," he said, with a wry grin. "We are a couple of idiots."

Nick pulled him into his arms, and they held each other for a long moment. "Christ," Nick murmured. "I can't imagine what Eric would've said if I'd gone home, and had to tell him you'd canned me!"

Jeff chuckled, patting Nick's back. "I'd probably have had him to deal with as well as Monica!"

"So you and Peter are OK now?" Nick asked, releasing Jeff from their hug.

"Yeah, we're good." Jeff sat down, then looked up at his partner. "And, in case you might not have noticed, I really did appreciate how you and Eric supported us both."

Nick shook his head. "That was a given. Okay, I'll give Monica the good news." He opened the door, and yelled into the reception area, "You can come in now. Jeff and I kissed and made up ... but that darned guy always wants to give me all of his tongue!"

Too late, he noticed out of the corner of his eye, a pair of female legs wearing sensible shoes. "Oops." He peered round the corner. A rather prim older lady looked back at him with a disapproving stare.

"This is Miss Anders, Nick," Monica informed him, trying to keep a straight face. "She has a twelve-thirty appointment with Jeff."

"Hi, Miss Anders," Nick said, his face getting redder by the second. "Go right on in. Jeff's waiting for you." He closed the door behind the woman's ramrod-like back, then collapsed into the seat she had vacated. "Oh, my God," he said, struggling to control his laughter. "Is that what you call a faux-pas?"

"It is," Monica giggled. "And nobody does it better than you!

John Hammond's gaze swept the interior of the bar Nick had suggested for their next meeting. It was Friday, after five, and the bar was busy with a mixed crowd of gay and straight patrons. Hammond spotted Nick, and gave him a tentative wave. He was still a little wary of Nick—not quite sure where his loyalties lay.

Oh, who am I kidding, he thought, as he walked toward Nick. That guy's loyalties are to his boyfriend first, his partner second, then everyone else—then me, way down at the bottom of the list. He barely managed to return Nick's smile as he sat down at the table.

"So, how's it goin' John?" Nick held out his hand, and Hammond took it, trying not to wince as Nick's big hand enveloped his.

"Okay, I guess. You?"

"Been busy ..." He signaled the drinks waiter. "What'll it be, John?"

"Uh ... I'll have a Manhattan."

"A Manhattan, and a Dewars on the rocks," Nick told the waiter.

"How are things ... uh ... with your partner and his boyfriend?" Hammond asked.

"Couldn't be better," Nick replied, grinning. "You know what they say ... half the fun of breaking up, is the making up that comes after."

"Yeah, I've heard about that." Hammond looked away, sighing.

"Feeling blue?" Nick asked.

Hammond nodded. "I guess I'm still smarting from that scene in your office the other day. I made a fool of myself, and I can't quite get over it."

"Hey, forget it ..."

"I wish I could," Hammond sighed again. "I think I need to see someone about anger management, or something."

Nick sat back as their drinks were placed in front of them. "Well, I have a friend who might help you."

"No thanks." Hammond waited until the waiter had gone. "My company provides that kind of service, free of charge."

"Good. Well, cheers."

"Yeah, cheers. So ..." He looked at Nick as he put his glass down. "You have some news about Robert's murder?"

Nick nodded. "Let me ask you something, John. Did you ever see this guy at The Racket talking to Robert?" He pushed the sketch Peter had drawn the day before across the table. Hammond picked it up, and for a second, his eyes widened. Then he shook his head.

"Who is he?" he asked.

"Name's Tom Skinner. You sure you don't know him?"

Hammond glared across the table at Nick. "I just said I didn't. Are you saying he was a friend of Robert's?"

"Bernie, the bartender, ID'd him right away from this sketch. Said he was in the bar a lot, always hanging around Robert. A friend of Robert's, Frank … you know him?" Hammond shook his head again, no. "Anyway, Frank tells me Skinner was hustling drinks from Robert, and there was something going on between them."

"So you think this guy killed Robert?"

"No … this guy is dead. In fact, he's the guy they dug up in Laurel Canyon—not Robert Landon."

"What?" Hammond looked stunned. "You mean Robert's not dead?"

"Well, let's put it this way—he's not the guy in the morgue."

"How do you know all this?"

Nick was not about to tell John Hammond of Peter's involvement. "I've been talking with the detective on the case—your friend, Bob Morales. He let me know that Robert Landon's dental records did not match the body."

"My God," Hammond muttered. "So Robert could be out there some-where … in hiding maybe?"

"Why in hiding?"

"You don't think he killed this Tom Skinner?"

"I have no idea," Nick said. "What I want to know is, why he was up there, in Laurel Canyon, in the first place. If he was on his way to see you, then why take that detour?"

Hammond shook his head then said, "I guess that's what I'm paying you to find out."

CHAPTER 11

The following morning, after Nick returned from his regular early morning run, there was a note from Eric on the kitchen table saying he had run down to the corner store for fresh milk. There was also a message on his cell phone:

"Hi Nick, it's Peter. Give me a buzz on my cell when you have a chance."

The message was recorded only ten minutes before he got home. Nick got the feeling that Peter didn't want anyone else to know about this call. 'Anyone else' being Jeff ... and Nick was suffused in a feeling of guilt as he punched in Peter's cell phone number. After what he and Jeff had gone through the day before, he did not want any further complications to affect their relationship—on the other hand, Peter rarely phoned him about inconsequential trivia. Oh wait, he thought, there was that question on Jeopardy they'd argued about.

"Hey Peter," he said quietly, when Peter picked up. "I got your message."

"Nick ... glad you called me back." Peter sounded tense. I've been having these dreams ... nightmares, really."

"Yeah, Jeff told me. I'm really sorry, Peter."

"No, no, it's OK. I just wanted you to know what they're about. You have a minute?"

"Of course."

"It's kind of a jumbled mess, noise, yelling, that kind of thing. But then I'm aware of two guys ... young surfer types. They are terrified, Nick, absolutely terrified. Someone, or something, is holding them down, and they're screaming for help. There's this horrendous suffocating feeling, a drumming noise in my head that makes me want to scream—and then I wake up."

"Jesus, Peter ... I'm sorry."

"It's OK, Nick, don't feel bad. If this is of some help to you, then I'll feel that at least these nightmares have been useful in some way."

"You said these guys were surfer types," Nick said, thinking. "Could you draw them too, like you did Tom?"

"No, I don't think so. It's more of an impression that I get, rather than a clear picture. I can't see their faces at all, but the feeling I get is that they are young and fit."

"Bernie, the bartender at The Racket, mentioned that two young hustlers had disappeared about the same time as Robert Landon. It could be them you're seeing. I'll follow up on that angle with the LAPD. Morales didn't seem interested when I mentioned their disappearance before, but maybe Joe could get me some information."

"It might be worth a shot," Peter said.

"Definitely worth a shot. Peter ..." Nick paused, unsure if he should ask the question that had popped into his mind.

"Yes, Nick?"

"These nightmares ... are they the same each time, or does there seem to be some kind of progression? I mean, is the nightmare with the two kids played over and over, or are there other things ... like other situations and people involved?"

"Well, the first nightmare was mostly about Tom Skinner trying to attack me. That played over and over, but then last night, I dreamed about the two guys. To be honest, this bothered me more, because I didn't know who they were, but it was like I was a witness—a bystander almost. I was watching them die."

"Christ," Nick muttered. "Do you feel OK today?"

"Apart from the fact I can't seem to forget it."

"Did you tell Jeff?"

Peter chuckled. "I didn't have to tell him, Nick. Last night, I think I made him my human punching bag. He had to lie on top of me to stop my fists flailing around." He chuckled again. "You see? Every bad dream can have its compensations!"

"You're the man, Peter," Nick said with admiration. "Not everyone could take all this in their stride like you seem to do."

"Well, I've had almost six years of off-the-wall experiences, so I guess I'm ready for anything. Well, almost anything."

After his conversation with Peter, Nick took a long shower, and thought over what Peter had told him. First off, was there any validity in these nightmares? Nightmares were generally a product of stress or trauma, and Peter had certainly suffered from both those symptoms in the last few days. It was understandable that his experience up at Laurel Canyon would have had some impact on his mind. But the dream of the two young men—that was something else. Nick had never mentioned the two hustlers to Peter. Or had he? No, he was pretty sure he hadn't … but even if he had, it would only have been in passing. Okay, so if the hustlers were tied to Landon's disappearance and Tom Skinner's murder, what part in all that, did they play?

Nick turned off the water and grabbed a towel from the rail. Drying his hair briskly, he mulled over the various possibilities. In Peter's vision, Tom Skinner had been waiting for Robert Landon. For what reason? Had Landon killed Skinner? Or had it been someone who had gone with him to Laurel Canyon … the two hustlers maybe?

Nick combed his hair back, noting that it was almost time for a haircut, then lathered his face with shaving cream. He gazed at his reflection in the mirror, razor poised over his left cheek. Again, he came back to that first persistent question. Why was Landon there at all, when he should have been on his way to Westwood? Why did he change direction to go so far out of his way? Why go there to meet with Tom Skinner when he could have seen him any night at The Racket? What had been so all-fired important that made him decide he had to go to Laurel Canyon to meet with Skinner?

Sighing, Nick began scraping off the last twenty-four hours growth of beard. As he finished up, he heard Eric call him from the bedroom.

"Yeah, I'll be out in a minute, babe." He splashed his face with cool water, toweled off, and pulled on a pair of sweatpants. It was Saturday, and he and Eric usually made a slow start on those mornings. Eric didn't have to be at the gallery until noon and Nick tried to keep Saturday mornings free of appointments.

The aroma of fresh coffee greeted his nostrils as he opened the bathroom door. Eric was in the kitchen, preparing their breakfast. Nick wrapped his arms around him and kissed the back of his neck.

"Good morning," he murmured.

"It is now ..." Eric turned and smiled into Nick's eyes. "Mmm, you smell good." Their kiss was long and sensuous. "Have a good run?" he asked, nibbling at Nick's earlobe.

"Excellent. The beach was deserted."

"No John Hammond lurking behind the sand dunes?"

Nick chuckled and kissed Eric's nose. "No, thank God. I think he got the message."

"Okay, go sit down and have some waffles while I scramble the eggs."

"You workin' out today?" Nick asked, chewing on a waffle.

"Uh huh. Andrew's picking me up in about an hour. What are you doing?"

"Peter called me earlier."

"Oh, yeah ... what about?"

"You probably know he's been having nightmares."

"He told me yesterday, yes."

"Well, he came up with something I find very interesting."

Eric froze. "Nick ... tell me you're not going to involve him in this again. God, we just got over that whole trauma with you and Jeff."

Nick looked pained. "Eric, he called *me*. Believe me, I wasn't about to even talk to him about this again. But last night he had another nightmare, and it's got me thinking about this whole case in a different light."

"What d'you mean?"

"I'm not sure yet. I want to talk to Joe French. That Morales character is just too hard to deal with. Once I have a clearer picture about what was really going on, you'll be the first to know."

Jeff was already in the office when Nick showed up around eleven. Monica had the weekend off, so they had to field the phone calls by themselves.

"Hey, Nick," Jeff greeted him. "You've got a couple of messages over on your desk."

"Thanks, pardner." He sat down and scanned the messages—nothing that couldn't wait. He cleared his throat. "Jeff ... uh, Peter called me this morning."

"I know."

"You know ... oh good, you know."

"Yeah, I asked him who he was talking to, and he said he'd called you about the nightmare he had last night."

Nick smiled. "Honest Pete."

"That's right." Jeff sighed. "I'll be honest too, Nick. I am not happy about what's going on with him."

"I understand."

"You should've seen him last night, Nick. Thrashing about, yelling, scared. I just know it's no good for him. He was covered in sweat, shivering. I finally had to take him to the shower. He was calmer after that."

"Jeff, I ..."

Jeff held up his hand to stay what Nick had to say. "I know you're sorry, Nick. We won't go there again. I know Peter ... he'll do his best to help you with this. But when it's over ..."

"I know." Nick flicked at the corner of his desk with his thumbnail. "If I so much as mention to him any case I'm working on, you have my permission to punch my lights out."

Jeff grinned at him. "I may just take you up on that, *pardner.*"

"So, you obviously know what the nightmare was about."

"Yeah, two young kids getting tortured, he said."

"Right." Nick stood, and went to sit in the chair at Jeff's desk. "Here's the thing. The bartender at The Racket told me that two young hustlers went missing same time as Landon. You know, of course, that the body they found wasn't Landon's."

Jeff nodded.

"In his vision, Peter saw this other guy, Tom Skinner, get killed. Landon was there. Peter seemed to feel more than just one other presence.

Now I'm thinking it's possible that the hustlers were there also. Maybe one, or both of them, killed Skinner."

"Okay, but what was the motive, and where are they?" Jeff asked. "They've all been missing for three months."

"The missing part I don't have a clue about," Nick said. "They could be anywhere—Mexico, Canada, the Deep South, who knows? Landon is, *or was*, from New Orleans originally. As for motive, I'm inclined to think blackmail. If Skinner was blackmailing Landon, that might explain why Landon went out of his way to make that detour up to Laurel Canyon the night he was supposed to have dinner with John Hammond."

"From what you've told me about Landon," Jeff interjected, "he doesn't sound like the kind of guy who gets blackmailed. Didn't you say everyone liked him, he had close friends—the guys at the bar, his boss ..."

"Yeah ... but there's this relationship, if you could call it that, with Tom Skinner. I spoke to a friend of Landon's, and he told me he thought there might be something sexual in it. Maybe Landon had a darker side than anyone knew."

"Possible," Jeff agreed. "We've both seen our share of people who were not altogether on the level. It might be worth delving a bit more into Landon's background."

"That's what I thought. Only problem is it's either Houston, where his mother lives now—or New Orleans ..."

"Where everything's been wiped out—or close to it," Jeff said.

"Yeah ..." Nick nodded and steepled his fingers under his chin, thinking. "It might be better if I checked out Skinner's background for starters. He's a little closer to home—or was, I should say."

"A guy like that is bound to have some kind of record," Jeff remarked. "Maybe just petty stuff, but something for you to go on. Give Joe a call—see what he can dig up."

"Good idea ... easier than dealing with Morales. I think I'll head back up to The Racket, *again*. Tom Skinner spent a lot of time there. I'll give Joe a call when I'm on the road.

Bernie looked a little surprised to see Nick walk into The Racket later that day. "Hey," he said, his startled look being replaced quickly with a passable leer. "Is it my animal appeal that keeps bringing you back?"

Nick grinned at him. "Something like that …"

"Just a Coke?"

"Just a Coke—and hopefully some more information."

"Oh yeah?" Bernie handed him an ice-cold glass of Coke. "Still looking for Robert's killer?"

Nick leaned closer and lowered his voice. "We don't know that Robert Landon is actually dead."

"What?" Bernie gaped at him. "According to the cops …"

"They haven't released the fact yet that the body they dug up was Tom Skinner's, not Landon's."

"Holy crap." Bernie busied himself wiping down the counter. "So, you're saying Robert could still be alive?"

"Possibly," Nick told him, watching Bernie's agitated movements with interest. "I'm beginning to think that Landon, Skinner and the two hustlers were somehow involved with one another."

Bernie stopped wiping and stared at Nick. "No *way*. Robert was a nice, quiet guy …"

"But he did have a fixation about Skinner," Nick said. "His buddy from the office, Frank—he told me he thought there might have been some sexual connection between them.

"Naw, no way," Bernie insisted. "Not Robert and that deadbeat. I can't see it."

"Or maybe you just don't want to see it, Bernie." Nick looked at him keenly. "You were *fond* of Robert Landon, weren't you, Bernie?"

The bartender nodded and gave Nick a sad smile. "Yeah, I liked him. He was a good guy—wouldn't hurt a fly. He had class … a Southern gentleman. He'd never run around with somebody like Tom Skinner."

"What about the two young hustler guys?"

"What about them?"

"You ever see Landon with them?"

"No, I told you that already." Bernie looked piqued.

"Right." Nick downed the last of his Coke. "Skinner ... he have any friends join him here?"

Bernie shook his head. "Not that I know of."

"Yeah, you do, Bernie ..." From the other end of the bar came a disembodied voice. Nick peered through the gloom at the man who slowly approached them. He was in his fifties, needed a shave, and was sadly out of shape. "You remember that guy ... what's-his-name ... they shared an apartment round the corner."

"No, I *don't* remember. I never talked to Tom if I could avoid it. I couldn't stand him, if you want to know the truth"

"Ah, he wasn't so bad ... bought me a drink a coupla times." He shot Nick a hopeful smile.

"Lenny ..." Bernie glared. "Quit actin' like a bum. Nick here is a private investigator."

"That's OK," Nick said. "What'll it be, Lenny?"

"Whisky. Irish, with a splash." Lenny licked his lips in anticipation. "See, Bernie? Some guys have hearts, as well as looks."

Bernie rolled his eyes while picking up a glass already filled with ice. "Rocks?" he barked.

"Of course," Lenny said, with a wave of his hand. "How else would you serve it?" He turned to Nick. "It's tough getting good help these days."

"So you knew Tom pretty well?" Nick asked, as Lenny savored his whisky.

"Pretty well ..."

Bernie snorted his displeasure, wiping the bar down even more vigorously than before.

"And the guy he shared with?"

"I never knew his name," Lenny told Nick. "He only came in here a couple of times ..."

"You know their address?"

"I can point it out," Lenny said, giving his empty glass a mournful look.

"Bernie ..." Nick pushed Lenny's glass toward him, along with a twenty-dollar bill. Bernie glared at Lenny, and poured another shot.

Nick took the refilled glass, and held it lightly between his thumb and forefinger. "You wanna show me where he lives?" he asked Lenny.

"He doesn't know," Bernie said sourly. "How would he know? He's just playing one of his games—ain'tcha Lenny?"

"I know, 'cause I followed them outta here one night," Lenny protested. He stared at the drink Nick was holding from him. "I can show you, right now."

Nick slid the drink toward him. "Okay, let's go."

Lenny gulped the whisky down then wiped his mouth with the back of his hand.

"He's fulla shit," Bernie growled as they left. "Fulla shit."

Nick rammed his sunglasses on as he followed Lenny out into the glaring sunshine. "Why'd you follow them, Lenny?" he asked, as they walked to the corner and turned right.

The other man squinted up at him. "You ever see Tom?"

"Only a drawing of him."

"A drawing?" Lenny shook his head. "He was one sexy man. I guess I kinda had the hots for him. 'Course, he wouldn't give me the time of day, but I'd had a few, one night, and thought I'd give it a try. You never know till you ask."

"And did you? Ask, that is."

Lenny grimaced. "No—I guess I hadn't had enough. I lost my nerve—but I did see him, and his buddy walk into this building right here." He pointed to a shabby stucco fourplex. Together, they walked through the rusty wrought-iron gate, looking around at the neglected exterior of the two-story building.

"I think they went upstairs," Lenny said. "And by the way ..." He put his hand on Nick's arm. "Don't believe what Bernie says. I saw him talking to Tom many times. Mostly when Robert was there."

"Is that right?" Nick stared into Lenny's rheumy eyes, trying to discern if the man was telling the truth or not. Lenny's eyes slid away from Nick's intense stare.

"Okay, I'm goin'," he muttered.

Nick watched as he shambled off, then took the stairs two at a time. He peered at the faded nameplate by the doorbell. He could just about make out the name Riley. The second name had almost been erased, but what remained was enough—S i n r. He rapped on the door and waited.

No one answered his knock, so he peered through a window to the right of the door. Removing his sunglasses, he shaded his eyes with his hand. He could just make out the shadowy shapes of a couch and a TV.

"Help you?"

The voice behind him startled Nick for a second, then he shot a friendly smile at the man climbing the steps to the apartment. Slender, with brown hair cut military short, wearing a white tee, shorts and sandals, and carrying a paper grocery bag. He stared at Nick with a wary, and not altogether friendly, expression.

"Hi." Nick held his hand out. "Nick Fallon. I'm a private investigator from Laguna Beach."

"Oh, yeah?" He took Nick's hand in a cool, firm grip. "Mike Riley. If this is about Tom, I haven't seen the s.o.b. in over three months."

"He lived here with you?" Nick asked, handing Riley his card.

Riley nodded, and unlocked the apartment door. "Come on in. Believe it or not, this dump has A.C.—one reason I stay."

Nick stepped inside, feeling the relief of the cool air. The apartment was small but surprisingly neat. "You live here alone now?"

"Yeah," Riley said, laying the grocery bag on the kitchen counter. "I kinda like living on my own, so I didn't bother to rent to anyone else."

"What d'you suppose happened to Tom?" Nick asked.

"He skipped town, most like." He gave Nick an appraising look. "You know something I don't?"

"How close were you two?" Nick figured the information he was about to pass on, just might cause an emotional outburst, if the two men had been more than just friends.

Riley shrugged. "We were close, I guess—on and off. We were in the Marines together."

"Were you guys lovers?"

"He would tell you no. Tom's not the lover type, believe me. So, what's the deal with him?"

"Well ..." Nick leaned against one of the two leather-covered barstools at the kitchen counter. "There was a body found up in Laurel Canyon about a week ago ... been there about three months. The cops thought it was a guy named Robert Landon. Mean anything to you?"

"Rings a bell ..." Riley sat on the couch and stared at Nick.

"Anyway, turns out it wasn't Landon," Nick continued. "I don't have proof positive yet, but I'm pretty sure it was your buddy, Tom, they dug up."

Riley gasped and slumped against the back of the couch. "Jesus," he whispered. "Tom ... dead?" He was quiet for a moment or two, then he said, "So, someone finally had enough."

"What d'you mean?"

"Tom was into a bunch of stuff," he said finally. "Stuff that I didn't really want to know about, quite frankly. Hustling, procuring ... that kind of thing. Girls as well as guys. I told him never to bring it home—and he never did. But he'd get these calls late at night. A couple of times he wasn't here, so I'd answer the phone, and whoever was on the other end was like ... man ... creepy, is the only word I can think of."

"You talked about this to him, of course," Nick said.

"Damned right I did—and he'd just make out it was nothing. Some drunk, he said, looking for some late night delight. But that's not what it sounded like."

"What did it sound like?"

"I don't know really—something *sinister* maybe. Tom would laugh ... said I had a vivid imagination ... but I don't know—especially now." Riley sat on the barstool next to Nick. "You're sure it was Tom they found?"

"Pretty sure, like I said. I have a friend with the LAPD—he's goin' to let me know when they have positive ID on the body."

Riley shuddered. "Don't tell the cops about me—I don't want to have to identify his body. Christ, after three months, what could be left? He was always so proud of his body ..."

"Would you happen to have a photograph of him?" Nick asked.

"Yeah … a couple from when we were still in the Marine Corp. I'll get them." He slid off the stool and walked the few steps to his bedroom. Nick got up and followed him, standing in the doorway of the small room while Riley rummaged through a dresser drawer.

"Tom have his own room?" he asked, looking down the narrow hall at a closed door.

"Yeah. You can take a look in there if you like. I straightened it out about two months ago when it looked like he wasn't coming back—but everything's still in there."

"Thanks." Nick opened the door and stared into Tom Skinner's bedroom. No doubt, that Mike Riley was a neatnik—there wasn't a thing out of place. A double bed was pushed into one corner, a nightstand and lamp alongside. A television sat on a dresser at the foot of the bed, and a couple of pictures hung from one wall. Nick opened the closet door, staring at the row of jackets, shirts, pants and jeans that hung from the rail; the shoes and boots that were arranged neatly on the shelf above. He was suddenly aware that Riley had entered the room, standing close to his side.

"Didn't it seem strange to you that Tom would just leave all of this behind?" Nick fingered the sleeve of an obviously expensive leather jacket.

Ignoring the question, Riley held up a photograph of himself and another, taller man in service uniform. They had their arms around each other's shoulders, smiling broadly for the camera. Mike Riley's head was tilted just a little toward the other man's shoulder.

"We were on a tour of duty in Afghanistan," he explained, his voice suddenly husky. He moved even closer to Nick who stepped back a little, as if to see the photo more clearly by the window. He knew where the young man was going with all this closeness, and didn't want to have to rebuff him too strongly. He stared at the image of the two young men. Tom was well built, broad and muscular with an arrogant, cocky air behind that big smile. Although he had said they were not lovers, it was evident to Nick that Riley had loved his soldier buddy, a little more than he admitted. He handed the photo back.

"Nice picture," he said. "Tell me, did he leave any papers, letters, that kind of thing, lying around?"

Riley laughed without humor. "Tom never wrote a letter in his life— and I should know." A trace of bitterness entered his voice. "After we got discharged, I wrote him often, but never heard a thing. Then out of the blue, he shows up here at my door." The sudden shrilling of the phone in the living room caused Riley to jump nervously. "I ... I better get that." He rushed from the bedroom, leaving Nick alone. Without hesitation, Nick started opening the nightstand and dresser drawers. Socks, underwear and tees were arranged neatly in the top two drawers of the dresser. It was almost as though Riley had laundered all of Tom's clothes in anticipation of his return. The third drawer revealed something very different ... a stack of videotapes. Nick paused, listening for any movement in the hall, but it sounded like Riley was involved in an animated conversation with some friend or other. Satisfied, he resumed the task oft rifling through the video stash. The first few titles revealed little. Mambo Kings, Zorro, The 13th Warrior ... It was obvious Tom Skinner had been an Antonio Banderas fan. He was about to close the drawer, when one tape caught his eye. The letters U.S.F.N.F. were printed on the homemade label. Nick frowned. What did that stand for? United States something ...? Maybe something Skinner had from his time in the Marines.

Just then, he heard Riley say goodbye to whomever he was on the phone with, and with an almost automatic reflex, Nick shoved the tape into the inside pocket of his bomber jacket. Quickly he pushed the drawer closed, and walked to the bedroom door. He collided with Riley in the narrow hall.

"Sorry," he muttered, trying to get out of the other man's way.

"Don't be." Riley gripped Nick's arm, trying to pull him closer.

"Uh ... you don't want to start that," Nick said, pulling himself free.

"Why not? You're hot."

"Thanks, young man, but I'm spoken for." He walked back into the living room with Riley at his heels. "Okay Mike, just so you know, the cops are going to want to talk to you about your association with Skinner."

A look of alarm registered on the other man's face. "Why? I didn't have anything to do with that stuff."

"Maybe so ... but you probably know more about him than anyone else. They're going to need background information on him, and you're their best bet. Let me give you some advice ..." Nick picked up his sunglasses from the kitchen counter. "Don't try to withhold any information—tell them everything you know about Skinner." He turned to go. "Oh, and one more thing—if a Detective Morales comes a'calling, don't try to put the make on *him*." Then he grinned. "On second thoughts, maybe you should, and let me know what happens!"

Nick rammed his sunglasses on as he stepped out into the bright sunlight outside Riley's apartment. As he ran down the steps, his cell phone rang. He checked the caller ID ... Private number ...

"Nick Fallon ..."

"You're going to have to start looking outside the box," a man's voice, sounding like it came from under piles of gauze, whispered in Nick's ear.

"Who is this?"

"Someone who knows where Robert Landon is."

"So, where is he?"

"Well, that would save you a lot of work, now wouldn't it?"

"Yeah, it would. Where is he, and how do you know he's not dead?"

"I just know ..."

"Look, quit monkeyin' around," Nick rasped. "Tell me, or get off the line."

"My, such ingratitude."

"I have nothing to be grateful for, yet."

"Well, let's just say he didn't run home to Mother."

"What's that supposed to mean?"

"Figure it out ... you're the detective."

The line went dead.

"Shit ..." Nick slapped his cell phone closed, and stood for a moment on the hot sidewalk, thinking.

He didn't run home to Mother.

Landon's mother was in Houston, but originally from New Orleans. Did it mean Landon had gone to New Orleans? But why, with the city still in a mess? But why not, with the city still in a mess? He could hide out there quite easily, if in fact, that's what he was doing ... if he killed Tom Skinner ... if ... There were still a lot of 'ifs' Nick groused to himself. Too damned many ...

CHAPTER 12

Driving back to Laguna, Nick called Joe French to see if he'd dug up anything on Tom Skinner.

"Not a lot, I'm afraid," Joe told him. "One arrest on a drug charge with no time served, and a minor traffic infraction."

"He was careful I guess," Nick remarked. "I just spoke to his roommate, and he tells me Skinner was into a bunch of stuff—hustling, procuring—that kind of thing."

"Hmm ... Morales should know about this."

"He'd know about a lot of things, if he'd call me," Nick said. "That guy has a fistful of hairs up his butt."

"He got his knuckles rapped for disclosing wrong information to the press. I think he's still smarting from that reprimand."

"Anything on Landon?"

"Not a thing. If he's still alive, he's managed to drop out of sight really well. He could be anywhere by now."

"I think I know where."

"Do tell."

"Just a hunch—but if I'm right, I'll let you know right away."

"Okay Nick. I'll tell Morales to call you."

"Only if he can take time out of his busy schedule, of course."

Joe laughed. "Keep in touch, Nick."

Nick punched in John Hammond's number. "Hey, John—Nick. How's it goin'?"

"Fine ... what's up?"

"Did you know Robert Landon was from New Orleans, originally?"

"Uh, no … not exactly." Hammond sounded distracted. "Why do you ask?"

"I think he might have gone home to New Orleans."

"But why? Especially with the mess that city's in. Why would he go back now?"

"I'm working on the theory that Skinner and Robert Landon were involved in something illegal. Whatever it was, Landon and Skinner fell out and Skinner got killed—by Landon or by some third party, I'm not yet sure. Chances are though that he ran after Skinner was killed. He could disappear in New Orleans very easily, what with all the chaos."

There was a protracted silence from Hammond's end. "New Orleans," he said finally. "You want to fly to New Orleans. How much is this going to cost me?"

"Dunno yet … fare plus hotel—if I can find one …"

"I don't know, Nick."

"Well, here are our options, John. Either I follow this through, and that means playing out my hunch that he's in New Orleans—or we call it quits, and I hand everything I know so far over to the police. If they ever solve the case, you'll read about it in the papers. It's up to you, John."

"And supposing you find Robert there, what then?"

"I'll ask him what his involvement with Skinner was, and did he kill him?"

"Right … like he's going to admit it!"

Nick chuckled. "No, but I have ways of finding out."

"Okay then," Hammond said. "But if you don't find him in two or three days, come back and we'll forget the whole thing."

"Gotcha. I'll be in touch. Bye, John."

Jeff was in the office when Nick got back about an hour later. "Any luck in LA?" he asked as Nick threw his jacket onto the chair in front of his desk.

"Some. I talked with Skinner's roomie. He had a few interesting little gems of information to pass on—mainly that Skinner was one big asshole into procuring girls and guys for prostitution."

"Nice," Jeff said.

"Right—and I have a feeling Landon might have been mixed up in it somehow. Although the roomie didn't seem to know him ... said the name rang a bell, that's all. Oh wait, I brought a souvenir from their apartment." He picked up his jacket and removed the videotape from the inside pocket.

"Removing evidence Nick?" Jeff frowned. "That's not like you."

"I know, I'm terrible." He pushed the tape into the recorder, and he and Jeff leaned forward to watch the television screen as it flared into life. The images on the screen were startlingly clear, almost professional in quality. Whoever held the camera knew what he or she was doing.

"Looks like a party or something ..."

"Hi guys!" They looked round to find Peter standing in the doorway. "What are you watching?"

"A tape Nick purloined from a dead man's apartment," Jeff told him as he sat on the edge of Jeff's desk.

"What's it about?" Peter asked.

"Not sure yet," Nick said, concentrating on the TV screen. "Some kind of party ... a masked party. Holy crap," he muttered as two naked young men appeared on the screen.

"Is this porno, Nick?" Peter started to laugh. "Is this what you guys do in the office when Monica's not here?"

"No, of course not," Jeff chuckled. "We just watch the stuff she brings!"

"You guys ... keep it down," Nick muttered. "Something's screwy here."

"What are they doing?" Peter asked.

"It looks like they're drugged. See, that one ... he's having a hard time standing up."

"Oh, my God," Peter gasped "Those guys ... I don't believe it!"

"What is it?"

"This is like that nightmare I told you about!"

As they stared transfixed at the images upon the screen, the two young men were grabbed by others wearing party masks. They were then stretched out on the carpeted floor, and a circle was formed around them.

As the two young men made dazed attempts to fondle each other, those in the circle began to masturbate.

"You gotta be kiddin' me," Nick gasped. "What kind of bullshit is this?"

But much worse was to follow. From behind the circle of men, a robed figure appeared. He was carrying thin cords, looped at one end to form nooses. He slipped a noose around the neck of the young man lying in front of him, then with excruciating slowness, began to garrote him.

Peter moaned aloud. "Oh, God ... he's killing him. He's *killing* him!" He turned away from the screen, unable to watch his nightmare being reenacted in front of his eyes. As the young man struggled to stay alive, several in the circle climaxed over his writhing body.

Then the screen went black.

"Jesus H. Christ," Nick whispered, visibly shaken by what he had just seen. He looked at Jeff, whose face was rigid with shock. "I thought I had seen everything ... but that ..." He got up and removed the tape from the recorder. He looked at the label again. "U.S.F.N.F.—that's what's written here," he said aloud. "U.S.F.N.F. What the hell does that mean?"

"It's an anagram," Jeff said, quietly. "An anagram for 'snuff'—as in snuff movies."

"So that's what Skinner was up to," Nick seethed. "That's what he was procuring for—movies like this aberration. What a scumbag. Man, he sure got what he deserved!"

"And what about the other men in the video, Nick? Jeff asked. "The ones who actually killed those kids—and all those others who stood around getting their jollies while those young guys died in front of their eyes. What about them, Nick?"

"Well, we don't know if those kids were really killed, now do we? If I remember right, a lot of those snuff films were proven to be fakes—no one really died."

"*They* did," Peter said quietly. "The ones in that video died, Nick. I'm sure of it."

"Oh, Jesus." Nick buried his face in his hands, thinking hard.

"You have to give that video to the police, Nick," Jeff said. "They are not going to like the fact that you took it from Skinner's apartment."

"You're right," Nick agreed, looking up at his partner. "Morales hates me as it is. He'd just love to throw me in the slammer for this."

"Couldn't you just mail it to him?" Peter suggested. "Anonymously?"

"I could," Nick said. "But Morales would guess it came from me—especially when he finds out I was in Skinner's apartment talking to his roommate. He's not *that* slow. I guess I'll just have to bite the bullet and tell him how I got it, after I get back from New Orleans."

"You're going to New Orleans?"

"I think Landon's gone home to hide out from whatever he was involved in with Skinner."

"But finding him in New Orleans, Nick ... that's going to take a lot of footwork, and luck."

"Right. So wish me a lot of the latter."

When Nick got home that night, Eric was already there, a color chart laid out on the kitchen bar. After their kiss hello, and a Dewars on the rocks prepared, Eric pushed the color chart in front of Nick.

"Okay, now I was thinking ..."

"Not tonight, babe," Nick said, trying not to sound disinterested. "I'm flying to New Orleans tomorrow, so I have to get on the computer and book me a seat."

"New Orleans! What the heck for?"

"I got an anonymous tip on the phone that Robert Landon's there. I need to talk to him regarding Tom Skinner's death."

"You think he did it?"

"That I'm not sure of yet.... but he was involved with Skinner in something, and after seeing a pretty nasty video today, I surely want to know just how deep his involvement was."

"But how will you find him?" Eric asked. "New Orleans is a big city, and most of it's still a mess."

"I know. It won't be easy—easy, get it? Big Easy?"

Eric groaned. "Nick, I love you ... but not for your jokes."

"Huh. What's for dinner?"

"Lasagna and salad."

"Yum." Nick leaned across the bar and kissed Eric's cheek. "You're the best. I'll be right back—just have to book a flight." He carried his drink into the den, and turned on his computer. After deleting most of the emails he found in his mailbox, he clicked on Google then typed in Flights Orange County to New Orleans. He grunted with satisfaction as a host of different options appeared on the screen. He settled for a Continental flight that left early in the morning, arriving mid afternoon. That would give him some work time on the first day. The travel website also offered a hotel, so he booked three nights at the Renoir in the French Quarter.

Next, he logged on to the private investigator website he subscribed to, and typed in Landon's name and home city. About a dozen Robert Landons showed up, none of them with criminal records. Nick tapped his teeth with his forefinger, thinking. What was his mother's name? Elizabeth, wasn't it? Okay ... Elizabeth. Chances were that even though she had moved to Houston after Katrina, her name would still be in the New Orleans' database. And there it was—Elizabeth Landon, age 55, 222 Green Street, New Orleans, 614-555-5654.

"Let's see who's living there now," he muttered, punching in the number. There was no reply and no answering machine. That would just have been too easy. Still, he pondered, Green Street—an excellent place to start.

He smiled as he felt warm hands slip inside the front of his shirt. "Hi, babe. Missing me?"

"Yes." Eric laid a kiss on his forehead. "You get your flight?"

"Uh, huh. *Early* in the morning, while you're still fast asleep."

"No, I'll drive you to the airport." He sat on Nick's lap, gazing into his eyes for a moment or two. "This isn't going to be dangerous is it?" he asked, concerned.

"Not unless there's another hurricane while I'm there."

"Don't kid me, Nick. What exactly d'you think this Landon guy has done?"

"I don't know yet—but whatever it is, I don't think he's the dangerous type. Only to himself maybe."

"What does that mean?"

"It means—and I'm speaking only from my own hunches—I think he got in over his head, panicked and ran."

"Can I come with you?"

"No, Eric. Absolutely not! Do you think for one moment that I would put you through anything *remotely* dicey after what happened to you last year?"

"You said it wouldn't be dangerous."

"You're not coming … end of story."

"Nick …"

"No, Eric. Besides, Peter needs you at the gallery. You can't up and leave him right now. I think he needs to take some time off."

"Why? What happened?"

Nick sighed. "Well, Peter will probably tell you anyway, so …" Quickly, and without a lot of elaboration he told Eric what he, Jeff and Peter had witnessed on the video he had taken from Skinner's apartment. Eric listened, his face registering his dismay.

"And Peter saw all of this?"

"Yes, unfortunately. If I had known he was going to walk into the office, I'd never have put the tape on."

"Oh, dear God." Eric rose from Nick's lap. "You know, of course, that this will probably cause him to have even more nightmares. Jesus, Nick."

"You sound like you're blaming me, Eric."

"No, I'm not blaming you. I just wish you'd never taken this goddam case!"

Nick stood up. "Eric, come here." He wrapped his arms around his lover, holding him tight against his body. "Most of the time, in this business, we're just looking for false insurance claims, helping divorce cases, boring things like that. But every now and then, we see things we wish we never had. We place ourselves—and sometimes the ones we love—in situations we would like to avoid at all costs. Hopefully, the end result is 'case solved, bad guy gets his'—but along the way, there are pitfalls that I can't always see coming. Sometimes, the bad guy gets too close …" He paused as they both remembered just how close, some months before.

"But please understand, I would never willingly place you, or any of my friends, in jeopardy. What happened this afternoon with Peter was unfortunate, for want of a better word. We can be grateful that he has Jeff there with him. He'll look after him."

Eric sighed, and laid his head on Nick's chest. "Why couldn't you have been an engineer, or a teacher, or something safe?"

Nick chuckled. "You think teachers are safe? Have you seen some of those kids they have to deal with?"

"You know what I mean," Eric said, tightening his arms around Nick. "Thank you though, for saying all of that. I love you."

"And I love you—even though you're depriving me of sustenance right now."

"Oh, right, the dinner ... it's probably burnt by now."

"That's okay," Nick said, laying a gentle kiss on Eric's lips. "I love burnt lasagna."

The tall silver haired man stretched out a languid hand to pick his ringing cell phone from inside the briefcase that lay at his feet. "Yes?" His tone was low and curt.

"It's time to bring Robert back," the caller on the other end said sharply.

"Why?"

"The police know it wasn't his body they dug up in Laurel Canyon. It won't be too long before they find him. He needs to be looked after."

"I see. Well, I'll leave it to you to make all the arrangements."

"Fine. I have your assurance he'll be taken care of?"

"Of course ... keep me informed."

The caller quickly dialed a number in New Orleans. After three or four rings, a wary voice answered. "Hello?"

"Robert ... it's me. Listen carefully, there's a guy who'll be in town soon looking for you. I want you to call him and arrange a meeting. Here's his cell number. He's going to ask you a bunch of questions—just remember to tell him everything, exactly as we agreed ... okay?"

"Okay ..."

"Don't make it sound too rehearsed. Let him think you're really nervous."

"I *am* really nervous ... and what happens after?"

"He'll want to bring you back—and you'll agree. Don't worry; you're not going to face any jail time. Our friends will take care of that. Just stay cool, and it'll be all right."

"Okay. I miss you."

"I miss you too."

CHAPTER 13

New Orleans in July, Nick thought, as he got out of the cab that had brought him from the airport to his hotel—was not the place to be with temperatures in the nineties, and humidity topping one hundred percent. It was late afternoon, and the air hung about him, hot and damp. The drive from the airport had been mind-blowing. So much devastation still so apparent everywhere he looked. An eerie atmosphere of desolation hung over the once bustling, vibrant city, now strangely devoid of the crowds of people that had given it its diverse appeal.

Nick checked in at the front desk of the Renoir, took his key and, on being told that the elevator was out of order, climbed the stairs to his room. A large ceiling fan in the middle of the room moved the warm, turgid air around. Nick looked around for a thermostat—there wasn't one. Great, he thought. Just great ... He pulled off his sopping shirt and pants, and headed for the shower where he stood under the cold spray for as long as he could stand it. As he toweled himself his cell phone rang.

"Probably Eric," he muttered, squinting at the ID screen in the half-light that filtered through the window shutters. "Nope, Mike Riley. Hey Mike, what's up?"

Mike was not happy. "Thanks a fucking bunch for telling the cops where they could find me!"

"You're welcome. Did you get to meet Detective Morales?"

"Detective fuckin' Moronic is more like it. What an asshole," Riley ranted. "He thinks he's so cool with the blackout shades and the preppy suit. What a jerk."

"Did he give you a bad time, Mike?"

"He came with a search warrant, and two other cretins, and practically wrecked the place. It's going to takes me hours to put this place right again." Riley sounded as though he were close to tears. "They took nearly all of Tom's stuff—even his videos. They said there might be stuff hidden in them somewhere—fuckin' Nazis! I'd like to meet that Morales character in a dark alley ..."

"I'm sorry, Mike."

"You should be—and by the way, I didn't say anything to that jerk, but I noticed one of the videos was missing."

"You did?"

"Yeah, I alphabetized them, and the last one—U.S. somethin', was missing. I figured you took it when I was on the phone."

Nick rolled his eyes. *Riley alphabetized videos stuck in a nightstand drawer*. What a freak.

"Anyway," Riley was saying. "You owe me, next time you're in town."

"Owe you?"

"Yeah—a drink, a date ... *something*!"

"Okay, I'll buy you a drink when my boyfriend and I are up there next time."

"Oh great." Riley sound a tad put out. "Just bring back the video."

"Do you know what's on that video, Mike?"

"No ... I just want it back."

"Believe me, you don't. Anyway, I'll have to hand it over to the police as evidence."

"Evidence of what?"

"You don't want to know, Mike. The less you know about what Tom was doing, the better off you'll be. Trust me on this. Gotta go Mike, someone's trying to get through."

"Hey, wait ..."

Nick sighed, and pushed the talk button. "Nick Fallon."

"Morales. I talked with Skinner's roommate. He said you'd been there. I told you already I don't want you snoopin' around my case."

"Hey, it was my lead, my hard work that got me there—and I passed it on to you. Don't forget, Detective, if it wasn't for me, you'd still be looking for Landon's killer, not Skinner's."

"Yeah, well I want you to back off now. Leave the investigating to me. Where are you anyway? This line's got a lot of static on it."

"Uh … I'm driving through the Laguna Canyon. The reception's bad here."

"Yeah? Well, like I said, don't get under my feet again."

"There's gratitude for you," Nick said. "But sorry, I can't back off. I have a client who's paying me to find the answers to Landon's disappearance."

"I'm warning you, Fallon …"

"What? You're breaking up, Detective. What did you say?" Nick cut the connection and threw his cell phone on the bed.

That son-of-a-bitch, he thought. He'd be nowhere in this case if it hadn't been for the information I passed on to him. Riley was right—the guy's a jerk. Just wait till he finds out what else I got. Woohoo!

222 Green Street, just off of Lafitte, was a modest detached one story home, that looked like it had been spared the worst of the flooding—as had a great deal of the French Quarter. However, there was an air of neglect surrounding the house, and indeed, the whole street. Very few porch lights were on, and over the porch at 222, no light shone. Bracing himself, Nick knocked on the glass paned door. After a few moments, he could hear a shuffling movement, and then the door swung open to reveal an elderly African American male with stooped shoulders and a shock of white hair.

Unless Robert Landon had employed a truly talented make over artist, this was not him.

"Help you?" the man asked.

"I'm looking for Robert Landon, sir. Does he live here?"

"Not the last time I looked. Heh, heh." He surveyed Nick through rheumy eyes. "Who is he?"

"I believe his mother owns, or owned, this house, up to the time of Katrina. Do you know Elizabeth Landon?"

The old man shook his head. "I wouldn't know who lived here before. House was empty when I came along, close to a year ago. Nice place though. You want to come in and see?"

"Thank you." Nick stepped inside, hoping the air would be cooler that it was on the street. It wasn't. He looked around at the sparsely furnished living room. "Nice place," he said.

"Looters took most of the furniture before I got here." The old man held out his hand. "William Dupree," he said.

"Nick Fallon." He handed William his business card. "I'm a private investigator from California."

"Come a long way lookin' for this guy. Landers was it?"

"Landon, Robert Landon. So you just took over this house?'

William Dupree chuckled. "Whole street's fulla squatters like me, son. Katrina took my house away—my dog too. I guess the lady that lived here got herself evacuated."

"Yeah, she's in Houston, I think. It's her son I'm looking for. He disappeared from California about three months ago."

"What makes you think he came here, and not Houston where his ma is?"

"I just have a hunch this is where he'd come. I figured he'd have some friends from school or college … someone he could go to for help."

"He in trouble?"

"He could be—but I'm not exactly sure what kind of trouble."

"Kinda vague all that, ain't it?"

Nick smiled. "Getting vaguer by the minute."

"Well, good luck with that. I'd say I'd call you if he came around, but the phone doesn't work—just like everything else."

"The other rooms, Mr. Dupree … was there one that looked like a boy or a young man might have occupied it at one time?"

"Like I said, looters took most everything—but you're welcome to look, if you like."

"Thanks. I won't be long. Down here?" he asked, pointing to the hall.

"That's right. My room is on the left—you can take a peek in there. I ain't got nothin' to hide."

Nick opened the door to Dupree's room and looked in. A bed, a nightstand, and a lamp that didn't work were all he could see in the fast fading light.

"Got no power," Dupree said, behind Nick. "Couldn't pay the bill anyway, even if they ever get it fixed. The other room's just over there ..."

The bedroom Nick figured was Robert Landon's was smaller than he had imagined. There was no bed, no dresser. A pair of drapes, hanging at the window had a Star Trek motif—Captain Kirk and Mr. Spock were well featured, with smaller images of Scotty and Uhura just visible in the folds of the material. On one wall, a poster, peeling from the damp, showed the old and the new Enterprises, with images of William Shatner and Patrick Stewart smiling at one another across the endless regions of "Space—the Final Frontier". If this was Robert Landon's room, there was no doubt he'd been a Trekkie when he was a kid. A small closet revealed nothing—it was completely empty. Nick turned to go.

"Thanks, Mr. Dupree," he said, holding out his hand. "You've been a big help."

"Think so?" Dupree's eyes twinkled as he shook Nick's hand. "Good luck with the searchin'—and watch out for the rats. It's gettin' dark, and they ain't scared o' nothin'."

Nick walked quickly back to the brighter lights of Lafitte. Rats, huh? he thought. What the hell was going on with this town? Lights, spilling out on to the street ahead of him, mingled with the sounds of music and laughter, drew him to a bistro filled with the ambiance for which New Orleans was renowned. Despite the heat and humidity, Nick found himself enjoying the press of people inside. A jazz combo swung mightily from a corner of the bar, some couples danced to the beat, but most mingled, talking, drinking, trying to forget the chaos that lurked outside.

"You lookin' for someone, handsome?" The question came from a tall drag queen, teetering on four-inch heels, and supporting a two-foot high blonde wig that threatened to lay waste to anyone who came too near.

"Robert Landon," Nick replied. "And the bartender."

"The bartender I can help you with. Follow me."

Nick was happy to step into the path cleared by his new friend's enormous presence. "Thanks," he said, on reaching the bar. "What's your name?"

"Lynn Oleum ... and yours?"

"Nick ... Nick Fallon. I'm a private investigator from California."

"Are you now ... and tell me, is that a gun in your pocket?"

Nick grinned. "No, I'm just happy to see you."

Lynn laughed heartily. "I like you. Let me buy you a drink."

"Thanks. Dewars on the rocks."

"Harry!" Lynn bellowed. "Get over here and fix a drink for my new man!"

"Keep your hair on." Harry, a muscular and shirtless young man, grinned at Nick. "It comes off you know. What'll it be?"

"He'll have a Dewars on the rocks," Lynn said sharply. "And make sure it *is* Dewars, and none of that piss you serve the tourists—and I'll have my usual." Lynn preened in front of the bartender. "Please, *sugar* ..." He turned to Nick. "So, who's this Robert Landon?'

"Someone who grew up here. He disappeared from LA about three months ago. I'm following a hunch he came back here."

"What'd he do—rob a bank?"

"No, he was mixed up with some hustler who ended up dead. I want to know if he did the deed, or if he knows who did."

"Got a photo of him?"

"Yeah." Nick showed him the one and only photograph he had—a copy taken from the newspaper report John Hammond had brought him. "It's not very good."

"He's cute," Lynn said, holding the picture close to his face. "I wish I did know him, but I'm afraid I've never seen him in here. Hey, Harry ... you seen this guy in here?"

Harry placed Lynn's martini on the bar and looked at the picture. He shook his head. "Nope, can't say I have. He a friend of yours?"

"Nick's a private eye, sugar," Lynn told him. "He's looking for his man."

"Aren't we all," Harry said, laughing. "Good luck."

"Let's pass the photo round the bar," Lynn suggested. "Maybe somebody's seen him around."

"Okay—but I don't want it to disappear. It's the only one if have."

"Don't worry, sugar. I'll take it round myself." Lynn heaved himself up onto his precarious heels, and wobbled round the bar, shoving the picture in various people's faces with the barked demand; "You seen this guy?"

Nick chuckled as some startled tourists were accosted by the Amazonian drag queen, demanding they give their full attention to the photograph he was showing them. Some time later, Lynn reappeared, wig slightly askew, and handed the picture back to Nick.

"No luck, sugar, I'm afraid. Most of these deadbeats wouldn't know their own mother if she walked in here with her hair on fire."

"Thanks anyway. How many bars have opened in the Quarter?"

"Too many, if you ask me. Too many—and not enough people to fill 'em."

"It must have been terrible," Nick said. "Katrina, I mean."

"Sugar, terrible doesn't come close. It was a fucking nightmare. That bitch nearly killed me. My apartment was in a basement, and I nearly didn't get out in time. I'm staying with Harry until I can get a new place—whenever that might be. Things are moving real slow around here. Real slow." He eyed Nick sharply. "You look like your itchin' to get out of here, sugar …"

"Well," Nick said, "I only have a couple of days here, and I'd like to cover as much ground as I can."

"Gotcha. You go sugar, but you come back and see me, before you leave. Okay?"

"Okay." Nick slid off the barstool. "Thanks for the drink."

"You got a boyfriend, sugar?" Lynn asked.

"Yes, I do. His name's Eric."

"Figures." Lynn heaved a long, theatrical sigh. "Bye, sugar. Be good to him."

"I will. Thanks again."

With so many bars, restaurants and nightclubs to choose from, Nick felt he was going to need a lot more than just good luck if he was going to get any kind of lead on Robert Landon, within the next couple of days. And then again, suppose Landon just never went out? Suppose he stayed holed up in someone's house or apartment, not even venturing as far as the corner store?

Feeling a tad footsore after visiting his fifth bar on Bourbon Street, he decided to call it a night. He could strike all those off his list—no one had seen Robert Landon in any of those bars, nor on the street, nor waiting for a bus. No one had seen him, period. Okay, there was still tomorrow—and the day after. It was way too early to start feeling this had been a dumb idea. He just wished it would cool down. Trying to get some sleep in that sweltering room was not something he was looking forward to.

He retraced his footsteps back to Lafitte, and the Hotel Renoir. The elevator was still out of order, and the temperature of the interior of the hotel hovered around ninety degrees.

"Oh, man ..." Nick pulled off his clothes as soon as he closed the door behind him, and headed for the shower. Could he ever get used to this? he wondered. Maybe he'd check out tomorrow, and look for a hotel with air—they must have them here, surely, he thought, stepping under the cool spray.

CHAPTER 14

Nick wasn't about to let the grass grow under his feet. He had two days and nights to accomplish what he had come to New Orleans to do—and he was confident that he would succeed. So far, he reckoned close to three hundred people had already seen Landon's photograph, and by the time he was finished, several hundreds more would. All he needed was a lucky break—like meeting another Miss Lynn Oleum. Those 'girls' saw and knew just about everything that went on in town—gay or straight.

Inevitably, he was going to get some false leads; some joker calling him pretending to know Landon, or sending him on a wild goose chase just for kicks, just like the jerk who had called him in the wee small hours of the morning saying he was friend of Landon's. A couple of quick questions had made it clear to Nick that the guy was just looking for a quick buck. That was par for the course, but if Landon was in New Orleans—and Nick was almost certain he was—he would find him.

He found a coffee shop on Royal Street, bought a newspaper and settled down with a cup of hot, strong java. The local paper was full of the trials and tribulations that the people of New Orleans faced on a daily basis. Nick had celebrated Mardi Gras on a couple of occasions, when his first lover, Martin, was still alive. Then, the city was alive, vital and vibrant. Now, although most of the people seemed upbeat about the future, New Orleans remained a shadow of its former self.

"Ahem ..."

Nick looked up through his sunglasses at the tall young man who stood at his table, smiling down at him.

"Do I know you?" he asked.

"You sure do, *sugar*—or are you an early study for Old Timer's?"

"Lynn! Jeez, sorry ... I didn't recognize you without the ..."

"Frock, sugar ... I know. But the people I work with at the office wouldn't recognize me with it on. Can I sit?"

"Of course. Can I get you something?"

"Just coffee—I'm on my way to ... ugh ... work."

Nick found himself staring at the radically different Lynn Oleum. Without the two foot high blonde wig, four inch heels, two inch eyelashes and a generous amount of rouge, he looked like a very ordinary, fresh faced guy in his mid-twenties—slightly overweight, but with the prettiest blue eyes Nick had ever seen on a man, Eric included. Although he would never tell Eric that—never!

"Didn't your Mama tell you it was rude to stare?"

Nick chuckled. "I was mesmerized."

"By my beauty ... but of course you were. Did you forget my coffee?"

"Totally ..."

"I have that effect on men. Black with sugar, *sugar*."

When Nick returned to the table with his coffee, Lynn was studying the newspaper. "Shit ... it just frosts me the way everything takes so long to get done here." He threw the paper aside. "But enough of that. How d'you do last night after you tore yourself from my side?"

"I hit about five more bars, and I got a crank call at three in the morning. So far, that's it."

"Hmm … Well, I'll keep asking around."

"Thanks. I'll appreciate any help I can get."

"And just how do you intend to show that appreciation?" Lynn asked, sipping his coffee delicately.

"Uh … I told you I had a boyfriend."

"Just kidding …" He smiled coquettishly. "Do you have a brother?"

"Sorry, no. Aren't you and Harry an item?"

"An item … how quaint a term. Let me see, how would I describe Harry, apart from the obvious? We've known each other since grade school; he was my first love. Still is, as a matter of fact, but he's moved on, emotionally, he says."

"I'm sorry."

"Don't be. We're still best friends. I don't know where I'd be without him, right now."

"Is your name really Lynn?"

"Lyndon actually—yes, after the President, but I've been Lynn all my life. Even my Daddy called me that, before he kicked me out of the house. But you don't want to hear that story this time of the morning—and I have to get to work."

"Where's work?"

"Royal Insurance, just down the road there." He glanced at his watch. "Time for another long, boring day at the office."

"I would have thought an insurance office in New Orleans would be real busy."

"It is … but it's all so worthless. Half those people will never see any money. There are just too many loopholes in their policies. Ah, well … *life* …" He stood with a dramatic sweep of his arms. "It goes on … and on … and on … one hopes. See you at the bar later? I'm performing tonight."

"Yeah, I'll stop by on my rounds," Nick said, grinning.

"I will live for that moment. Bye."

Nick watched as Lynn sashayed down Royal Street. He shook his head, wondering just how an exotic creature like that could exist in a dreary insurance office cubicle.

He looked at his watch. Not quite nine, and the sun was already heating up the humid air. It was going to be another scorcher, for sure.

Innumerable bars, retail stores and restaurants later, and feeling like he had covered every one of the eighty blocks that comprise the French Quarter, Nick made his weary way back to the Renoir, ready for a cool shower and a fresh change of clothes. Another bust, he groused to himself, as he climbed the stairs to his room—the elevator still being out of service. How many dozens of people had stared blankly at Landon's picture, and then shaken their heads no ... He'd lost count, and frankly, at that moment, didn't give a damn.

Pushing his way into his room, and muttering under his breath about the lack of air conditioning, and why hadn't he found another hotel, he pulled his sodden clothes off, and stood under the cool shower spray until, at last, he began to feel almost human again. He'd picked up two ice-cold beers on the way back, and now he chugged one down, relishing the sensation of the icy stream making its way down through his insides.

"Yeah," he sighed, flopping, naked, onto the bed. He picked up his cell phone and punched in Eric's number. "Hey, babe," he murmured when Eric picked up. "I miss your sweet buns."

"I think you have the wrong number, sir!"

"Does this mean we can't have phone sex? You know you love that."

Eric's laughter filled his ear. "Nick, it's three in the afternoon here, and I'm at work."

"So, what's the problem?"

Eric laughed again. "How's it going out there?" he asked.

"I just got out of the shower, and I'm already hot and sweaty."

"Mmm ... I'll be on the next plane out. Seriously though, are you making any progress?"

Nick sighed. "Wish I could say yes, but so far, nothing. I've got a couple of local guys helping me out though, so somethin' might pop before long—I hope. Anyway, I just wanted to say 'hi'. I'll be home day after tomorrow ..."

"I can't wait. Oh, Andrew and David want to go see a movie, Friday. Are you up for it?"

"Sure ..." He paused as his phone beeped signaling another call. "I'll call you back later, babe," he told Eric. "Someone's on the other line ..."

"Okay. Talk to you later. Love you."

"Love you too." He pressed the flash button. "Nick Fallon."

"Mr. Fallon, I understand you've been asking a lot of people about me. What do you want?"

Nick sat bolt upright on the bed. "Robert Landon?"

"That's right. What is it that you want to know?"

"Well, let's start with why you disappeared three months ago; leaving your job and your friends—without a word."

"What's that got to do with you?"

"Do you remember a guy named John Hammond?"

"John Hammond?"

"You had a dinner date with him the night you disappeared," Nick said. "You met him at The Racket. Ring a bell?"

"Oh, yes. I remember him."

"He hired me to find out why you'd been murdered—only, you're not dead. Tom Skinner is. You remember him of course?" There was a prolonged silence on the other end. "Hello ... you still there?"

"I'm here. I guess we should meet."

"That's a great idea. Where and when?"

"Tonight, I guess ... there's a bar on Bourbon Street called Mama's. I'll be there in about an hour."

"So will I. See you there."

"How will I know you?"

"Don't worry about that," Nick said, chuckling. "I'll know you. I keep your picture next to my heart."

Another silence, then Landon said, "You're trying to be funny, right?"

"Right. Just don't stand me up the way you did John Hammond."

Without another word, Landon broke the connection, and Nick rolled off the bed, heading for the bathroom, and another shower.

A fine drizzle was coating the sidewalks of Bourbon Street as Nick made his way to the bar where Landon had suggested they'd meet. Ever since Landon's call, he'd wondered if the man would actually show up. What had prompted his call? If he were involved with Skinner's snuff movies, wouldn't it make more sense for him to go deeper into hiding? Or was he simply tired of trying to live anonymously in a town he'd once called home. Did he just want this to be over, regardless of the consequences? Well, he'd soon find out, he thought, looking at 'Mama's' neon sign, its reflection flashing off and on in the wet pavement. His eyes scanned the interior of the busy bar, the air conditioning a welcome relief from the humidity outside. A jazz quartet played mellow music in one corner, surrounded by a group of appreciative listeners, while at the bar a more boisterous bunch was engaged in a birthday celebration.

Of Landon, there was no sign, so Nick ordered up a Dewar's rocks, and found a table in a corner where he could watch the door. A few minutes later, Nick saw Landon standing in the doorway. He walked over to the bar, ordered himself a drink, then stood studying the crowded bar with a careful eye. His gaze paused on Nick, as though he had guessed this was the man he'd come to meet. Nick nodded. Landon crossed to his table, a wary look on his face. He looked very much like his photograph, light brown hair topping a pleasant, though unremarkable face. He was slim, but not athletically built, and for a moment, Nick found himself wondering what John Hammond had been so crazy about.

"Mr. Fallon?"

"That's right—but you can call me Nick." He held out his hand, and Landon took it in a nervous grasp. His hand was damp. "Relax," Nick said, smiling. "I'm not here to arrest you."

"I haven't done anything," Landon protested.

"So tell me why you left California in such a hurry."

"It's complicated."

"I have plenty of time," Nick said. "Why don't you start telling me about your relationship with Tom Skinner?"

"It wasn't a relationship—at least not in the strict sense of the word. I used to hang out at The Racket with my friends from work, and Tom … well, he sort of caught my eye one night. He wasn't really my type, but he had a way about him."

"Your friend Frank told me he frequently hustled drinks from you."

"You spoke to Frank? I think he was kinda jealous."

"Of you, or Skinner?"

"Frank had a thing for me," Landon said. "He didn't like Tom for that reason."

"Did you know what Tom Skinner did in his spare time?" Nick asked, leaning forward.

Landon looked away. "Not really …"

"I talked with his roommate the other day—Michael Riley. You know him?"

Landon nodded. "I met him a couple of times in the bar."

"Riley told me Skinner procured young hustlers and hookers, for wealthy clients. You didn't know this about him?"

Landon flinched. "No, no … I didn't know that."

He's lying, Nick thought. "Did you know Tom Skinner was dead, before I told you earlier tonight?"

"Y … yes."

"How did you know? Were you there when he was killed?" Landon looked around him as if he was ready to make a run for it. "Robert," Nick said quietly. "Why agree to meet me here, if you're just about to tell me a bunch of baloney? You knew what Skinner was—and, I think you helped him find the right clients for his hustlers."

"*What?*" Landon lurched to his feet. "I'm not talking to you about this anymore. Next thing, you'll be saying I killed Tom."

"Didn't you?" Nick leaned back in his seat and studied the trembling man through narrowed eyes. "Your ID was found on Tom Skinner. How'd it get on his body if you didn't leave it there?"

"This is crazy," Landon whispered. "I didn't kill him." He sank back down on his seat and stared at Nick, his mouth slack, his forehead slick with perspiration.

"Okay, Robert … take it easy," Nick said. "Tell me why you came back here, without letting anyone know you were leaving."

"They told me it was best that I got out of town. That they were going to make it look like I was dead, so that no one would connect me to Tom's disappearance."

Now, we're getting somewhere, Nick thought. "Who're they?"

"Eddie Keegan, and his friend, Billy. They hustled at The Racket."

"The hustlers who disappeared?"

Landon nodded. "They worked for Tom. They helped him put together the stable of young guys and girls that Tom used to hire out to his clients."

"And these clients, Robert … How did someone like Skinner have these wealthy contacts?"

"I don't know."

"You don't know." Nick shook his head. "So tell me; what was your connection to all of this? Why was Tom Skinner so darned interested in you?"

"I told you, I bought him the occasional drink."

"And he gave you the occasional blow-job?"

Landon started to get up again. "I don't have to listen to this."

"No, you don't," Nick said calmly. "But the police will want to listen to it, Robert—so sit down, and tell me why I should believe you didn't kill Tom Skinner."

Landon fell back onto his seat, tears filling his eyes as he stared at Nick. "I came here tonight so that you would stop looking for me. Stop asking questions …"

"So you thought, tell the dumb P.I. a few lies; just enough to make him start looking for the murderer in a different direction—and you'd be in the clear. Right? Except, I'm not that dumb, Robert. Your whole demeanor, your total body language tells me you are scared, and ready to lie your way out of this situation you've made for yourself. Now, either you tell me the truth, or I go to the cops with what I've got—and believe me, that's enough to put you in the slammer for quite a spell."

"I don't believe this," Landon sniveled.

Nick handed him his drink napkin. "Blow your nose—then tell me what really happened."

"I have to use the restroom," Landon said, rising.

Nick got up. "Fine, I'll come with you."

"What?"

"I'm not having you run out on me now, Robert. We're just getting to the good part."

"There is no good part." Landon sat down again, wiping his face with the palms of his hands. "It's all shit … all of it."

"Tom Skinner got you into something bad, didn't he?"

"Yes … only, I didn't know just how bad it was until Eddie told me. He showed me a tape … I couldn't believe it … what I saw, was worse than I could imagine."

"Same again, guys?" Both Nick and Landon were startled by the sudden appearance of the drinks server; a busty blonde who reminded Nick of Lynn Oleum, except this was the real thing.

"Uh, yeah," he said. "Dewars rocks, and …"

"I'll have a vodka tonic," Landon said, his expression morose. "A double …"

"Be right back," the blonde chirped cheerfully, and was gone leaving a trail of cheap perfume in her wake.

"How did this get started?" Nick asked.

Landon heaved a heavy sigh of resignation. "Tom … He made a big play for me the first time we met. He must have found out from someone what I did for a living. In my line of work as financial advisor, I came in contact with a lot of wealthy people. Sometimes, I'd be invited to their social gatherings, clubs, bars … mostly to talk business, but quite often, after they'd had a few drinks, some of these guys would open up about how lonesome they got—their wives weren't interested anymore. You know, the usual bullshit. I didn't really pay much attention to it, until one night, Tom and I were sitting at the bar, and later when I thought about it, I realized he kinda led the conversation into that subject. He said he had what a lot of wealthy men would pay big bucks for—and he would cut me a deal, if I would provide him the leads. At first, I thought he was talking about himself. I knew he hustled at one time, but frankly I thought, although I found him attractive in a rough kind of way, he was getting too old for that particular game. Then he said he had some young 'friends' that could take care of these guys."

"So you mentioned this to your clients at the next opportunity."

"Right." Landon paused as their drinks were delivered, then he gulped down half his vodka and tonic before continuing. "I couldn't believe how fast these guys jumped at the offer. Most of them were interested in girls, but as word got around some of the other men asked if I could get guys too. This went on for over a year, and I was making a nice … commission, for my part. At first, I was nervous about it—it never felt good to me, but I kept thinking of the money, and I justified it by telling myself that the hustlers were getting paid too—so everyone was happy. Then Eddie showed me the tape …"

Landon threw back the rest of his drink. "I couldn't believe it," he said, wiping his mouth with the back of his hand. "I just fell apart. I recognized the two kids that they had snuffed …"

"You mean, they really killed those guys on the tape?" Nick asked, his jaw clenched in a sudden fury.

"Oh God, "Landon quavered, seeing Nick's expression. "I didn't know what was happening until I saw the video. Tom told Eddie they didn't really die—that it was all a fake. As soon as the camera was turned off, he said, the guys were revived, given their money, and stayed for the rest of the party. But Eddie knew who the guys were, and tried to find them—he never did. He told me he thought his friends had been murdered, and I … well I told Tom I wouldn't have anything else to do with it, and that I would go to the police if he didn't quit. He got madder than hell—said he and Mike, his roommate, would beat the shit out of me if I so much as said a word to anyone. I had no doubt he meant every word of that, so I kept my mouth shut—and I have to tell you, I hated myself for my cowardice.

"Then Eddie came to me one night, and told me that Tom had asked him and Billy to attend one of those 'parties'. He was scared, and I told him no way should he go. The house it was being held in, was up in Laurel Canyon. Tom had said he'd meet him and Billy at the entrance to Wildacre Park, and then drive them to the house—the location had to be kept secret, of course. He asked me to go with them to tell Tom to either give it up, or we'd all three go to the police, and turn him in."

"And this was on the night you were going to John Hammond's place for dinner?"

Landon sighed. "Eddie didn't know what night the party was set for—these guys had a network to organize the time and place. All Tom knew at that time was the place, not the date. It just so happened that the night I was on my way to John's apartment, Eddie and Billy caught up with me, and told me it was to be that night. Of course, I had to go with them."

"So, you drove them up to Laurel Canyon to meet with Skinner," Nick said. "Did you really think he was going to listen to reason?"

"I guess I thought the threat of the police would be enough, but I was wrong. When we got there, he acted like he was glad to see me. He said, 'Robert, I knew you'd want to get into this sooner or later'. I started to tell him what I had rehearsed, but he just laughed, grabbed me, started kissing me, smacking me, tearing at my clothes—then all of a sudden, this shocked look spread all over his face. He stared at me for what seemed like an eternity, then he just crumpled up, and fell at my feet. I saw Eddie standing there, holding a tire iron in his hand. He said, 'I had to stop him, Robert, I had to'. I remember I just nodded, and kept looking at Tom lying there … dead. The three of us stayed amazingly calm afterward. We sat in my car, trying to sort things out." He looked around for the blonde waitress, and pointed to his empty glass.

"I wanted to go to the police and tell them everything," he continued, "but Eddie freaked when I mentioned it. He said we'd all go to jail, even if we claimed self-defense, because of our involvement with the snuff movies. He said we should just get as far away as possible—just disappear. He and Billy apparently had already decided to split before all this happened. They had talked about going to San Francisco, he said—and I could go along with them. But I just wasn't into this whole Thelma and Louise routine. If I was going to leave town, it would be on my own.

"Then Billy came up with the idea of switching IDs. 'If we bury Tom,' he said, 'it'll be weeks, maybe months, before they find him. He'll be hard to identify after all that time, so we can make it even harder by dropping your ID in with his body. The cops'll think it's you—and it could take weeks for them to find out it's not. They'll be looking for suspects in all the wrong places.' Of course, at the time, we didn't factor John, or you, into the equation."

He fell silent as Lynn's look-alike delivered his drink. "Somethin' for you, honey?" she asked Nick.

"Thanks, I'm good," he said, smiling up at her.

"You sure are," she sighed, picking up Landon's empty glass. "Just holler if you need me, and I'll be right there."

Nick watched Landon start to chug his drink. "Take it easy," he said. "I need you coherent, till you tell me everything."

Landon gave him a watery smile. "It feels kinda good to get this off my chest. I've been keeping all this inside me for months now. There was no one I could tell."

"What about your mother?" Nick asked, trying not to sound too accusatory. "Shouldn't you at least have let her know you were still alive? The cops called her when they found what turned out to be Skinner's body, but at that time, they thought it was you. She must have been devastated."

Landon's eyes slid away from Nick's questioning gaze. "I know ... I'll call her soon. She's with my aunt in Houston. You have to understand—I really didn't know what to do ..."

"Okay ... so, Eddie and his buddy talk you into this screwball idea of pretending you're dead ... what then?"

"We went back to where we'd left Tom. We didn't really have anything to dig a hole with, but we got the tool kits out of both cars, and after about an hour or so, we had gouged out enough to bury him. It had been raining and the ground was real soft ...

"Eddie asked me for my billfold. He took out all the cash and credit cards. 'This'll make it look like a robbery,' he said. 'Throw the cops off some more'. He emptied Tom's pockets, then we covered him up, and threw a bunch of leaves and dead branches on top of the grave." He shuddered at the memory, and took another gulp of his drink. "Eddie said I couldn't use my credit cards, ever, because they could be traced. Then he and Billy got in Tom's car, and took off. I never saw them again. I guess they made it to San Francisco."

"What did you do?'

"I went back to my apartment. I felt sick ... filthy. I took off all my clothes, bagged them, and took a long shower. It was then I decided to come home. I knew Katrina had left New Orleans in chaos. There was still very little law and order. I thought I could just simply disappear here. I took a couple of shirts and underpants, socks, that kind of thing but left nearly everything ... didn't use a suitcase, just a brown bag from the supermarket. I cut up all the credit cards and flushed them down the toilet. I had money ... cash ... in the apartment. What I got from Tom I never banked. I thought it would look suspicious, these periodic large amounts being deposited, so I kept it all on a shelf at the back of the closet. I was amazed at how much there was when I counted it ... plenty to keep me going for a while ...

"It was then I realized I had lost my cell phone. I must have dropped it when we were digging the hole. At first I panicked, was that incriminating? Should I go back and look for it? And then, I thought, no wait a minute ... if it's supposed to be me up there and they find my phone, so what? That's when I got in the car and hit the road. I was here three days later ..."

Landon finished his drink, put his glass down, and with some hesitation asked, "What do you think I should do now?"

"Tell me something, Robert," Nick said, quietly. "What do *you* think you should do?"

"Well ..." Landon fidgeted with is glass. "I know I should have gone with my first instincts to tell the police. What we did was wrong ... but honestly, Nick, Eddie scared me. He was fired up after killing Tom. I got the feeling afterward, that he had planned the whole thing, and that he got me involved as the fall guy. I mean, they drive away together in Tom's car with all his cash and credit cards, but I'm suddenly a dead man, with no ID, and no one I can safely tell that I'm still alive. I should have gone to the police, right there and then, and told them the truth—but I didn't. And now ... now surely it's much worse, isn't it?"

"It certainly wasn't the brightest idea," Nick said. "If you go to the police now, you're going to be arrested on a bunch of charges—obstruction of due process, falsifying your own death, not reporting a crime you witnessed, fleeing the state, not to mention the prostitution racket you were a part of. I have to be honest, Robert, you *will* serve time, unless you get yourself a really good attorney, and you turn state's witness against the two hustlers—if they can ever be found."

"Oh God." Landon put his head in his hands and started to sob. "I don't know what to do."

"Do you want to hear what I think you should do?" Nick asked. Landon did not uncover his face, but nodded through his sobs. "I think you should come back to California with me, and give yourself up to the police. Get yourself a good attorney. If you don't know one, I can recommend a friend. Give the police a statement telling them exactly what happened, just like you told me. They're going to want names of the people involved in those videos ..."

"Oh, my God," Landon gasped, staring at Nick through fear filled eyes. "I can't do that! They're powerful men—they would have me killed!"

"You'll have protection. Believe me, Robert, this is the best way out for you." Nick looked at the terrified man, feeling something close to pity for him. What an unholy mess he'd gotten himself into, he thought. He couldn't quite bring himself to like the guy. Anyone who was willing to sell the bodies of young girls and guys for profit was low-life in Nick's book. Landon had been willing enough to go along with what Skinner had been doing, as long as the money, and no trouble, kept rolling in. And was he now telling him the truth? Maybe he had known about the snuff movies all along. Right now though, it was up to him to persuade Landon to return to California with him.

"What are the alternatives, Robert?" he said, pressing the point. "To stay in hiding for the rest of your life? To make your mother swear never to tell anyone that you're alive; never be able to see her or any of your friends again? How long can you really live that way?"

Landon shook his head miserably. "You don't know what it's been like ..."

"I can guess, Robert. Now it's time for you to make things right. Will you come back to California with me?"

"Will you go with me when I turn myself in?"

"I'll do that. D'you have an attorney?"

"I know a couple of guys—but you said you had a friend."

"Yeah, Johnny Pedersen ... he's great." Nick stood, and helped Landon to his feet. "Come on, you need some fresh air. Let's go for a walk."

"What's wrong with your friend?" Lynn II asked, as they made their way to the exit. "You been mean to him?"

Nick nodded, smiling. "But he loves it."

"I would too, honey," she said, slipping the bills he gave her into her cleavage. "Need any change?" she asked with a suggestive wink.

"Uh, uh ... it's all yours."

The rain had helped cool the temperature a little, but it was still too muggy for Nick's taste. Still, he didn't want to let Landon out of his sight. He was afraid the guy just might have a change of heart, and do another disappearing act. He knew he was dealing with an extremely fragile psyche. Landon had been thrown into a situation that many stronger men would find unbearable—that Landon had not cracked under the strain, Nick found remarkable. Maybe he was a tougher cookie than he looked.

Their walk took them in front of the bar where Lynn was appearing that night. "Let's go in," Nick said, taking Landon's arm. "I have to say goodbye to someone."

An enthusiastic crowd was roaring their approval as Nick and Landon entered the bar. The dynamic Lynn Oleum was regaling them with a rendition of "Stormy Weather", and Nick was impressed when he realized Lynn was not lip-synching to a tape. That low down sultry sound was actually his voice, not Judy or Lena.

"Where's your friend?" Landon asked, at his side.

"That's him." Nick indicated the outrageously coiffed Lynn. Tonight the wig was pink.

"You have a drag queen for a friend?" Landon regarded him with amazement. "Who knew?" He was swaying on his feet; the drinks had obviously taken their toll.

"I just met him last night," Nick explained. "He's a riot."

"They usually are," Landon said, with a disinterested expression. "I need another drink."

"Easy," Nick said, gripping Landon's arm to steady him. "I think you've had one too many already."

"What're you—my mother?" He pulled away and headed for the bar, Nick right behind him.

"Hey, Nick!" Harry yelled. "How's it goin'? You come to see Miss Lynn? She'll be takin' a break in a minute or two."

"Yeah, good. This is Robert, Harry. He'll have a vodka tonic."

"Yeah, make it a double …" Landon's speech was becoming decidedly slurred. "And easy on the tonic."

"And a Dewars rocks, right?" Harry set to filling two glasses with ice.

"You come here often?" Landon asked clutching at the edge of the bar for support.

"No, last night was my first time," Nick told him. "It always amazes me how bartenders remember customer's names and drinks so fast."

"It's their job, isn't it?" Landon slurred, looking around the bar through bleary eyes.

"Sugar! You remembered!" Nick was practically knocked off his feet by the exuberance of Lynn's bear hug. "Did you catch my set?" he asked, his candyfloss hair waving on top of his head like a pink cloud.

"Just the last song," Nick told him. "You were great. Lynn, this is Robert."

"*The* Robert, as in the *missing link* Robert?"

Landon opened his mouth to say something, but instead, fell flat on his backside.

"Jesus," Nick muttered, bending down to hoist Landon into an upright position.

"I have that effect on a lot of men," Lynn remarked.

"I think I'd better get him out of here," Nick said, supporting Landon by putting an arm around his shoulders. "Sorry about this, Lynn. I'm leaving tomorrow, and taking this guy back with me. Wish me luck."

"Oh, sugar ..." Lynn bussed Nick's cheek. "And we were just getting acquainted. Come back and see Harry and me again some day—we'll still be here!"

"It's a date," Nick said, lugging Landon to the door. "See ya!"

Ignoring the scowling night desk clerk at the Renoir, Nick heaved Landon up the stairs to his room, and threw him down on the bed. Great, now on top of everything else, he was going to have to spend the night, either on the floor, or on the one lumpy chair, the room provided. He pulled Landon's shoes off and loosened the top buttons of his shirt. He glanced at his watch—it would be eight-thirty in California. Picking up his cell phone, he punched in his home number.

"Eric, it's me, babe ..."

"Hi. Are you all right? You sound tense."

"I found Robert Landon ... he's here with me now, and he's flying back with me tomorrow to talk to the police."

"That's great ..."

"He's passed out on my bed."

"What did you do to him?"

"He's passed out drunk. I guess the stress of coming clean about everything made him drink more than he's used to."

"Are you sure he'll still want to talk to the police when he wakes up in the morning?"

"He's gonna have no choice."

"Nick ..."

"Don't worry, I'll be nice. Friendly persuasion, and all that jazz."

"Just hurry up, and come home. I miss you. This bed's way too big for one person."

"Don't worry," Nick said, chuckling. "I'll make it all up to you when I get there—in more ways than one."

"I can't wait … just please be careful."

"Always. Okay, gotta go. I want to call Johnny Pedersen to see if he'll take Landon on. He's gonna need a good defense attorney."

"Okay … I love you."

As Nick punched in Johnny's number, Landon moaned, punching the air above his head, as if trying to ward something, or someone, off. Nick shook his head. He had no doubt Landon was plagued by nightmares—either from fear, or a guilty conscience.

"Hi Johnny, it's Nick Fallon."

"Nick … are you all right?"

"Yeah, I'm fine. Sorry to call you this late. Do you and Gloria have company?"

"No, no, we're just watching some TV. What's up?"

Quickly, Nick filled him in on the details surrounding Robert Landon's disappearance, and the fact that he had found him in New Orleans.

"He's willing to give the cops a statement, Johnny, but he's really going to need some legal help. I'd like you to listen to his story, and maybe represent him when he goes to Los Angeles. There's a Detective Morales handling the case, and he is totally non-simpatico, if you catch my drift."

"Got it. Okay Nick, bring him by my office soon as you get back, and I'll see what I can do."

"Thanks Johnny … Oh, and one more thing. Jeff is holding a tape I think you should see. Call him and ask him to drop it off to you, so you're aware of what's on it. I have to warn you, though—it's not pretty."

"I understand. I'll call him in the morning."

Nick put his cell phone down, and looked again at Landon. His eyes were open and staring back at Nick.

"Whydonyoucometobedwitme," he slurred. "I'm lonesome …"

"Forget it," Nick growled. "I never put out on the first date!"

CHAPTER 15

"Okay …" Jeff gave Nick a searching look as they stood outside Johnny Pedersen's office, taking a coffee break. "Tell me what's on your mind."

Johnny had asked if he could have a word with Landon alone—legal technicalities that involved client/attorney privileges.

"What d'you make of Landon?" Nick asked

"He strikes me as someone who got in way over his head," Jeff replied. "I guess the easy money appealed in the beginning, but now he looks freaked out by what he's facing."

"Right … and there's still this bunch of other creeps out there that are putting kids in danger with this snuff movie crap." Nick's jaw clenched as he thought about it. "Those are the guys I want to see hung out to dry."

"That's the LAPD's job, Nick," Jeff said. "They're the guys with the inside track on that kind of thing."

"You'd think so, right?" Nick shook his head. "But nothing's been done, and meanwhile, kids are dying. We saw one example, but you know as well as I do, that they don't stop with just one night of getting their rocks off. I'll bet you anything that someone, somewhere is setting up one of those 'parties' even as we speak. Tom Skinner was just one asshole in a team of many assholes. I don't think, for one minute, that just because he's toast, that the game is over."

Jeff nodded. "You're right … the Skinners of this world are ten-a-penny. But look at the other side of this, Nick. Skinner and Landon both disappeared, along with the two hustlers. Maybe the guys who depended on their services got nervous, and decided to call it a day."

"I'd like to think you're right, but once some perverts get a taste of something that really turns them on, no matter the danger or the expense, they just want to keep on doing it. Maybe the group is smaller … that's a possibility, but I'm willing to bet they're still around." He broke off as Johnny opened his office door and stepped into the hall with them.

"I just called Detective Morales. He wants us to bring Landon in now."

"I figured he would," Nick groaned.

"He sounded pissed, Nick."

"He always sounds pissed, Johnny. He's perpetually pissed."

"Well, I told him we'd bring Landon to his office right away. Sorry …"

"Not your fault," Nick said. "I should have figured he'd want it on his terms. Okay, let's do it. I'll see you tomorrow at the office, Jeff."

"Right. Good luck with Morales. I'll give Joe a call, and bring him up to date. Maybe he can sit in on Landon's statement."

"That'd be great. Oh, and would you tell Eric what's happening? I'll call him when we're on our way back."

Bob Morales looked grim as Joe French approached his desk.

"Hey, Bob." Joe gave him a big smile. "I just had a call from my buddy, Jeff, down in Laguna."

"Oh yeah?" Morales's expression did not flicker.

"Yeah, he says Nick is bringing Robert Landon in, along with his attorney, to make a statement about Tom Skinner's death. That's a real break for you, isn't it?"

"I suppose it is." Morales narrowed his eyes. "What's your interest in it?"

"Oh, just making conversation, but I was wondering if I could sit in with you when Landon makes his statement."

"Why?"

"Just curious—and besides, you need someone else there anyway. Might as well be me."

Morales stared at Joe for a moment, then he said, "Okay. I'll let you know when they get here."

"Great ... thanks, Bob."

"No problem, and besides ..." Morales leaned back in his seat, and smirked at Joe. "I could use a little moral support when all those fags get here."

Joe looked Morales in the eye, and shook his head. "Bob, you really need to drop the attitude."

"Excuse me?"

"You heard me. Maybe you'll take a bit of advice from someone who's older, and been in this game a deal longer. Arrogance can sometimes blind a guy to what's right in front of him. You've got a chance here to come out smellin' like a rose, after screwing up that first press release ..."

"How the hell was I to know it was the wrong guy?" Morales protested. "He had ID on him."

"The *wrong* ID, Bob ... and you didn't wait for the lab to finish its tests. You jumped the gun, and ended up making the department look foolish."

"Look," Morales growled, "I don't need this from you."

"No, you don't. You already had your reprimand—but what I'm saying is, Nick Fallon has done you a big favor in bringing this Landon guy to you. He's a good cop, and I'd be careful using that kind of deprecating language around him if I were you. You don't want to get his Irish dander up, believe me."

"Those guys don't scare me."

"They shouldn't scare you, Bob. That's the whole point. Let me tell you something ..." Joe sat at Morales's desk, and leaned across, looking the other detective squarely in the eye. "I've known Jeff Stevens for close to ten years. We were cops on the beat together, and one thing I discovered about him, real fast, was that I could rely on him in a crisis. He was the ideal partner, steady and sane. He took a lot of shit from some of the other guys, but he never backed away, never gave ground. The department lost a good man the day he went private.

"Now, Nick Fallon is cut from the same cloth—except he's a little more fiery than Jeff. A little quicker on the draw, if you get my meaning ... but he's a good guy, Bob. And one you could benefit from knowing—if you can get rid of your prejudices."

"Thanks for the lecture, Joe," Morales said, unable to hide his irritation.

Joe sighed and stood up. "It wasn't meant as a lecture, Bob ... but if you want to see it that way ..."

"I'll let you know when Fallon gets here," Morales said.

"Okay." Joe turned to walk back to his desk. "Oh, by the way ..." He paused, and smiled at Morales. "Johnny Pedersen, the attorney, is straight. I thought you should know that, just so you don't make any stupid comments in front of him."

A little after seven, Nick sighed with relief as Johnny pulled up outside the LAPD headquarters at the Parker Center building in downtown Los Angeles. Morales was waiting for them, grim-faced, at his desk. He got up as Nick introduced Johnny as Landon's attorney—and Landon himself. Nick was glad to hear that Joe was to sit in while Landon's statement was taken. Maybe Morales wouldn't be quite so much the heavyweight with Joe around.

It went pretty much as Nick expected. Landon's story matched the one he'd told Nick the night before. Was it only last night? Nick stifled a yawn.

Landon droned on and on, prompted occasionally by Morales, and by Johnny, when he thought Landon was giving too much information. Johnny was looking for a plea bargain—Landon's testimony for a lighter sentence, but it was obvious from Morales's expression that he considered it too early in the game for that.

In the end, Landon was arrested on a variety of charges, the more serious of which were failing to report a homicide, aiding in the flight of the alleged perpetrators, and accepting money from a purveyor of illicit sex. As Morales read him his rights, Landon looked like a deer caught in the headlights.

"Nick," he said, trembling, his face pale and sweaty. "They're going to put me in a cell—you said I could stay with you."

"You'll be arraigned tomorrow, Mr. Landon," Morales told him.

"We'll ask for bail, Robert, don't worry," Johnny said, trying to placate him.

"But I don't want to go to jail," Landon whined, as he was led a way. "Nick, help me ..."

Jeez, Nick thought, did he really think they were just going to let him walk away after that statement? Was he that naïve?

"The district attorney's office will ask that bail be refused," Morales was saying to Johnny. "He's definitely a flight risk."

"Well, I'd like the DA to see the bigger picture," Johnny said, snapping the lock on his briefcase. "Robert Landon could be used to expose the members of these prostitution rings."

"If they still exist," Morales said, unimpressed.

"Guys ..." Nick pulled the tape from his jacket inside pocket, and handed it to Morales. "You should both see this."

"What is it?" Joe asked.

"Something that might change the course of this case," Nick said, bracing himself for the blast to come.

"How'd you come by it?" Morales asked, a suspicious gleam in his hard stare.

"Well, I kinda borrowed it, when I went to Skinner's apartment."

"You removed evidence from Skinner's apartment?"

"Well, I didn't know it was evidence at the time," Nick said, trying to look innocent. "But once I saw what was on it, I knew I had to get it to you right away."

"*Right away?*" Morales moved in for the kill. He waved the tape in Nick's face. "You went to Skinner's apartment three days ago! D'you know the kind of trouble you're in Fallon? I'm gonna bring you up on charges for this!"

"Hold on, Bob," Joe said. "Nick is trying to help you with this. He brought Landon in, now he's handing over a piece of evidence. Okay, how he got it is not something we should normally overlook, but you need to cut him some slack, Bob, after the help he's given you."

For a moment, Morales looked as if he were about to tell Joe to back off, but then he turned to Johnny and asked, "Do you know what's on this tape?"

Johnny nodded. "Yes, but I could only stand a few minutes of it."

"What the heck is on there?" Joe asked.

"Let's find out," Morales said, pushing the tape into the player sitting in the corner. The room became charged with tension as the two detectives watched the flickering images on the TV screen.

"Holy God ..." Joe sucked in a gasp of surprise, while Morales remained immobile, as though carved from stone. When it was over, he turned and glared at Nick. "I should have you arrested for withholding this," he snapped. "Do you know what we have here?"

Of course I know, you moron ... Nick swallowed what would have been his knee jerk response, and remained silent.

"Boy, I've seen some things in my time," Joe remarked quietly. "But that ... that was bad ... really bad."

"Those guys standing around watching and ... whatever," Nick said, "are all wealthy clients of Landon's. He put them in touch with Skinner. Now I'm not saying that all the guys that contacted Landon were involved in this kind of sick setup, but I want to find out who was."

"Sometimes stuff like this is fake," Morales said. "They can revive the victims when they stop filming."

"Yeah, that's true," Nick agreed. "But ..." He looked at Joe. "You know Peter Brandon, right Joe? Well, he seems to think those guys were killed. He had a nightmare ..."

"Jesus Christ!" Morales all but screeched. "Who the hell else saw this fucking tape before we did, Fallon?

"Peter is Jeff's friend," Joe said, as if this were the only answer Morales needed. "He's got some psychic ability—he's helped out a couple of times in the past."

Morales looked at Joe as if he had just grown three heads. "I don't believe this," he seethed quietly. "I'm trying to solve a murder, and you're telling me about fucking psychics—and *you* ..." He leveled a poisonous look at Nick. "*You* will stay out of this, you understand? Your work here is done! You get under my feet one more time, and you will find yourself in your own private cell—for the duration!" With that, he pressed the eject button on the remote, and strode from the room, clutching the tape in his hand.

Johnny's chuckle broke the silence in the room, after the door had slammed shut behind Morales. "Nick, I think he'd have pointed that remote at you, if he thought he could make you disappear."

"Man, Nick ..." Joe shook his head. "You could have been in a world of trouble there. Please don't do anything like that again."

"I won't." Nick appeared contrite. "And thanks, Joe, for backing me up. I owe you one."

"Yes, you do. Now, it's time to go, fellas. It'll be a big day tomorrow."

It was dark when Johnny dropped Nick off outside his home in Laguna Beach. "Wanna come in for a drink, handsome?" Nick kidded the attorney.

Johnny chuckled. "'Fraid I'll have to decline, but give Eric my best."

"Sure will—and thanks again, Johnny," Nick said, opening the car door. "Landon is going to need some serious help."

"I'll do my best. G'night, Nick."

"'Night ..." He closed the car door and walked up the path that led to his and Eric's home. Just as he was about to put his key in the lock, the door swung open and Eric fell into his arms.

"Oh, thank God," Eric sighed. "I was beginning to think you'd never get here."

"I called you." Nick chuckled and held Eric tight. "You going to let me in?"

"That's a loaded question," Eric said, pulling him through the door, slamming it shut.

"They arrested Landon," Nick told him, shucking off his jacket. "He's in the pokey."

"Poor guy ..." Eric started to unbutton Nick's shirt.

"I need a shower, babe. It's been a long, long day."

"So what are his chances?" Eric asked, following Nick into the bedroom.

"Johnny's got his work cut out for him, and no mistake. He's shooting for a plea bargain, but I don't know if the DA will go for it. Some of those charges are pretty damning."

Eric sat on the edge of the bed watching Nick get undressed. "Mmm, that's what I've been missing for the past three nights"

Nick grinned and flexed a bicep for him. "I won't be long."

"You hungry?"

"I could eat something ..." He leered at Eric. "But maybe a sandwich first?"

The phone rang as Eric started fixing Nick's sandwich.

The caller sounded tense. "Is Nick there?"

"He's in the shower. Can I have him call you?"

"Uh, yeah ... it's John Hammond. He has my number."

We all do, Eric thought, but said brightly, "I'll have him call you."

"Thanks." Hammond hung up.

When Nick entered the kitchen, wearing only a pair of sweatpants, Eric whistled in appreciation, then told him Hammond had just called.

"Shit … I guess I should call him back," Nick groused.

"I said you would."

"Better get it out of the way, I suppose. I'll call him from the office. Would you fix me a drink, babe?"

"You got it."

Hammond must have been sitting by the phone, as he picked up on the first ring.

"Hey, John—Nick."

"How'd it go in New Orleans?"

"Well, I found Robert. Unfortunately, the cops wanted his statement right away, and they're holding him for arraignment tomorrow."

"You mean he confessed to killing Skinner?"

"No …" He smiled up at Eric who'd just delivered his drink. "He says two other guys killed him, kinda in self-defense. He was involved in a prostitution ring that Skinner set up. Robert supplied him with wealthy clients. Things got hairy, Robert wanted out, and Skinner came on like a heavy."

"Robert was involved in prostitution?"

"Looks that way …"

Hammond breathed out a long sigh. "I suppose I should be grateful knowing what happened. It's just not what I hoped for." To Nick's ears he sounded close to tears. "Just send me the rest of your bill, and I'll take care of it."

"Thanks, John. Sorry it didn't turn out better. Jeez," Nick muttered, after Hammond had hung up. "Someone else I've managed to make unhappy …"

"You're not blaming yourself, surely?" Eric said, kneading Nick's shoulders with skillful fingers.

"Oh, that feels good …" Nick leaned back and gave in to the comfort Eric was supplying. "No, I'm not blaming myself, but I would have felt better if this had worked out differently."

Eric laid a kiss on the top of Nick's head. "Eat your sandwich. I'm going to make myself a cup of tea." Nick followed him to the kitchen and sat at the bar, enjoying his sandwich

"You know," he said, between mouthfuls, "I bet if we could get those two hustler guys to verify that part of Landon's story, he'd face lesser charges. I've seen guys get away with just a stiff fine, for being involved in prostitution—and if he cooperates with the police, and gives the names of some of those wealthy perverts, it could go along way to getting him off the hook—or at least part of it."

"Do you think the two hustlers would admit to being the ones that killed the Skinner guy?"

"They'd claim self-defense. Skinner was threatening Landon, slapping him around. Eddie just tapped Skinner on the head too hard."

"But where are these guys now?"

"San Francisco, so Landon says."

"Nick, San Francisco is huge. Where would you start to look?"

"Well, that's the problem. Morales kinda warned me off the case—said he throw me in the slammer if I got 'under his feet again', as he put it."

"Well, that's that then."

"Yeah, but I was thinking …"

"Nick! You are not going to get yourself thrown in jail," Eric raged at him. "Let the LAPD do their job. Please, don't get up that cop's nose any more than you already have."

Nick leaned across the bar and kissed Eric's cheek. "I won't, don't worry."

"Promise me …"

"I promise."

"You're not crossing your fingers behind your back, are you?"

"No, 'course not. But it just so happens that Jeff has a contact in the SFPD. If he'd put a word in his buddy's ear … both Eddie and his friend have records—petty stuff, but it's on file, photos and everything. He just might be able to run a trace on them."

"As long as you don't go flying off to San Francisco to try and drag them back to LA all by yourself."

Nick affected a wounded look. "I just promised you, didn't I? Now come round here and say you're sorry."

Eric chuckled. "You do that so well," he said, sitting astride Nick's lap. Their kiss was long and sweet. "Now that I have given you food and drink, are you strong enough to carry me to bed?" he teased.

"I have the strength of ten men," Nick said, grinning.

"All right," Eric's sigh warmed Nick's neck. "Ten men ... then I guess we'll be up all night."

CHAPTER 16

Sam Goddard, relaxing with a cup of coffee and the morning newspaper, swung his feet off his desktop, grabbing the phone as it rang.

"Detective Goddard," he said, cursing silently as he slopped his coffee onto the newspaper.

"Sam, it's Jeff Stevens. How are you?"

"Jeff? Man, haven't heard from you in a coon's age. How the hell are you?"

"Just fine ... how're the wife and kids?"

"Doing great. You still with the artist fella?"

Jeff chuckled. "Believe it or not, yes I am. You got a minute, Sam?"

"Sure, what can I do for you?"

"My partner, Nick Fallon, is investigating a case down here that might be leading him to your neck of the woods."

"Oh yeah?"

"He's trying to track down a couple of gay hustlers he thinks might have been involved in a murder. Actually, he's not sure if it was murder or self-defense. Right now, he's hedging his bets, but they're kinda crucial to corroborate another guy's story."

"You got names for these guys, Jeff?"

"Eddie Keegan, and Billy ... we don't have his last name."

"Eddie Keegan, huh?" His fingers flew over the keyboard to his computer. "Here he is. Eddie Keegan, arrested on May 12th, 2006 for drug dealing ... Oh, oh ... deceased May 19th, 2006 ...

"Deceased," Jeff repeated. "Overdose?"

"No … Suicide. In his cell, awaiting sentencing … tore a strip off his blanket and hung himself."

"Jeez," Jeff muttered.

"Nothing in the report 'bout anyone called Billy. If you can find me a last name, maybe I can find out some more."

"Okay …"

Nick, who had been quietly by Jeff's desk, listening to the conversation on the speakerphone, said, "Hi Sam, this is Nick, Jeff's partner."

"Hey … you got anything more?"

"Not really. But, I'm curious. Was there an investigation into Eddie Keegan's suicide?"

"No more than usual—just says, 'Coroner's verdict, suicide.'"

"Hmm …" Nick scratched his chin while he thought. "Just seems strange that a young kid like that would commit suicide."

"Maybe he was scared of going to jail," Sam said. "Good lookin' kid, by the looks of his mug shot. He'd probably heard all kinds of stories about what goes on inside."

"Maybe," Nick murmured. "From what I've heard about the kid, though, I'd have thought he could take care of himself."

"Well, if you like, I'll do some poking around," Sam said. "Don't know how much more I can dig up, though. Unfortunately, as you know, hustlers, hookers, homeless kids, drugs … it's an endless parade in this city, just like everywhere else. Not enough manpower to deal with it. Same old story; never changes."

"I understand," Nick said. "But I'd appreciate if you find the time to come up with anything else."

"Leave it with me."

Jeff picked up the receiver. "Thanks Sam. Appreciate your time. Tell Sarah 'hi' from me, won't you?"

"Will do … Take care, Jeff."

Nick looked at Jeff and shrugged. "Oh well, those are the breaks … Suicide, huh? Why does my suspicious mind make me not believe that?"

"I know what you mean—kinda convenient, isn't it?"

"Right. One less loose end."

"Sam will probably look at it the same way, now we've got his interest piqued. Who would know Billy's last name?"

"Landon maybe … or Bernie."

"You should let Morales know about Eddie Keegan."

Nick frowned. "I'm getting a little tired of doing that flatfoot's work, then having him threaten me with the slammer." He stood up impatiently, looking at his watch. "I gotta call Johnny, and find out what happened with Landon this morning. His arraignment was set for ten."

"Okay …" Jeff stood and stretched. "Hey, don't forget we're meeting Peter and Eric for lunch …"

"I'll have to pass. Too much to do … I'll see you later."

Nick called Johnny on his cell phone and got his voice mail. He was probably still in court with Landon, Nick thought, as he left a message for Johnny to call him

Next, he called Bernie at The Racket. "Hey Bernie, it's Nick—how goes it up there?"

"The usual crap." Bernie sounded out of sorts. "What can I do for you?"

"I'm trying to trace Barney, the hustler that used to hang with Eddie Keegan. Would you happen to know what his last name is?"

"Can't help you there. I never did know it."

"Bernie, I just spoke to a cop in San Francisco this morning. He told me Eddie Keegan committed suicide in a jail cell, a couple of months back."

"Oh, shit … that poor kid."

"Yeah … and I was trying to locate Billy to see if he was still around. There was no mention of him on Eddie's charge sheet, so I need his last name."

"I'll ask around here, but you know how it is … kids come and go. Sometimes we never know their first name—and their johns aren't about to ask!"

"Well, if you hear anything …"

"Sure, I'll let you know."

Nick hung up, and sat brooding at his desk. Something didn't smell right in any of this. Okay, Landon admitted he was in this setup with Eddie and Billy. They killed Skinner because he was threatening all three of them—the kids with the snuff movie, and Landon with bodily harm. That was Landon's story anyway ...

His cell phone shrilling startled him for a moment.

"Nick Fa ..."

"Yeah, hi Nick, it's Johnny."

"How'd it go with Landon?"

"Well, there's good and bad news here. Bad news is, the judge wouldn't go for releasing him. He set bail at $500,000."

"Ouch."

"Yeah, that's what I thought. But the public prosecutor presented a pretty good case for flight risk."

"And the good news?"

"The DA's office is willing to work with us on a plea bargain. If he'll give the names of the guys involved in the making of the snuff movies they'll move for a lighter sentence—say five years plus probation instead of the twenty he's facing now."

"What'd he say?"

"He wants to think about it, he said. He's scared of these guys, Nick."

"But if they're convicted, he'll be in the clear when he gets out."

"He said something to me to the effect that those guys would never be convicted. That they were just way too powerful."

"Remember the name Eddie Keegan?" Nick asked.

"Yeah, one of the hustlers, right?"

"Right. He died in jail in May—suicide, they said."

"That's convenient."

"That's what I think. Something stinks in all of this, Johnny. I wish I could figure it out."

"Well, you're going to get the chance," Johnny said, chuckling. "I need for you to do some work for me on this case."

"But Morales already warned me off."

"I'll clear it with the DA's office. Shouldn't be a problem—after all, you're the one who's brought most of the evidence, *and* the missing suspect in."

"Well, okay, if you think you can swing it," Nick said, trying to suppress a feeling of glee at the thought of Morales's sick expression when he got the news.

"By the way," Johnny added, "I'm going to ask for protection for Landon while they're waiting for his answer," Johnny said.

"Good idea. Hey, where is Landon now?"

"Waiting for me in one of the side rooms ... I get to talk to him one more time, before they lock him up again."

"Ask him if he knows the other hustler's last name. Billy something ..."

"Okay, will do ... I'll call you later."

"Thanks, Johnny."

Nick looked up as Jeff and Monica walked into the office. "Good lunch?' he asked. "Where'd you go?"

"*Peter* took us to the Montage," Monica said, with a superior air.

"It was great." Jeff sat down and patted his stomach in appreciation.

"How come I wasn't invited?" Nick groused.

"You were ... you said you were too busy."

"Well, if I'd known you guys were going all gourmet, I might have been persuaded."

"Too late," Monica crowed. "But Eric enjoyed it very much."

"So what was the occasion?" Nick asked.

"Honestly, Nick!" Monica shook her head in despair. "Eric's *birthday*."

"*What?*" Nick jumped up so fast he thought he'd given himself a hernia. "Eric's ...? Wait a minute ... his birthday's in November." He fell back into his chair, glaring at Jeff and Monica's laughing faces. "You guys!"

"Oh God," Jeff chortled. "You should have seen your face!"

"Pure terror written all over it," Monica said, laughing so hard, she almost fell over.

Nick forced out a laugh. "All right, all right, you've had your fun. Tell me, do you two rehearse this stuff in advance?"

"Yes … but, voila! We brought you back a plate." Monica laid it on his desk with a flourish.

"Well, thanks …"

"It was all Eric's idea."

Nick grinned as he unwrapped the plate. "Yeah, that's my boy. Did he also send me some wine?"

"So what happened in court with Landon," Jeff asked, as they got back to business as usual.

Nick filled him in on what Johnny had told him. "But the guy's really scared about naming names," he added. "And I don't know if I blame him."

Jeff frowned. "But just how powerful can these guys be, Nick? Some celebrities seem to circumvent the law from time to time, but not usually when it comes to murder."

"Well, now …" Nick looked across the office at Jeff. "I can think of a couple of instances where an ex-football player, and a deadbeat actor, did just that … right here in California."

Jeff nodded. "Yeah, you're right. What was I thinking?"

"We both know from experience, Jeff, that there's a bunch of characters out there who can get just about anything they want done—legal or otherwise. They have the money, and then there's another bunch waiting with outstretched hands to collect—cops, politicians, judges—they can all be bought for the right price."

"That's a bit harsh, Nick."

"Well, maybe not all," Nick conceded. "But enough to make law enforcement a hit and miss affair, sometimes. Anyway …" He paused as Monica buzzed in.

"Nick, John Hammond's on line one."

Nick picked up. "Hey, John …"

"Nick, hi … I just wondered how it went for Robert, today. You said something about an arraignment."

"Yeah, not so good, I'm afraid. They set bail at $500,000, but his attorney is trying to get some kind of plea bargain going."

"What does that mean?"

"Uh … well, if he cooperates with the DA's office, and provides names that lead to arrests, he could come up with a lighter sentence."

"Oh, I see." Hammond paused for a moment, then said, "I just wondered if maybe I could talk to him, or go see him, even—if that's allowed."

"He's allowed visitors, John, but it takes time to get clearance. If you want to just talk to him, I could ask Johnny Pedersen, his attorney, to arrange something."

"That would be great." Hammond sounded enthused.

"John, don't get your hopes up, expecting some kind of romantic reunion with Landon. He's pretty messed up …"

"He's upset, Nick. Anyone would be."

"It's more than that, John. I really don't think you know the man."

"Oh, and you do?" A sharp edge, Nick recognized, had crept into Hammond's voice.

Nick sighed. "Okay … let me see what I can do. I'll call you later." He hung up, and rolled his eyes at Jeff, who'd been listening to his end of the conversation. "Hammond … he wants to talk to Robert Landon."

Jeff grimaced. "I would think Landon has enough on his plate without John Hammond adding to the pressure."

"You're right. Still, if Landon wants to talk to John, I guess it can't do any harm."

Monica buzzed through again. "Nick? Johnny Pedersen on line two."

"Thanks, Monica. Hey, Johnny, you still up there with Landon?"

"Yes." Johnny sounded tired. "The guy's a total pain, Nick. He keeps changing his mind about the plea bargain. I can't get him to see sense. Now he tells me he thinks he'd be safer in jail."

"Just like Eddie Keegan was," Nick remarked. "Did he remember Billy's last name?"

"Oh yeah … it's Pulaski. Billy Pulaski."

"Well, that's something, I guess. Not too many with that name around. By the way," Nick added. "Landon has a friend named John Hammond. He's the guy who hired me at the beginning of all this. He'd like to talk to Landon."

"Okay, let me have his number. I can have Landon call him on my cell. There's always a line that would choke a horse for the payphone."

"Thanks, Johnny. Here's his number …"

John Hammond was just clearing his desk, ready to leave the office, when his cell phone rang. "Hi, this is John Hammond," he said, not recognizing the number showing on the ID screen.

"John … it's me, Robert."

"*Robert.* I'm so glad you're back."

"It's been a while, for sure. How are you?"

"Never mind me, Robert … how the hell are you? What's happening up there?"

"Oh, it's been pretty terrible. But I know it'll be over soon. I'm just a bit nervous right now."

"Look, it's going to be just fine. I'll come up and see you, if you like."

"That would be great."

"Are they treating you OK?"

"Yeah. My attorney … he's letting me use his phone. He's really nice." He lowered his voice. "Cute too. But the cops … one is pretty nice, but that Morales guy, he's mean."

"I know," Hammond said, his voice mirroring his dislike. "I've met him."

"I mean, he's good looking … you'd think he'd be more … I don't know …"

"Don't worry about him, Robert. Just think about getting out of there. I can't wait to see you again."

"That is so nice, John. You've made me feel a lot better. Oh, Johnny's signaling. I have to go."

"No problem. I'll find out from Nick the best way about getting to see you real soon. Okay?"

"Okay … bye, John."

Hammond was smiling as he replaced the receiver.

"Yeah, Sam," Jeff spelled the last name. "P-u-l-a-s-k-i, Pulaski. Billy Pulaski."

"Got it," Sam Goddard, Jeff's friend with the San Francisco police department, typed in the name. "Pulaski … yeah, he's here. Arrested for lewd behavior, sentence set aside. Let's see, what else. Drug trafficking … he's in the State pen for a year."

"And still alive?"

"So far, according to this. What is it exactly you need from him?"

"I'll let Nick tell you, Sam."

"Okay, Nick, shoot."

Nick started by telling Sam of Landon's connection with the two hustlers, and how they felt Tom Skinner was coercing them into taking part in a snuff movie.

"The three of them—Landon, Keegan and Pulaski decided to face off with Skinner and the end result was, according to Landon, Eddie Keegan killed Skinner who was starting to beat up on Landon. Self defense, Landon claims, but there's no one there to corroborate his story—and that's just one of the charges he's got against him."

"So, you want me to talk to this Pulaski kid, and see if he wants to admit to any of this … right?"

"Right … I know it's a long shot. I mean, if the kid knows what happened to his buddy, Eddie, he's probably scared shitless as it is. But, it's worth a try."

"Okay," Sam said. "I'll get back to you guys, soon as I have something. It may take a day or two."

"Thanks, Sam."

"What's your next move?" Jeff asked, putting the phone down.

"Not sure," Nick replied. "Johnny needs some more information to strengthen his case, but I'm running out of people to talk to. Landon's friends don't seem to have any idea of what he was up to, and Bernie's become tight-lipped all of a sudden. What I need is someone who actually knew the guys involved in those movies. If Landon doesn't talk, it'll be almost impossible to get near them—and if Billy Pulaski doesn't cooperate, this could all go nowhere."

"You think Landon won't take the DA's offer?"

"He should ... twenty years in the slammer with a bunch of hardened criminals is not something to look forward to, and besides ..." Nick allowed himself a low chuckle, "... even John Hammond won't wait that long."

Jeff grimaced. "*John Hammond.* I'll be glad when you wind this case up, and I don't have to hear that name again." He paused, remembering. "You know, Nick, when I think back on that night when I went back to his place, and how close I came to ... actually ... you know ..."

"Well, now that you've brought it up—and of course, I was never going to, for fear Eric would beat the shit outta me ..." Nick grinned at his partner. "Just what the hell *were* you thinking? I mean, Hammond's cute, I guess, but he's nowhere in Peter's class."

"Thanks for reminding me of that," Jeff said, with a glare in Nick's direction. "I wasn't thinking; that was the whole point. Shit, the whole thing still makes me cringe ... and then when he was here, screaming at me in front of Peter, saying that I had begged him for a blowjob ... Jesus, but the guy is a total ass, capable of just about anything."

"He has a mean streak in him, that's for sure," Nick agreed.

"So ..." Jeff was ready to change the subject. "What're you and Eric up to tonight?"

"Movie with Andrew and David. Wanna come along?"

"No thanks. Peter had a meeting down in San Diego, so I'm taking him out to dinner when he gets home."

"Has he made up his mind about that new gallery?"

"Not completely. Johnny pointed out a couple of possible problems with the lease, so he's down there, trying to clear things up with the landlords."

Nick nodded, stood up and stretched; ready to go. "I'll see you tomorrow. Tell Peter hi, won't you?"

Peter pulled into the parking lot outside Jeff's office, his mind a jumble of regrets, and relief. Getting out of his car, he pushed his way through the glass doors that led to the reception area. Jeff was sitting at Monica's desk, checking the computer for the coming week's appointments.

"Hey babe," he said, looking up at Peter with a smile. "How'd it go in San Diego?"

Peter leaned across the desk and kissed Jeff's lips. "It didn't." He sat down on the seat in front of the desk, and stared fixedly at his lover. "I canceled the whole darned thing."

Jeff did a double take. "But why? You were so jazzed about this new gallery."

"I was …" Peter sighed. "But dealing with corporate bullshit today, it kind of soured me on the whole deal."

"What happened?" Jeff asked, turning off the computer.

"Well, the problems that Johnny saw in the lease—the major one being the extra percentage points they wanted from my profits, on an annual basis …"

"Yeah, that looked kinda strange to me," Jeff agreed. "Is that something new in leases?"

"Only if you let it happen. I'm glad I had Johnny look the contract over. I don't think it would have registered with me right away. Anyway, when I brought it up today, they got all pissy on me, and wouldn't negotiate. More or less told me that I should consider myself fortunate that they would deem to have my gallery in their more than prestigious building."

"Are you kidding me?"

"No, I'm not." Peter chuckled at Jeff's incredulous expression. "They sat there, looking fat and ridiculous, in their fat and ridiculous suits, and I told them, in no uncertain terms, exactly what they could do with their building. I tore my copy of the contract into bits, threw them up in the air, and swept out!"

"Oh, my God …" Jeff started to laugh. "What I would have given to have seen that!"

"I was good," Peter said, his eyes glinting. "And you know something? I feel so much better now it's done. I had no idea just how much stress this was all causing me, until I was driving back home—and I was like, Yes! I can concentrate on all the more important things in life …" He stood and walked around to where Jeff sat, smiling up at him. He sat on Jeff's lap and kissed his cheek. "And that means, you ..."

Jeff held him tight and kissed him hard on the mouth. Then he leaned back, his eyes searching Peter's. "Are you sure this is what you want?" he asked, his voice husky with emotion.

"Kissing you? You bet," Peter said, grinning.

"I mean, the gallery ... you were so into it."

"Yes, I was," Peter murmured. Then louder, he said, "But I think the relief I felt today tells me I did the right thing. Opening a new gallery, going to Europe, keeping the gallery here, and the art classes going—it's just all too much ... even for me," he added with a smile.

Jeff tightened his embrace, holding Peter pressed to his body, as their lips met again in a tender, loving kiss.

"Are you closing up shop soon?" Peter whispered against Jeff's mouth.

"Mmm ... any minute now. Did you want to go to dinner right away?"

"I was wondering ..." Peter's smile was sly and sensual. "If, first, you'd like to take me into your office, and show me your credentials."

Jeff grinned at him. "Just let me lock the doors, sir—and I'll be more than happy to oblige."

CHAPTER 17

Nick received the call at a little after nine, Monday morning. He had just pulled into his parking space outside the office, when his cell phone rang.

"Joe French," he muttered, checking the caller ID. "Hey Joe, what's up?"

"Nothin' good, I'm afraid," Joe replied, his voice low as if he did not anyone near to hear him. "The Assistant DA's talkin' to your friend Johnny Pedersen right now, giving him the news ... so I guess he'll be calling you any minute."

"Go on, Joe ..."

"It's Robert Landon. He was found dead in his cell this morning, around five."

"*What?*"

"Yeah ... looks like he hanged himself."

"Bullshit, Joe!" Nick raged. "Why the hell would Landon hang himself? God dammit, something stinks here. *How* did he hang himself—by ripping a piece off his blanket?"

"No, he used the wire from the bed springs."

For a moment, Nick was stunned. "He unwound a *bedspring,* then hanged himself with it? I don't believe that horseshit for one minute. I'm telling you, Landon just wasn't the type to put himself through that kind of agony."

"Take it easy, Nick."

"No Joe … *no,* I won't take it easy! This is the second guy in this case to '*hang himself*. I'll be damned if I'll take it easy! Eddie Keegan—and now Robert Landon. Doesn't that smell to you? Tell me you weren't about to call it a coincidence!"

"I admit it doesn't look good … even Morales was stunned …"

"Oh, my God," Nick sneered. "You mean he actually registered a flicker of surprise?"

"Well, yeah, considering as how Landon finally said he was going to take the plea bargain that his attorney was shooting for."

"He did?" Nick pushed open the doors to his office. "Listen, Joe … sorry I went off the deep end at you. I appreciate you letting me know."

"Yeah … what was that saying about not killing the messenger? Don't worry Nick, I'll keep you up to date with anything I hear."

"Thanks, Joe."

He closed his phone, shaking his head. *Landon,* he thought bleakly. *As much as I didn't care for the guy, this is not what I'd have wished for him. Christ, how was John Hammond going to take this news?*

"Nick …" Monica was looking at him with total concern. "What on earth is wrong? You look like someone just ran over your foot!"

Nick sighed, his eyes focusing on Monica's sweet face. "The guy I brought back from New Orleans … Robert Landon. He was found dead in his cell this morning. Joe French just called with the news."

"Oh, wow … that's terrible," Monica said sadly. "Do they have a suspect?"

Nick stared at her, then sat down on the chair in front of her desk. "Tell me something, Monica, why did you ask that?"

"Sorry?" Monica blinked as she saw the intensity in Nick's eyes. "Was that a dumb question?"

"No, it wasn't at all," Nick said. "I'm just curious as to why you'd think it was foul play, instead of suicide."

"Well, I guess it could've been suicide—but isn't it kinda hard to kill yourself in a prison cell? I mean they take everything away from you, and give you all plastic things to use, don't they? No knives or any kind of sharp object."

"That's right … but he hanged himself."

"With what?"

"One of the springs off his bed."

Monica shuddered. "Oh, but that would have cut him … his throat and … how could he have stood the pain … hanging there?" She shook her head in disbelief. "That's just too horrible to even think about."

"And totally out of character for Robert Landon," Nick said, getting to his feet. "So your question about a suspect was not at all dumb. That's exactly what I'm going to ask Detective Morales, the arresting officer … Who did this?"

The ringing phone interrupted them. "Good morning, Stevens and Fallon Investigations," Monica said, putting a smile in her voice.

"Hi, Monica … it's Johnny. Is Nick there?"

"He sure is. Just a moment and I'll transfer you. It's Johnny," she told Nick.

"Thanks …" Nick strode to his desk and grabbed the phone while he sank down on his chair. "Hey, Johnny … Yes, I just heard the news."

"Can you believe it?" Johnny sounded madder than a hornet. "The total, fucking, crass, ineptitude of these people. Knowing the state of mind he was in, and still not keeping him under surveillance 24/7. I just can't fucking believe it."

"First Eddie Keegan," Nick said slowly. "Now, Robert Landon. What d'you think, Johnny?"

"You're thinking it wasn't suicide."

"If it was, in either instance, I will eat that tie I know you're wearing right now. It all sucks, Johnny. Big time."

"I tend to agree, but listening to Morales you'd think there was no other option. He's convinced ..."

"He's an asshole," Nick interrupted. "He's too in love with his own opinions, and he's sloppy ... too eager for the quick fix. If you want this investigated properly, you're gonna have to go to the top—way over Morales's head."

"Right. Hang in there with me, Nick," Johnny said. "It's not over yet. I've an appointment with the Assistant DA this afternoon, so I'll express my concerns then, and let her know I'm going to conduct my own investigation."

"Good. She might just put some fire under Morales's tail. Let me know how that goes."

Valerie Newcomb, Assistant District Attorney, pushed her chair back from her desk, and gave the man who stood in front of her a long, searching look. Her narrowed eyes gleamed with appreciation as she took in his well-honed physique; evident even beneath the well-cut suit he wore. *Too bad he's an asshole*, she thought, with a slight twist of her lips. Still, for a night's company, he might just prove adequate enough. The boss had insisted she took the guy along—so she would.

Bob Morales, made momentarily uneasy by his boss's obvious sexual inspection of him, frowned and coughed into his hand to break the silence that pervaded the office.

"So, Detective Morales," she said finally, "I just had Johnny Pedersen on the phone. You know who he is, right?"

"Yeah." Morales tried appearing nonchalant. "He's the attorney for the guy who committed suicide this morning."

"You mean Robert Landon, right? Did you forget his name already?"

"No, I didn't forget ..."

"Only Pedersen doesn't think it was suicide, Detective Morales. He wants the DA and me to meet with him about Landon's ... uh ... demise. And he's concerned, because apparently another guy, perhaps also related to this case, died in his cell two months ago up in San Francisco. What d'you know about that?"

"Yeah ..." Morales shifted uncomfortably. "Pedersen told me that. He's got some investigator working for him and ..."

"The investigator who has done most of your work on this case, so Pedersen tells me," Newcomb said, her voice sharp and critical. "Nick Fallon brought Landon in ... yes?"

"He also withheld evidence," Morales blurted, his face reddening under Newcomb's scrutiny. "The guy has been under my feet since I got this case."

"Just as well, from what Johnny Pedersen tells me."

"That's not fair."

"But probably true." Newcomb rose and walked around her desk until she stood within a few inches of Morales, who stared at her as if mesmerized. He wanted to take a step back, but didn't dare, for fear of antagonizing her even more. What am I supposed to do? he thought, feeling beads of perspiration break out on his forehead. She was simply standing there, gazing up at him, a little smile on her lips, saying nothing. Did she want him to kiss her? She's OK looking, I guess, he said to himself. Not my type, older than me, but not bad. His eyes widened as he felt his crotch being massaged. Holy crap ... she's coming on strong. This could be good for me. He pulled her into his arms, his mouth clamping on hers, then opening wide in a squeal of pain as he felt his testicles being squeezed— way, way too hard.

"Owww!" He twisted away from her, a look of fury on his face. "You bitch!"

Newcomb laughed in his face. "You really are as big an asshole as everyone says you are, Morales. "You think for one minute, I wanted you to *kiss* me?"

"You were coming on to me," he spluttered, rubbing his crotch.

"But I had no intentions of kissing you." She smirked, enjoying his discomfort. "That, I reserve for men I respect. However, I do know some women who might be tempted by those big lips of yours—women you'd like, *influential* women." She leaned on the edge of her desk as she continued. "Quite frankly, Morales, you're going to need influential people around you, if you're going to stay in law enforcement. You have a knack for getting up people's noses. Your associates, your *superiors*, are not at all happy with you right now ... did you know that?"

"No ... wait ..."

"Because you're too full of yourself, Detective," she continued, ignoring his protest. "You're too interested in your appearance, your body, your haircut, your clothes—all the things that make people expect certain things from you, and are disappointed when you fail to deliver. In other words, Detective, you do not live up to the image you have created for yourself."

"I ... I don't understand," Morales muttered. "Are you firing me?"

"Not if you will do something for me."

"What's that?"

"I have to attend a party tomorrow night, and I need an escort—someone young and attractive enough to turn heads." Valerie Newcomb allowed herself to laugh lightly. "You fit the bill quite nicely, Detective."

Morales stared at her for a long moment. What the hell is going on? he wondered. First, she nearly takes my balls off, then she invites me out as her date. What's with this bitch?

"Well?" Newcomb was staring back at him, an amused look on her face.

"I ... I guess so." He tried to smile. "I just don't quite understand why ..."

"You don't have to understand, Detective. Just let me lean on your arm tomorrow night, and you'll meet some of the most interesting people— people you never dreamed of knowing."

"Okay. What time?"

"Eight o'clock. Wear your best bib and tucker, and a big smile." Morales nodded, and Newcomb patted his arm gently. "Sorry about ... earlier. I hope it has already recovered."

"Good as new," Morales said, pushing a grin to his face.

"Don't worry about Pedersen." Newcomb sat back down at her desk. "I'll take care of him. Just make sure that now Landon's dead the case is closed quickly. All this bad publicity does the Department no good, what-soever."

Nick met Johnny at the DA's office later that afternoon. Deputy District Attorney Mario Lombardi, was anxious to avoid adverse publicity for the department, and had agreed to meet with Johnny to answer the questions he had regarding the lack of supervision that had led to Landon's death. After been ushered into the office with Johnny, Nick was introduced to Lombardi, who in turn, introduced him to Assistant District Attorney, Valerie Newcomb. As they all sat around Lombardi's desk, Nick found himself aware of the feral-like gaze Newcomb was casting on him. He looked back at her, one eyebrow raised just slightly.

Oh, now, Newcomb thought, crossing her legs and settling back in her chair, this one's a winner. This guy's no fool ... no wonder Morales hates him. I'm going to have to watch this one.

"So, gentlemen ..." Lombardi was saying. "There seems to be some misconception about what happened this morning."

Nick glared at him. "Misconception? You mean Robert Landon is still alive?"

"No, of course I didn't mean that," Lombardi said, frowning. "What I meant was, you apparently are harboring the notion that Landon did not commit suicide."

"I'll bet everything I own, that he didn't. Do you have an autopsy report, yet?"

"Not yet ..."

Nick looked at Johnny. "Isn't this meeting a bit premature then?"

"We have a short statement from the coroner," Newcomb interrupted, "based on a cursory examination." She smiled at Nick, while handing the document to Johnny. "I asked him to speed up the process, so we can lay this to rest."

"Along with Landon," Nick said, wryly.

"It says here ..." Johnny read from the report, "... that the cause of death was strangulation. I would have thought that hanging from a wire would have caused deep lacerations."

Valerie Newcomb nodded. "You'd think so, but apparently he padded a piece of his shirt around his neck first, so the wire didn't actually penetrate the skin."

Nick and Johnny exchanged glances. "Why d'you suppose he did that?" Nick asked Newcomb.

She shrugged. "I have no clue. Perhaps he couldn't stand the sight of blood."

Nick barked out a laugh. "According to you guys, he was about to kill himself. Why would he care about a little thing like blood?"

"Well, we'll know more when we get the full autopsy report," Lombardi, mopping his forehead with a wad of Kleenex.

"Does it say anything about his fingers, Johnny?" Nick asked, ignoring the Deputy.

Johnny scanned the report. "Nope, nothing about his fingers ... why do you ask?

"He's hoping to prove Landon was murdered," Newcomb said, the trace of a sneer in her tone. "If so, his fingers would be cut, trying to pull the wire away from his throat. Right, Mr. Fallon?"

"That's right," Nick agreed, meeting her eyes. "But even if he wasn't murdered, he still had to pull the bedspring out of the frame, unwind it to a suitable length, then wrap it around his neck. All of that would have put severe pressure on his fingertips. So, even if he didn't cut himself, there would be signs of abrasions at the very least. Landon was not a laborer with calloused hands. He wouldn't have reacted very well to having his fingers shredded by what he had to do in order to kill himself." His steady gaze was fixed on both Johnson and Newcomb. "I spent some time with Landon—enough time to know that he was not the kind of guy to inflict physical pain on himself."

"But it goes to the state of mind," Lombardi protested. "He was obviously distraught ..."

"Yet, he had just agreed to accept the plea bargain and name names," Nick reminded them. "Add to the mix, Eddie Keegan, also an apparent suicide, also involved with Landon. Doesn't all of that make you wonder just what the real story is?"

"Of course we're anxious to clear this up ..."

"I hope by that," Nick remarked caustically, "you don't mean, sweep it under the rug."

"Just what are you implying?" Newcomb snapped, her face flushing.

Johnny could not resist a chuckle. "I don't think Nick's *implying* anything, Miss Newcomb. He very rarely implies—merely states."

"Well, there won't be any kind of cover-up here, I can assure you," Lombardi said.

"Presumably, the duty guards have been questioned?"

"Of course. They saw nothing unusual."

"Amazing." Johnny shook his head in disgust. "A man dies a slow agonizing death, whether by his, or someone else's hand, and no one saw or heard anything unusual."

"Maybe you should send 'em all for eye exams," Nick said with a deal of sarcasm. "And throw in a hearing test, while you're at it."

Lombardi glared at them. "We will, of course, apprise you, Mr. Pedersen, of any new developments." He rose to his feet, indicating the meeting was over.

"Thanks for your time," Nick muttered, heading for the door. He held it open for Johnny, who winked at him as he exited.

Valerie Newcomb stood for a long moment, staring at the closed door, then turned an angry look on her assistant. "That was not well done, Mario," she rasped. "They are going to cause us problems we don't need right now."

Lombardi gaped at her, his face slick with sweat. Pulling another wad of Kleenex from its box, he wiped his face nervously.

"I don't know why I asked you to sit in on this," she continued. "Look at you, sweating like a pig ... like you have something to hide. What the hell's the matter with you?"

"N ... nothing," Lombardi gasped. "I think I'm starting a cold, or something."

"Jesus," Newcomb muttered, walking toward the door. "Keep on that coroner until we have a final report. I don't want any loose ends in this investigation. Pedersen's smart—and so is that investigator. Make sure we're smarter!"

"Robert Landon is dead." The speaker's voice was flat, without emotion.

There was a prolonged silence before the other man asked, "Was that really necessary?"

"Of course. What he knew could have far reaching effects. We couldn't afford the possibility of him talking to the DA, now could we?"

"I suppose ..."

"You *suppose?*"

"Eddie Keegan ... and now Robert Landon. Don't you think the cops are going to make the connection, eventually?"

"No more than they would connect you to Tom Skinner's death. Besides, Detective Morales is not known for his acumen ... plus, after he is *compromised*, he'll be of no further use to the department."

"Still, I don't like it."

"It is done ... now make sure you do your part, *well.*"

"It's all arranged. We've got the girls lined up, and the camera. We just have to make sure Morales shows."

"Oh, he'll be there, I have the assurance of those in the proper places that he'll be there."

"Valerie Newcomb?"

"Good Lord, no. She is a mere pawn in the game. She's merely following orders from her superior. From you I expect results—and a copy for my own collection."

"I'll see to it."

"Make sure you do."

CHAPTER 18

"So, what d'you think?" Nick asked, as he and Johnny walked to their respective cars.

"I think you had them rattled," Johnny said, grinning. "They don't like to be put on the defensive when they haven't got the answers." He glanced at Nick. "What do *you* think?"

"I think they know Landon didn't commit suicide, and they're trying to figure out how the hell someone could've gotten close enough to kill him. If I'm right, that means someone inside did the deed ... one of their own."

"It's been done before."

Nick nodded his agreement. "True ... but it's gotta be unsettling for the DA's office to know that it's just that easy to take a person out. Someone they are supposed to be safeguarding; someone who was going to help them bust this case wide open. I mean, how many people knew Landon was ready to cooperate? You, the DA's office, Morales ..."

"And you," Johnny said.

"Right ... and we didn't do it, so that leaves Morales and ..." Nick paused, remembering. "Son-of-a-bitch!"

"What?"

"John Hammond. I told him that they'd offered Landon a deal."

"Who's John Hammond?"

"He's the guy who talked to Landon on your cell phone, Friday," Nick said, thinking fast. "The guy who hired me in the first place, asking me to find out what happened to Landon, when we all thought it was his body they'd dug up in Laurel Canyon. Wait ..." Nick shook his head. "This doesn't make any sense."

"Slow down, Nick," Johnny said, leaning against his car. "Some of this I don't know about, so fill in the blanks for me. Start at the beginning ..."

Driving back down the Interstate 5, Nick mulled things over in his mind. Even after he had filled Johnny in on all the details surrounding Hammond's involvement with Landon, he'd found it hard to convince either Johnny, or himself, that Hammond might be the one behind Landon's death. It still didn't make any sense.

His cell phone's shrill ringing tore him from his thoughts. "Jeff," he muttered, checking the caller ID. "Hey, Jeff ..."

"Nick, I just heard from Sam. He talked with Billy Pulaski."

Nick came to full alert. "Oh yeah? What's the scoop?"

"The kid came apart apparently. Sam said he looked terrified when he mentioned Tom Skinner, but he denied taking part in the murder. Said he'd take a lie-detector test to prove he had nothing to do with it. He said Landon, and another guy, killed Skinner. He didn't know who it was— he'd never seen him before. Couldn't describe him—it was too dark, he said."

"Okay, but he was there when Skinner got whacked, right?"

"Yes, both him and Eddie were there."

"So, what were they doing? According to Landon, Skinner was taking them to a 'snuff' party that they didn't want any part of."

"Yeah, that part's right. But Billy said it was Landon and the other guy who were trying to force them into going. Skinner was just there for the money, and some kind of argument blew up about payment. Skinner started to slap Landon around, and the other guy brained him. The two kids ran for it, taking Skinner's car. Pulaski doesn't know what happened after that. Eddie and he kept driving till they got to San Francisco—then Eddie got the bright idea of blackmailing Landon."

"But Landon was in New Orleans."

"Right, so Eddie started calling people he knew were involved with the 'parties' he and Billy had been to. Must have scared somebody enough, because Eddie started to get money, but then, as we know, he 'committed suicide'."

"Sam say he believed Pulaski's story?"

"He said the kid seemed genuinely scared to death."

"Boy, that's a radically different story from the one Landon told me," Nick said, pursing his lips in thought. "So, he was a big fat liar—just like John Hammond. And speaking of Hammond ..."

"Do we have to?" Jeff sounded pained.

"No. I'll keep it till later. Something I want to check out. Jeff, thanks for letting me know all this—and thank Sam for me, will you?"

"I will. You comin' back to the office now?"

Nick glanced at the dashboard clock. Almost five. "Later maybe. There's something I just want to check on first."

"Okay, I'll see you tomorrow."

As he had expected, the gates to the townhome complex where John Hammond lived were closed tight, so Nick pulled over to the side and waited. Only a few minutes went by before a car cruised up and the gates swung open, allowing Nick to follow close behind.

"Let's see," he muttered, looking at the back of Hammond's business card where he'd scrawled the address. "2445 Oakdale ... should be right over there." He skirted the front of the townhome and walked through the landscaped grounds to the back patio. Good, he thought, nobody home, by the looks of it. Jimmying the patio door lock with an expert's ease, he slipped inside and looked around. The place was a mess.

"Tsk, tsk, John ... you're a slob," he chuckled, looking at the piles of old newspapers and magazines strewn on the couch and floor; at the paper plates with the remains of fast food stuck to them. "Yuck ..." He walked quickly into the bedroom. "Figures ..." The bed was unmade and piled with dirty clothes—the bathroom, even worse. "Jeez ..."

A desk sat in the corner, also piled high with papers and envelopes. Nick rifled through them quickly, but found nothing incriminating, apart from some unpaid, overdue bills. He pulled open the drawers and flipped through their contents ... more nothing. Sighing, he retraced his footsteps into the living room. He wasn't quite sure what he was hoping to find— just something maybe, that linked Hammond to Landon in ways that had been hidden from him thus far. He stood in the center of the kitchen and gazed about him, then walked over to where a bulletin board was hung by the refrigerator. For a moment, he gazed at the score or so post it notes pasted in haphazard fashion of the board's surface.

One read: *Call Bernie at home.*

Bernie ... bartender at The Racket, Bernie? Another was scrawled with—*Mike's home # 310-555-5756*—Mike Riley, maybe? But the one that really jumped out at him, and made him draw in a deep breath of surprise was—*Thursday, 18th, 8pm: Newcomb/Morales.*

"Newcomb and Morales," Nick muttered, staring at the names. Why would Hammond be meeting with those two, he wondered. Quickly, he pulled out his cell phone and speed dialed Joe French.

"Hi, Joe ... it's Nick. Listen, do you happen to know if Morales has an interview with John Hammond tomorrow night, around eight o'clock?"

"Tomorrow night is unlikely, Nick," Joe said with a chuckle. "He'll be way too busy trying to impress the Assistant DA, to be bothering with the likes of John Hammond."

"Morales and Newcomb?" Nick stared again at their names of the board. "They're dating? Is that allowed?"

"Well, to hear Morales tell it, they're practically engaged." Joe lowered his voice slightly. "Nick, he was so damned full of himself right here in front of my desk, bragging about how Valerie had come on to him, begging him to go out with her. At first, I thought he'd finally cracked under the pressure, but then he said they were going to some fancy-schmancy party tomorrow night, and he was to be her escort. Why the heck she'd choose him to be seen with is beyond me, frankly."

"Well, he does clean up kinda well."

"And that's about all. That guy is an airhead. Man, was I wrong about him!"

Nick laughed. "I have to agree. Okay, Joe ... thanks for the info."

"So what's with John Hammond?"

"Oh ... uh ... nothing really. Just something he said about wanting to talk to Morales. He probably changed his mind."

"Right. Okay Nick. Anything else I can gossip with you about?"

"Maybe later," Nick chuckled. "See you, Joe."

Nick closed his phone and tapped it lightly against his teeth, trying to put this latest piece of news in focus. Newcomb and Morales were going to a party together, and John Hammond knew about it—and was most likely also going to be there. Something about that didn't seem right. Hammond couldn't stand Morales, and to the best of Nick's knowledge, had never met Valerie Newcomb—at least he'd never mentioned knowing her. If he did know her, even just as an acquaintance, why hadn't he contacted her when he was trying to find out what had happened to Landon? Nick frowned, trying to make sense of it. If his suspicions were right, Hammond and Landon had known each other much longer than Hammond admitted, and had been involved together in the snuff parties. Hammond could have been the 'other guy' Pulaski had talked about. If so, then Hammond killed Tom Skinner, and persuaded Landon to disappear … but why then hire Nick to find out what happened to Landon if he already knew that the body dug up in Laurel Canyon was Skinner, not Landon?

His thoughts were abruptly interrupted by the sound of the garage door opening. "Time to go," he muttered, walking quickly to the patio door, and sliding it closed behind him As he headed to where his car was parked, he punched in Jeff's number.

"Hey, Jeff …"

"Nick, what's up?"

"I'm just on my way home after checking out Hammond's townhouse."

"Uh … was he there?"

"No dummy, I broke in."

"Nick …"

"I know, I'm terrible …" Nick chuckled, reversing his car out of the parking space. "But here's the thing. My suspicious mind has him involved somehow in Landon's killing—and maybe Tom Skinner's also."

"What brought that on?"

"Johnny and I were talking about just who knew Landon was going to take the DA's deal, and I remembered that I had told Hammond, just before he talked to Landon. Plus, your news about Pulaski talking about 'another guy' at the scene of Skinner's murder … Coincidence? You know I don't believe in them thar things, so I figured a little physical search of his home might just yield some surprises—and guess what?"

"Okay, I'm listening."

"I found a couple of post-it notes. One said, call Bernie at home, and another had Mike's phone number."

"Who're those guys?"

"Bernie's the bartender at The Racket who says he doesn't know Hammond at all well, and Mike—if it's the same Mike—was Tom Skinner's roomie. Now isn't all that just too cozy? But here's the kicker—one of the notes read; Thursday 18th, 8pm—then alongside that, the names Newcomb and Morales."

"Newcomb … wait … you mean Valerie Newcomb, the Assistant DA?"

"None other. So, I called Joe French—and guess what?"

"Will you stop with the 'guess what', and just tell me?"

"Joe says that Newcomb and Morales are going to some big party tomorrow night, which happens to be the 18th. Now, why d'you suppose Hammond has a note of that?"

"He invited them?"

"Hammond can't stand Morales. No, I'm thinking it was Newcomb who was invited. Joe said she asked Morales to escort her."

"You don't think she'd have passed that by Hammond first?"

"You're right, 'cause how else would he have known … and apparently he's okay with it. Man, something is screwy here. Hammond, Morales and Newcomb partying together."

"Doesn't sound like a load of fun and games."

"Unless it's one of *those* parties."

"Surely not," Jeff protested. "Not with Morales and Newcomb there."

"What if Hammond's setting them up for blackmail?"

"Seems kinda way out, Nick."

"The whole thing's way out, but the more I think about it the more convinced I am that Hammond's in this up to his neck—which incidentally, I will wring, if I'm right."

"So, what's your next move?"

"Well, I was thinking I need to go to this party tomorrow night. Wanna be my date?"

"Not really. Just how are you going to get us invited?"

"We'll gatecrash, of course."

"But you don't even know where it is."

"Right, but we'll tail Hammond tomorrow, and he'll take us right there."

Jeff groaned. "Oh, man. Here we go again. If you're right about the kind of party it is, the place will be hopping with big security guys, carrying big guns—and every one of them, a karate expert."

"Jeff ..." Nick sighed heavily. "Surely you're not scared of a few wannabe Steven Seagals, are you?"

"Would it matter if I said, yes?" Jeff chuckled quietly. "Just make sure that neither of our respective partners know anything about this crazy scheme of yours."

"I won't tell, if you won't." Nick turned off Coast Highway, and began the steep climb to his house. "I'm almost home, Jeff. So we'll talk more tomorrow. Thanks for your help."

"I'll see you at the office. I can't wait to hear more of this fabulous plan of yours."

"Have faith, Jeff my boy. I'll think of something." Grinning, Nick punched in the number he'd copied from Hammond's wall. The answering machine clicked on after one ring:

"*Hi, this is Mike Riley, leave me a message.*"

"Well, well, well ..." Nick muttered, breaking the connection. "Little fishes, all in a row."

Nick sat in his car for a few moments after he turned the engine off. He suddenly felt drained, and vaguely depressed. If he was right about all this, Hammond was an even bigger dirt-bag than the one he had him already figured to be. And why did he have a post-it reminder to call Bernie at home—a guy he hardly knew? He pushed himself out of the car, and walked into the house.

"Hi," he called. "I'm home ..." He looked across the living room, out through the French doors to where he could see the shimmering glow of the pool light. He stepped out onto the patio, watching Eric's sleek body cut smoothly through the water. He sighed, trying to push the turmoil of the day from his mind, letting his senses be filled with the sensuous image before him. Not wanting to disturb Eric in his time of relaxation, he sat on one of the patio chairs to watch his lover's rhythmic and graceful strokes, as he swam lap after lap without effort. Not until Eric had finished and stood up, pushing his streaming hair back from his eyes, did Nick lean forward and say, "Hi, babe ..."

"Hi ... you're not coming in?" Eric smiled up at him, and Nick felt, as he did so many times, that little pulse of joy at the sight of him.

"I'm kinda beat," he said, shaking his head. "It's been a rough day."

"I bet." Eric pulled himself out of the water. "I saw on the news that Robert had killed himself. That is so sad … the poor guy."

Nick stared at him for a long moment; then he nodded. "Yeah, the poor guy."

"Nick …" Eric came and knelt by him. "What's wrong, honey? You look really down."

"Nothing that a kiss from you won't cure." Nick pulled him into his arms.

"I'm all wet," Eric protested, then gave in as Nick's lips met his. "Mmm …" He unbuttoned Nick's shirt and teased his left nipple between his thumb and forefinger. "Why don't you join me in the shower, and I'll massage away all your cares."

"As only you can." Nick smiled into Eric's eyes. "That's an offer I'm not about to refuse."

"Come on then." Eric stood, and held out his hand. Nick, accepting it gratefully, hauled himself to his feet. He cupped Eric's face in his hands, and kissed him tenderly on the mouth.

"I love you," he murmured. "You bring me sanity in this crazy world."

Gently, Eric steered him toward the bathroom, helping him out of his clothes, before turning on the hot spray in the shower. As if by mutual understanding, they had fallen silent as Eric worked up a soapy lather in his hands, massaging Nick's tense shoulders with gentle but deep strokes.

"Feels so good, babe," Nick sighed, beginning to unwind under Eric's touch.

"Good," Eric whispered, kissing Nick's shoulder blade. "Just relax now …"

Nick chuckled. "It's difficult to relax when I can feel something poking me in the butt."

"Sorry," Eric muttered, stepping back a little. "Can I help it if that's the effect you always have on me?"

Nick turned round, and took Eric in his arms. He pressed his own burgeoning erection against Eric's. "Guess what? The feeling's mutual," he said, grinning. "What the heck are we going to do about this dilemma?"

Eric leaned past him, and turned off the water. "I'll show you—soon as we get out of this shower."

"I knew you'd think of something," Nick said, his grin widening. "That's why I claimed you for my own."

Eric fairly pulled him through the shower door. "Sometimes my man, you know just the right thing to say. Let's go!"

Lying in each other's arms, Eric's head resting on Nick's chest, they both sighed with contentment, suffused in the afterglow that only great sex could bring.

"You are incredible," Nick whispered.

"You are too," Eric mumbled, kissing Nick's left nipple.

"But you're more incredibler ..."

Eric giggled, and raised his head to look at Nick. "Listen, there's something I've been wanting to say to you for days."

"Yes?"

"Years from now, when you talk about this," Eric intoned. "And you will—be kind."

"Huh? Speak of what?"

"You know, what we just did ... made love."

"Why would I speak of it? I never discuss what we do. It's totally private."

"Oh, Nick ..." Eric sighed with impatience. "It was a line from a movie Peter and I watched on TCM, when you were in New Orleans. Deborah Kerr ..."

"Who?"

"*Deborah Kerr* ... you know from the fifties movies?"

"Oh, some old broad ... Ow!" He jumped as Eric tweaked his nipple, hard.

"Deborah Kerr is *famous*. Anyway she lets some young college guy make love to her, to cure his homosexuality."

"That'd do it, all right," Nick chuckled. "Ow! Cut that out, or ..."

"And that's when she says it …" Eric ignored Nick's threat. "Just before they do it, she says, "'When you talk about this, and you will … be kind'. Isn't that great?"

"Hogwash!"

"What d'you mean?"

"I'll bet that kid ran around the whole school telling everyone what a terrible lay the old broad was!"

"*Nick*, you are a barbarian."

"You know, I've heard that before—and you know what? You're right." He grabbed Eric, and threw him on his back, covering his struggling body with his own. "Resistance is futile," he growled in Eric's ear. "Prepare to be assimilated."

"Mmm …" Eric smiled up at him. "Ain't life grand …"

CHAPTER 19

Nick spent the next day keeping tabs on John Hammond. He figured the only way they were going to find out just where this party was being held, was to track Hammond, and have him lead them there.

Hammond worked for a financial company in Newport Beach. The building was easy to find, being the tallest one on the street. Parking his car, he made his way into the impressive marble hall that served as a reception area. A young girl smiled as he approached her desk.

"Can I help you, sir?"

Nick glanced at her name badge. "Hi, Jessica. Is John Hammond in today?"

"Yes, he is … but he's with a client right now. Do you have an appointment?"

"No, I'm a friend of his. Just thought I'd stop by … say hello … that kind of thing. Will he be long?"

Jessica looked at her computer screen. "He should be finished real soon, and he doesn't have another client till eleven. Why don't you go on up, and wait outside his office? It's on the third floor, Suite 330."

Nick stepped off the elevator on the third floor and found his way to the waiting area for Suite 330. He sat near the door, listening to the low voices on the other side. A few minutes later, the door opened and Hammond ushered his client out. His face registered complete surprise on seeing Nick sitting there, a big smile on his face.

"Hey John," Nick greeted him, getting to his feet. "You got a few minutes?"

"Well …" Hammond looked at his watch. "I do have another appointment."

"At eleven," Nick said. "I checked." He gestured to Hammond's office door. "Shall we?"

Hammond walked ahead of Nick, and sat at his desk. "What can I do for you?"

"I just stopped by to see how you were." Nick sank into a chair opposite Hammond, rocking in it slightly as if testing the springs. "I figured you'd be kinda upset after hearing about Robert's death, so I thought I'd come take you to lunch, or something."

Hammond blinked in surprise. "Oh, gee … that's really nice of you Nick, but I have a really full day ahead of me."

"What about tonight, then … dinner, maybe?"

Hammond shook his head, as though he was really sad about having to refuse the invitation. "Again, I'm sorry. I have a dinner party with friends … it's been arranged for some time."

"Oh, that's good," Nick said, smiling. "I'm glad you won't be on your own, you know … brooding too much … that kind of thing."

"Can I take a rain check?" Hammond asked.

"You bet. So, you're OK, then?"

"Yeah, well it was a shock, of course. I mean, after everything he'd been through, and all."

Nick nodded. "I know what you mean. And what gets me is, I'd never have figured Robert as the suicidal type. Know what I mean? Especially, how he did it."

Hammond looked across his desk at Nick. "How he did it?"

"Yeah, strangling himself with a piece of coiled wire from the bedsprings of his bunk. You know how painful that would've been? Hanging there for what must have seemed like a lifetime … slowly watching everything go dark around you. Wondering if anyone in the world is going to miss you … maybe changing your mind about the whole damned thing … only, it's too late …"

"Stop it!" Hammond was glaring at him, his face pale, fists clenched.

"Sorry, John." Nick tried to look contrite. "It just sorta gets to me, you know. Whoever did this, trying to make it look like suicide."

Hammond grew even paler. "What are you saying?"

"I'm saying, Robert Landon was murdered, John. Murdered to stop him from naming those he was involved with." For a long moment, Hammond stared at Nick as if he had never seen him before. Then, he shook his head, pasting what he may have hoped was the semblance of a supercilious smile on his face.

"That is the stupidest thing I've ever heard of in my life," he said, his voice sharp and edgy. "What are you trying to do now? Have me put you on a retainer, so you can go on concocting variations on a theme. So you can bleed me dry? So you and your partner can have a damned good laugh at my expense? Give me a break. Robert committed suicide, because he couldn't face the shame and humiliation of what his life had become—end of story!"

Nick smiled, got off the chair and leaned across Hammond's desk. "Just so you know, no I don't want you to put me on a retainer so I can bleed you dry. I'm working for Johnny Pedersen, Robert Landon's attorney. See, like me, he's not at all convinced that Landon committed suicide—and, like me, he wants to see justice done. Robert Landon may not have been a model citizen, but he deserved his day in court just like anyone else charged with a crime. I aim to make sure that whoever took away that right from him, pays the penalty."

"How noble," Hammond sneered.

"Glad you think so," Nick said, ignoring Hammond's attempt at sarcasm. He pushed himself away from the desk. "You better watch your back, John," he added, heading for the door. "Whoever killed Robert, might just know of your association with him … as a friend I mean."

Hammond let out a hollow laugh. "Believe me, Nick, I have nothing to worry about. I knew nothing of Robert's nefarious dealings."

"Good, John. Well, sorry about lunch. Maybe another time." He opened the door. "Enjoy your party tonight." He stepped into the hall, closing the door behind him. As he walked to the elevator, he could almost see Hammond pick up his phone, and frantically dial whomever he had to answer to.

Nick smiled grimly as he punched the elevator 'down' button. He'd shaken the little bastard up just enough to make him feel less invincible— and this was only the beginning. Tonight, at the party he was so looking forward to, little Johnny Hammond was in for a big surprise.

Morales looked around the crowded room, a smug smile of satisfaction lurking at the corners of his mouth. He looked good tonight, he thought, catching a glimpse of himself in one of the many mirrors hung around the spacious room ... better than most of the other guys here. Older guys most of 'em. Some of the women were hot, though. If he could just dump Valerie, he might score easily enough.

Valerie Newcomb stood at the bar; exchanging some small talk with two women, she didn't know. From her vantage point, she studied Morales with a contemplative eye. He really was a handsome bastard, she thought. Too sure of himself, though ... totally aware of his good looks, and the effect he had on women—some women, anyway. Trouble was, men like that were usually lousy in bed. She knew that from bitter experience. Still, when he sees me home, she mused, it might be worthwhile just to check it out. She looked toward the door as a large mixed group of men and women arrived. There were lots of hugs and kisses; exclamations of obviously feigned surprise all around her. Jeez, but people were such phonies, she thought, fixing a smile on her face as the host, whose name she couldn't quite remember, descended on her, introducing her to a couple who promptly engaged her in yet another boring conversation.

Only half listening, her gaze swept the room, looking for Morales. There he was, preening in front of two younger women, who were staring up at him with what seemed like rapt attention. What the hell could he possibly be saying that was worth listening to? she thought, uncharitably. She'd hardly been able to get two words out of him on the way over to this place. She threw back the remnants of her champagne, then grabbed another from a tray on the bar. Woopsie … she steadied herself, a hand clutching the edge of the bar. This stuff is too good!

John Hammond, watching the proceedings on a monitor in a small adjacent room, smirked with pleasure as his eyes fell on Detective Morales. There he is, he thought, the son-of-a-bitch who's going to wish he'd been a whole lot nicer to me. He doesn't know just what he's in for tonight … or that it's going to be his last night with the LAPD.

He turned as a man entered the room, and stood alongside Morales, watching the monitor.

"So, the fucker showed up, huh?"

Hammond grinned. "His boss wasn't about to take no for an answer."

"You got her under control?"

Hammond nodded. "She's well on the way, already. The lady's a lush."

"Okay, let me know when you're ready." He left, closing the door quietly behind him.

Hammond kept watching the monitor, bringing Morales into close-up. The memory of that day in the park, came back to haunt him again. When he'd found himself face to face with the detective who'd smiled at him—a sensuous, sultry smile that had lured him into the bushes. He'd been so enthralled by the wide set eyes, fringed with long thick lashes, the man's mouth, those full, pouty lips … Anger welled inside him as he remembered the harsh voice telling him he was under arrest. Well, Detective Roberto Morales, tonight you're going to finish what you started.

Nick and Jeff sat in Nick's car just outside the gates of the big house where the party was being held. They had followed Hammond from his office to this exclusive area, in the hills above Glendale. They had watched the guests arrive, some in private cars, others in cabs or limos. They reckoned about fifty or so people were now in the house.

"Let the games begin," Nick muttered.

"You figured a way in there yet?" Jeff asked.

"No, but it's time to reconnoiter, wouldn't you say?"

Jeff groaned. "*You* reconnoiter, then, when you've worked it out, come back and get me."

"Jeff, buddy, we're partners aren't we? Come on, it'll be fun!"

"You have a decidedly warped idea of what constitutes fun, my friend," Jeff muttered, climbing out of the car. "Some date this is!"

Nick chuckled, giving his gun in its shoulder holster, secreted under his black bomber jacket, a reassuring pat. "Let's go," he said, walking quickly over a grassy bank that separated the road from the wall of the house. "Up and over," he told Jeff, holding his hands as a cradle for Jeff's foot. He gave his partner a boost, and Jeff was able to grab the top of the wall, then pull himself up the rest of the way. He leaned down to grab Nick's hand, helping him scramble up beside him.

"Been here, done this—many times," Jeff muttered, peering into the darkness of the grounds that lay before them. They jumped down, then remained perfectly still, waiting for the possible eruption of dogs barking or electronic alarms going off. Nothing, save the sounds of music and laughter from the house itself, wafting across the lawn to the trees where they crouched, waiting.

"Now what?" Jeff whispered.

"I don't see any bozos hanging around the house, do you?"

"No, but they're bound to have someone at the door, checking invitations. I forgot mine—did you bring yours?"

"Smart ass. Look, there's a door at the back, probably for deliveries. Let's check it out ..." Nick took off running, Jeff hard on his heels. The door was unlocked. Nick took a deep breath then stepped inside. He was in a small hallway ... ahead of him he could see, and smell, the kitchen. Jeff slid in beside him, and together they walked, as nonchalantly as possible, toward the kitchen. Like most kitchens preparing for a large party, chaos reigned. Nick and Jeff stood in the doorway listening to the shouted orders, clanging pans and dishes, and trying to look like they belonged.

A young girl gave them a startled look. "Security," Nick told her, and she smiled and nodded. Following Nick's lead, Jeff shouldered his way through the milling crowd with many a "Sorry", 'Scuse me", "My fault", on the way. Once outside the kitchen, they could see a flight of steps leading to what could only be the main floor. Knowing they would have to stay out of sight of Morales, Newcomb, and possibly John Hammond, they were cautious as they climbed the stairs.

"Hey guys!" They both froze, turning slowly. A sweet-faced young man carrying a tray of hors d'oeuvres gave them a big smile. "Like to try my wares?" he asked, his eyes full of mischief.

"No thanks," Jeff said, but Nick reached in front of him, and grabbed a pastry off the tray, biting into it with gusto,

"Mmm, good," he said, grinning.

The kid beamed at him. "Plenty more where that came from. You security?"

"Yep ..." Nick winked at him. "We're undercover, so don't tell anyone you saw us."

"Wow ... I'm Tony, by the way. Come by the kitchen when it's all over. I'll save the best for you."

"I'm Harry," Nick said, with a straight face. "And this here, is ... Larry."

"Harry and Larry ... that's funny," Tony said, giggling. "Well, I better get going. Come see me later, won't you?"

"You bet I will ... I mean, *we* will." Nick gave him another wink.

"What the hell are you doing?" Jeff asked, when the kid had gone. "We're out here, where everyone can see us, and you're flirting with the help."

Nick rolled his eyes. "Yeah, I should've screamed in his face, and told him to fuck off. That would have been a whole lot better, right?"

"Come on," Jeff muttered, grabbing Nick's arm. "Let's check the place out, or do you want another hors d'oeuvre?"

"Party pooper ..." Nick followed Jeff through the door he'd cautiously opened. In one corner, a television monitor flickered with images.

"Interesting," Nick said. "They got surveillance of the main room. There's Morales ..." He pointed to the detective for Jeff's benefit. "Oh wow, look at Valerie Newcomb. She looks hammered." They both watched with some amusement as a very drunk Assistant DA staggered across the room, obviously unsure of where exactly she was heading. Several people had to dodge out of the way as she careened from one side of the room to the other.

Nick chuckled. "Is she ever gonna have the head from hell tomorrow morning!"

"Your friend Morales is totally avoiding her," Jeff remarked.

"Can't say I blame him ..." He stiffened suddenly, gripping Jeff's arm. "There he is ... the man himself ... your friend and mine, John Hammond." Nick fell silent as he recognized the man standing at Hammond's side. "Son-of-a-bitch," he whispered. "No wonder he didn't tell Morales I took that tape."

"Looks like Hammond's talking to Morales, and those two girls," Jeff said.

"Does Morales look kinda funny to you?"

"Yeah, like he's asleep on his feet, almost."

"He's been drugged ... I'm sure of it. Wait, where are they going?" They watched as Hammond, and his companion, led Morales, accompanied by the two young women he had been talking to, toward a door at the far end of the room.

"Let's go," Nick turned, and made for the door.

"Wait a minute!" Jeff grabbed his arm. "We're just going to rush out there, without knowing where we're heading?"

"We'll work it out," Nick said, jerking his arm free. "Faint heart never won ... whatever."

"Fair lady ..." Jeff finished for him. "And what the hell has that got to do with anything?"

"Nothing!" Nick snorted. "Now, come on!"

They both walked rapidly into the main room, looking around for the door Hammond had exited through with Morales.

"Oops ..."

Nick recoiled as Valerie Newcomb barged into him, slopping her champagne over his shoes. "Lady, you better sit down," he told her."

"Don' I know you, han'some?" she slurred, peering up at him through bloodshot eyes.

"Not very well," he said, taking her arm, and practically throwing her onto a nearby sofa. "Stay there, till we get back."

"'kay, but hurry back ..."

"You're so masterful," Jeff chuckled as they made their way through the crowded room.

"Just comes naturally," Nick said, grinning. "Okay, two choices ..." They looked at the two doors ahead of them. "Left or right ..."

Hammond, his hand on Morales's arm, guided him down the long hallway they had entered from the main room. He liked the feel of the detective's hard bicep, but even more, he liked the easy acquiescence of the man. No resistance was what he enjoyed most. He hated it when they screamed and struggled, and begged him not to hurt them. That turned on some people, he knew, but he liked it when they came to him, as if in supplication.

He smiled at the two young girls who followed behind. They would love their part in this too, he thought. Well, up to a point, he supposed. Of a sudden, he remembered again, Nick's visit to his office, and once again, the memory rankled. What had that been about? No way, would Nick arrive, out of the blue, just to take him to lunch. Well, whatever it had been about, he couldn't think about it right now. They had reached an open door at the end of the corridor. Hammond hustled everyone through; then stood, for a moment, regarding the small, select group of men and women who had been waiting quietly for their arrival.

"Here we are," he said jovially, to no one in particular. "Are you ready for a good time?" A chorus of assent filled his ears. He beamed at them. "We have a very special guest tonight. His name is Roberto ..." He gestured to the girls, and nodded. They stepped forward, and removed Morales's coat. "Masks everyone," Hammond said. "Camera will roll in a moment."

A digital video camera on a tripod had been set up, along with some sophisticated lighting. Morales was bathed in the lights as they were switched on, and the crowd audibly gasped, as the two girls unbuttoned his shirt, revealing his toned, hard torso. Next, his pants were removed, his shoes, his socks, then lastly his briefs.

Through all this, Morales remained stoically unmoved by this forced exhibition of his naked body. His eyes seemed to be focused on something no one else could see, a small smile lingered on his lips, as though he was inviting the stares and lewd comments that were now coming thick and fast.

One of the girls, knelt before him, taking his penis in her hand, then placing her lips around it. Again, the crowd gasped as it hardened and grew almost instantly. Hammond smirked. That new drug worked wonders, he thought. Not the greatest dick ... but not bad. He found himself wishing that he could have brought Jeff here tonight, instead of Morales. Wouldn't that have been sweet revenge—even sweeter than this. Jeff was maybe just a little older than this mob generally liked, but with Jeff, they might have made an exception. He was still a beautiful man, and his endowment—well, much better than this.

At a signal, the crowd moved forward; hands pawed at the young detective's body, mouths scoured his skin, fingers probed into every orifice, everything lewd and lascivious was perpetrated upon him, yet he remained, still strangely unmoved by what was being done to him. Now, the girl lay prone at his feet, while the other helped him sit astride her. She drew him inside her, her legs entwined around his hips, her body moving in rhythm, coaxing him into an almost robotic form of copulation. The crowd applauded, several of them were masturbating, some enjoined in their own sexual unions—all the while, the video camera capturing everything. Hammond, masked as the others, stepped forward, placing Morales's hands on the girl's throat ...

"Now," he said quietly.

The camera zoomed in on Morales's face, from which sweat was dripping steadily onto his 'victim'. The girl moaned, seeming to struggle beneath him, pulling at his hands, gasping for breath. The crowd grew quiet in anticipation. Morales groaned, the first sound he had uttered since he had been brought into the room. His body bucked in the throes of orgasm, his hands tightened in reflex around the girl's neck. Her eyes bulged in their sockets, a sound of desperation escaping her lips.

"Cut," Hammond said. Morales was pulled off the girl and deposited on a chair. The girl glared at Hammond.

"That was too close," she whined, rubbing her throat.

"Get over it," Hammond said dismissively. He turned to the cameraman. "Give me the disc …" Carrying it, he walked over to where Morales sat, still dazed and unfocused. Hammond took him by the arm, leading him into a small nearby room.

"Well, well, Detective Morales," he said, when they were alone. "That was quite a performance you gave. Not the best, but it will look terrific on the DA's television, don't you think? Such a pity," he said, rubbing his hand over the other man's chest and abdomen. "You are quite a honey, especially when you're like this." He leaned forward, teasing Morales's lips with his own. He smiled, as the detective seemed to respond, pressing his lips against Hammond's. "Oh yes," he sighed against the detective's mouth. His hand cupped Morales's testicles; he started to kneel before him …

"John, John, John …"

Hammond froze at the sound of Nick's mocking voice behind him. He whirled round, and gaped at the sight of Nick and Jeff staring back at him with hard expressions.

"So, what's this?" Jeff asked. "Another one begging for a blow job?"

"How the hell …?" Hammond croaked, his eyes darting around for a means of escape.

"Don't even think of leaving," Nick said. He grabbed the disc from the other man's hand, and stowed it in his jacket pocket. "Watch him, Jeff …" He walked over to where Morales stood; still unaware of what was going on. Nick waved his hand in front of the detective's eyes, then with a shrug, he slapped him hard on the face.

"*Fuck*," Morales gasped, staggering back from the blow. "What the …" He looked at Nick, Jeff and Hammond, then at his naked body. "Jesus Christ … you fucking perverts!"

"Calm down, Morales," Nick said. "We didn't touch you … well, Jeff and I didn't. Now John here, that's a different story."

"Where are my clothes?" Morales all but screamed, keeping his hands over his crotch.

"I'll get them," Hammond said, trying to get to the door.

Jeff grabbed him by the scruff of his neck. "Not likely, scumbag."

Nick pulled his gun from his shoulder holster, and strode into the other room. "All of you are under arrest," he yelled. "Stand back over there in the corner. You …" He fixed Hammond's companion with a hard stare. "Mike Riley … bring the detective's clothes over here. He watched as Riley gathered up Morales's strewn clothing, and brought them to him, his face a scowling mask.

Morales grabbed them, and started to hastily dress. "You call for back-up?" he asked, through gritted teeth.

"Of course," Nick growled. "What d'you think we are—make-believe cops?"

Any further conversation went out the window, as the door burst open, and a dozen or so armed cops swarmed in, Joe French leading the way. While the officers read the mob, including Hammond, their rights, Joe, trying to hide his amusement, said, "So Bob, you all right? You look a mite shaken up."

"I'm fine …" But Morales didn't feel fine. He had to admit to himself, that he still felt dazed, confused, and for the life of him, he couldn't remember how he ended up naked, with all these people around him. *Christ* … "Where's Valerie … I mean Miss Newcomb?" he asked.

"Passed out on a couch back there," Joe told him. "What the hell were you guys doing?"

"I think you'll find her drinks were tampered with," Nick said. "Most of the people out there, probably don't have a clue about what was going on in here …"

"Which was?"

Nick hesitated. Morales still looked so out of it. If the authorities ever saw the disc he had in his pocket, it would wreck his career, without a doubt. Not that he owed Morales anything—in fact if he were the vindictive type, it would give him a lot of pleasure just to see the moron's face crumple like a kid's when he found out just what was on the disc. But Nick wasn't the type to kick a man when he was already down.

"Drugs and sex," Nick said. "Hammond slipped Morales here some kinda drug in his drink … made him not know what was going on; then he led him in here to video him having sex with two girls. Jeff and I were next door … we called you as soon as we realized what was going on."

"They videoed me?" Morales flushed with anger and embarrassment. He looked like he was going to launch himself at Hammond who was, along with Mike Riley, being led away by police officers. "That son-of-a-bitch pervert …"

"Where's the tape?" Joe asked.

Nick turned to Jeff. "You see any tape?"

"They were using a digital camera," Jeff said, keeping a straight face. "The disc is probably still in there." He walked over to the camera, and opened the side of the case. "Nope, no disc …"

"You mean, one of *them* has it?" Morales looked stricken. "Oh my God … if anyone sees it …"

"We'll search 'em all when we get them to the station, Bob," Joe said. "Don't worry, we'll find it." He grinned at Nick and Jeff. "Good work, lads. You need a ride, Bob?"

"No, I've got my car outside."

"I'll order a cab for Miss Newcomb," Joe said, then paused. "Unless you'd like to drive her home, Bob."

Morales shook his head quickly. "No, I should get to the station … make sure these freaks get charged properly."

"Okay, see you there. Thanks again, guys." He winked at them, then left them with Morales, who seemed to be having difficulty looking at either Nick or Jeff.

Nick broke the silence. "Before you thank us, Morales, we have something for you." He pulled the disc from his pocket, and handed it to the detective.

"This is … it?" he croaked, his hand visibly trembling. "But how …?"

"I grabbed it from Hammond before the cops got here," Nick explained. "Jeff and I figured you wouldn't want it to fall into the wrong hands … so, it's yours to do with whatever you want."

Morales stared at them both, his face working with conflicted emotions. "Guys … I … I …"

"It's okay, Morales," Jeff said quietly. "You've been through enough."

"But this is evidence," Morales whispered. "Of what they did. I should hand it over …"

Nick rolled his eyes at Jeff. "Don't be a schmuck, Morales. You hand that in, and you'll never be able to live with the humiliation. You know as well as I do, someone will make a copy of that, and it'll be all over the precinct before you can say 'dick'. And that's what they'll all want to see."

"You saw me doing that … stuff?" Morales's face went pale.

"No, we didn't," Jeff said quickly. "There were too many people in the way. We didn't see anything."

"Morales …" Nick sighed with impatience. "Look, you do what you want with the disc. If it was me, I'd destroy it."

"You would?" Morales suddenly looked young and vulnerable—and filled with indecision. He looked at Jeff. "What would you do?"

"Same thing," Jeff assured him. "It'll serve no purpose to hand it over. Most of those men and women arrested tonight—with a good attorney, they'll get off with fines, probation, and at the very most, thirty days, time served. You, on the other hand, will spend the rest of your career wondering who's seen that disc, and laughing up their sleeves every time you walk by. Give yourself a break—get rid of it."

Morales nodded. "And you … you'll both say nothing?"

"If we were going to blab, guy, we'd have kept the damned thing," Nick said, turning to go. "Wait …" Morales stepped toward him. "I didn't thank you for … for what you did."

Nick nodded. "You're welcome. But, if you really want to thank us, find out just exactly what happened to Robert Landon."

"You don't think it was suicide, right?"

"Do you?"

"Joe and I have talked about it … and it doesn't make sense to either one of us."

"So you'll make sure it's thoroughly investigated?"

"Yeah. You can count on it."

"Excellent … here's a little tip. You might have to look no further than John Hammond and Mike Riley."

"And you have them both in custody," Jeff prompted.

"For the moment anyway," Nick said. "Hammond's a smart little weasel."

Morales had regained his composure, and the thought of what Hammond had tried to do was making the young detective seethe with anger. "I'd like to take him apart," he said, grinding his teeth.

Nick chuckled. "That makes three of us—just let me have first dibs."

Morales managed a tight smile. "We'll draw straws."

Eric was sound asleep when Nick got home later that night. After undressing, he eased himself into the bed alongside him, trying not to wake him. Sometimes, he thought, staring up at the darkened ceiling, life just seems surreal. A couple of hours ago, he and Jeff had stood side by side, watching what was really a porn movie in the making. Only, the movie's star was none other than Detective Roberto Morales, drugged out of his mind to be sure—but there he'd been, large as life. Well, not that large, Nick thought with a quiet chuckle.

Now, he was back home, lying next to his lover—and all that other stuff just somehow seemed unreal. The party; Valerie Newcomb's hostile surprise when she'd been so rudely awakened by Joe French—that part, at least, had been priceless. Watching her stagger out supported by Joe and another police officer; her hair a mess, her dress soaked from her spilling champagne all over it—knowing she was going to have the hangover of all hangovers the next day. Funny, but he couldn't feel remotely sorry for her.

And Hammond, ready to have a taste of Morales all to himself … what a creep.

Beside him, Eric sighed in his sleep, turned over, and snuggled against him. Nick smiled, holding Eric close. Yeah, he thought, this was what made it all worthwhile. All that madness he'd been a part of earlier belonged in another world … not here. Not anywhere near Eric—or Peter for that matter. Not ever again.

CHAPTER 20

Morales called Nick early next morning with the news, that just as Jeff had predicted, almost all of the orgy participants had been released. Only one or two remained, facing further charges of resisting arrest.

Their attorneys had argued that a party in a private home, with no one forced to do anything against his or her will, did not constitute an illegal act. The fact that Morales had been drugged could not be proved, as he had not submitted to a drug test that night, and all the witnesses swore he had been a willing participant.

"I couldn't believe they'd just walk." Morales sounded bitter. "It was like the judge was on their side … kept looking at me as though I was the pervert or somethin'."

"Just be glad they didn't have that disc," Nick said. "Did you destroy it?"

"I watched some of it," Morales admitted. "Then I threw it in the microwave and nuked it."

Nick didn't believe him for a minute. "So, John Hammond's on the loose … better put a tail on him. He might try to leave town."

"Why would he do that? That arrogant s.o.b. thinks he can get away with anything now."

"But he's got to be feeling less sure of himself, after we busted him last night," Nick persisted. "He knows we're on to him. Why didn't you keep him for questioning with regard to Landon's murder?"

"What do I have on him? Only your hunches."

"It was my hunches saved your ass—in more ways than one, last night," Nick said. "What d'you suppose Hammond was proposing to do, when he thought he had you alone in that room?"

"I'd have beaten the shit out of him, if he'd laid a hand on me."

"You were out of it, Morales." Nick stopped short of telling him that what Hammond *had* laid on him—were his lips. "Anyway, just a piece of advice ... take or leave it. Don't let him slip away."

After talking with Morales, Nick thought he'd better keep an eye on Hammond himself. It wouldn't hurt to make the man nervous—that way, he might just make another mistake. For in Nick's mind, what Hammond had done by trying to involve Morales in a sex video, and presumably use it to blackmail him, showed poor judgment on Hammond's part. What Valerie Newcomb was thinking by asking Morales to escort her to the party, was another story entirely. That kind of thing was totally frowned on by the Department, and could have resulted in disciplinary action.

Nick shook his head ... the arrogance of some people. Hammond was definitely in that category. Morales was right. Hammond probably did think he could get away with just about anything. Well, he was going to make sure he didn't. If he could just tie him to Landon's death ... And what was Mike Riley in all of this? Well, Nick thought grimly, if Morales isn't going to bring them in for questioning, there's nothing to stop me from dealing out some third degree. What were they gonna do—call the cops?

For two days, Nick dogged Hammond's every movement, following him as he drove to work, and back home. On the first night, Hammond stayed home, but at the end of his workday the following evening, he took the 405 North to Los Angeles. Nick followed, already figuring where Hammond was headed. He was not surprised when the man parked his car behind The Racket and went in through the back door. A meeting with Bernie, perhaps? Nick was sorely tempted to walk in and confront the two men he was now sure were in league with one another, but instead he sat in his car, patiently waiting. He was rewarded when Hammond and Bernie suddenly appeared in the parking lot, looking to be involved in a violent argument. Bernie's arms were waving about like a windmill's sails as he yelled into Hammond's face. Hammond shoved him away, Bernie swung at him but missed, and Hammond stalked off toward his car.

"Well, well," Nick murmured, watching as Bernie slammed back into The Racket, and Hammond took off, burning rubber, as he flew out of the parking lot. Slipping his car into gear, he pulled out; following Hammond back onto the freeway, making sure the man was headed home.

Sometimes, Nick thought, as he drove up to Newport Beach the following day, surprise confrontation could produce great results. Anyway, there was no harm in trying. He had considered visiting Hammond in his messy condo the previous night, but had ultimately thought better of it. Hammond would be less likely to pitch a fit in his office, not wanting the prying eyes and ears of his co-workers, to hear tell of his nefarious little ways.

I'm going to enjoy this ... He pulled into the parking lot, noting with satisfaction that Hammond's car was already there.

Here I come ... Giving the secretary a little wave, he marched over to the elevator, and punched the up button.

Ready or not ... He tapped lightly on Hammond's door and let himself in. Hammond's chair was turned toward the window. A faint, familiar, coppery smell permeated the air.

"Hey, John ... how're you doin'?" Instead of the expected lurch of the chair as Hammond spun round to face Nick, there was no movement at all.

"John?" Nick moved to Hammond's side, staring down at the front of his shirt, dyed a dark red by the blood that had poured from the wound in his throat.

"Wow ..." Nick stepped back, knocking his thigh painfully against the corner of Hammond's desk. "Ouch ... son-of-a ..." He grabbed his cell phone, and punched in Morales's number. "Morales? Nick Fallon. Hey, I'm over at John Hammond's office and ... he's dead. Homicide for sure."

"What are you doing over there?" Morales yelled.

"He owed me money," Nick lied. "I came to collect, in case he skipped town."

Morales made a grunting sound. "Don't touch anything."

"Don't worry. You want me to call the Orange County Police? It's their jurisdiction."

"*I'll* call them. Just stay put till I get down there. You'll need to make a statement."

"No kidding."

"And don't alert anyone there to what's happened."

"No sir, yes sir ... Jeez, I know the procedure."

"Cut it out, Fallon."

"Sounds like you don't love me anymore, Bob."

Click! The line went dead. Nick grinned, and closed his cell. He looked around the office for signs of a disturbance. Whoever did this, either took Hammond completely by surprise, or it was someone he knew—and trusted enough to turn his back on. He stood, his back to the window, his hands in his pockets, looking down at John Hammond's body. What further craziness had you gotten yourself into, John, he thought, staring at the man's blood soaked shirt and tie. Did you really think you could handle it all, or were you just in way over your head? He sat down on a chair by the wall, keeping his hands in his pockets, making sure he didn't touch anything. So, now what? Landon was dead, and now Hammond was dead. That left Mike Riley. Was he also sitting in a chair somewhere with his throat cut—or had he done the cutting? He flipped open his cell, and punched in Morales's number again.

"Hey Morales, me again ..."

"What now?"

"I'm lonesome ... just kidding. Mike Riley—remember him? Skinner's roomie slash the other night's cameraman?"

"What about him?"

"Maybe you should check out his place."

"No need. He's still in custody. He was one of 'em who resisted arrest. Punched a police officer on the mouth."

"Okay. You on your way?"

"Yeah, why?"

"I told you, I'm lonesome." He grinned as he heard Morales's heavy sigh. "Come on, Bob, you really need to lighten up."

"How can you be so damned nonchalant," Morales asked, tersely, "When you're sitting there with a dead body?"

"Well, actually I'm terrified. Being jocular helps keep my spirits up ... ooh, spirits ..."

Morales groaned. "Fallon ... will you cut it out?"

"Sorry. I'm terrible, I know. Eric tells me I'm irascible."

"Eric?"

"My partner."

"Oh ... that ..."

"Yes, that. He's a nice guy. You'd like him—but he wouldn't like you."

"What? Why not?"

"Just kidding ..."

"Fallon, for God's sake. Do you ever take things seriously?"

"I take life seriously, Detective Morales. And, believe it or not, I take death seriously too—seriously enough to find out just who is killing these guys. See? I'm on the same page as you, after all."

"I'll see you in a few minutes," Morales said. "... And Fallon?"

"Yeah?"

"What's irascible?"

"Darned if I know," Nick chuckled. "I always figured it was a compliment, though. You know ... like rascal."

"Yeah." Morales said after a pause. "That's you, all right."

Before very long, Nick heard the sound of sirens getting closer, and the parking lot below him quickly filled up with police cars. A minute or two later, the office door was flung open, and Morales accompanied by four uniformed police offers, burst into the room.

"You touch anything?" Morales barked at him.

Nick sighed. "Hell, no ..."

"Step outside." The detective's eyes swept the room then he walked around the desk, and stared at Hammond's body. "Barron, get Forensics in here," he said to one of the cops who waved at two men in white coats. Morales jerked a thumb at Nick, and said to the cop. "Get his statement." Then he strode off, pulling out his cell phone as he went.

"Charming fellow," Nick said, as Officer Barron opened his notebook.

"You don't know the half of it," Barron muttered under his breath.

"Joe French here?" Nick asked.

"Yeah, downstairs in the lobby. He's talking to the receptionist."

"Okay, good."

"So, let's have it …"

Nick began giving his statement, at the same time watching Morales who seemed decidedly jumpy as he talked on his cell. Whoever was on the other end, was giving him a bad time. Nick was pretty sure it was Newcomb. After he'd given his statement, he decided to hang around, and wait for Joe French. Morales, his conversation over, approached him, a scowl on his face.

"Hey, Bob," Nick said with a grin. "What's with the unfriendly face? I thought you and I were buddies now."

"What gave you that idea?"

"Well, I figured we bonded over what happened to you the other night."

"Keep your voice down, Fallon," Morales all but snarled at him.

"Show a little gratitude, then," Nick said. "Unless you want all your underlings to know I saw you without your skivvies on."

"Shut the fuck up," Morales hissed at him, his face livid.

"Yeah, I guess it's true." Nick sighed. "A leopard can't change its spots—and an arrogant jerk can't change his attitude." He looked away as he heard the elevator door open. "Hey, Joe," he called out. "Finally, a friendly face."

"I think I've had just about enough of you, Fallon," Morales seethed.

Nick turned back, slowly looking him up and down. "And I've had way too much of you, Morales. Don't forget," he said quietly. "I may have given you the disc, the other night, but I remember everything that was on it—every *little* thing." Stung into speechlessness, Morales could only stare at Nick, looking as if he were about to implode. Joe, who had been watching their interchange from a few feet away, now stepped forward between Nick and Morales.

"Bob, what the heck's the matter with you?" he rasped.

"Detective Morales is suffering from a bad case of memory loss," Nick said, holding Morales's stare. "The other night …" Nick broke off as the expression on the young detective's face changed from anger to a kind of panic. "Uh, he thanked Jeff and me for calling the cops when things were getting kinda out of hand. Now, he seems to have forgotten all that ... not that I'm surprised, of course."

"Bob ..." Joe glared at Morales. "When the heck are you going to learn ...?"

"Okay, Joe," Morales interrupted. "No need for another lecture." He looked away for a moment, then with a seemingly supreme effort, he said, "You're right, I'm acting like an ingrate. I apologize ..."

Wow, Nick thought, that must have just about killed him. He only hoped the little rat had learned something from it. He stepped out of the way, as Hammond's body was wheeled out of his office on a gurney. The forensics guys did not look too happy with the findings. Nick listened as one of them spoke to Morales.

"Too many prints, all over the place. No sign of a struggle ... hardly anything under his nails ... not much to go on really ..."

"Can I ask a question?"

Morales swung a reluctant stare Nick's way. "Go ahead," he said, his mouth set in a tight line of frustration.

"No sign of a struggle. Could that mean he knew his attacker?

The forensic guy nodded. "Most likely. The victim's throat was cut left to right, meaning the perp was standing behind him, his back to the window. You don't usually let total strangers get behind you like that."

"You've still got Riley in custody," Nick said to Morales. "He needs to come clean about his involvement in this. It's my humble opinion that he, Hammond, Landon and Skinner were all in this pornography hustling ring together. Somewhere along the way, there was a falling out. Now Skinner, Landon and Hammond are all dead—that leaves Riley, either as the murderer, or the next possible victim."

"How could he have murdered Hammond or Landon?" Morales objected. "He's in a cell, so he couldn't have killed Hammond. And Landon died in jail. No way could Riley have gotten close enough ..."

Nick didn't expect to be asked to accompany the two detectives when they talked to Riley—and he wasn't. Still, he thought, I have another fish to catch this morning.

He arrived at The Racket around eleven. Bernie was just opening up, and didn't look at all surprised to see Nick.

"So, still on the case, I see."

"Yeah …" Nick looked around the empty bar for a moment. "John Hammond was murdered this morning."

"Oh?" Bernie picked up a glass, and started polishing it. "So, you getting closer to finding the answers?"

Nick stared at the bartender for a long moment. "If people would stop lying to me, I might be able to put this one away."

"Yeah …" Bernie met Nick's stare without blinking. "There's a bunch of liars out there."

"Well, you would know."

"What the hell does that mean?"

"It means, Bernie my boy, that you've been spinning me a few good yarns yourself, ever since the first day I came in here."

The bartender looked away. "Don't know what you're talkin' about."

"Okay, I'll refresh your memory for you. When I asked you if you knew Robert Landon, you said, yeah, he's the guy they dug up in Laurel Canyon."

"So? It was in the papers, wasn't it?"

"Right—but you knew it wasn't Robert Landon they'd dug up, Bernie. You knew Landon was still alive, didn't you."

Bernie shook his head. "Bullshit—how could I have known that?"

"Because you're the one person, apart from John Hammond, who knew he'd gone to New Orleans."

"John Hammond?" Bernie grimaced. "I hardly knew that guy."

"Tsk, tsk, Bernie … that's another lie. You knew John Hammond because of his involvement with Landon. They both went to a lot of trouble trying to convince people, including me, that they'd just met a few days before Landon disappeared—but, in fact, they'd had an ongoing affair for some time. Something that you didn't like at all ... Am I right?"

"No, you're all wrong! I told you I liked Robert, that much is true."

"And you didn't want him getting involved with John Hammond, because you thought the guy wasn't good enough for Robert."

"Okay, I'll admit that."

"Will you also admit that you knew what they were doing, along with Tom Skinner?"

Bernie paled. "I told Robert to keep away from Skinner ... that he'd fuck things up for us."

"Right, Bernie ..." Nick sighed, and leaned forward across the bar. "And what was your connection to all this?"

"Nothing. I had nothing to do with it."

"So, how could Skinner fuck things up for you and Robert?"

"I ... I didn't mean it the way it sounded."

Nick paused, thinking. Landon had told him that Skinner had approached him first about procuring for his wealthy clients, but maybe he was just keeping Bernie out of the equation, out of loyalty maybe.

"You and Landon were close. How close, Bernie?"

"Not like that ..." Bernie's eyes glistened. "I loved Robert. We got along great, but he was into younger guys. I didn't blame him for that—then he got into three-ways with Skinner ... and John Hammond."

"The same John Hammond you hardly knew?"

Bernie nodded, and had the grace to look ashamed. "Yeah ... him ..."

"So, let me make a wild guess here, Bernie." Nick pushed himself away from the bar, and studied the older man for a moment. "You and Landon had a nice little gig going. You produced the boys and girls, and Landon introduced them to his clients. Then Skinner got wind of it somehow, and threatened a little blackmail if he wasn't included. Landon caved, Skinner got involved, then Landon met John Hammond, and boom—it all kinda got out of hand. Now there's too many people in on this for your liking. Somebody had to go."

"Wait a minute," Bernie yelled. "You're saying I killed Skinner?"

"No. I'm saying John Hammond killed Tom Skinner—but you killed Hammond, Bernie—this morning, 'bout three, four hours ago. Am I right?"

Bernie's laughter was strident. "Oh, Jesus, Mary and Joseph! You *are* nuts, you know that? How the hell could I kill Hammond? I don't even know where he works."

"Oh Bernie, Bernie ... did I say he'd been killed at his office? No, I'm sure I didn't mention that."

"Fucker!" Bernie grabbed a bottle from under the bar, and swung it at Nick's head. Nick caught the man's wrist, twisting it until he dropped the bottle, a low moan of pain escaping his lips. "Oh dear God," he whimpered. "Let me go, please let me go." Nick released him, and Bernie slumped against the bar, rubbing his wrist and crying quietly.

"Why'd you do it, Bernie?" Nick asked. "Did you hate him that much?"

"He killed Robert," Bernie sniffled. "He had him killed ... I know he did."

"Why don't you start at the beginning, Bernie?" Nick said, gently. "Just tell me everything ..."

"I better lock the door."

Nick nodded, watching Bernie trudge to the door with his keys. "What did you do with the murder weapon?" he asked.

"It's back there." Bernie gestured at the bar. "I washed it up good ... no blood." For a moment, it looked to Nick as if he might try to run for it. He slid of the barstool and stood, muscles tensed, ready to give chase. But Bernie locked the door, and with a defeated sigh, walked slowly back to where Nick waited.

"Let's sit over here," he said. "Getcha somethin'?"

"No, I'm good." Nick sat at the small table opposite Bernie, and looked at him expectantly. "So, how did this all start?"

Bernie grimaced. "I've been arranging this kinda stuff for years, on and off. Young kids, lookin' to make a fast buck ... I'd see 'em in every bar I've ever worked in. I'd fix it so they didn't have to be out on the streets ...

safer that way ... less disease, less chance they'd get beaten up ... though sometimes that happens anyway.

"Anyway, Robert and me, we'd get to talkin' on the nights he'd come in here alone. He mentioned he had some real wealthy clients. He'd laugh about how drunk they'd get at the parties he had to attend. I guess some of them knew he was gay. One or two of them propositioned him ... offered him money. He'd say, no way ... but I told him if they were serious I could supply what they were lookin' for—boys or girls. That's how it started, and then that son-of-a-bitch Hammond horned in, and turned it all around. They started doing that dangerous stuff, you know, suffocating the kids." Bernie shook his head, remembering. "I told Robert that Hammond and Skinner were going to ruin it all, but he said that the kids weren't in any danger, and that the clients paid more to watch the struggling. Jesus ..." He paused to wipe his damp forehead with a bar napkin.

"So, none of the kids were hurt," Nick said. "Nobody died, as far as you know."

"Until they started to make movies ... and that's when things went wrong. It was Hammond's idea to film the kids. He was mean, Nick, really mean. He wanted Skinner to strangle the kids for real. Shit, even Skinner said he wouldn't do that, but Hammond said he'd seen movies— 'snuff' movies they call them. He said people paid a lot of money to see those things. When Robert told me about this, I hit the roof. I yelled so loud, I scared him, but Hammond told me to take a hike if I didn't want in. Robert said no one would get hurt—it was all going to be faked. Realistic looking is all, he said. Then Eddie told me two of his buddies who'd gone to one of the parties weren't around no more. No one had seen them for weeks ... Zack, one of them was called, I can't remember the other kid's name ... they never did show up again ..."

"And no one reported them missing?"

Bernie shrugged. "Not as far as I know, and you know how it is, the cops could care less about missing hustlers. Tom Skinner came in here one night, drunk as a skunk, muttering about those stupid shits who'd fucked everything up, and how he was going to have to get out of town. That was good news to me, but I figured something bad had happened—and I was right. A little prodding, and Skinner told me two kids had been snuffed. Hammond had got too rough ..."

"Jesus," Nick whispered. "That must be the tape we watched. *Hammond* killed them?"

"Yeah. Then he planted a copy in Skinner's apartment. As surety, he said."

"You mean, Skinner didn't know he had that tape?"

"He never had a chance to find it. He was dead ... Hammond killed him. Skinner was running scared and ready to blab, Hammond said. He arranged to meet him, along with Robert, on the pretext of offering him more money, just to keep him quiet. At least that's what Robert thought the meeting was about. Skinner showed up, drunk, and started to get ugly. He smacked Hammond, then began mauling Robert. Hammond swung a tire iron at him ... and that was that."

"Whose idea was it to make it look like Landon was dead, and not Skinner?"

"It was Hammond's idea. He told Robert it would confuse the police, if and when the body was ever found. In the meantime Robert should get out of town for while, and he, Hammond, would take care of things here."

"Wait a minute," Nick interrupted. "Robert agreed to this? It makes no sense ..."

"It didn't to me either, when he called me and told me he was leaving. I said, why you? Why not Hammond?"

"Why anybody?" Nick shook his head. "Why leave town at all? Why throw your driver's license in with a dead body?"

"I think John Hammond had Robert confused," Bernie said sadly. "I know Robert was in shock when Skinner was killed. I think Hammond figured he'd be a nervous wreck, waiting for the cops to come get him, so the best way was to persuade him to leave town. Hammond had an enormous influence over Robert. He'd do practically anything Hammond asked him to."

"So Hammond knew Robert was in New Orleans all the time," Nick muttered. "Son-of-a-bitch. He was probably the one who called me about Robert being in New Orleans ..."

234 A DEADLY DECEPTION

Bernie shook his head. "All that yelling and screaming he did in here, pretending Robert had stood him up on their dinner date—all that was baloney, just for the benefit of witnesses. See, he never came in here with Robert—not once. That story he told you 'bout meeting Robert here … baloney too. He even had Robert tell his friends at work he was having dinner with a 'new boyfriend'. If you ask me, he already knew he was going to get Skinner out of the way that night. He thought he was so damned clever. He told me he'd left messages on Robert's phone, yelling about being stood up and all. But then, the mucky-mucks that hosted those parties, they got on his ass about the lack of thrills since Robert and Tom Skinner both split, so he decided to go it alone."

"He had those kind of contacts?" Nick asked surprised.

Bernie looked down at the table as he replied. "Well, I'm ashamed to admit it, but I sent him some girls and boys. Then he came to me with this asinine idea of getting that detective on film servicing some whore. Man, I was dead against it, so he told me I'd become useless, and he'd got himself some recruits on his own"

"So you guys were all in it together from the beginning. Mike Riley too?"

"Not Mike so much. Tom Skinner tried to get Mike involved …"

"He was the cameraman the other night," Nick told him.

"Yeah … Hammond persuaded him, along with a lot of cash. I think Mike liked the idea of that cop, Morales, being humiliated. He gave Mike a bad time …"

Nick grimaced. "He gives everybody a bad time, including himself. So, getting back to this morning … you said Hammond had Robert Landon killed. How do you know that?"

"The same way he had Eddie killed. The kid tried blackmailing Hammond—big mistake. Those guys Hammond was involved with, they can arrange just about anything, anytime they want. They have connections everywhere. A prison guard killed Eddie. They made it look like a suicide—same as Robert. No way would Robert commit suicide. Hammond most likely called his clients and told them Robert was going to take the plea bargain … name names …"

"Tell me something Bernie," Nick said. "Something that's been bugging me since I figured Hammond was behind all of this. Why d'you suppose he came to me, asking that I investigate Robert Landon's murder, when he knew all the time Robert wasn't dead?"

Bernie averted his eyes from Nick's searching gaze, and shook his head. "He was crazy, y'know. Liked living on the edge … I tried to tell Robert he was dangerous, and he should dump him. But Robert, man … he was in too deep with him. All I can think is the s.o.b. wanted you involved just to see how he could manipulate the situation."

Nick thought about that for a moment. It just might have appealed to Hammond's arrogant ego to see just how long he could play the game, trying to keep one step ahead, but not really caring about the consequences. During the time he'd been a cop, both in Pittsburgh and New York, Nick had seen his share of bizarre behavior from criminals. Often, the recklessness of their actions could almost be seen as a desire to be caught—to be the victim. Hammond's crazy involvement with Morales had shown how unhinged he'd become—trying to compromise or blackmail the detective. Nick wondered just who was behind that scenario. Who was Hammond involved with—and had he realized that they regarded Robert as a loose cannon, wanting him out of the way, permanently? Hammond had thought he was being clever, but it was obvious he had misunderstood the other men's motives.

Later, driving Bernie to police headquarters, Nick called Morales. "I'm on my way over with Bernie Kaminsky," he said. "You remember the bartender from The Racket? He'll confess to killing John Hammond."

Nick heard Morales suck in a deep breath between his teeth before he said, "Okay Fallon. Does he have an attorney?"

"No, says he'll go with the public defender. What's the news on Mike Riley?"

"He's talkin' to the DA right now …"

"How come you're not in there?"

A pause. "He said he wouldn't talk with me in the room." Morales sounded puzzled.

"He might have thought you were biased, after the other night," Nick suggested.

"Maybe, but he's not comin' up with much. I'm listening to what's going on, and he seems to be clueless as to what the rest of them were doing."

"So, what was he doing behind the camera? He was the one recording your performance, for Chrissakes, Morales. Get in there and squeeze him."

"Hey, who died and put you in charge of me? Valerie ... I mean Miss Newcomb's in there with him."

Nick chuckled. "She remember anything about the other night?"

"Not much," Morales admitted. "She's been kinda glaring at me, like all this was my fault ..."

"Well, you did leave her side for a younger woman."

"Fallon, cut the comedy," Morales rasped. "I'm in enough trouble as it is."

"Gee, I'm sorry. So, you want me to bring Bernie to you, or ..."

"Yes, to me. I'll take it from there."

I'll bet you will, Nick thought, hanging up. *He has to look like he's doing somethin'.* He glanced at Bernie who had been sitting silently in the passenger seat ever since they'd left the bar.

"You all right, Bernie?"

The bartender's hands were clasped tightly together on his lap. "What d'you think they'll give me?" he asked. "Life?"

"Honestly? I'd say that was a possibility," Nick said, slowing as they approached a busy downtown intersection.

"Yeah ... life, that's what I thought." He turned and gave Nick a sad look. "You know, I'm just a bit too old for all that shit, so if you don't mind ..." Before Nick could grab him, Bernie had opened the car door and jumped out, running with surprising speed into the intersection, and the oncoming traffic.

"Aw, Jesus ..." Amid squealing tires and blaring horns, Nick leapt from his car trying to reach Bernie, but the older man had darted into the path of a UPS truck. The startled driver, trying to swerve at the last moment, clipped Bernie's shoulder, sending him headfirst into the side of a passing car. All traffic ground to a screeching halt, and a crowd gathered around Bernie's crumpled body. Nick could tell he was dead even before he knelt by him, feeling for a pulse. After he called 911, he redialed Morales's number. Sorry, Detective, he thought, listening to the ring tone, I guess your shot at vindication just died, along with Bernie Kaminsky.

CHAPTER 21

Nick sat at his desk, thinking about the events of the day; of the questions he still had that now would most likely remain unanswered. Mike Riley had been released on bond—the only charge against him, resisting arrest. Bernie had said Riley hadn't been in so deep, and that was probably true. So, with all four of the men involved now dead, how was he ever going to uncover the trail that led to the other criminals—the rich slime buckets who got their jollies watching young men and women brutalized, and sometimes killed?

He could 'visit' John Hammond's condo again to look for any clues to their identities, but the police were probably there already digging around—and besides, it was unlikely that Hammond would leave stuff like that lying about. The last time Nick had investigated this kind of furtive operation, there had only been one phone number, one contact—and those who organized the meetings had committed that name and number to memory. He was certain this sleaze had been run the same way.

There was one possibility, however. He glanced at his watch … almost five. He might still be in the office. Flipping through his billfold, he found the number he was looking for. When the operator answered, he asked for Frank Jessup, and was put on hold.

A moment later, "This is Frank Jessup. How may I help you?"

"Frank, it's Nick Fallon, the private investigator. We met at The Racket a week or so ago."

"Oh, yes … hi. How are you?"

"Okay, listen, you've probably heard about what happened to Robert."

"Yes …" A long pause followed. "It's been terrible here … everyone is so upset. Steve, that's my supervisor, and me … we just can't believe it."

"You mean, his suicide."

"That, of course ... but what he was mixed up with. I just can't believe it. Was it that Tom Skinner guy? I bet he got Robert into ... that."

"It was a lot of guys, Frank. Bernie, the bartender ..."

"*Bernie?* Oh, my God. He's such a nice old guy. Will he go to jail?"

"He's dead, Frank. He was killed this morning—road accident."

Another long pause. "I just can't believe it ..."

"Listen Frank ..." Nick had had enough of Frank's disbelief. "I need a favor from you."

"Oh, yes?"

"Are your calls monitored?"

"Uh, sometimes ... you know for quality of service."

"Can you meet me somewhere?"

"Gee ..." Frank sounded flustered, and excited. "I guess so, but tonight I ..."

"That's OK," Nick said smoothly. "Tomorrow would be just fine."

"Okay ... where?"

"How about ..." Nick wasn't that familiar with LA, but he remembered a place Jeff said was pretty good. He'd get directions from him later. "... The French Market?"

"Oh, yes, I know it."

"Good ... about five-thirty?"

"I'll be there."

"Good. See you there, then."

"Bye, Nick."

Nick hung up and gave a rueful sigh. Shit ... He'd just got that kid all jazzed, thinking he had a date. But as he wasn't going to get what he was probably hoping for, he'd give him something else to set his knees a-trembling. He looked up as Jeff walked into the office.

"Aha!" Nick grinned at his partner. "Just the man I want. Whatcha doin' tomorrow, late afternoon?"

Jeff gave him a wary look. "If it's another one of your hare-brained schemes, I'm busy ... *very* busy."

The French Market, a popular restaurant with a large gay clientele, was bustling with activity when Nick and Jeff pushed their way in through the doors, the following day. Frank Jessup was already there and waved to Nick from his table. He looked surprised to see Nick wasn't alone, but his smile grew bigger as Jeff held out his hand and introduced himself.

"Jeff and I are partners," Nick said, sitting next to Frank so the young man could have his fill of looking at Jeff.

"Oh." Frank sounded disappointed.

"*Business* partners," Nick added, picking up the menu. Jeff raised his eyebrows at him, but Nick ignored him and started reading the menu. "What's good, Frank?"

"Well, I'm vegetarian, so I can't really recommend too much of anything. Do you like meat, Jeff?"

"Does he ever," Nick said chuckling.

"Nick ..." Jeff gave him the evil eye.

"Oh, well ..." Frank winked at Jeff. "I understand the fillet is really good, or so I've been told."

"I'll just have a salad," Jeff said, gruffly. "And a glass of wine." He glared at Nick. "The best, since you're picking up the tab, Nick. Right?"

"Oh, right." Nick grinned at him. "So, Frank ... Jeff and me ... we need your help."

"You do?" Frank was all-agog.

"Yeah ... you know I was investigating Robert's murder when we all thought that was him, up in Laurel Canyon?"

"Yeah ..."

"Well, Jeff and me ..."

"It's I," Frank said.

"'Scuse me?"

"It's Jeff and I, not Jeff and me. Oh, sorry, that's a bad habit of mine ... correcting other people's bad grammar, I mean."

"No, that's okay," Jeff said, chuckling. "You go right ahead; correct him all you want."

"Ha, ha …" Nick glared at his partner. "So, Jeff and *I* … want to find who's behind his death this time around—in prison, I mean. And that's where you come in."

"Oh, but I don't have a clue about that," Frank said, his mouth twitching with nervousness.

"No, but you might just have a lead as to who does."

"Really?"

They paused as the waiter came over to take their order. After they'd ordered, and the waiter, a cute young Latino, had flirted shamelessly with them all, Nick explained what it was he needed Frank to do.

"Who took over Robert's accounts?" he asked.

"I did …"

"So, you have access to all of Robert's prior clients, right?"

"Uh … yeah."

"We need a list of those clients, Frank."

"Oh, I couldn't do that. That's confidential information."

"Frank." Jeff leaned across the table, and gazed into the young man's face with a gentle, but earnest, expression. "You liked Robert didn't you?"

"Yes …"

"And you'd like to see whoever killed him, behind bars, wouldn't you?"

"Of course." Frank was staring into Jeff's light gray eyes as though mesmerized.

"You see, Nick and I … we tend to think that some of Robert's clients might be responsible for his death."

"Are you serious?" Frank whispered.

"Dead serious," Nick said, matching his voice tone to Jeff's. Frank's head swiveled to meet Nick's eyes.

"Oh, my God."

"We don't need everyone's name," Jeff said, capturing Frank's attention again. "Just the ones Robert probably had book-marked. Have you seen any of those?"

"Why … yeah … but I didn't know what that meant."

"Probably better that way, Frank," Jeff said. He straightened up as the waiter came over with their drinks. After some more flirting, they were left alone again to talk.

"So, Frank …" Nick squeezed his arm gently. "Can you help us out—for Robert's sake?"

"Shouldn't the police be looking into this?" Frank asked, not moving his arm away.

"Yes, they should," Jeff told him. "But they're not convinced yet that Robert was murdered."

"Why d'you think he was?"

"Remember Eddie, the hustler at The Racket?" Nick asked him.

"Yes …"

"He was murdered in his jail cell, just like Robert—made to look like he'd hanged himself."

"Oh, my God …"

"He was blackmailing some of the guys involved in the prostitution ring."

Frank looked like he was about to faint.

"You okay, Frank?" Jeff asked gently.

"This is all too much for me to comprehend," Frank gasped, reaching for his glass of water and gulping half of it down. "People dying everywhere … oh my God."

"Take it easy, Frank," Nick said gruffly, still holding his arm. "All we need you to do, is give us those names. We'll take care of it from there. Are you in?"

Frank nodded. "Yes, yes. They have to be stopped, right?"

"Right," Nick said, and placed a smacking kiss on Frank's forehead. "Jeff, you kiss him too!"

"Nick," Jeff growled as they pulled out of the French Market's parking lot. "I don't think I have ever met anyone as shameless as you."

"What do you mean, shameless?"

"Using that kid the way you did, is what I mean—and don't play Mr. Innocent with me. I know you, remember?"

"He loved it," Nick chuckled. "He'll do anything for you."

"Nick, I don't need some love-struck kid thinking he's going to get lucky."

"Maybe you shouldn't have kissed him so hard."

"Cut it out ... and did you have to give him my cell number?"

"Of course I had too," Nick said. "I gave him mine too. But guess who he's gonna call?" he added, grinning.

"Jeez. You just love rattling my cage don't you?"

"That's 'cause you're so uptight all the time. You should be more like me—irascible."

"Irascible? Why would I want to be a short-tempered grump?"

"You saying I'm short tempered?"

"That's what irascible means, Nick. Irritable, grumpy ... that kind of thing."

"It does?" Nick frowned at him. "You sure about that?"

"Yes, I'm sure. Who called you that, anyway?"

"Uh ... I don't recall ..."

"You've gone all red in the face."

"Have not."

"Have too."

"Oh, all right. Eric said I was irascible, one night. Shit, I thought it meant rascal, or something cute like that."

Jeff roared with laughter. "Oh my God, that's priceless. Well, he's right of course ... you do have a short fuse."

"Sez who?"

"Sez Eric, apparently."

"Wait till I see him," Nick muttered, under his breath.

"Yeah ... you can show him just how irascible you can really be!"

CHAPTER 22

Frank could hardly wait to get to work the following day. All night he had fantasized about the two hot private detectives he'd had dinner with. Both of them were dreamy, he thought. Jeff was a doll, and so gentle. Nick, well he was just to die for. He'd almost creamed himself when they'd both kissed him. Who would have believed it?

He knew what he was going to do for them was wrong, and could get him fired. But, hey, everyone needs a little excitement in their lives now and then. Let's face it, Frank, he mused, this is probably the one and only time a little diversion like this is going to come along.

Flinging himself into his ergonomically correct chair, he fired up his computer, and brought up the list of clients the two guys were so interested in. He'd wondered why some names had been highlighted. There were ten in all—eight men and two women. Could one or more of them really be the ones to have had Robert killed? He shivered slightly. How could Robert ever have been caught up in something so sleazy—and dangerous? He'd seemed so nice. Boy, he really fooled me, Frank thought bitterly.

He transferred the names to another document, then sent Nick an email with the document attached. He hoped Nick and Jeff would call him again ... maybe go for a drink together. He wondered if they'd be into three-ways.

"Look at this," Nick said, waving a copy of the email Frank had sent him at Jeff, as he entered the office.

"Frank came through?"

"And how. You wouldn't believe some of these names. Between them, they could buy and sell Saudi Arabia. Landon was right—these guys are power players."

Jeff took the copy and scanned it, whistling in surprise. "Harold Forsythe? Holy cow ... You think he could be mixed up in this? Isn't he a Presidential hopeful for 2008? And Barbara Van Duesen ... just the richest woman in Los Angeles." He handed the copy back to Nick. "Okay, so now we have the information, just what are we going to do with it?"

"Well, Morales isn't going to do squat with it if we hand it over to him, you know that. So, I figure one of us should call these guys, and make some kind of overture."

"What kind of overture?"

"A sex overture, of course. That's what they're into, isn't it?"

"And just how are you gonna deliver the sex?"

"I'm not—*you* are."

"*What?*"

"Just kidding; there won't be any sex, real sex, that is. Here's what I thought. I can call these guys and say, 'Oh so sad about Robert and John, but I was a silent partner in their 'business' and have the same kind of connections—are you interested?'"

"Why don't we just hand this information over to the police," Jeff suggested, "and let them deal with it? That way, they can set up their own 'sting' operation."

"They won't. There's not enough to go on here, apart from our hunches." Nick sighed heavily. "Okay, I'll just have to take care of it myself."

"What does that mean?"

"It means you don't have to worry about it. I'll take care of it."

"Oh no, you don't." Jeff fixed his partner with a mean look. "You are not going off on your own, doing something stupid and dangerous."

Nick shrugged his wide shoulders expressively. "What choice do I have? My own partner won't help me out. 'Course, there was a time that I recall when you were being held hostage, in dire need of help, and who came galloping to the rescue, *all the way from New York City?*"

Jeff groaned. "Not that again. Every time we get in an argument, you throw that up at me. Jeez, haven't I done enough penance by now?"

"Almost." Nick grinned at him. "Helping me now will clear the marker completely."

"Christ ..."

"Jeff, such profanity. I'm shocked."

"Okay ... okay, I'm in. Now what?"

"Great. So here's what we'll do ..."

Harold Forsythe's secretary, Leticia, liked the sound of the man on the line asking if it would be at all possible that he might speak with Mr. Forsythe. He had a deep sexy voice, and was extremely polite.

"I know this may be an intrusion," he said, "but I think Mr. Forsythe will welcome my call."

"Well," Leticia cooed into the phone, "he's actually between appointments and phone calls, so let me see if he will speak to you. May I tell him what it concerns?"

"Certainly—tell him I'm a friend of John Hammond."

In a moment, she was back on the line. "Mr. Forsythe says if you leave your name and number, he will call you directly."

"Sure—it's Nick Lamont, and my number is 949-555-3467. That's my cell …"

"I'll give it to him right away, Mr. Lamont."

"Nick Lamont?" Jeff guffawed. "Where did you come up with that name?"

"I think it sounds a bit more sophisticated than Fallon," Nick said, grinning. "Nick Lamont … I like it."

Jeff shook his head. "You are too much. What's my name?"

"I was thinking Jeffrey Dahmer."

"Thanks a million. Nothing like being named after a pedophile cannibal. I'll stick with what I got, thanks."

They both tensed as Nick's cell phone jangled. "Hello?"

"Is this Nick Lamont?"

"Yes it is. Mr. Forsythe?"

"Right. I'm on my private line. So what's this about?"

"I helped John … uh … arrange some of the parties you attended, before his unfortunate demise. I'm thinking of picking up where he left off, and wondered if you might be interested."

"I might be … if I can be assured of total privacy and safety."

"Oh, you can depend on that, Mr. Forsythe. My partner and I have all the bases covered."

"Then, yes—I'm interested."

"Excellent." Nick gave Jeff the thumbs up. "My partner and I have access to some fine boys and girls who like to party—only problem is, we need somewhere discreet, out of the way, as it were, in which to meet."

"No problem, I have a house in the hills." Nick could scarcely believe how eager the other man sounded. "Tell me, will it get ... uh ... edgy?" Forsythe asked, his breathing becoming heavy. "You know, a little *dangerous*?"

"That can be arranged," Nick replied, trying not to sound like he wanted to strangle Forsythe with his bare hands.

"Okay, I'll let my friends know. Call me when you've got it put together. Here's my private number ..."

Nick threw his cell phone onto his desk and slumped back in his chair. "That dirt bag," he said, scowling. "He's totally into it, the son-of-a-bitch. Wants it to get *dangerous*, he said. What a creep."

"Well, at least we know he's the one we deal with," Jeff said.

"Right, and he's got a place in the hills we can use, he says. So, now to the second part of our plan—and this is where it gets tricky."

"Tell me," Jeff said, frowning. "Just where are we going to get a bunch of guys to go along with this charade?"

"I think we should get Morales involved, after all." Nick chewed on his lower lip as he thought. "If he can provide some undercover cops, it would look good for him if he could put this one away."

Jeff was dubious. "D'you think he'll go for it?"

"Let's find out shall we?" Nick said, with a grin as he punched in Morale's number.

Harold Forsythe sank back into his leather high backed chair with a smug smile. So the fun wasn't over yet, he thought running a hand over his perfectly combed silver hair. John Hammond and the others might be gone, but there was always someone else there to pick up the slack. Money talks, he mused, and money was something he had plenty of. He drummed his long, beautifully manicured fingers on his desk, and then picked up his phone.

"Hi," he drawled after the other party answered. "Looks like we're back in business ... Are you up for it?"

"How did you get this information?" Morales exploded into the phone after Nick had told him of his plan to trap Forsythe and his cronies. "Didn't I tell you to back off of this case?"

"So, it's a no?" Nick asked him. "I thought you'd jump at the chance of putting these guys away—and with you leading the operation, it would do a lot for your reputation in the department. You need a break, Morales, and this could be it."

There was silence on the other end for some time while Morales was obviously thinking over what Nick had just said. "What would I have to do?" he asked finally.

"What we'll need is some young looking guys and girls. They should be used to undercover work ... you know, able to keep cool under strange circumstances."

"I can't think of anything stranger than that weird setup they had the last time." Morales went quiet again. "I don't know. I should talk to the Chief about this first. Undercover cops are fine, but we'll need back up."

"Right. Talk to him and get back to me. Believe me, this will do you a power of good—and get those rats out of the way for a long time."

"Okay, Fallon. I'll call you when I get an answer for you."

Nick sat back in his seat with a satisfied grunt. "He's going to talk to the Chief to get the green light on this."

"Good idea," Jeff said. "That way, we're covered if something goes wrong."

Morales flicked nervously through the magazine he'd picked from the stack on the table outside the Chief's office. He wasn't at all looking forward to this appointment, even though he knew that if the Department went with Fallon's idea, it just might help put him in a better light. There had been way too many rumors flying around the Department of late—rumors that made Morales sweat inside the seventy-five dollar shirt he couldn't really afford. He needed a break, just like Fallon said—loath though he was to admit it to that smart-ass.

"Chief Robertson will see you now, Detective Morales." Robertson's secretary buzzed him in, after giving him a tight little smile.

"Thanks," he muttered, straightening his tie as he walked through the door into Robertson's office.

"So, Detective ..." Robertson looked up from his desk as Morales appeared in the doorway. "What can I do for you this morning?" He gestured toward a seat in front of his desk as he spoke.

"Uh, it's about the guy who committed suicide in his cell last week ... Robert Landon?"

"What about him?"

"Well sir, I'm sure it came to your attention that he was involved in a prostitution ring—providing young men and women for high rollers. He got his clients through his job as a financial consultant where he had access to some pretty important people's accounts. It seems he got a small group of these people into something even more hardcore ... filming kids while they were being 'snuffed' ..."

"Go on," Robertson said, his eyes narrowing as he stared at Morales.

"I've been talking to a private investigator who was involved in the case early on ... Nick Fallon. Seems he's come up with a list of these people, and he wants us to take action."

"What kind of action?"

"A sting operation, where we set them up with the kind of scene they like, using some of our undercover people as bait."

"This Nick Fallon ... where did he get this list?"

"Uh ... I don't know ..."

"Do you know who's on the list?"

"No, sir."

"Do you have Fallon's phone number, at least?"

"Yes, sir ..." Feeling foolish, Morales dug in his wallet, fished out Nick's card and handed it over. Robertson immediately dialed the number listed under Nick's cell.

"Nick Fallon."

"Mr. Fallon, this is Chief Robertson of the LAPD. I have Detective Morales here telling me you want us to conduct a sting operation against what he calls 'some pretty important people' who apparently are involved in some kind of 'snuff' movie setup."

"That's right," Nick said.

"Tell me, Mr. Fallon … just what kind of important people are we talking about here?"

"You want me to tell you the names over the phone?"

"This is a secure line, so yes, I want you to give me two names you consider important."

"Okay … how about Harold Forsythe and Barbara Van Duesen for starters?"

Morales, watching Robertson, but unable to hear what Nick was telling him, was more than a little surprised to see the Chief's face flush a deep red as he listened to what Nick was saying.

"That is *preposterous*, Fallon," Robertson said, his voice low and deadly. "Who gave you those names?"

"I'd rather not divulge my source."

"I just bet you'd rather not! Do you know what you'd be doing by accusing these people of a crime as heinous as this? We couldn't afford to fight the lawsuits, Fallon. They would hang the Department out to dry! Just what proof do you have?"

"Well, right now I'm working on a hunch, but …"

"A hunch? I should risk the Department's reputation on your hunch?"

"But if you catch them in the act …"

"Forget it!" Robertson shouted into the mouthpiece. "Take that list and put it through a shredder. There will be no sting operation—and Fallon …" Robertson's voice took on a distinctly threatening tone. "If I hear of you trying to proceed in any way against these people, I will shut you down. Do you understand?" Without waiting for Nick to reply, he flung his phone down and glared across his desk at Morales who was visibly quaking.

"I should fire you, Morales," he hissed, his face beet red with rage. "You come in here on some crazy PI's whim, and tell me with a straight face that you think we should mount a sting operation against two of the most powerful people in California—and without one shred of evidence to support it."

"I … I'm sorry, sir. I thought Fallon had proof."

"Don't think, Morales ... *ever again*. Now get out of here, before I use my better judgment, and fire your ass!"

Robertson sat very still for a few moments after Morales had beat a hasty retreat through the door, then he picked up his cell phone and punched in a private number.

"Harold?" His voice was strained and terse. "We need to talk ..."

Nick turned off his cell phone, got out of his chair, and stared out of the window onto the busy street below. Jeff, seeing his partner obviously pissed off, got up and crossed to where Nick stood by the window.

"I'm guessing that the Chief of Police didn't buy the story," he said, putting his hand on Nick's shoulder.

"You guessed right." Nick turned to face Jeff. "And not only that, he warned me off any further investigation into the matter. Said he'd shut us down ... the bastard. Something stinks here ... big time! Maybe Robertson's protecting those shits ..."

"Nick ..."

"I know, I know ..." Nick heaved a sigh, and stuck his hands in his pockets. "Don't worry, I'm not about to put our livelihoods in jeopardy. They'll never know it till it hits them, but one day I will get those bastards. If we're all drawing Social Security when it happens—I'll get 'em!"

It was late when Nick arrived home. His dark mood was lightened somewhat by the mellow music on the stereo, and the smell of some delicious cooking coming from the kitchen.

"Mmm ... what's that?" He kissed Eric, and held him close, glad as always to be home with his lover.

"Chicken cordon-bleu—I thought I'd try something different." He stroked Nick's face gently. "Had a bad day?"

"Yeah, but you're making me feel better by the moment."

"Glad I still have my uses," Eric said, his eyes twinkling. "Like a drink before dinner?"

"That'd be great ..." He leaned against the bar while Eric poured their drinks. "By the way, I have a bone to pick with you, young sir."

"Oh yeah? What'd I do now?"

"What does the word irascible mean?"

"Huh?"

"Irascible, Eric. I've been meaning to ask you this for days. What does it mean?"

"Uh, kinda grumpy, short tempered, I think. Why?"

"Because that's what you said I was," Nick huffed. "And all this time I thought it meant something different."

Eric chuckled. "You sure I didn't say you were irresistible?"

Nick snorted. "Oh right, now you're just buttering me up." He cupped Eric's face in his hands. "Irresistible ... really?"

"Of course you are." Eric's eyes gleamed as he gazed at Nick. "Irascible sometimes—irresistible, always."

"God, but I love you," Nick said, kissing Eric long and hard.

"What did you think irascible meant, by the way?" Eric asked when they came up for air.

"Uh, don't laugh, now. I thought it meant, like rascal."

Eric chuckled. "Oh yeah, that's you all right ... you rascal, you. Let's go to bed."

"What about my dinner?"

"Like me, it's simmering." Eric jumped into Nick's arms. "*Un*like me, it can wait!"

978-0-595-47768
0-595-47768-2

Printed in the United States
143110LV00004B/125/A

9 780595 477685